Love's Bright Tomorrow

Eagle Harbor Book 6

Naomi Rawlings

Love's Bright Tomorrow: © Naomi Mason 2018

Cover Design: © Clarissa Yeo 2016

Cover Photographs: Shutterstock.com

Editors: Melissa Jagears; Roseanna M. White

Formatting: Polgarus Studio

To those who wear a badge—like my late, beloved grandfather—who spend their lives serving their communities and protecting the innocent.

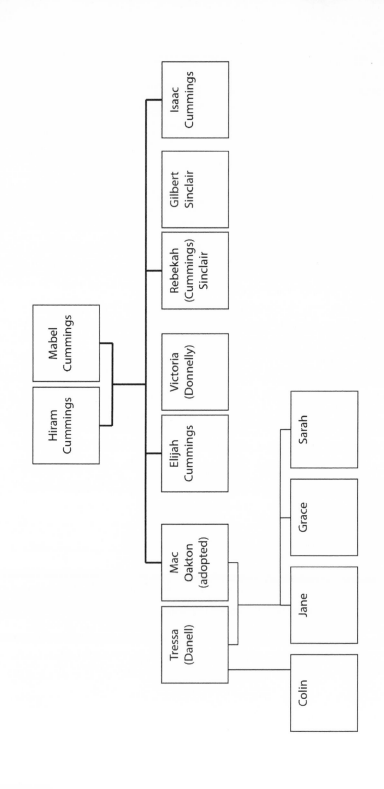

Chapter One

Eagle Harbor, Michigan; June, 1884

The dream came in waves, soft and gentle at first. The sun from a hundred different afternoons, beating down until her skin darkened with freckles while she worked the land. The crackle of the fire in the hearth, the sound of her da's voice. The hunched form of her brother seated at the table with Da, studying the checkerboard. The feel of potatoes in her hand as she scrubbed them for dinner.

The still form of her ailing da as he lay in the corner, barely strong enough to raise himself on his elbows as he mumbled something at her.

From her position beside her father, Aileen leaned closer inside the hot, stuffy cottage, straining to hear her father's frail voice where he lay in bed. "What was that, Da?"

Sweat beaded on his forehead, and his face held the gray color of death. "The window. Look out the window."

Not again. She sat back in her chair. "Later, Da. I'm too busy tending ye right now. How about I get another cloth for yer forehead?"

"I told ye, look out the window, lass." The faint words nearly disappeared before they reached her, but his eyes held a glassy sort of determination.

She swallowed her sigh and rose, then headed over to the closest of the cottage's two windows. She knew what she'd see, had been staring at it since she was four and old enough to push a chair to the window and peek outside.

The rolling landscape of Ireland filled her vision, a vast expanse of emerald fields sloping softly down toward the crystal blue ocean in the distance. Birds swooped above, calling to each other as they scoured the countryside for food, and a hare peeked around the corner of the stable, then hid again.

"Everything the sun touches, it'll be ours one day." Somehow Da's weak voice still traveled across the room to her, as though her going to the window had given him a sudden burst of strength. "One day I'll buy those fields for meself. One day the land we work will be ours."

A sheen of tears glazed her eyes. The land wasn't ever going to be theirs, not when they couldn't even afford the rent. At this very moment, her brother Conan was in town, trying to talk the land agent into giving them more time to come up with the money.

Money they weren't going to have this year, not with Da so ill, not with the falling crop prices, not with the surge of rain they'd gotten over the summer. Half their potatoes, turnips, and carrots were rotting from the moisture in the soil.

"Da, we're not…" She turned back to face her father, the once strong man who'd caught a fever over the winter. Despite his bloodshot eyes and wheezing breaths, his gaze held such hope. She swallowed her words of truth and forced out others instead. "Aye, Da, the land will be ours one day, and ye'll be the best farmer in all of Ireland, ye will."

And then she was no longer eighteen, but six, standing in the field with her father, her apron full of seeds for planting while the rich scent of freshly plowed soil filled the air.

"Close yer eyes and lift yer face up to the sky." Her father's booming voice rumbled from his chest, strong and hearty.

She did as asked, letting the faint breeze off the ocean ruffle her hair and drawing in a breath that tasted of moist soil and salty sea.

"Do ye feel the sun on it?"

The sun's spring rays kissed her face with their warmth, and she nodded.

"Now open yer eyes and look out over the fields."

She did so, staring out over the gentle knolls of rich brown earth dotted with patches of green, both of which gave way to blue ocean in the distance.

"Everything the sun touches, it'll be ours one day."

Tears streaked her face, and she took a step back from him, then another, until the land behind him blurred, until the towering form of her father disappeared into a swirl of brown and green and blue. *It won't be ours, Da. It won't. Don't tell me lies. Don't fill me head with nonsense. Don't make me hope for things that will never be.*

But he had filled her head with nonsense anyway, and Conan's too. Every time they worked the fields, every time they took a wagon of vegetables to the land agent to pay their rent, every time they set up a booth at the market to sell their goods. It didn't matter how old they were, what they were doing, or the time of the year, there was one thing Da never stopped talking about—

Crash!

Aileen woke with a jolt, the fields of her homeland slipping away as she sat up on the narrow bed and pressed a hand to her heart. It stampeded against her palm like sheep running down a hillside.

"What did you do?" A man's voice invaded the darkness.

She froze.

"I didn't do nothing. It fell all on its own." Another man's voice joined the first, this one a little deeper.

Were the men downstairs in the bakery? Her gaze found the door to her room, and she stared at the handle. The fear in her chest rose into her throat, so thick and suffocating she nearly choked.

"Clean this up, and be quick about it."

No, the voices weren't coming from downstairs or the hall outside her room, but from the alley. She moved her gaze to the window, and her stampeding heart slowed a wee bit. That was normal enough, wasn't it, voices outside the window? Truly, she had nothing to be alarmed about. People could use the alley at any time of day or night.

But in nearly a year of renting rooms above the bakery, she'd never been awakened by people behind the building.

Should she go to the window and look? What if they were trying to break in?

Her heart pounded anew, and she twisted her sweaty hands in the tangled sheets.

There was a time that the idea of strangers forcing their way into her room seemed unfathomable, but someone had broken into the bakery just this past winter. A chill swept through her despite the muggy heat filling the room. The perpetrator had been caught, aye, but another man could attempt the same.

More talking sounded from the window, where the gauzy curtains fluttered in the nighttime breeze. The voices were lower now, more secretive, more… suspicious.

Probably because they were trying not to wake half the town. Aye, that was the reason the men outside were being quiet, not because there was something sinister going on.

"Hurry before someone sees us."

Or mayhap not. She glanced down at the sheets tangled around her lap, then at her pillow, still bearing the indent of where her head had lain. She'd not be able to sleep now. Shouldn't she at least try to figure out what the men outside were doing? Drawing in a shaky breath, she shoved her covers down and swung her legs over the side of the bed.

Humid air, unusual for so early in the summer, surrounded her. The thrum of blood in her ears was so loud it nearly drowned out the voices as she crept toward the window. She paused by the wall, her back pressed to the white plaster, then drew in a steadying breath before she peeked outside.

The silver moon slanted a shaft of light between the buildings and into the alley, where a group of men clustered beneath her window. There were more than two, but how many? Four? Five? It was hard to tell given the way thick shadows cloaked almost everything in sight.

The men appeared to have a large crate that had somehow split open. Two of them picked up objects shrouded in shadow and set them into a second crate which appeared to be loaded onto a handcart of some sort.

It almost looked like they were dockworkers taking cargo to the warehouse. Except dockworkers didn't work at night, and the pier and warehouse were several blocks from the bakery. There'd be no need to haul cargo this far from the beach. She attempted to swallow the lump stuck in her throat, but it lodged there, unmovable.

Two more men approached from the direction of the harbor, pulling their own handcart. "What are ye still doing here?"

Irish. Aileen sucked in a breath. That voice was unmistakably Irish.

"Ye take much longer and someone'll spot us."

It was too late for that. She twisted the fabric of her nightdress in her hands.

"We're hurrying the best we can." One of the men below moved to pile things into the open crate. "Just be careful of that there rock so your crate doesn't topple as well."

Two more men with a handcart approached from the opposite direction. "Only one more load left. We'll see you at the wagon."

The wagon? What were these men doing that needed a wagon? And why use the alley instead of the road that ran along the front of the building? Aileen leaned a bit closer.

Two of the men passed the ones working to clean up the spill, then hurried down the alley toward the harbor. Through the patchy moonlight, she could just make out the shadowed forms heading to...

Not the harbor.

Had they stopped at the back of the bank?

She gripped the molding beside the window. Surely she wasn't watching the bank being robbed.

She glanced down at the objects littering the alley. Could it be money? It seemed too heavy, but mayhap the bills were bundled together.

She shifted nearer the window. If she could find a spot where the moonlight reached the ground, mayhap she could see—

One of the men jerked his head up in her direction.

Her heart thundered against her ribs, its beating so loud the workers below likely heard it.

The man stayed where he was, his head still angled up. She shifted back just a bit, then froze.

He didn't move.

She shifted another little bit, then paused again. Silence filled the street below. The next time she moved, she shifted far enough that the wall blocked the man from view.

"We need to be done. Now. Get a move on it," a terse voice echoed from below.

She didn't know how long she stood there, her back pressed to the wall, her chest heaving with frightened breaths she didn't dare let all the way out. It might have been minutes or it might have been hours before footsteps thudded on the packed earth of the alley. If the handcart moved, its wheels gave nary a creak.

And yet she stood there, perfectly still, as though if she moved an inch someone would burst through her bedroom door and haul her away. When her hands finally stopped trembling and her breathing calmed, she shifted to peek out the window. The night that greeted her was as still and dark as the burial shroud that had covered her father back in Ireland.

What should to do? She wasn't about to step foot outside the building now to alert the sheriff, not with strange men about. Morning would be here soon enough, and she could go then.

But what if that man had seen her? Would the robbers realize she'd turned them in?

⌐.⌐.⌐.⌐.⌐

Ding-a-ling. Ding-a-ling.

Isaac Cummings twisted on his bed and groaned. What had possessed him to hang a bell pull outside the sheriff's office below his apartment?

Ding-a-ling. Ding-a-ling.

Well, besides the part about wanting Eagle Harbor to be a secure town where people didn't fear for their safety.

Ding-a-ling. Ding-a-ling.

But he also wanted sleep. Was there anything wrong with that? He cracked an eyelid to glance out the second-floor window where the bell hung.

Morning. Kind of. He yawned and rubbed his eyes. Though after a night of staying up late to break up three different bar fights, the faint pink hue spreading across the sky shouldn't count as morning.

Ding-a-ling. Ding-a-ling.

He groaned again. Putting a bell up had seemed like a good idea when he'd done it. But

the bell had lost its appeal on the third morning after it had been installed, when Mrs. Kainer had woken him at four-thirty to help search for her missing cat.

Ding-a-ling. Ding-a-ling.

He sighed and forced himself out of bed, then reached for the shirt hanging over his bedpost. *Please don't tell me someone's dog is missing.*

Though in truth, being woken up for a lost dog would be better than having someone be in danger.

"Sheriff Cummings, are ye in there?"

That voice, he'd recognize it anywhere, lilting and soft and unmistakably Irish. A voice he'd like to hear more than just at church on Sunday or when they happened to see each other around town. He shoved his arms through his shirtsleeves, then thudded across the floor while he started on his buttons.

He stuck his head out the window, revealing only the top of his shirt as he worked to button the bottom half. "Miss Brogan."

She looked up at him, her rich red hair shoved hastily into an updo that looked as though it might come falling down any second. Even in the early morning light, her face and hands were the color of fresh cream.

"What's wrong?" He furrowed his brow, his heavy eyelids suddenly having no trouble staying open. "Did someone break into the bakery again?"

"Nay." She glanced around the empty street, then twisted her skirt in her hands. "Let me in. We need to talk."

"I'll be down in a minute." He turned and grabbed his trousers hanging on the bedpost, then pulled them on along with his boots.

What was so wrong that Aileen couldn't tell him through the

window? This past fall there'd been a rash of robberies, and someone had broken into the bakery where she lived, leaving her an eerie sort of message.

But the man responsible had been caught just after Christmas and was now sitting in jail for the rest of his life.

Outside of the weekly drunken brawls at one of the town's two bars, Eagle Harbor had been quiet until about a month ago, when a bit of vandalism had started. So far he'd dealt with ink being poured onto Mrs. Ranulfson's dress while it hung on the line, Mr. Foley's wagon bed having an ax taken to it, Mrs. Kainer having a rock thrown through a window of her boarding house, and a dead mouse on Mrs. Runkle's doorstep.

Though that last one might have been a cat.

Had someone vandalized the bakery? He strapped on his holster and gun and headed downstairs into the sheriff's office below his apartment, then hurried across the wide plank flooring and slid back the deadbolt.

Aileen wore a white shirtwaist and plain blue skirt. With the unusually pale shade of her face, the smattering of freckles across her nose and upper cheeks stood out like charcoal against snow. She twisted her hands together and looked around the empty street before stepping closer.

"Miss Brogan, what is it?" He nearly reached out to grip her hands, to see if he could stay the trembling, but stopped himself. Last time he'd tried reaching for her when she was upset, she'd jumped away from him so quickly she'd sent both herself and a chair crashing to the floor.

"I… th-think someone robbed the bank."

He nearly choked. A bank robbery? In Eagle Harbor? He glanced around the street that suddenly seemed too still and peaceful, then stepped out onto the porch, pulling the door shut behind him.

"Let's get Deputy Fletcher." Fletcher could keep her safe, question her, and then escort her home while he and Deputy Granger had a look at the bank. "Tell me what you know on the way."

He extended his arm to Miss Brogan, then started down North Street, a sick feeling twisting his stomach. He had his savings in that bank, as did his brother Elijah, and just about everyone else in town. The thick forest that rimmed Eagle Harbor offered too many places for criminals to hide. If someone truly had robbed the bank, he and everyone else in town would likely never get a lick of their money back.

Chapter Two

She was a fool, an utter and complete fool.

Aileen stood with her back to the wall of the bank while the bank owner, Mr. Ranulfson, talked with Sheriff Cummings. Behind them, the safe door was open, and two bank workers and both of the sheriff's deputies counted money—for the second time.

Yet nothing seemed to be missing. Here everyone had been woken up and called to the bank two hours early and she'd left Ellie to start work at the bakery by herself, and all for nothing.

Aileen took a step toward the door. Deputy Fletcher had already questioned her, but rather than let her return to work, he'd brought her to the bank, saying the sheriff probably wanted to speak with her. But then, Deputy Fletcher had also assumed the bank had been robbed when he'd said that.

No one seemed to notice the first step she'd taken toward the door. Deputy Fletcher was just as busy counting money as Deputy Granger, and the clerks hadn't so much as glanced at her. Sheriff Cummings and Mr. Ranulfson had their backs to her while they studied the alley's entrance to the bank.

She took another step, then another. Mayhap she'd come back during her lunch break and apologize for disrupting everyone's morning. Or better yet, she'd bake an extra batch of cookies and deliver them when she apologized.

One more step took her out of the offices and into the empty lobby. The room was lovely, with rich dark walls and fancy rose-colored carpet that must have cost a fortune to ship to Eagle Harbor.

But nothing inside this lavish, showy room was for her. She'd never once had enough money set by to save it in a bank, and she probably never would. Why bother with an account when she could just stash her extra money beneath one of the old floorboards in her room? And once she got enough to book passage to Ireland, there'd be no reason to stick the money in a fancy bank—she'd be buying her ticket immediately.

She pushed out the front door, and the mugginess of the air outside hit her like a wall. The heat and misery contrasted with the peaceful harbor that stretched out its green-blue waters before her. Beyond lay Lake Superior, an endless expanse of wavy blue, large enough to rival an ocean. The golden morning sky painted the sand and street and town pier with a yellow brush, and the gulls above called out against the sound of gently lapping waves.

She might not have had a choice about leaving the emerald slopes and sparkling sea of County Mayo, but she could hardly complain about replacing the view from her childhood home with the one from Eagle Harbor.

She hurried along Front Street, taking a last final glance at the water before she turned away and started down Center, where the bakery lay three blocks ahead. She'd been in such a rush to find the sheriff earlier, she'd not even left a note for Ellie about where she'd be or why she'd left. Hopefully Ellie wasn't too far behind with the morning's baking. And hopefully she could make up the two hours she'd spent with the deputy. She needed to be working more hours, not fewer.

"Aileen Brogan, stop right there."

Aileen slowed and turned toward the female voice, but no one was in the street. All she could see was the large Sinclair family mansion towering over the town. Who had—?

"I'll be down in a flash," the voice called again. A flurry of auburn hair and yellow dress disappeared from one of the mansion's second story windows.

Aileen couldn't stop her smile. Looked like Rebekah Cummings— or rather, Rebekah Sinclair—had returned. If only the woman had stayed in the window longer, then she'd have told Rebekah to meet her at the bakery. But Rebekah had never been good at standing still for more than two seconds.

Aileen looked toward the bakery, then back at the elaborate gray mansion with fancy gables and trim. She didn't have time to wait. Should she just go to the bakery and hope Rebekah found her?

The front door opened, and out stepped Gilbert Sinclair. Despite the early hour, his three-piece suit was immaculate, his shoes polished to perfection, and his blond hair slicked down and perfectly pomaded until it was almost glossy beneath the morning sun.

"Aileen, is my wife shouting you down in the middle of the road?" A gentle smile tilted the corner of his mouth, and his angel blue eyes danced. He reached for her hand, then bent and pressed his lips to it. "I fear she lost all semblance of manners the second we disembarked from the ship last night."

Aileen grinned, even if she tugged her hand back a little quicker than was proper. Had Gilbert really been successful in teaching Rebekah manners? She could only imagine how those lessons had gone.

"I didn't know ye were back, so I don't mind her calling out to me, except that I'm late for work. Can ye tell Rebekah to—?"

"Aileen." The slam of the mansion's door reverberated through the still morning, and Rebekah strode straight toward where she stood with Gilbert. "Good to see you."

Aileen blinked. It was rather odd seeing a woman who'd had trouble wearing the simple serving uniform skirt the Sinclairs had required in Chicago now swathed in a fancy yellow dress made of fine fabric. Though admittedly, the dress did lack the puffed sleeves, ruffles, and flounces that adorned most rich women's clothes. And Rebekah's deep auburn hair was pulled back into a thick braid that looked like something a woman in a plain gingham dress would wear.

Rebekah drew her into a hug—though hug might be too mild of a description, seeing how Rebekah's arms clamped around her as tight and hard as iron fetters. True, they'd not seen each other since Rebekah had married almost a year ago, but that didn't mean the woman had to crush the breath from her.

Then, as quickly as the hug started, it was finished. Rebekah leaned back studying her, eyes narrowed as they ran from the top of her head down to her hem and back up again. "You look too thin. Have you been eating enough?"

Had she? Aileen glanced down at herself. "I… don't know."

But her skirt did seem a little loose, now that she thought about it.

Rebekah's brow knit. "Your letters made it seem like you were faring well enough."

"I'm fine," she answered quickly. A bit *too* quickly. She was certainly trying to be fine, though the news she'd received from Ireland this past week hadn't helped. Aileen looked back at her friend—or at least the closest thing she had to a friend since coming to America. "And how have ye been?"

"Away too long." Rebekah scanned the street, then peered down the road toward the harbor. "I suppose Elijah's left for the day already? I wanted to fish with him this morning, but someone here forgot to wake me up before dawn." Rebekah jabbed her elbow into Gilbert's side.

"Yes, I completely forgot, darling. Maybe I'll do a better job of remembering on a day when you've had more than four hours of sleep." He dropped a quick kiss onto his wife's forehead. "But you do look lovely this morning, even with this." He tugged on her braid.

Judging by the glare Rebekah gave him, the tug hadn't been all that gentle. "The maid took too long."

"You've not been in Eagle Harbor a full day, and already you're turning into a hooligan." Gilbert raised an eyebrow at Rebekah, the gesture oozing with the arrogance of society's upper crust.

"That's because hooligans have more fun, isn't that right, Aileen?" Rebekah winked in her direction.

"I… ah…" Aileen twisted her hands. Being a hooligan hadn't turned out all that well for her brother Conan. But then, she doubted Rebekah had ever been a true hooligan.

Rebekah narrowed her eyes at something down the street. Then a smile broke across her face, as wide and brilliant as the sun at noonday. "There's Isaac. I'll be right back."

Making no effort to take dainty steps the way most women of her station would, Rebekah strode toward her brother, Sheriff Cummings, who was headed in their direction. A few seconds later, she threw herself into her twin brother's arms, pushed up onto her toes to place a kiss on his cheek, then wrapped her arms around him for a long hug.

Gilbert sighed and rubbed at his temple. "Maybe one day I can convince her not to clobber people on the street."

Aileen coughed. "Good luck with that one. I count it success enough ye got her into a dress."

"Yes, now if only I could get her to make use of her lady's maid and stop braiding her hair." His voice was dry, but his eyes were riveted to his wife.

Aileen tilted her head to the side. "Methinks she looks nice with a braid."

"She always looks nice, even in trousers and a flannel shirt, with her hair free and tangled, and her cheeks sunburned from a day of sailing."

A smile split Aileen's lips. She'd done more smiling in the few minutes Rebekah and Gilbert had been back than she had in... well, that probably didn't bear thinking about. "Ye love her."

"Unequivocally."

Leave it to Gilbert Sinclair to use a fancy word like that to describe his love for his wife.

Gilbert turned his eyes on her then, and gone was the tenderness. In its place was an assessing gaze that belonged to the inventor-turned-businessman whose wealthy family she'd once worked for. "Have you truly been well? I have a feeling what you told Rebekah isn't the whole of it."

How was she supposed to answer that? She looked away from him, but doing so didn't stop the flood of memories from last summer. Pain and fear and uncertainty bombarded her until she could hardly draw a lungful of the thick air surrounding them.

"Aileen?" Gilbert stepped closer.

She took a panicked step back, then pushed the air from her lungs and clamped her teeth down on her tongue. The sharp bite of pain cleared her mind. She was being ridiculous. Gilbert Sinclair, of all people, wasn't going to hurt her.

"Aye." She forced the word out, because it seemed the right thing to say, even if so many things in her life were wrong. "Aye, I've been..." She hugged herself, and a strange coldness invaded her despite the muggy heat. "Doing better."

She couldn't quite claim she'd been well, but she was certainly better today than she'd been at this time last summer. That counted for something, didn't it?

"But I need to go. I'm late for work." It was true, never mind she'd tell a blatant lie if that's what it took to get her away from this conversation. She moved to step around Gilbert.

"Aileen!" Rebekah's voice echoed down the street. "Wait a minute. Isaac needs to talk to you."

She pressed her eyes shut. She did need to tell the sheriff she was sorry for waking him so early and causing a commotion about nothing, but she'd have been better off telling him that after she'd baked him a batch of cookies.

She turned around to face the twins, their auburn hair, hazel eyes, and fair skin declaring their blood relation to all the world.

The sheriff's eyes were full of questions, of course, but at least these questions would be easier to answer than the one he'd asked last winter—the one where he'd asked to court her.

The only trouble was, ever since she'd refused him, he'd taken to looking at her in that soft way he had, the way that showed too many of his thoughts, the way that held too much concern.

The way that made her feel heartless for refusing him.

But she wasn't being heartless, she was being smart and sensible. So why did she feel like wrapping her arms around her middle and huddling into herself whenever he was near? Either that, or reaching out to smooth the unruly tuft of auburn hair that always hung down over his forehead.

Sheriff Cummings pulled out his notepad and pencil, the stray tuft of auburn hair bobbing in its usual awkward place. "Miss Brogan, tell me again what you saw last night."

"You saw something unusual? What?" Rebekah's gaze moved between her and the sheriff.

"Nothing." She curled her fingers into her palm lest they reach up on their own and smooth away the hair from the sheriff's brow. "I'm sure it was nothing now. I'm really sorry to have disturbed you and Mr. Ranulfson so early in the morn, especially since it was all for naught."

"But you did see something in the alley, correct?" The sheriff raised his head from his notepad. "You told me a noise woke you."

At least he was keeping things official rather than asking her on another walk. "Aye, 'tis as I told you earlier. I saw men moving crates on handcarts. I thought they were going to and from the bank, but I was wrong, and 'tis sorry, I am, for waking you."

"You said one of the crates broke?" The sheriff stopped his writing and moved his clear hazel gaze to hers.

Did he realize how pretty his eyes were? How they swirled brown and green together into a color that looked like the richly plowed fields of Ireland mixed with the greenest pasture? She looked away. "Aye, just behind me window. I didn't look before I went for ye, so ye might find something if ye search the alley."

"And what time did you see the men?" He started writing again.

"Three, mayhap four." It had seemed like an eternity as she'd waited for the sky to lighten. "I thought of coming to get ye sooner, but last time ye said to wait until I thought things were safe."

"Last time?" Rebekah crossed her arms over her chest and stepped in front of her brother. "What happened last time?"

Aileen swallowed. Yet another thing she didn't want to talk about, but knowing Rebekah, the woman wouldn't let her leave until she told her every last detail. "We found some—"

"What time did your ship dock last night?" The sheriff was looking at Gilbert now, a shrewd gleam in his eyes.

"Nearly eleven." Gilbert didn't pause before he answered.

Sheriff Cummings scrawled something more on his pad. "Why so late?"

Gilbert shook his head. "It's not my ship, if that's what you're after. Rebekah was anxious to get here, so we took the first ship from Chicago bound for Eagle Harbor."

"Who owns the ship?"

"My father. I agree that it docked abnormally late though."

Aileen looked between the two men. They seemed to be speaking about something more than just the ship, but she couldn't quite grasp what. Why would the sheriff be so interested in the ship in the first place? And what did that have to do with the men she'd seen in the alley?

"Did it make any unusual stops?" The sheriff went back to writing in his notepad again, the breeze from the harbor ruffling his hair so that two other tufts joined the one already lying across his forehead.

Gilbert moved closer to the sheriff, peering over his shoulder to see the notes. "It stopped in Marquette yesterday afternoon, and it took so long to load and unload, I assumed we'd dock there overnight. But the captain called the crew back around dinner time, and we left for Eagle Harbor."

Chatter sounded from the direction of the harbor, and a group of sailors turned from Front Street onto Center, likely coming from the same ship the sheriff and Gilbert spoke of. One of the sailors shoved another as they rounded the turn. Then the second sailor shoved the first sailor back, which prompted a larger man to get between the two brawlers and bark something about behaving.

Aileen narrowed her gaze at the sailor on the far side of the group. There was something familiar about the way he moved. Was he one of the men from last night? With his hat pulled down and his face half hidden behind the other sailors, she couldn't tell.

And what did it matter if he was? It wasn't as though whoever had been outside last night had committed a crime.

The group passed without even a nod in their direction, likely on their way to the bakery.

The bakery. The ship in the harbor. Oh, what had she been thinking? Or mayhap the better question was, what *hadn't* she been thinking? The morning after a ship docked, they usually had a rush of sailors wanting breakfast, and Ellie hadn't had a lick of help from her.

"I'm sorry, but I have to get to work before the Oaktons up and fire me." She dashed off without giving either the sheriff or Rebekah a chance to bid her farewell.

~.~.~.~.~

"Miss Brogan, wait." Isaac glanced up from his notepad where he'd been scrawling Gilbert's information about the ship docking in Marquette. "I want you to…" *Show me the alley.*

But she was already halfway down the road.

Rebekah scowled up at him. "You need to be nicer to her. She's all alone. Don't you know her brother died last year, and a cousin is the only relation she has in America? And I doubt she's seen him since she left Chicago."

Isaac raised his hands, his notepad included. "Be nicer? All I did was ask what she saw last night, and I was perfectly nice while doing so."

Rebekah's chin tilted up—evidently her fancy husband hadn't been able to cure her of such defiant gestures, even if the man should be commended for getting her into a dress. "Then why does Aileen seem so anxious to get away from you?"

Probably for the same reason she was always anxious to get away from him, not that he had a clue what it was. He glanced over to see Miss Brogan rushing down the street, her plain blue skirt swishing about her ankles.

"I didn't do anything to her, I promise." Unless asking to court her last winter counted against him. But when she'd said no, he'd left her alone, as simple as that.

Except it really wasn't simple. Not in a town the size of Eagle Harbor, where he saw her at church every Sunday and where she was always invited to his family's gatherings on holidays. Not when she was the last thing he thought of most nights before he drifted off to sleep, and the first thing he thought of in the morning.

And the main thing he thought of during lunch.

And walking down the road.

And—

"Then why are you staring after her like that?"

He blinked and forced his gaze away from Miss Brogan pulling open the door to the bakery just ahead of a group of mariners. "Like what?"

Rebekah planted her hands on her hips. "Don't treat me like I'm an imbecile, Isaac. You know exactly what I'm talking about."

"Rebekah," Gilbert's voice held a warning note.

Rather than look at her husband, Rebekah kept her gaze pinned to him, eyes narrowed accusingly.

Sisters. He supposed it was nice to have his back for a few months, but it would be even nicer if she needled her husband instead of him. "I haven't done anything other than try to be kind and helpful and occasionally question her when troubles come up, as any sheriff would. That's it."

Rebekah glanced down the street toward where Miss Brogan had disappeared into the bakery and furrowed her brow. "Is she really that frightened of you?"

"I wouldn't call her frightened, but she's never been comfortable with me, no." He tucked his notepad into his shirt pocket, since Rebekah didn't seem apt to let him get back to work anytime soon.

"Is she that way with everyone?"

"Ah…" He scratched the side of his head. "She's a mite better with Elijah than she is with most men, but besides him…"

Rebekah bit the side of her lip, her gaze still latched onto the bakery. "But I don't understand. Things were supposed to be better for her here." When she looked back at him, her eyes shimmered with moisture. "Coming to Eagle Harbor was supposed to help."

He sighed. How was it his sister could be as tough as an anchor rope one minute and as soft as pie filling the next? "Help what?"

"I think it has helped, darling." Gilbert reached for his wife and pulled her to his side. "Not everything can be fixed overnight."

Rebekah's shoulders rose and fell on a sigh. "It's not overnight. It's been almost a year. I suppose I was hoping…"

"To find her married with a child on the way?" Gilbert rubbed the side of her arm and looked down at her, the gaze in his eyes so tender Isaac nearly turned his back to give the couple a bit of privacy. "You knew better than to expect either of those things from her letters."

"Maybe not married with children, but I wanted her to be happy." Rebekah looked up at her husband. "Did she seem happy to you?"

"I…" Gilbert shook his head and sighed. "Not really, no, but we only saw her for a few minutes, and it seemed like she'd had a difficult morning."

Rebekah turned back to Isaac, her shoulders sagging. "Does she seem happy in Eagle Harbor?"

Isaac coughed. "I… ah, don't really know her well enough to say."

But that had been her choice, not his.

Her words from last winter drifted back to him. *If such a thing as a good man exists, Sheriff Cummings, then I'm sure ye're one of them. But me, I'm just not the type to make a good wife. I don't think I'll ever be, at least not anymore.*

The snow had sparkled around them that day; the previous evening's dusting of several inches still lying pristine over the town. Her hair had flamed against the whiteness, a single, unmistakable splash of color so vibrant he'd nearly reached out and fingered one of the flyaway strands hanging by her ear. Even now, in this wretched humidity, he could almost taste the crisp winter air on his tongue, almost smell the wood smoke curling up from nearby chimneys.

"What aren't you telling me?" Rebekah took a step closer to him, myriad thoughts churning behind hazel eyes the same shade as his own. "Has being in Eagle Harbor helped her or not?"

He clenched his teeth. "I already said I don't know. I don't even know what being in Eagle Harbor is supposed to help her with in the first place."

Rebekah and Gilbert shared a look, but neither spoke.

He raised his hands, only to let them fall back to his side. What was it about Miss Brogan no one wanted to tell him? "At least tell me what happened to her in Chicago."

There wasn't any question that she'd been hurt in some way. He'd figured that out the very day she'd arrived last summer with Rebekah. She'd been too skittish to even say hello to him then.

Rebekah's shoulders rose and fell on a sigh. "If it were up to me, I'd tell you. But it's her story, and she probably doesn't want you knowing."

"Yet both of you know." The words tasted bitter on his tongue.

Rebekah looked up at Gilbert, but Gilbert just pressed his lips together.

Fine, then. He had work to do. Both of his deputies were supposed to head this way after they were done questioning those who lived near the bank. And he should have been searching the alley already.

He rubbed a hand over his face. He didn't yet have evidence of a crime being committed, but so far the clues were all pointing in one direction—a direction that seemed utterly impossible. But with a ship docking abnormally late and men running boxes away from the harbor in the dead of night...

He couldn't possibly have smugglers in Eagle Harbor, could he?

Chapter Three

Isaac stared down at the worn piece of wood in his hand, running his thumb over the half-formed letters on the broken board he'd found tucked against the bakery wall. Or maybe wedged was a better word since he'd had to yank it free from behind the giant flowerpot sitting by the back door.

"Looks like it came from a crate." Deputy Fletcher left the patch of packed dirt he'd been inspecting with Deputy Granger and scampered across the alley to where Isaac stood near the bakery.

Isaac nearly winced. No question Fletcher was on the young side for a deputy, but the man had been working for him for over two months now. When would he learn to walk a little slower, carry himself with a little more authority?

"If it came from a crate, then it matches Miss Brogan's story." On the other side of the alley, Granger picked up a splinter of wood, frowned at it, then set it back down near the base of the Lunsfords' house.

"That it does," Isaac muttered. Miss Brogan had said the men appeared to be cleaning up a broken crate. If only he could make out enough of the letters to know what the board said. But the board had shattered, leaving him with a foot-long, four-inch wide splinter with only the bottoms of letters printed on it.

Did it say *Canada*, perhaps? Or perhaps the board said *nada*, which could certainly be part of *Canada*.

Yet even if he had the full board with *Canada* written on it plain as day, that didn't prove smugglers had been behind the bakery.

But it didn't disprove smugglers either. If there were any about, they'd likely be running goods between Canada and the United States.

He slapped at a mosquito feasting on the back of his neck. Still, the whole notion seemed a little far-fetched to him. Men intent on smuggling had hundreds of miles of wilderness shoreline they could sail to on Lake Superior. Would something specific have made them decide to use Eagle Harbor? Or had they randomly picked this port and could have ended up in Copper Harbor or Ontonagon or Baraga just as easily?

"I don't see anything else out of place." Granger still hunched low, inspecting the alley beside the Lunsfords' house.

"Here. See if you can make out what these letters say." Isaac handed the board to Fletcher.

A wide grin spread across his deputy's face, highlighting the smattering of freckles on his cheeks. "Yes sir, Sheriff."

The man would learn to be a little less eager with time too, wouldn't he? Isaac bit back his sigh and swept his gaze over the alley. What kind of clues would smugglers leave? He wanted Eagle Harbor to be safe, yes, but he'd only been sheriff for seven months. He could handle robberies, fights, disorderly conduct, public intoxication, and he'd hopefully have the town vandal caught by the end of the week, but smuggling?

His imagination was likely running away from him and nothing more.

"So what exactly do we think happened last night?" Fletcher rubbed his forehead beneath his hat brim.

Isaac gave a slight shake of his head. "Don't know. Can't even say it was anything. But I'm thinking one explanation could be smuggling."

Granger dropped the rock in his hand and stood, his gaze steady.

"Smugglers in Eagle Harbor?" Fletcher's voice pitched high. "I don't believe it."

"I'm not sure I do either." Isaac scanned the alley once more, an alley that appeared to be too clean. Where were the rocks and clumps of dirt that should litter the center of it? It was almost as though whoever had been here last night had taken a broom and swept the packed dirt clean before leaving. "But smuggling is the only guess I have—if anything happened worth guessing about."

Granger leaned against the wall of the Lunsfords' house and tapped his chin. "Could be there was some kind of bet, a bunch of drunk fools racing each other through the alley wagering on the winner, or something along those lines."

Isaac stifled a yawn. The three hours of sleep he'd had last night was catching up to him. "Maybe, but don't forget there was a ship that docked after dark."

"And Miss Brogan said she saw more than one crate being moved, but only one broke." Fletcher held up the board they'd found as though it could somehow tell them more about the mysterious crate it had come from.

"Sheriff! Sheriff Cummings!"

Isaac looked up just as two skinny bodies trapped somewhere between childhood and adulthood scrambled around the corner of the bakery.

"There's a dead man, Sheriff. You gotta come quick!" Martin Spritzer rushed toward him and pulled on his sleeve, the youth's red hair flopping over one eye.

"Where?" Was he allowed to pray that the boys were mistaken? That there wasn't really a dead body somewhere in Eagle Harbor?

"In the woods," Martin blinked up at him, his skin pale against his bright hair. "We were in the woods—"

"Exploring." Leroy gave a stiff nod of his head. "That's what we were doing, exploring."

"Yeah, we were in the woods exploring." Martin scratched the back of his neck. "And then we heard a gunshot, so we went looking."

"You heard a gunshot, and then you ran *toward* the sound?" Isaac clenched his jaw and glared at the brothers.

Martin frowned. "We thought someone shot a deer."

"We were wondering if the hunter would give us a hind roast." Leroy blinked earnestly from beneath the thick thatch of reddish-blond hair that hung over his eyes. "Ma's been ill, and the money Ellie brings home from the bakery only goes so far."

He looked over the boys' heads and met his deputies' gazes. "Looks like we've got a body to investigate."

⌐.⌐.⌐.⌐.⌐

Afternoon sunlight glinted off tree leaves and blades of grass, giving the entire forest a golden hue. Above, a bird chirped happily from a tree branch and two squirrels chased each other. If only the scene in the little patch of grass below matched the rest of the forest. Isaac ran his gaze slowly up the body lying on the forest floor before forcing himself to look at the man's face. Though calling the mass of mangled flesh and blood and bone a face was a bit generous on his part.

"Any guess who he is?" Granger squatted near the body, his face grim, though his dark eyes hid his thoughts.

Isaac drew in a breath of air tinged with the stench of blood and squatted on the other side of the man. "Search his pockets. Hopefully there'll be something we can use to identify him."

"Do you think he's from town?" Fletcher stood several feet away and kept his face averted. The young man had turned pale the instant he'd come upon the body.

"Can't tell." Isaac turned the man's hand over. The thickness of his skin along with the lack of lines and wrinkles said the man wasn't any older than him, though the roughness of his fingers spoke of someone accustomed to hard labor.

He laid the man's hand to rest over his chest. "Could be he's a Cousin Jack from Central. Could be he's a dockworker only in Eagle Harbor for the summer months. I don't feel as though he's anyone I know particularly well. He's the wrong size to be Jake Ranulfson, and outside of you…" Isaac jutted his chin toward his squeamish deputy. "…I don't know of too many other people in town this age."

"Nothing in his pockets or boots." Granger sat back and ran his gaze over the body with a steadiness that told Isaac this wasn't the first dead person his mysterious deputy who'd sailed into town last fall had come in contact with.

"Let's roll him, see if we find something that might help us determine who he is." Isaac looked at the man once more, trying to commit as many details as he could to memory before they moved the body. Nothing seemed out of the ordinary except the pistol lying about three feet away from the man's shoulder.

"Do you think it was a suicide?" Granger's gaze flickered to the gun. "He obviously took a gunshot to the side of his head."

"Gun seems a little far away for a suicide, but why would a killer leave it behind?" Isaac slapped at a mosquito on his arm, then shooed another away.

"C-could be a gun would fall that far when it drops from a standing man's head." Fletcher still wouldn't look directly at the body.

"Could be," Isaac muttered half to himself. "Fletcher, why don't you head back into town and question Leroy and Martin again, see if they left out any information before." He'd questioned the boys while they led him and his deputies to the body, but had sent them back to town so they didn't have to stay with the dead man any longer than necessary. Had he known how Fletcher would respond, he'd have sent his deputy back too. "You also might give Leroy and Martin another lecture or ten about running away from gunshots in the woods, and not toward them."

If this man's death wasn't a suicide, the two Spritzer boys had been dangerously close to a killer. What would a killer have done if Leroy and Martin had happened upon him? Isaac set his jaw. One body was enough to bury in Eagle Harbor's cemetery.

"I'll let the doc know there'll be a body to examine too." Fletcher gripped the brim of his hat, then scampered off without so much as a glance at the dead man behind him.

"I like Fletcher, I do," Granger drawled. "But I'm not sure the boy is cut out to be a lawman."

"Maybe in another month…" Isaac sighed. How much time should he give Fletcher to adjust before he looked for another deputy? "All right. Let's roll him."

Isaac walked around the other side of the body before kneeling and helping Granger push the man over. But the stranger's back didn't give away any more clues than his front.

He had brown hair, at least from what Isaac could tell of the matted mess. On the young side, probably closer to twenty than thirty. Around a hundred and sixty pounds and about five-foot-ten.

Why couldn't the man have been six-foot-five and skinny as a rail? Or five-foot-two and grotesquely large around his middle? Then maybe they'd have a chance of someone knowing who he was with only a description. But there was nothing remarkable about this person, whoever he was. Not too tall or too short, not too heavy or too skinny, and a hair color that described half the people living in Copper Country.

"Let's look for tracks." Isaac pushed to his feet. "If he wasn't alone, then it could be a murder."

Murdered by smugglers? He rubbed at the back of his neck. A foolish notion, that. Smugglers probably only existed in his imagination.

But if this man's death wasn't a suicide, a killer was somewhere in the area. And a man who'd killed once wouldn't have a hard time killing again.

Chapter Four

Isaac yawned and rubbed his eyes, the scraggly grass underfoot crunching along with the twigs as he made his way across the yard toward the workshop. Behind him, the rambling log cabin his pa built sat like a watchman against the boulder-strewn shore of Lake Superior.

If only he didn't have to stare at the lake every time he came to visit his brother or ma. Even now, the sound of waves washing onto the rocks echoed through the woods despite the fact he moved farther and farther away from the water.

He yawned again and blinked a bit of the exhaustion from his eyes. His shoulders ached, his neck was stiff, and his head pounded. He should probably be home in bed, getting a few hours of rest before the revelry at the bars started tonight and he had to go back out on patrol. But he had to talk to his older brother, Elijah.

And Rebekah had said something about Miss Brogan coming for dinner tonight.

Though he didn't know why he was eager to see her again. She'd hardly been thrilled with his questions earlier, and she'd probably be even less happy to see him at dinner. He pushed open the door to the workshop.

"Isaac?" Elijah called from the back of the room. "Didn't realize you were coming."

Isaac stepped inside. The scent of wood and sawdust twined around him, the familiar smell almost as relaxing as an afternoon of angling at the river.

He headed toward the workbench on the far side of the building where Elijah and their adopted brother Mac were both huddled, weaving his way between the haphazard tables filled with handmade toy wagons and trains and horses. He'd carefully sawed, assembled, and sanded each one before he'd been elected sheriff. He needed to ship them off at some point and see what price they'd bring in Chicago rather than let them sit here and collect dust. He scratched the back of his head. He still had to paint the toys on the back table, but when would he have time? Being sheriff was a round-the-clock job that didn't seem likely to give him a break anytime soon.

Isaac stepped around the final table, and Elijah turned to face him, his dark blond hair and gray eyes nothing like the features Isaac shared with Rebekah.

Did Elijah realize how lucky he was to look like their ma? To not see Pa staring back at him every time he glanced into a mirror?

Elijah set his pencil down atop the papers scattered across the workbench. His overgrown hair and bushy eyebrows gave him the rugged look of a mariner that hadn't visited a barber for half a year. "Dinner ready?"

"No, they're just starting the potatoes."

"Why didn't they start those a half hour ago? I'm hungry." Mac turned, and only then did Isaac see Mac's youngest child, Sarah, in his arms. The babe reached for a scrap of wood lying on the workbench, then made a gurgling sound when her fist tightened around it.

"Victoria isn't helping, is she?" Elijah grimaced. "I love my wife, but I don't know that she'll ever have Ma's way in a kitchen."

"Or Tressa's or Rebekah's," Mac muttered.

Isaac laughed, which only caused Mac to glower.

"You think it's funny, but you didn't have to eat her biscuits when Tressa was laid up before Sarah was born. They're like eating sawdust."

"Rocks," Elijah muttered. "Sawdust is too soft."

"Fine, like biting into a rock that tastes like sawdust." Mac tried to take the wood from Sarah, but she squealed in protest.

Elijah nodded. "That's pretty close to it."

Isaac laughed again, and it felt good. When was the last time he'd had a conversation about something so mundane? Instead his days were filled with vandalism and drunken brawls—and now dead bodies.

"Heard about the body in the woods." Mac leaned against the workbench, his hulking frame so large Isaac half expected the bench to crack beneath Mac's weight. Mac's wide chest, thick arms, and towering form probably caused people who first met him to think he was a miner or logger rather than the town lightkeeper who'd married Eagle Harbor's bakery owner. "You figure out who the dead man was?"

Isaac shook his head. When he'd sent Fletcher back to town, his deputy hadn't just told the doctor he'd be examining a body, he'd also told the entire town about the dead man. Half the townsfolk had shown up to see the stranger taken to the doctor's office, but no one had recognized him. "Probably going to take a few days since he doesn't seem to be from around here."

"And you think he killed himself?" Elijah leaned back against the workbench with Mac. It didn't so much as creak beneath the added weight.

Isaac sighed and rubbed the back of his neck. "Seems most likely."

Elijah blew out a low whistle and shook his head. "I'm always sad to hear when a person takes his life. A man would have to be caught in a mighty hopeless spot to do something like that."

"Hopeless, yes, but I'd rather have the death be the man's own doing than have a murderer on the loose." *Please God, if there is a murderer out there, let me find him quickly.*

"What was in those crates Aileen saw last night?" Mac jostled Sarah, still content to gnaw on her piece of wood. "Did you find out?

"No, and I doubt I will considering the investigation didn't turn up any extra information."

Did the dead man have anything to do with the men Aileen had seen in the alley? The last thing he needed was for Miss Brogan to have witnessed something that might put her in danger.

And there he was getting ahead of himself again, because as far as he could tell, the men in the alley hadn't committed a crime. But he wasn't quite ready to lay that particular incident to rest just yet.

He drew in a deep breath, then looked at Elijah and forced his next words out. "Are you taking the *North Star* to Houghton anytime soon?"

Elijah raised one of his bushy eyebrows. "Are you asking me to take the boat out?"

"Not exactly. I asked if you were planning to." Isaac swallowed. "Don't take it out on account of me."

Whatever you do, don't take that boat out because of me.

His mind screamed the words, but he kept his mouth clenched tight. The *North Star* was the fastest way to get what he needed done, and since Elijah didn't have any qualms about taunting the great monstrosity of a lake to their north, he'd figured there was no harm in asking. But the last thing he needed was for Elijah to go to Houghton on his behalf. What if a storm came up? What if Elijah couldn't get to safety? What if—?

"Isaac."

Isaac drew his gaze up to Mac, then sucked in a breath and pushed it out. When had his breathing grown so hard?

"You all right?" Concern filled Mac's tawny eyes.

"Fine." Or he would be as long as he didn't think about boats and water... and death.

"What do you need me to do in Houghton?" Elijah's voice was calm—too calm—as though he spoke to a skittish kitten rather than a grown man.

Rather than the man charged with protecting Eagle Harbor.

Isaac didn't need to look in his brother's direction to know Elijah watched him with a keen gray gaze that saw far too much. He reached into his shirt pocket and pulled out the folded piece of paper. "I have a telegram that needs sending. But if you're not headed down to Houghton or Ontonagon or somewhere else soon, I'll figure out how to send it myself."

Elijah narrowed his gaze. "Why can't you send this telegram from the office in town?"

"Mrs. Runkle's almost as big a gossip as Mrs. Ranulfson." With the town already talking about the dead man, he hardly needed the telegraph operator spreading another rumor.

Elijah held out a hand for the paper. "What exactly does this telegram say?"

Isaac handed over the missive, and Elijah read while Mac peeked over Elijah's shoulder.

"You think there're smugglers here?" Mac hefted little Sarah higher against his chest. The babe screwed up her face and threw the piece of wood she held onto the floor.

"I'm supposed to report all suspicious activity to the U.S. Customs Service and let them handle any investigations. But it's the best explanation I can think of for what Miss Brogan saw last night, as far-fetched as it seems." Isaac turned to survey the table full of toys nearest him, grabbed a rattle, and held it out for Sarah. "If you have any other ideas, I'm open to hearing them. But I'd prefer to keep

Mrs. Runkle, Mrs. Kainer, and Mrs. Ranulfson from telling everyone in Copper Country there're smugglers afoot. It'll probably turn out to be nothing."

Elijah kept his gaze trained on the paper. "Suppose I could run down to Houghton after I set my nets tomorrow. I've been doing some fishing south of Eagle River anyway. But if I take this telegram, can you spend a few hours clearing your things out of here?" Elijah gestured to the room overflowing with toys. "I need some space."

Isaac opened his mouth to agree, then stilled. "Space for what?"

He was probably better off not asking, especially considering where they were standing. Even so, it was a fair request for his brother to make, since the property now belonged to Elijah and Victoria.

Mac jiggled the rattle for Sarah. "For a project Gilbert asked us to help with."

Isaac's throat turned dry. If they were helping Gilbert, there was only one kind of project they'd want to use this building for—the reason they'd built the workshop in the first place.

A boat.

But one of the boats they'd built in this very room had taken their pa to his grave.

The *North Star* had washed up on shore shortly after the storm that had taken Pa's life, battered but salvageable. It was the boat Elijah still fished in.

Isaac's stomach churned with a sickening sensation.

Every time Elijah took out that boat, it was as if he dared the stormy black clouds to gather and the angry gray lake to swallow him up as it had Pa. He could still see it in his mind, the churning sea that capsized the small boat, his father swimming toward shore, one huge wave washing over him, then another and another, until he disappeared beneath the waters of the harbor...

And all the while, Isaac stood rooted to the iron platform in the lighthouse. Too terrified to move. Too terrified to help.

Air. He gulped in a breath. He needed air, to be out of this building, to be away from the memories. He turned and strode toward the door.

Elijah called out to him, followed by Mac, but he didn't stop. The fear might be irrational, might be crazy, might be any number of things. But it felt as though an anchor sat atop his chest, pressing on his lungs until he couldn't breathe. He reached the door and lurched outside, forcing his eyes to focus on the grass beneath his feet instead of the lake that lay beyond the cabin, deceptive in its peacefulness on a day such as this.

Breathe. He needed to breathe through the panic threatening to choke him. He couldn't afford to be weak, not when he had a town to protect.

Chapter Five

She'd forgotten the cookies. Aileen drew in a breath and let it out again as the breeze off the lake twined through her hair. She stood outside the Cummings family cabin poised to go inside to dinner. Should she go in without the sheriff's cookies and simply apologize for ruining his morning? She could always give them to him tomorrow.

"Aileen Brogan, wait right there. I need to talk to you." A familiar voice hollered through the window.

Rebekah rushed outside a moment later, flyaway strands of hair hanging from the braid that had seemed so perfect that morning. A large, stained apron covered her fancy yellow dress. And was that mud splattered on the hem?

"There were too many people around this morning or I would have said something then." Rebekah dug around in her dress pocket. "Have you seen any papers from Chicago lately?"

At the mention of the crowded, blustery city, something cold swirled through her. "Nay, and I don't intend to either."

But Rebekah was already pulling out a folded section of newsprint. "There's a court case in the news."

A simple glance at the headline told her all she needed to know. Gilbert's brother, Warren, was involved in a trial. A small picture of the woman accusing him sat in the corner of one of the columns. She was pretty, of course, and poor. A kitchen worker in the restaurant of some fancy hotel, which explained how Warren would have met her.

Aileen didn't need to read the whole of the article to know what the rest would say. And she didn't need to see the headline that would be splashed across the paper a month from now to know who would win the case. She handed the paper back to Rebekah.

"Have you thought about—?"

"Nay." Her answer was short and clipped, though her throat had suddenly turned thick.

"But what if—?"

"Nay."

Rather than fold it, Rebekah crumpled the paper in her hand. "I figured as much, but I still wanted to ask."

Giggles and shouts sounded from the other side of the house near the water, where the O'Byrne children likely played with the Oaktons' wee ones.

"Nothing will happen to him if I do." The words tasted bitter on her tongue, but that didn't make them any less true. "It never does with rich people like that."

"Maybe if someone else testified, if someone else…"

Aileen shook her head. "If ye stop and think a spell, ye'll see I've the right of it."

Besides, she couldn't entertain thoughts of going to Chicago— for any reason—not when she planned to return to Ireland. But she'd yet to tell Rebekah that.

"It's not right." Rebekah shoved the crumpled paper back into her pocket, her jaw suddenly hard. "He should answer for what he did."

Aye. There were a lot of things not right with the world, but an immigrant woman like her didn't have the power to change them.

She slipped her arm through Rebekah's and turned her toward the house. If they stood outside any longer, people would ask them what they were talking about. "Sometimes it's best to leave the past in the past and move on."

Or rather, make the best of what was left. Because some things a person couldn't ever move on from, not really.

They climbed the porch steps and headed inside, moving through the entryway that was full of boots and coats, even though they wouldn't be needed again until fall. When she stepped inside the kitchen, the scents of frying fish and potatoes, fresh biscuits, sugary cookies, and pie mixed into such a tantalizing aroma her stomach growled.

"Sorry I took so long." Rebekah headed straight to the stove, where her mother Mabel stood. On the top, pans with frying fish and potatoes sizzled.

"Not a problem, but we're ready for another batch of potatoes." Mabel looked over her shoulder and smiled. "Hello, Aileen. Glad you could come for dinner."

Aileen smiled in return. "Thank ye. 'Twas right kind of you to invite me, it was."

On the other side of the stove, a couple dozen cookies sat cooling on the hutch beside two pies. Victoria Cummings, Gilbert Sinclair, and her boss, Tressa Oakton, were all hunched over a large roll of parchment on the table.

Victoria rose in an elegant gesture and swept toward her, her arms extended for a hug. "I'm happy you could join us as well. I was w-worried about you when I heard about those men behind your shop last night. Are you all right?"

Every eye in the house turned to her, but at least they were asking about what happened at the bakery and not about what Rebekah had talked to her about in the yard. "I'm, ah… fine."

"You look a bit pale." Victoria leaned back, her eyes filled with concern, the air tinged with an expensive smelling perfume that matched the elegant green dress draping her tall frame.

How exactly was it that a woman as elegant and regal as Victoria had ended up married to the town fisherman? And a man as rich as Gilbert Sinclair had married the fisherman's sister? She'd been living here almost a year and had yet to hear the full story. All she knew was that Gilbert and Victoria had once been engaged, but Victoria had broken the engagement when her father's shipping company had fallen on hard times and married Elijah instead.

Her boss, Tressa Oakton, rose to give her a hug as well, and only then did Aileen see the babe settled on her hip.

Something twisted inside her, and it only wrenched more when Tressa leaned in to hug her, pressing little Sarah against her side.

Tressa pulled back after only a few moments, a concerned smile on her face. "Isaac stopped by the lighthouse to tell us what happened. I'm glad it wasn't a bank robbery like you first thought."

"Me too. I hope you don't mind I was late to start work this morn after fetching the sheriff, but I stayed late and gave the kitchen a good scrubbing, I did."

"No need to worry about such things. I'm not going to get upset because you had to get the sheriff." The small woman waved her off.

But Aileen followed Tressa to the far end of the table. This was just as good a time as any to ask about more hours at the bakery. "Might ye have any extra work to do around the bakery this summer? Something that needs cleaning out mayhap, or extra bread I can bake to stock the mercantile. They'll sell more when the town is busier."

"I—"

"No need to spend extra hours scrubbing floors for Tressa. You can scrub mine. Bet I pay more than Tressa anyway." Gilbert sat back from the table and winked, a playful smile turning the edges of his lips up.

Aileen didn't smile back. Instead, her throat turned dry. The last time she'd worked for the Sinclairs, things had turned out terribly for her.

"Do you mean to hire her for the mansion or the hotel?" Rebekah turned from the stove long enough to look at her husband, then went back to frying fish.

"The hotel?" Aileen furrowed her brow at Rebekah. "What are ye talking about?"

"Gilbert bought two mansions this week, the one his parents owned, and the one that belonged to my parents." Victoria slipped back into her seat beside Tressa.

He had? She met Gilbert's gaze across the table.

He sat there in his immaculate three-piece suit that didn't look as though it had picked up a speck of dust all day. His eyes almost sparkled with excitement. "My parents have been talking about selling their mansion for a while, and considering my wife wants us to spend our summers here…" He sent Rebekah a look that caused a blush to spread across her cheeks.

"As for buying the old Donnelly mansion, Eagle Harbor needs more lodging." Gilbert turned back to her. "The boardinghouse is always full, and people who come into port hoping to travel farther inland often don't have a place to stay. Rebekah mentioned buying the Donnelly place and turning it into a hotel, and I thought it a good idea."

"Don't let him fool you into thinking he takes my word for anything." Rebekah left the stove with a bowl of potatoes and set them on the table. "He spent an entire day laying out business projections and ciphering numbers before he decided I was right."

Gilbert raised his hands. "One should do research before making an investment of this magnitude. But now I'm in need of someone to ready the hotel. Will you come work for me, Aileen?"

Tressa's head shot up. "You mean after she's done with her shift at the bakery? You do want to keep working at the bakery, don't you, Aileen?"

Aileen glanced between the man rich enough to buy two dozen farms in Ireland and the fiery bakery owner who paid her every week. She bit the side of her lip. "I…"

Gilbert sent her a wink. "Whatever Mac's paying you, I'll double it."

Double it?

Tressa stood, her chair screeching across the floor as she plopped a hand on her hip. The babe whined at the commotion. "It's my bakery, not his. I'm the one paying her."

"In that case, I'll triple it."

Triple it? Surely he couldn't mean that. But if he were serious, a few months of working for him would solve her troubles. She could be in Ireland before winter.

Tressa's eyes narrowed into two thin slits. "Just see if you get any more cookies from me, Gilbert Sinclair."

It was the wrong threat to utter, especially considering how Gilbert sat on the side of the table where the cookies were cooling. He merely winked at Tressa, grabbed a cookie, and sank his teeth into it.

Aileen couldn't stop her grin. How did Rebekah stand being married to someone like him? Arguing with Gilbert would be akin to telling the ocean to stop making waves.

Then again, disagreeing with Rebekah would be much the same.

Tressa stomped her foot on the floor. "You'd better enjoy that one, seeing how it'll be the last you get from me."

Sarah squawked again, but Gilbert just raised an arrogant

eyebrow. "Aileen's a hard worker, and I bet her cookies are every bit as good as yours."

Tressa's mouth dropped open. "Why you—"

"Don't pay him any mind." Rebekah set a platter of fish on the table. "You'll only encourage him."

Gilbert moved quicker than a cat pouncing on a mouse. His hand shot out to yank Rebekah's arm, and he scooted his chair out from the table just in time to catch his wife as she fell into his lap. "Hush now, darling, or you'll give away my secrets."

He clamped an arm around her waist to pin her in place, then pressed his lips to Rebekah's temple and moved his mouth to her ear and whispered something. Rebekah's cheeks turned red and her gaze latched on her husband.

A dull ache spread through Aileen's heart. Did they realize how sweet they were together? How easy they made it seem to be in love?

How impossible love was for certain people in this room?

Rebekah swatted Gilbert away and tromped back to the stove, a secret smile on her lips.

Aileen drew in a breath, then met Gilbert's eyes. "What would working for you entail?"

Please, God, let it be something I can do so that I can get back to Brenna quickly.

Her cousin needed her help, and the sooner, the better.

"Oh sure, just leave the bakery the second this buffoon strolls into town." Tressa huffed, yet her voice lacked heat.

A good thing, that, since she couldn't afford not to consider Gilbert's offer.

"For now, I need someone to clean out the rooms, catalogue supplies, and make a list of furnishings we'll need to order." Gilbert scooted his chair closer to the table. "I'd like to have as much furniture as possible made locally so the hotel can be running by August. I've a mind to use it more as a boardinghouse in the winter, when we don't get many newcomers."

"So the job would only last until August?" If she left the bakery, Tressa would replace her right away. So if she didn't earn enough to buy passage back to Ireland by August, what would she do to make up the rest?

"Not necessarily." Gilbert settled his arms across his chest, his voice serious enough he might well be negotiating a ten-thousand-dollar business deal in Chicago rather than a temporary job for an immigrant woman. "I'll need someone to run the hotel once it's finished."

"Run the hotel?" She blinked. "But isn't that a man's job?"

"You forget I married a fisherman." Gilbert's voice was dry.

Rebekah looked over her shoulder and sent Gilbert another one of her secret smiles. "Fisherwoman."

Gilbert snorted. "If my wife can be a sailor, I daresay my hotel manager can be a woman too."

Except she didn't have a lick of experience with managing hotels—or managing anything really. "I... ah..."

The door opened, and Elijah and Mac tromped inside.

"Is dinner ready?" Elijah scanned the table, which was already half filled with food.

Mac rubbed his belly. "I'm starved."

"Go call the children." Rebekah's mother turned from the stove and wiped her hands on her apron. "We'll be ready to eat in just a minute."

Rebekah brought the final platter of fish to the table. "Where's Isaac?" Her gaze landed on Elijah. "Didn't he go out to the workshop with you and Mac an hour ago?"

Elijah and Mac shared a look, then Elijah dropped his gaze to the floor and rubbed the back of his neck. "He, uh... went off into the woods before Mac brought Sarah in. Should be back any time."

Aye, Isaac. The man whose day she'd upset by telling him about a non-existent bank robbery. Getting woken at the crack of dawn had to be easier than finding a dead body in the woods, but even so… Aileen twisted her hands in her skirt. Mayhap she wasn't as eager to apologize as she'd thought.

"Call him in when you call the young'uns then." Rebekah's mother shooed Mac back out the door.

The kitchen transformed into a flutter of movement as Gilbert and Elijah headed into the living area to set up a table for the children. Aileen moved extra chairs to the large kitchen table for the adults, while Victoria set the table and Tressa went to lay down a sleeping Sarah in one of the bedrooms.

Then Sheriff Cummings came in, and the entire room stilled…

At least for her.

Everyone else, however, moved about readying the house for the feast Rebekah and her mother had prepared. Aileen drew a breath into her tight lungs and reached for the bowl of biscuits on the hutch. She was being a wee bit ridiculous, she was. Once she apologized for sending him on a goose chase, she'd feel less awkward around him.

The children bounded into the house, causing childish chatter and giggles to fill the room. Aileen soon found herself seated between the sheriff and Rebekah. With all the other adults at the table married except for Isaac's widowed mother, she couldn't exactly complain about being paired off with Isaac.

They all joined hands while Elijah bowed his head at the front of the table. Elijah's voice boomed through the house as though he were trying to tame Lake Superior, and yet his prayer still held an undeniable note of thankfulness. Then Elijah's hearty amen echoed through the room, and he reached for the platter of fish in front of him.

It all felt so charming and homey and perfect. If only she could smile as easily as Mrs. Cummings or laugh as freely as Rebekah. If only she could feel like she belonged at this table surrounded by the Cummings family.

But what was the point of getting comfortable when she'd be leaving for Ireland, hopefully sooner than expected?

"Did you get the hotel all planned out with Victoria and Gilbert?" Across the table, Mac settled a hand across his wife's shoulders.

"We were close, but then Gilbert decided to try stealing one of our employees away from us." Tressa shot Gilbert a glare.

"Is that so?" Mac reached for his water glass, then looked across the table at her. "You have a better job offer, do you, Aileen?"

She squirmed. "Aye, mayhap I do."

"How soon will you be leaving us?" Mac jerked a thumb toward Gilbert. "Knowing him, he probably convinced you to start work for him tomorrow."

Aileen stared down at her plate. The delicious scent of the fish wafted up to her, but she'd not yet taken a bite. Would the Oaktons really not mind if she quit the bakery and started working for Gilbert? They'd been good to give her work in the first place, and she'd still need to rent the room above the bakery.

"She's still thinking about it." Gilbert lifted a forkful of fish but paused before it reached his mouth. Then his gaze found hers from down the table where he sat on the other side of Rebekah. "Let me know what you decide."

"You don't have to work for him." Sheriff Cummings leaned close, his voice low so as not to be overheard. "You're free to make your own decisions. Gilbert can be a bit, um, convincing at times, but you're allowed to tell him no."

Aileen swallowed. "Aye, I understand well enough, but thank ye."

Except she really couldn't say no, not if Gilbert meant what he said about paying her triple what Tressa paid.

She glanced up to find everyone watching her, as though waiting for her answer though Gilbert had just said she didn't need to give one. And really, why keep everyone wondering what she would decide when she already knew?

She squirmed again, then blew out a breath. "I got a letter from me cousin Brenna in Ireland at the beginning of the week. Her husband died of a fever this spring, and she's got four wee ones. I'm going back to Ireland to help her, though it will take almost a year to earn enough. So if ye're serious about paying me more than the Oaktons, Gilbert, and if it won't be too much of a hardship for Mac and Tressa, then I'll take yer job to ready the hotel and head back to Ireland before winter."

"Why didn't you say something about your cousin being in such a predicament?" Victoria set her water glass on the table without taking a drink, her eyes filled with that familiar look of concern again. "I had no idea."

Gilbert wiped his face and set his napkin down beside his plate. "You don't need to work at my hotel, Aileen. If you want to go back to Ireland, I'll have passage arranged by the end of the week. No need to concern yourself with the cost."

Her fork clattered to the table. It was too much. But she was hardly in a position to refuse. How long had it been since little Daithi had curled onto her lap or Nora had asked her to play with her rag dolls? Cathal would be nigh on eight now, and she'd never even laid eyes on wee Ide.

Even if she had to work a long time to pay Gilbert back, she'd rather take his money and go to Brenna than stay here.

But would there be work for her in Ireland?

The table exploded into chatter, questions and voices and offers all bombarding her. Did she want clothes to take to her cousin? How old were the children? Could the town hold a bake sale to raise money for Brenna, or maybe set up a special booth at the Thimbleberry Festival in August? Everyone seemed to have a question of some sort—everyone except Sheriff Cummings, that was. He stayed silent beside her, though she could feel his gaze warming the side of her face.

Aileen held up her hands until the table quieted. "I'll be thanking ye, I will. But 'tis all a mite fast. Brenna's brother Morley lives in Chicago, and I sent off a letter yesterday to see if he wants to go back to Ireland with me. He's a sailor, so it might take a bit before he makes it back to Chicago and finds me letter."

Or mayhap she should just go back to Ireland now. Morley could always follow later.

"What kind of situation would you be going back to in Ireland?" Rebecca sent her a probing look while reaching for the platter of fish.

The kind that didn't involve memories of last summer. But Ireland held a different set of unwelcome memories. Conan's trouble with the constable, her father's funeral, losing the land she'd tended for as long as she could remember.

With Ennis dead, would Brenna lose the farm? What if she ended up being more of a burden to Brenna than a help?

"Would your cousin rather come here instead? Gilbert could pay for that." Rebekah reached over and clasped Gilbert's hand atop the table. "Couldn't you, darling?"

Gilbert raised an eyebrow at Aileen, with nary a comment about how eager his wife was to spend his money. "Do you think your cousin would want to come here?"

"To Eagle Harbor, ye mean?"

"You already have friends here." Victoria refilled her water glass. "So why not bring your family too?"

"I can have passage for her and the children arranged just as easily as I can for you, though it will take a few weeks to get word across the Atlantic." Gilbert took a small sip of water. "And again, don't worry about the cost. I can see to everything."

Her gaze shot up at that. Was he doing this in an attempt to make up for what happened last summer?

"And if it's her finding work you're worried about," Gilbert continued, "I'll need a housekeeper for my hotel before winter, and someone to run the restaurant too once that gets underway."

She toyed with a forkful of green beans on her plate. He owed her nothing—last summer hadn't been his fault—yet how could she turn down his offer?

"Thank ye, I'll write me cousin on the morrow and let ye know what she says, though I can't imagine her saying nay. Her brother and husband were both saving to come to America, and so was Conan before he…" Her throat grew thick at the thought of her brother's death. "Well, as I said, thank ye, but we'll pay ye back, we will."

Gilbert opened his mouth as though to argue, then clamped it shut and gave her a quick nod. "I'm sure we can work something out, if that's what you want."

Was it what she wanted? It seemed like a solid plan, but everything had happened so fast. And yet, how could she say no to a well-paying job and a chance to bring her family to Eagle Harbor?

But would staying in this town bring peace to her heart? She looked around the table, filled with smiling faces and light chatter, filled with a sense of family and home.

If she had a good job and could put a bit of money aside every month, if Brenna were here with her wee ones, would she finally feel as though she belonged in Eagle Harbor?

Chapter Six

"Everything's clear. You can come in." The sheriff's voice echoed out the door of the bakery to where Aileen stood in the gathering shadows of the alley. He'd been kind enough to walk her home after dinner and check inside for anything out of place.

Perhaps it was more than she should have asked of him, seeing how her suspicions about the men in the alley had turned out to be nothing. But with a dead body showing up, it didn't hurt to be cautious.

She took a tentative step inside, then another, and glanced around the dimly lit kitchen. Everything seemed normal, from the scent of the sourdough bread rising on the counter to the big oven that would be hot first thing in the morning.

The sheriff returned through the swinging half-doors that led from the storefront to the kitchen. "I searched the first floor, but not the second." He looked toward the stairs on the far side of the kitchen. "Figured it'd be safer for you to wait in here while I go up there."

She should probably tell him not to bother. She'd already taken up enough of his time, but a vision of her nightgown, stolen jewelry, and a kitchen knife laid out on her bed last winter swept through her mind. "I-if ye wouldn't mind looking upstairs, I'd be much obliged."

He turned without a word and headed slowly up the stairs, gun drawn. His footsteps soon sounded on the floor above, and she forced herself to draw a calming breath. Or rather, she wished it were a calming breath, but it didn't do much to settle her nerves.

The sheriff's footsteps thudded as he moved from one room to the next. She forced herself to take another slow breath, then turned to inspect the kitchen for herself. Indeed, everything seemed right as rain, it did. Even down to the sack of cookies sitting on the counter.

The cookies! She hurried toward the bag. As if forgetting them before heading to Elijah and Victoria's wasn't bad enough, here she'd had the sheriff standing in her kitchen a few moments ago, and she'd still forgotten them.

His footsteps sounded at the top of the stairs, and she turned, bag of cookies clutched in her hand.

"All clear. There's no sign anyone was here while you were away, and no sign of any new trouble in the alley."

Which was good, definitely good. Except she felt like a fool. She'd been so nervous about coming inside, yet once again naught had happened.

All the more reason to give him the cookies and apologize for wasting his time. "I made these for ye. I meant to bring them to Elijah's, but forgot."

"You made me cookies? But I thought…" His quiet voice echoed through the kitchen, and his eyes scanned her face, then a small smile tilted the corner of his lips. "Thank you."

Wait, he didn't think she'd made the cookies for him, did he? Well, she had, but not in the way he was thinking. "'Tis sorry, I am, that I woke ye this morn, and all for naught too. 'Tis why I made ye the cookies, not because… because…" Because I have any kind of attraction to ye.

And yet, if she was going to be attracted to a man, if she was going to let her heart free to feel for someone, it would be him. Not even a man like him, but him alone.

The half-smile dropped from his lips, but his eyes turned even softer, which was somehow worse. Better for him to make a joke or even have a bit of hope in his gaze instead of the concern lingering there now.

He took a step closer and reached out, almost brushed a hand against her shoulder, but he let it fall instead. "You don't need to apologize, Aileen."

Aileen. The way he said her name, all soft and tender, made her breath still. The night suddenly seemed too quiet, the air too thick, and she couldn't take her eyes off him.

"It's my job to investigate things." Isaac cleared his throat, and the stillness surrounding them vanished. "Never apologize for coming to me with suspicions."

She looked down to where he held the cookies. "I feel like a fool, is all. About last night and now."

"You're not a fool."

A man couldn't touch a woman with his eyes. The thought was utterly ridiculous. But it sure felt as though his hands were cupping her cheek given how his gaze brushed her skin, how he stood so close his breath teased her face.

Then he took a step back and nodded toward the door that led to the alley. "I have rounds to make. Thanks again for the cookies, now I won't get hungry while I'm working."

He headed to the door, then turned back and touched a hand to the brim of his hat. "Just remember, anytime you have need, anytime you're nervous or frightened, don't hesitate to ask for help. It's not only my job to assist you, but I'm happy to do it."

She drew in a breath and nodded. "Thank ye, Sheriff."

"It's Isaac. Didn't I tell you that last winter?"

He probably had, but she'd chosen to ignore it then. "Isaac," she said softly. "Thank ye, Isaac."

A small smile tilted the corners of his mouth. "Sleep well tonight. I'll keep an extra watch on this place, so you have nothing to worry about."

He tipped his hat toward her. His gait was strong and confident as he walked out the door and pulled it shut.

She stood for a moment, staring after him. It wasn't as though Isaac Cummings had no cares or worries. But the man carried himself as though he could handle whatever came at him, while she… she…

Oh, she didn't feel like she could handle anything these days. When had she become so helpless? So scared?

It seemed like part of her had died the day her father had passed, another part had withered when she'd lost Conan, and the tiny bit left over had shriveled last summer.

But all that was going to change. She was going to take the job Gilbert offered and see that Brenna and her children came to America. She was going to earn money and save some while still paying Gilbert back. And mayhap, in another year or two, she'd be carrying herself with the same kind of confidence as Isaac and Rebekah. After all, with her cousin coming to Eagle Harbor, she had just as much to look forward to as anyone else.

So why did a hollow ache still fill her chest? Why did the thought of her future make her want to wring her hands and slump into a heap on the floor?

The door handle turned, a soft, barely discernible rustle.

She jolted and pressed a hand to her heart, a scream building in her chest.

But instead of releasing the scream, she blew out a long breath. It was probably just the sheriff returning for one reason or another. Dead body in the woods or not, she needed to stop being so skittish.

Yet when the door opened, Isaac Cummings wasn't standing on the other side, but Jack O'Byrne.

"Jack!" She rushed toward the boy who couldn't be much older than twelve. "What are ye doing out so late?"

"I'm sorry to bother you, Miss Aileen." A slight Cornish accent trickled through his words. "But I was wondering if you had a loaf of bread or two to spare."

"Sure, I do." But why was the boy coming to her for bread? Was his father not feeding him? His two younger siblings, Alice and Toby, had been at the Cummingses' earlier, but she'd not seen Jack sitting at the table. She went into the storefront and found two loaves of day-old bread in the darkness, along with a half-dozen cookies, and brought them back to the kitchen.

"Thank you." The boy looked at the food as though he was ready to devour it right then and there.

"Why weren't ye at the Cummingses' tonight?" She handed him the bread. "Ye could have eaten your fill there."

Jack's gaze slid to the side. "A boy as big as me needs to earn his keep, leastways that's what Pa says."

"You're not old enough to worry about earning yer keep." Aileen crossed her arms over her chest. "If ye ask me, a boy your age shouldn't be about town this time of night by himself either."

Jack took a step back toward the door with the bread. "You don't need to worry none, I promise."

She sank her teeth into her bottom lip, as though she could stop herself from worrying at someone's command. Jack's father hadn't been around when the doctor's wife had found the children living in a lean-to in the hills last fall. Elijah and Victoria had opened their home to the children, but it had taken months of searching and numerous newspaper advertisements before they'd found their father, Virgil O'Byrne.

Hadn't Isaac mentioned something about how if Jack's father wasn't doing a good job of taking care of the children, Jack and his siblings would go back to living with Elijah and Victoria?

Then again, it seemed like Jack's younger brother and sister were pretty much living with Elijah and Victoria anyway. She'd not seen them with their father once since school released for the summer.

"Just what kind of work does yer pa have ye doing?" Aileen ran her gaze down Jack. His pants were about an inch too short, his shirt was torn, and his hair so shaggy it hung into his eyes. Would the sheriff count that as Mr. O'Byrne not caring for his children?

Jack's eyes shifted to the side again. "I best be going now, but thank you for the bread." He reached behind him and opened the door.

"Wait. Ye could eat here. Do ye want some jam?"

But Jack was gone before she reached the door, leaving her to stare at nothing but the long shadows of night.

She shut the door, locked it, then checked the lock. But knowing the door was secure didn't quench the flicker of worry igniting inside her.

What wasn't Jack O' Byrne telling her?

⌐.⌐.⌐.⌐.⌐

Isaac's feet weighed as heavily as anchors as he headed up Third Street, away from the bakery. He didn't have any evidence that Aileen was in danger. Yes, men had been in the bakery's alley last night, but that wasn't a crime. Yes, there'd been a dead body in the woods earlier, but that was more likely a suicide than a murder.

So why did he feel like he'd just left a fawn surrounded by a pack of wolves?

Maybe it had something to do with the vulnerable look in Aileen's eyes before he'd unlocked the bakery and gone inside to search it, as though she'd half expected him to laugh at her rather than help.

Or maybe it had something to do with the way she'd acted like he'd handed her the moon when he'd reported the building was clear. Or how she'd jumped away from him as though he'd scalded her during the split second he'd thought she'd baked him cookies just to be kind, and not as some kind of penance for waking him up that morning.

Heaven forbid she made him cookies just to be nice, just to show a little interest in him. He scrubbed a hand over his face. She seemed so vulnerable and yet so determined to keep her distance. How could he help someone who didn't want help in the first place?

He couldn't. That was the answer, plain and simple. All he could do was offer.

And keep a close eye on the bakery. There was no harm in watching the alley closely tonight or looking around the place for a few extra minutes on his patrols.

But first he had a meeting with his deputies—one for which he was already late. He headed through the deepening shadows toward North Street, where the sheriff's office, mercantile, telegraph office, and the Rusty Wagon Bar all sat. Farther down the road, just past the town limits, sat the Pretty Penny Brothel, which also doubled as a bar.

Once on the main road, lights from the Rusty Wagon across the street chased some of the shadows away. He strode toward his office two blocks down.

"Sheriff, there you are." Ian Fletcher descended the office steps and met him in the road, the star pinned to the young man's chest catching the lantern light from the porch. "We didn't know what you wanted us to do when you didn't come, so Granger went to check the Penny while I waited for you." The deputy blinked his large blue eyes at him. "I hope that's all right."

"That's fine. I was searching the bakery for Miss Brogan to make sure there hadn't been any trouble in the few hours she was away."

"Heard about the break-in last winter." Fletcher looked out over the street, his gaze moving too quickly to catch much. The man needed to slow down a bit, to not always be in such an all-fired hurry. "You don't think the men in the alley had something to do with that, do you?"

"No. That was Frank Ebberhard." Yet even as he said the words, he wasn't quite sure he believed them. They'd suspected Frank had been working with other men last winter but had never found any evidence of it.

"You don't think… that is, er…" Fletcher shifted on his feet. "The dead body, and the men Miss Brogan saw last night, do you think…?"

"Suicide is still the most likely explanation for the body." And yet he had the same niggle of doubt worming through his own head, the same bit of apprehension stirring somewhere deep in his gut.

But without proof, apprehension and doubt were merely feelings, flimsy and slippery, constantly changing, and useless in a court of law.

Which was how things should be. It was hardly just for a man or woman to be incriminated based on another person's feelings.

"Suicide." Fletcher's swallow was so loud it could probably be heard clear down at the harbor. "Right."

"Was there any trouble while I was away?"

"No, all's been quiet."

But was there such a thing as too quiet? A chill swept through him, and he turned to study the shadows across the road. Everything was in its place, as normal as could be.

Isaac settled his hand on the butt of his gun. Was he imagining trouble where none existed? Or were there dangerous men afoot, and he'd yet to uncover their tracks?

Chapter Seven

She was late. Again. Ellie Spritzer turned from Front Street onto Center Street and walked as quickly as she could without tripping over the hem of her skirt. The yellow orb of sun hanging low in the sky chased her down the road. Usually she was headed to work at dawn, when the sky was lit with pinks and oranges and before the sun appeared.

What would Aileen think? The other woman had never once complained about her arriving late at the bakery, but today would make three times in a week.

Aileen had been gone yesterday morning, of course, but only because she was fetching the sheriff and reporting a possible bank robbery. Ellie had no better reason for being late than she'd been so tired even the cock's crowing hadn't woken her.

She rounded the side of the bakery, her hands brushing the side of her skirt. Something white fluttered to the ground. She paused and turned, bending to retrieve the wrinkled envelope with the strong, masculine handwriting that was becoming ever more familiar to her.

Probably foolish to carry it around in her pocket, but she'd not wanted to hide it with the rest of her letters quite yet. Hopefully there'd come a time when her entire family would learn of the letters she'd been exchanging, and there'd be no need to hide any of them anymore.

She slid the letter back into her pocket, careful not to wrinkle the edges any more than they already were after spending almost two weeks on her person.

The light coming through the window above the sink told her Aileen had already started the morning's baking. She tried the doorknob and found it unlocked, then rushed inside. "Sorry I'm so late."

Aileen looked up from where she was working streusel-topped muffins out of their tin. "Late night?"

They were always late these days. She tucked a stray wisp of bright red hair behind her ear and headed to the cupboards where the bread pans were stored. "Ma's still feeling poorly, so there was washing to be done after I left the bakery last night."

Washing and mending, and more washing and mending. Thankfully Suzanna was old enough to make dinner now, and Christopher had offered to help as well. But after everything was eaten and put away and she was hanging up the last batch of wash, Leroy and Martin had come home wanting food. But she'd not complain too much. Whatever job her thirteen and fourteen-year-old brothers had found for the summer seemed to pay well enough, even if the hours were odd.

Ma had lain on her bed for the entire evening, barely even acknowledging little Lynnette tucked against her side.

Ellie sighed. Being the oldest girl of ten siblings had never been easy, nor had burying her older brother Clifford, nor had growing up with a father who was gone more than he was home. Yet she'd somehow managed through everything—until her mother had fallen ill.

She stifled a yawn and carried the bread pans to where the giant bowl of sourdough sat on the counter near Aileen. "I'll be on time tomorrow." And she would. She just had to figure out a reliable way to wake up early since the noisy rooster was no longer helping.

Aileen set the last muffin from the pan on a platter. "Good, because I won't be here."

Ellie froze, her hands pausing over the sourdough. "What do you mean?"

Aileen ducked her head for a moment, then sent her a small smile.

Did the woman realize how lovely she was? No wonder the sheriff had his eye on her. Aileen's hair was a deep rich red, unlike her own locks that were so bright a person might wince at them. And Aileen's body was shapely rather than reed thin, with curves that gave her a lovely figure—and not because she tied her corset too tight. Her skin was the color of the rich cream they used when making custard, and the handful of freckles scattered across her cheeks only seemed to make her lovelier.

Ellie absently slid her hand into her skirt pocket and touched the letter. Would she have the attentions of a man one day too? If she went to Texas to marry Sam Owens, the cowhand she'd been exchanging letters with for four months, would he look at her the way Sheriff Cummings looked at Aileen?

She'd never be as lovely as the Irishwoman, not with her bright red hair and the garish freckles that warred for positions on her nose and cheeks. But Sam Owens seemed a decent sort. Polite and honest, to be sure. Maybe one day—

"Ye might not have heard, but Gilbert Sinclair bought the ol' Donnelly mansion." Aileen picked up another tin of cooling muffins and started working them from their pan. "Aims to turn it into a hotel, he does, and he asked me to work for him."

Ellie paused, her hands about ready to plunge into the sourdough. "So you're leaving the bakery?"

"The pay will be a bit better, and I think the job itself might suit more."

Aileen had never been happy working at the bakery. She'd done her work well enough, and no one would ever call her idle, but her eyes carried a constant sadness, her shoulders an eternal slump, and she didn't like serving certain men. How many times over the past year had Aileen rushed into the kitchen and busied herself with mixing up more cookies or muffins when a group of sailors walked through the door?

Ellie filled the first bread pan with dough. "I'll miss you in the kitchen, but I hope you're happier at the hotel than you are here."

And she did. Aileen leaving would mean more hours for her, and thus more pay, but she didn't exactly have more hours to give right now, not with Ma ill. She forced a smile onto her face anyway.

Surely she'd be smiling in truth as soon as Ma got better.

Pounding sounded from the storefront. "Are you open? Hello?"

Aileen's brow furrowed. "Did you forget to unlock the front door?"

Ellie glanced at the clock hanging on the wall. Was it six already? And here she didn't even have the bread in the oven yet.

"Forgive me. I'm not quite myself this morning." She stepped to the sink and pumped the faucet, rinsing the sticky dough from her hands with the chilly water. Then she rushed through the swinging doors that led to the shop while drying her hands on her apron.

"Is anyone in there?" The voice echoed through the door.

She pulled back the deadbolt, already speaking before opening the door. "I'm sorry. I lost track of—"

"Ellie Spritzer, I should have known you'd be the one running late."

She looked into the familiar brown eyes of Jake Ranulfson, her deceased brother's closest friend and the town banker's son. He must be home on break from college. She'd caught a glimpse or two of him around town over the past week but hadn't spoken to him. In fact, she couldn't recall speaking to him since Clifford died over a year ago. Had he come home from school last summer?

Jake stepped into the bakery. "I won't be long. Just stopped by for a strawberry pie."

She blinked. A strawberry pie at a quarter past six in the morning? "Ah… I'm running a little behind and don't have one yet." In truth, she rarely had them out before eleven, and that was on mornings she wasn't running late. "But I can make you one. You can pick it up this afternoon sometime."

"Sure, Ma just needs it for the beautification society meeting tonight. I figured I'd get one before going to the bank, but I can wait." He glanced around the dim bakery, then cocked his head to the side, his eyes studying her. "Are you all right? You look pale, and this is the first time I've seen you with your hair down."

Her hair? She reached to her shoulder where she felt the tresses dangling on her shoulder. She'd put her hair up so quickly that some of the pins must have fallen out while she'd dashed to work. She shoved a lock of the ugly red tresses behind her ear.

Jake sighed and leaned against a shelf, glancing down at his feet before bringing his friendly gaze back up to her. "Look, Ellie. I know I haven't been around much since Clifford died. Truth be told, it's a little hard seeing you or your brothers and sisters without my mind going back to Cliff. But if you ever need anything, I'm here for the summer. Come and get me. Cliff would have wanted it that way."

Her chest tightened. She couldn't blame him for not coming around. It wasn't exactly easy for her to see Jake without envisioning Clifford by his side. Her brother's tall, lanky form, freckles, and messy red hair had always called attention away from Jake's average height and plain brown hair and eyes.

"Thanks, but I don't think there's anything I need. Why don't I bring you the pie at lunch?"

He grinned. "Better make it two pies if you're bringing them to the bank. The first will be gone before I have a chance to take the other to Ma." He pushed himself off the shelf, then paused. "I still don't like the look of you, Ellie."

"I'm fine."

His forehead wrinkled in a way that seemed to shout something about him not believing her. He reached out and took the lock of bright red hair dangling beside her cheek, twirling it in his fingers. "Put your hair up before you do anything else, all right?"

"Of course. If I don't, its hideous color will scare away all the customers."

He dropped the strand and tilted his head to the side. "It's not hideous, Ellie. I promise. I was thinking you should put it up for a different reason."

What reason? Because it wasn't proper for a woman her age to leave her hair down? With the town banker for a pa and a woman like Mrs. Ranulfson for a ma, Jake had probably gotten lessons on propriety in his crib.

He tilted his head toward the door. "I'd best be going, but don't forget, if you need anything, come find me. I'd like to help. Seems like a good way to honor Cliff's memory."

She opened her mouth to assert things were fine once again, but how could she deny his offer when he was making it because of Clifford? "Thank you."

He winked and tugged on the strand of hair still hanging beside her ear. "I'll look forward to having a slice of pie around lunch time."

The door shut behind him, and she made her way across the storefront toward the kitchen, patting her haphazard hair. It seemed half her updo had slid out of its pins. She sighed. Jake had said he was willing to help, but more than anything else she needed her ma to get better, and there was little chance Jake Ranulfson could do much about that.

~.~.~.~.~

"I'm the best at scrubbing floors, Mrs. Sinclair. Just ask Ma if you don't believe me."

Aileen stifled a yawn, then smiled at Ellie's younger sister, Suzanna. A pail and scrub brush in her hand, Suzanna stood between her brother Christopher and Rebekah Sinclair in front of the old Donnelly mansion. The afternoon sun beat down on them, the heat unrelenting, though the gulls circling above didn't seem to mind.

Aileen had only met these two Spritzer children a couple times, but even if they'd been strangers, their bright red hair and freckles proclaimed them related to Ellie.

"Do we gotta clean the whole thing?" With a pail and rag in his hand as well, Christopher frowned up at the three-story white house that had once belonged to Victoria's parents.

Rebekah started to laugh, then covered her mouth and turned it into a half-coughing sound. She was dressed in another of her fine gowns made of expensive fabric and sewn to fit perfectly. Yet just like her dress from yesterday, this pale blue gown lacked the ruffles, flounces, and puffed sleeves that adorned the dresses most women of her wealth wore.

Suzanna elbowed her brother in the stomach and sent him a glare. "Christopher's not so good at scrubbing, Mrs. Sinclair, but he can move things around well enough. You won't regret hiring him, I promise."

Christopher pulled himself up straighter. "No, ma'am. I didn't mean to complain. I'll clean it all if that's what you need."

"I'm sure you will." Rebekah reached out and settled a hand on

65

each of the children's shoulders. "I've heard both of you are hard workers."

"You have?" Suzanna's face glowed with excitement. Aileen hadn't asked her age, but she'd guess somewhere around ten. This was probably the first real job the girl had been hired for.

"Of course." Rebekah reached down and smoothed a shaggy thatch of hair out of Christopher's eye. "All I ask is that you follow Miss Brogan's instructions. She's the one in charge of cleaning the mansion from top to bottom."

"Well, well, what do we have here?" Isaac headed up the walkway toward them, his wide-brimmed hat pulled low to keep the afternoon sun from his face. "Looks like a group of cleaners, if you ask me." He doffed his hat and gave her a little nod, then resettled his hat on his head. "A very pretty group of cleaners."

Aileen ducked her head as heat spread across her cheeks.

"Thank you, Sheriff Cummings!" Suzanna bounced up onto the balls of her feet, her smile bright enough to melt the sun.

"Boys aren't pretty." Christopher's ears were a slight shade of red.

"Handsome, then," Isaac ran his gaze over the lot of them. "Where are Leroy and Martin? Aren't they helping?"

Christopher shook his head. "Naw, they got themselves a job for the summer."

"Doing what?" Isaac shifted in the muggy heat.

Aileen took a step closer to Christopher. This was the first she'd heard of Leroy and Martin having a job too. It seemed odd Ellie wouldn't have mentioned such a thing, especially considering how concerned she'd been about their mother's health and the need for money now that their mother couldn't take in much wash or mending.

Susanna shrugged. "Working errands for a man or something."

Isaac scratched at his temple, though his hat brim shielded most of his face from view. "Must be an awful lot of errands if they're too busy to clean the hotel for a few hours."

Now it was Christopher's turn to shrug. "Don't know, but last week they brought home two pig roasts plus a dollar cash money. Said it was all payment for their work."

The familiar-looking sailor she'd seen yesterday morning turned onto Center Street. Aileen tilted her head to the side and took a step toward the road, Christopher and Isaac's words fading behind her. Like last time, she couldn't see all of him, yet there was something about the way he held his shoulders, about the unique tilt of his hat. She took several more steps, then found herself following. Could it be...?

"Morley!" Her shout echoed down the street. "Morley, is that ye?"

Several of the sailors stopped walking, and one or two of them turned. Then sure enough, her cousin stepped out from the middle.

"Morley." She rushed forward, blinking twice, clearing her vision to make sure it was really her cousin standing in front of her. He was as short and thin as she remembered, nearly her size, in fact. He wore his hat pulled low over his head, eclipsing most of his face from view. "Morley, what are ye doing here? Why aren't ye in Chicago?"

"Ye expect a sailor to be home during shipping season, do ye?" The rich brogue of his voice rolled over her. Then he opened his arms, and she was in them.

"I missed ye, I did." She clung to him, afraid to let go and lose the moment that felt so good and right and perfect. He smelled of Ireland. It shouldn't be possible, considering he'd been in America longer than she, and yet the scent clung to him anyway, soil and sun and peat mixed with the salty air of the sea.

"'Tis good, it is, to see ye, lass." He pulled away from her and chucked her under the chin, just like he had when they'd been children.

67

"How long are ye here for?" She glanced toward the harbor, though she couldn't see the pier. Had a ship docked that morn? But wait, had she not seen him—?

"Came in on a ship two nights ago."

"Two nights?" The warmth twining through her faded, and she frowned. "Why didn't ye come find me?"

Standing this close and peering up beneath his hat brim, she could see the sun had worn lines around his eyes and mouth, and his skin was no longer cream-colored, but as tan as the sand that lined the harbor. There was a sharpness to his features as well, a certain wariness that stayed in his gaze, even when he smiled at her. "Oh, that's right, it's here ye're livin' now, isn't it?" Morley scratched his head and took a step back from her.

A chill skittered up her spine despite the muggy heat.

"I was figurin' ye were in the next town down. But now that I think on it, ye're letters did say Eagle Harbor, not Eagle River."

Aye, the names were similar, but she'd memorized Morley's address months ago. Why hadn't he done the same with hers?

"Did ye get the letters I sent?"

Morley shook his head. "I've been gone since the season opened in April. Haven't been back to Chicago once."

"So ye've not heard about Brenna?"

He grew still, all except for a muscle at the back of his jaw, which pulsed with tension. "What's wrong with me sister?"

Aileen twisted her hands in her skirt. "'Tis more like what's wrong with Ennis. He took a fever this spring and... he didn't survive."

"Brenna's alone? With all the wee ones?" Morley's eyes turned darker, and he shoved his hand up beneath his hat brim, wiping his brow. "She say how she's supportin' everyone?"

Aileen shook her head. "Nay. I just got the news at the beginning of this week. I sent her a bit of money and told her I'd head back to

Ireland as soon as I could afford passage. I wrote ye, to see if ye wanted to go home with me, but last night—"

"That's yer answer? Goin' back to Ireland?" His eyes sought hers again, a mixture of emotions swimming there that she couldn't quite discern. Regret, perhaps, or mayhap a little disbelief. Then he shook his head. "She's supposed to be coming here, remember? Just as soon as we have the money. Don't be spending whatever ye've scraped together to go back to that rotting island. If anything, ye can put it together with the money I'm saving, and we can pay for her to come here sooner. Don't ye want to be in America? To have a chance to own yer own land like yer da always dreamed of?"

Dreams. Her da had been dead for two years, yet his dreams still haunted her. Mayhap owning a farm had been the plan once, but then Conan had died six months after moving to America, leaving her alone in a vast country save for the cousin who couldn't recall what town she lived in.

Dreams indeed. "How am I supposed to run a farm without Conan?"

Morley reached out to swipe a stray strand of hair from her face. "Don't ye be fretting now. I bet one day ye'll have that farm. Bet ye'll even have someone to help you run it too."

"I still won't have Conan back."

Morley's shoulders slumped. "'Tis sorry, I am, for yer loss."

She looked away, then blinked back the fierce bit of moisture welling in her eyes. She could almost see herself standing at the door of the tiny Chicago apartment she'd shared with her brother while two men in fancy suits apologized for an accident on the docks.

"I've a friend who offered to pay for Brenna and the children to come here, and he even has a job she can work. So if she's willing to come here, I won't be going back to Ireland." Hopefully once Brenna arrived, the three of them would find new dreams, make a new way for the Brogan family in America.

"A friend?" Morley didn't smile at the news. "That's an awful generous offer."

"Hello, I'm Sheriff Isaac Cummings."

Aileen jumped at the sound of Isaac's voice, then turned to find him standing beside her. Had he and Rebekah watched her talk to Morley all this time?

Isaac extended his hand, but her cousin didn't take it. Instead Morley looked back to her. "Is this yer friend? The one who's going to pay for Brenna to come?"

"Nay, he's—"

"I'm a friend, yes." Isaac's voice took on a deeper, official sounding tenor. "Now what did you say your name was?"

"Sheriff, this is me cousin, Morley Brogan." Aileen looked between them. "Morley, this is Isaac Cummings, sheriff of Eagle Harbor."

"A lawman?" Morley's jaw turned as hard as the boulders lining the shore by the Cummings's house. "I don't send ye letters for a couple months, and ye run to a lawman?" "I'm not sure what ye mean by running to a lawman, but the sheriff isn't paying for Brenna to come here, if that's what ye're after." Aileen dug the toe of her shoe into the packed dirt road. Why was Morley being so rude? If he was going to leave her to herself for months at a time, he could hardly complain about her making friends.

"Then what other friend have ye made? The one paying for Brenna to come here." Morley's features were sharp, his eyes watching her closely. "Seems awful curious that a friend would make an offer such as that." Heat flooded her face. Surely Morley didn't think she was doing something improper in return for bringing Brenna here.

"Watch yourself, Brogan." Isaac's voice was dark, his eyes narrowed. "I'll not stand by while you insult an upstanding member of my town."

Morley crossed his arms over his chest, his stance every bit as defiant as Conan's used to be when facing the village constable. "I want to know who's paying for Brenna to come here. 'Tis a fair question."

"Gilbert Sinclair," she blurted. "He's a businessman with more money than he knows what to do with, so there's no need for ye to think his offer is anything less than charitable."

"Charitable." Something in Morley's voice twisted the word until it sounded evil. "I'll bet it is."

She took a step closer to her cousin, causing their toes to meet, and stared into eyes so cold the emerald green depths almost seemed unfamiliar. "How dare ye imply I'd be inappropriate with any man, let alone Mr. Sinclair, who is happily married!"

"Wait, did you say Sinclair?" Morley scratched behind his head. "As in, owner of Great Northern Shipping?"

Aye, Morley would know of the family. Any sailor from Chicago would. "Gilbert is the second son of Byron Sinclair, and he—"

"Tell him nay."

The muscles across her back and shoulders grew taut. "Surely ye don't want Brenna to stay by herself in Ireland with all the children. Ide's just a wee lass, too young for Brenna to even go off and find a job. And that's assuming—"

"I don't want me cousin tangled with the likes of the Sinclairs." Morley made a slashing motion with his hand. "No good will come of it."

He didn't want her tangled with them? Didn't he know she'd worked for them last summer? She'd told him she'd taken a position as servant to the Sinclairs after Conan's death.

Mayhap Morley hadn't paid attention, just like he'd not paid attention to the difference between Eagle Harbor and Eagle River.

Isaac reached out and laid a hand on her arm. He might be keeping his mouth shut, but a quick glance at his clenched jaw told

NAOMI RAWLINGS

her he was as riled as she was, and not because of the muggy heat.

"Gilbert's wife, Rebekah, is one of me closest friends. I'll not deprive meself of the few friends I have on the word of a cousin who couldn't even remember what town I'm living in. Besides, I've already written Brenna about the offer." She'd also sent the last of her savings to tide Brenna over until Gilbert could arrange passage.

"I'll have money to bring Brenna to America by the end of the summer." The words shot out of Morley's mouth, quick and fierce. "I'm working a good job. Just wait a few more months and we can manage on our own. That'll be better, far better, than yer being beholden to a Sinclair."

"I'm not going to leave Brenna to scrabble by. If this job is as good as ye say, ye can pay Gilbert back yerself come fall."

"I said nay, and that's the end of it." Shoulders stiff, Morley whirled and stalked away from her.

"Wait." She took one step after him, then another. Her heart— so overflowing with hope a few minutes ago when he'd hugged her— turned as empty and hollow as a cave. "When do ye leave? Can ye at least come to dinner tonight? I let rooms above the bakery, but we could talk for a while, visit and…"

He didn't even turn.

…Be careful sailing, and don't go unloading any crates that are too heavy.

Without so much as a look over his shoulder, Morley reached his friends who were still waiting in the street.

"Hey." A hand reached out to touch her shoulder, and she turned toward Isaac, his gaze searching her face. "Let's get you inside, and—"

"I'm fine." She tried to take a step back, to put a bit more space between them, but he took her elbow, holding it with just enough pressure she'd have to yank to get away from him.

"You're not fine, and I wouldn't be either." He started toward the

72

hotel. "You have a sorry excuse for a cousin. No decent man would say those things to any woman, let alone kin."

Tears swam in her eyes, clouding her vision until she couldn't even see the walk that led to the mansion. She tried to stem the tears, truly she did. She shouldn't be turning into a watering pot, in front of Isaac no less. "Morley's all I have."

"He's not. You have Rebekah and Gilbert, Elijah and Victoria, and Mac and Tressa. You have me—if you want anything to do with me, that is. We might not be blood kin, but that doesn't mean we can't adopt you, same as we adopted Mac."

Adopt her? Oh, if he knew of her past—of the things that had happened, of choices she'd then made—he'd never offer such a thing. A sob welled in her chest, and a fresh bout of tears streaked her face.

"What's going on?" Rebekah's voice echoed through the mansion's foyer. "Isaac, what did you do?"

"Wasn't me. Turns out her long-lost cousin doesn't have much to commend him. Hey now, don't cry." Isaac slipped a handkerchief into her hand. "If my family's not enough, just think about Brenna. She'll be here by the end of the summer, and something tells me she won't treat you the way her brother did."

He was too kind, his words too much. He didn't know what he offered, not really. The truth was, if Brenna knew what happened in Chicago last summer, her cousin might want naught to do with her too. "Stop," she rasped. "Please stop. I need to be alone right now."

And with that, she bolted away from him and headed for the nearest room, closing the heavy door behind her.

~.~.~.~.~

She'd shut him out. Isaac paced around the desk in the sheriff's office, arms crossed and muscles tense. He shouldn't be surprised. This was

Aileen Brogan, after all. The woman had been shutting him out for almost a year.

He'd stood by her side, keeping his mouth shut—or mostly shut—as her cousin griped about how she must be doing something disreputable to account for Gilbert's offer. His hands had curled into fists, yet he hadn't used them, and all because he'd wanted to support her.

And yet what had she done as soon as they'd gone inside? Closed the door in his face. Just like she'd been doing since she'd first arrived in town ten months ago.

He should have just hauled off and planted a fist into Morley's jaw. Maybe then the man would have found something kind to say to Aileen.

Isaac glanced at the clock on the wall. Enough time had passed for Aileen to calm down. Maybe she'd be willing to talk to him now. At the very least, he needed to apologize for making her cry earlier, though he still didn't understand what he'd said wrong. Wouldn't most women without much family be comforted by the thought that a family as large and friendly as his would welcome her?

The door to his office burst open so hard it swung back and banged against the wall.

"I want more details about the man you found yesterday." Ernest Ranulfson grabbed the handle on the moving door and sent it crashing shut behind him. "Who was he, and how did he end up dead?"

Isaac scrubbed a hand over his face. He should have expected a visit from the head of the town council, who also happened to be the owner of Eagle Harbor's one and only bank.

"Don't know. The dock foreman is supposed to let me know if any of his workers turn up missing today. I've sent word to the lawmen in Central, Copper Harbor, Eagle River, and Calumet asking if a man who fits the description has gone missing recently." Isaac grabbed the paper pad with his notes from yesterday and scanned the top page, though it certainly didn't say anything new. "But if no more information turns up, there's not much I can do."

Which rankled, because something didn't sit right about the situation.

"Of course there's something you can do." Ranulfson planted his palms on the desk and leaned forward. "You can find the man who killed him. Do you think the council approved raising taxes and hiring more lawmen for you to sit around while people are being murdered?"

Heat climbed up the back of Isaac's neck, and he leaned forward to meet Ranulfson's stare. "First, I haven't been sitting around playing checkers. I've been working on the case." He waved his notes under Ranulfson's nose. "And second, like I said when we brought the dead man back to town yesterday, I don't know that there was a murder. The gun found near the man's body means it could have been a suicide. And if you don't believe me, ask Dr. Harrington. He did a post-mortem examination, and his report was just as inconclusive as mine. We know a bullet to the head killed the man, but we don't know who put the bullet there or why."

Ranulfson rubbed his brow, the gray hair at his temples glinting silver in the light from the window. "I hardly got a lick of sleep last night with the tizzy my wife was in. And you should have heard Trudy Kainer and Irene Runkle in the parlor this morning going on about the killer on the loose."

Isaac winced. No wonder the man was in his office. Mrs. Ranulfson caused more than enough commotion on her own. He could only imagine the fit she'd worked herself into with her two friends around. "I'm sure Doc Harrington has a tincture or two that will calm your wife's nerves."

Ranulfson muttered something about his wife already taking half the bottle. "None of this changes the fact that there's a killer out there somewhere. But despite being paid rather handsomely to catch him, you don't have the first notion where to look."

Isaac nearly choked. Yes, after the trouble the town had over the winter, he'd gotten a raise two months ago, which meant he was paid enough to live on now, but there was nothing handsome about his salary. Most of the extra money brought in by the new tax went to paying his two new deputies.

"As I already said, Mr. Ranulfson. I don't know if there's a killer involved."

Ranulfson threw up his hands. "Then declare his death a suicide and be done with it."

Did he really want to sign his name to a piece of paper that would forever state the death as suicide? What if he was wrong? What if Betty Ranulfson's fears were legitimate—for once in her life—and there was a killer lurking in the woods?

The town council meeting was two weeks away. He could only imagine the commotion at that meeting if there was a murderer on the loose. There'd be no question about the sheriff's office needing funding, but there'd be plenty of questions about whether he was the right man for the job. Now that the council had raised the sheriff's salary, surely they could find a man with more experience willing to be the top lawman.

Something tightened in his chest. And look at him, being ridiculous. He hadn't even wanted to be sheriff, so why did keeping the job matter so much?

Because he might not be able to go back and save his pa from that fateful storm, but maybe he could save the next person who found themselves in danger. "Tell you what, I'm going back to the scene of the death to take another look around, see if I can find anything that indicates someone besides our dead man and the Spritzer boys were in that section of woods yesterday." He and Granger had looked for tracks before the undertaker had arrived to take the body to town, but they hadn't seen anything proving more than one person had been there.

Then again, tall grass didn't exactly show footprints, only trampled paths. "If I come up empty, and no one's gone missing from the surrounding towns, I'll call it a suicide."

Ranulfson's shoulders fell with a sigh. "I hope for everyone's sake it truly was a suicide."

So did he. But how could he be sure when he had so few clues with which to work?

Chapter Eight

Elijah slanted a glance at Victoria in the front of the boat, then scanned the rich blue waters of Lake Superior before drawing in a breath of air. Did life get any better than this? Nothing beat the feel of the morning sun on his face, the wind in his hair, and the rigging in his hand as he stood on the little mackinaw fishing boat he and his brothers had made with their father.

They'd be back to Eagle Harbor in about a half hour though, never mind he'd rather stay on the water until dark. But at least he'd been able to take his wife down to Ontonagon yesterday so Victoria could visit her sister for an afternoon and evening.

A delighted giggle sounded from the boat's bow, where Alice and Toby O'Byrne—the children they were watching for the next few weeks—were playing with a couple of carved wooden figures their older brother Jack had made for them over the winter.

Victoria picked her way across the boat toward him, her steps not as confident as Rebekah's would be, but she was surer of herself in the boat than she'd been when they'd married a year ago.

Things had been busy, busy, busy since Rebekah and Gilbert arrived almost a week and a day ago. It seemed Rebekah was intent on stuffing a year's worth of missed family dinners and gatherings into her first few weeks back in Eagle Harbor. It had been nice to take this trip, to spend some time with just Victoria and the children.

"Thank you for t-taking me to see my sister." Victoria sank down onto the simple wooden bench near him, then sent him a smile.

He would say she was welcome, but visits to her sister's family were always hard on her, and this one had been doubly so since Beatrice now had not just one child, but two. "How are you doing?"

She blew out a breath, then dangled a hand over the side of the boat to let her fingertips trail in the water. "I'm all right. Little Meredith was so big I'm not sure I can call her Little Meredith anymore. I wish I could have seen her when she was younger."

Elijah's eyes scanned the water, though the rich blue of the clear sky didn't give him much to worry about, nor did the gentle wind that was just strong enough to fill his sails. "If Meredith would have been born in October, maybe we could have risked a late trip."

Even so, he'd have been nervous taking his wife the hundred miles down the coast at that time of year.

There were drawbacks to living in a town that was mainly accessible by ship—and only for six months of the year.

Victoria looked down at her empty hands, then up at him again, a glaze of moisture in her eyes. "I w-want a baby, Elijah. I know I'm supposed to wait for God's timing, I know I'm supposed to rely on him, I know I'm supposed to be content with what I have. But I still want a b-b-baby of my own."

"Ah, Vic." He left the sails, seeing as there was nothing but calm waves and open sea surrounding them, and sat to draw her close.

He wrapped both arms around her and held her as the boat swayed gently beneath them. The silence lengthened around them, but he didn't open his mouth to fill the quiet. Any words he could speak had already been said in the past year they'd been praying for God to give them a child.

He waited for the deluge, for the sobs to wrack her body, for her face to twist with emotions so very different than the joy he longed to see on her face. And yet she didn't sob, just sniffled and dabbed one of her fancy lace handkerchiefs to her eyes. "I got to hold M-Meredith for a little bit today. I should be thankful for that instead of crying over what I d-d-don't have."

"It's normal to want a child of your own." He stroked a hand up and down her arm. "And I'm sorry we don't have one yet, or at least one on the way."

"No, but we have Alice and Toby for a while. I can be thankful for that, right? And for how much their f-father has let us watch them."

He leaned over and dropped a kiss onto the top of her head. "Makes me wish we had Jack too." Virgil O'Byrne had been insistent Jack work with him over the summer. "But yes, I'm glad we've gotten to have them so much."

The children had moved in last November, shortly after their older sister had died and they'd been found abandoned in the woods without any sign of their father. The children had wormed their way into his and Victoria's hearts in the short time they'd lived together, but then their father returned, claiming he had the means to care for the three young'uns he'd abandoned earlier that year. But the man's shifty eyes and the way the children shied away from him said that the O'Byrne young'uns might be better off without the man, blood relation or not.

Nothing would make Victoria and him happier than making Alice and Toby's room in their house permanent, and having their twelve-year-old brother Jack join them.

Elijah sat back and scanned the shoreline, the thick trees, small inlets, and coves becoming more familiar the closer they got to Eagle Harbor. Given the way the boat was drifting closer to shore, he'd have to get up and move the sails in another minute or two.

"Why don't we stop and have the picnic you packed?"

Victoria snuggled closer. "The idea sounds lovely, but I'm really not that hungry, are you?"

He wasn't. Beatrice had served them an early breakfast the size of a feast before they'd left, but he wouldn't mind exploring one of the coves he hadn't been to for a couple years. "I know a little bay with a great patch of sand for swimming, and we've got several hours yet before dark. Didn't you pack the bathing dresses?"

"Swimming?" Alice called from the front of the boat. "I want to go swimming."

He stood and angled the sails so the nose of the boat tilted toward shore. "Give me about five minutes and you can be in the water."

The boat drifted closer to the sandy cove that broke from the boulders lining most of this section of shoreline.

A shot rang out over the water.

Elijah tensed, then looked around. Had that been directed at them? Surely not. A coyote had probably wandered too close to a hunter or—

Another shot rang out, the bullet splashing into the water several yards from the bow where the children were.

"Down, everybody get down!" His heart thundered against his chest. He stood only long enough to tighten the sails and swing the nose of the boat back out to the lake.

"What's g-g-g-going on?" Victoria's voice trembled.

"Is someone shooting at us?" Tears clogged Alice's words.

"We'll be out of range in just a minute." He glanced at where Alice and Toby had obediently huddled beneath the gunwale. "Stay down."

"I want my mama," Toby wailed.

Something pinched inside Elijah's chest. The child likely didn't remember his mother. Was he calling for his late sister Jenny? Or did he mean Victoria? "I need you to stay where you are for a few more minutes, champ. Then I'll have a special place on my lap just for you."

Elijah crouched beneath the gunwale just as a third shot sounded, this one striking the water farther from the boat. Either whoever had the gun was a terrible shot or warning them off.

But why? Had someone bought that little patch of land? It was awfully far from a town, and even if someone did own it, why fire shots at them? Why not just call out and tell them they weren't welcome once they got closer?

Heart still thrumming in his chest, Elijah peeked over the side of the boat. Once again, the blue sky and open sea surrounded them while the shore behind them grew distant.

But the peaceful water and calm wind seemed a mere deception now.

⌐.⌐.⌐.⌐.⌐

Eight days. It had been eight days since the Spritzer boys had found the body in the woods, and five days since he'd proclaimed the death a suicide and quashed the rumors circulating around town. Yet the case still haunted him.

Isaac leaned back in his chair and rubbed his bleary eyes. Late morning sunlight streamed through his office windows, and the open door revealed a street crowded with wagons and passersby.

He stifled a yawn and looked back at the open book in front of him, then slapped it shut and glanced at the cover. *The Law of the Office and Duties of Sheriff.* It had been in the former sheriff's collection of things. While it had several pages about procedures for after declaring a person murdered, it hadn't contained a single word about how a lawman could distinguish a murder from a suicide.

Maybe the difference between murder and suicide was something a sheriff was simply supposed to know? Something that should never even be a question?

Or maybe it didn't matter. He glanced out the door at the busy street. The town had certainly moved past the rumors and fear that had gripped it when the dead body had appeared. He should move on too. After all, he'd done the best he could, had examined the few clues he'd found. What more was there to do?

Isaac leaned back in his chair and slid the book into its spot on the bookshelf behind his desk, then brushed his fingers over the spine of the book next to it, a lawbook that had once belonged to his father. The one next to it was a lawbook as well, as was the one next to that, and next to that, and next to that.

He'd been twelve the first time he'd taken one of the lawbooks off the shelf at home and flipped through it. It had taken him another eight years before he'd spoken to Pa about them. He'd been twenty then, and full of dreams and hope—fool that he was. Even now, he could almost smell the tang of the lake on that summer afternoon, almost feel the gentle swell of the waves beneath the boat.

"What made you decide to go to law school, Pa?"

Pa planted a hand on the North Star's *gunwale and looked out over the rolling water. At his feet lay a tangle of fish from the net they'd just hauled in.*

"Justice." Pa said it as though only one word was needed.

"Were you treated unjustly?" Isaac crouched and looped the net over a fish's gills, then tossed the slippery whitefish into the tray holding the others needing to be cleaned.

"You've heard the story of Moses Pullman."

Isaac nodded. It was a tale he'd heard at least a hundred times. His grandfather's fishing partner in Milwaukee had been a black man, a former slave. When a wealthy white woman was murdered by a large black man, Moses was the first person accused. He'd been innocent though, and Pa and his father had gone to court, testifying they'd been with Moses at the time of the murder.

"I wanted to make sure that didn't happen again." Pa pulled at his beard, his face still turned to the sea while the fish lay forgotten at his feet. "Though I wasn't a lawyer, I was able to defend Moses, but only because the circumstances had been right. I didn't have a clue what I was doing, how to approach the judge, when I was allowed to interject, or anything else. The next time an innocent man or woman was accused of a crime, I wanted to know how to defend them better."

Isaac released another lifeless fish from the net and tossed it into the wooden tray with the rest. "The town charter, it's written all official-like. Mr. Fletcher said you wrote it."

Pa looked down and raised a bushy eyebrow. "What are you reading the town charter for?"

Isaac shrugged. "When Mr. Stillings had that heart attack and died last summer, I figured the council would appoint someone to replace him, but you didn't. You waited all the way until November and had an election."

Pa nodded, then crouched on the other side of the net and worked a fish free. "Seemed the best way to set things up. The town council is mostly businessmen. If they're able to appoint someone, who do you think they'll chose?"

"Another businessman."

"And one who probably does business with them. You get a bunch of friends running a town, and what kind of policies do you think they'll put in place?"

He barely needed to think about the answer. "Ones that benefit them."

"And probably no one else."

Isaac's hands stilled in the net, and he looked up to meet his pa's gaze. "I want to go to law school. Eagle Harbor gets more residents every year.

We've got ourselves a doctor and a sheriff and a town council, but we don't have a lawyer. We haven't had anyone falsely accused that I know of, but that day might come."

Besides, it seemed that a lawyer could help make sure the law was followed—by everyone, not just the poor people whose fathers didn't sit on the town council.

A slow smile spread over Pa's face, visible even beneath his bushy beard. Pa wasn't given to smiling at every little thing, but that smile was so big and sincere Isaac felt it somewhere in his own chest. "I don't regret leaving law school when I met your ma and moved here, but having one of my sons be a lawyer? Seems like God would be giving me my dream back times ten."

Pa bent back over the net, this time studying a hole in it rather than releasing another fish. "There's time enough to get you signed up for classes this fall. Your ma and I have some money put by. Probably not enough to pay for everything, but it could help."

Pa would help pay for law school? Isaac slid another tangled fish from the net, then sat back and stretched his shoulders. He shouldn't be surprised. Pa gave away money to anyone who had a half good reason, but Isaac couldn't quite suppress the warmth that swelled inside him at the offer. "I'm not going to leave you to fish alone. We'll wait until Elijah returns."

If Elijah ever returned. At the moment his older brother was off sailing the Atlantic. In part because he was upset about people with money—namely the Sinclair family—having too much control over the town.

But how much worse would Eagle Harbor be if Pa hadn't written the town charter? The charter said a person couldn't sit on the council unless they'd been a resident for five years. Though Byron Sinclair was rich and powerful, he only spent his summers here, which meant he couldn't be on the council.

Elijah would come back eventually, ready to settle down, have himself a family, and fish with Pa.

That's when it would be time to go to law school.

Except no one had counted on Pa dying before Elijah returned. Isaac reached for the mug on his desk and took a gulp of long-cold coffee. He'd lost more than just his pa four years ago, he'd lost his dreams as well.

But that wasn't entirely true. Being sheriff might not have been his dream, but what about his desire to see justice done? To have a town where people were treated well and fairly regardless of their last name, where they hailed from, or how much money sat in their bank account? He could do that now, even if being a lawman was a bit different than being a lawyer.

Would Pa be disappointed that he'd never gone to law school? No question Pa'd be thrilled with Elijah going out to rescue sailors in stormy seas, probably wouldn't care in the least about Elijah risking his life each time he went out either.

But would Pa be proud of him being sheriff?

Isaac stood from his chair and stretched, his back starting to ache from too many hours of sitting, then wandered onto the porch.

Since the bout of sticky heat had passed last week, it seemed that they were in for an ideal summer. The sun was bright but not hot, the sky a vibrant, cloudless blue that provided the perfect backdrop for the white gulls circling above the harbor.

Isaac leaned against one of the porch posts and crossed his legs at the ankles. He ran his gaze slowly over the street filled with people, some of whom had just disembarked from a passenger ship en route to Duluth.

Harsh laughter sounded above the chatter and clomping of horses' hooves. "Come on, hurry."

Isaac narrowed his eyes at Martin Spritzer, who darted out the door of the mercantile kitty-corner from where he stood, the boy's laughter ringing with trouble.

"Faster or she'll catch us." Leroy raced through the door and started down the steps at full throttle.

Isaac shoved off the post and rushed across the street, hastening around a mother with children and between two passing wagons.

"Hold on a second." He reached out and snagged Leroy's arm before the boy could dart behind one of the wagons and lose himself in the crowd.

Leroy looked up and twisted his lips together. A yellowish-brown circle surrounded his eye.

"Where are you off to in such a hurry?" Isaac kept his grip on Leroy's arm firm.

Martin stopped running and came back toward his brother. The boy's jaw sported a bruise about the same color and shape as Leroy's. "We were just… uh…"

"Knocking over a jar of jam and running off without paying for it." Mrs. Foley emerged onto the mercantile's porch and planted her hands on her hips. "Or without cleaning up the mess."

"It was Martin's fault," Leroy spat. "He tripped me."

"That's no excuse for running away." Mrs. Foley clomped down the front porch toward them, a rag spotted with a sticky red substance in her hand.

His back toward the shopkeeper's wife, Martin rolled his eyes; then Leroy snickered.

Isaac clenched his jaw. "How did you get the bruises on your faces?"

They exchanged glances with each other, then Martin curled his lip and sneered at his brother. "Leroy deserved it."

"Not as much as Martin," Leroy muttered.

Isaac shook his head. Their mother had been sick lately, yes. But if she didn't squelch this sort of behavior now, it wouldn't be long until these boys were fighting others instead of themselves. "You two owe Mrs. Foley for the cost of the jam, plus a nickel each for running off instead of apologizing and offering to clean up the mess."

Though her lips were still pinched, Mrs. Foley gave him a small nod. "That'll do nicely. Thank you, Sheriff."

"Best get into the store and start working." Isaac released Leroy's arm.

The boy just grimaced. "Now? But we got stuff to do."

"Should have thought about that before you broke the jam and tried running off." He glanced over Leroy's head at the shopkeeper's wife. "An afternoon of work from each of you should pay for everything, don't you think, Mrs. Foley?"

The woman gave another nod. "The back storeroom needs cleaning. If they work hard, they should be able to get it done before the store closes at five."

"Fine." Leroy scowled but trudged toward the store; Martin trailed him up the steps a moment later.

"And if I hear reports that you gave Mrs. Foley any trouble," Isaac called, "I've got a slew of chores around the sheriff's office you'll end up doing too."

Martin turned his head and sent a furious glare over his shoulder, but he followed Mrs. Foley and Leroy into the store.

Isaac blew out a breath and slung his hands on his hips. How could he make Leroy and Martin want to behave? They might be paying for the broken jam, but forcing good behavior from the boys was a far cry from them choosing right on their own. Pa probably would have found a way to have the Spritzer boys pay Mrs. Foley back for the jam plus feel sorry about breaking it in the first place.

"Isaac!"

He turned to see Elijah coming from the direction of the beach, his jaw set and gait clipped.

Isaac headed toward his brother, but rather than come to meet him, Elijah veered toward the sheriff's office. Isaac waited for a wagon to pass, then stepped behind a group of sailors before crossing the rest of the street and climbing the porch steps. Elijah reached the door first and pushed it open without so much as a pause in his stride, his shoulders as tight as a ship's sail at full wind.

Isaac entered a second later. "What's—?"

"Someone shot at the boat."

Isaac froze. "What…? When?"

"When I was coming back from Ontonagon. You remember that little cove about five miles west of here? The one where Pa used to take us swimming?" Elijah paced from one end of the office to the other, his boots echoing on the plain wood floor.

"I take it no one was hurt." Otherwise his brother would have gone straight for the doctor.

"No. Nothing hit the boat either. I think they were warning shots, either that or whoever was pulling the trigger is the worst shot in Copper Country."

Isaac headed around the desk and opened the second drawer, then pulled out a map of the coast. "This place here?" He pointed to the spot where they'd picnicked and played as children.

Elijah stopped pacing long enough to peer at the map. "Yes, that's the one. Did someone buy it? Is there a reason for us to be scared away from that bit of property?"

"I can check with the deeds office at the courthouse in Central, but as far as I know, the land still belongs to the state." He tapped a finger over the spot.

"Could this be related to the dead man in the woods?"

Isaac's throat tightened. "Don't know."

Despite scouring the woods, he'd not been able to find footprints indicating a second man had been with the stranger. But two shooting incidents near Eagle Harbor within eight days of each other? Something wasn't right.

"I'll grab Granger and go have a look around." Hopefully it was early enough he could still find Granger at the boardinghouse. Fletcher could keep an eye on things around town while he and Granger headed into the woods. He turned to the shelf behind the desk and grabbed his pouch filled with ammunition and other supplies.

"Do you mean to go by boat?"

"Not if I'll be shot at. We'll have surprise on our side going by land." Plus he doubted he could step onto a boat without having another fit like he'd had in the workshop last week, but Elijah didn't need to know that.

He started for the door, then paused and glanced over his shoulder at his brother. "Should be back by dinner, but if not, you know where to start looking."

Elijah stood in the center of the room, hands in his pockets, his face a mixture of emotions Isaac didn't quite want to think about. "I feel like I should go with you."

"No, dig a tin star out of the desk and keep an eye on Fletcher if you want to be helpful." He'd deputized his brother last winter when he needed some volunteer help. "There's no point in three of us going."

Or three of them dying if they were walking blind into a killer's den. He pulled open the door.

"Isaac."

He stopped and turned, only to have one of Elijah's strong hands clasp his shoulder.

His brother's steely gray gaze met his own. "Be safe."

"I plan to be."

"And come back."

His mouth turned dry. This was the part where he was supposed to promise he'd return. After all, Elijah promised he'd be back each and every time he went on a water rescue.

But the words stuck in his throat. What was the point of promising something he couldn't control?

Chapter Nine

Sam Owens had just inherited ranchland. Ellie swallowed as she read the letter Mrs. Foley had dropped off at the bakery when she'd stopped to purchase muffins a few minutes ago.

He hadn't been expecting to inherit any land, but evidently a rancher Sam had once worked for died rather suddenly, and Sam had been listed in the will. After working this year's cattle drive for another rancher, he'd have enough saved he would buy his own herd.

Ellie fanned away the heat of the bakery's kitchen with her hand. Would Sam ask her to marry him once he had his ranch? Surely he'd need a wife to help him cook and clean house. After all, the only reason they'd started writing was because he'd written the same mail-order-bride service that she had.

But what if his letters were lies? What if he was an outlaw or like Pa? Could she marry a man who once he got her with child ran off for years at a time, only to return when he decided it was time for her to be in the family way again?

But no, Sam's letters spoke of rolling land and grazing cattle, of wanting the same simple things she did. A home, a family, a little nest egg. And he wrote of God too. If Sam were trying to deceive her, then wouldn't he say he owned a ranch the size of Michigan's Upper Peninsula and thousands of cattle in an effort to entice her down there?

She reached for the paper and pencil on the counter. If the bakery stayed quiet for another quarter hour or so, she could get a good start on her letter back to him.

But what to tell him? That she'd always dreamed of being a rancher's wife?

The truth was, she'd always dreamed of a man looking at her the way Sheriff Cummings looked at Aileen, or Elijah looked at Victoria, or Mac looked at Tressa. She really didn't care if the man was a rancher or a fisherman or a lawman, as long as he was honest and treated her right.

The little bell above the bakery door tinkled. Ellie dropped the pencil onto the counter, then stood and pushed through the swinging doors to the storefront.

"How have you been?" Jake Ranulfson swept his gaze briefly down her before looking her in the eye. "Better, I hope. You seemed a little flustered last week when I stopped by."

Heat crept into her cheeks, and she reached up to make sure her hair was still coiled neatly on her head rather than escaping its pins. "I've been fine."

But had it really been a week since she'd seen him? She supposed so. A week since Aileen left to work for the Sinclairs, a week since she'd been running the bakery by herself.

"All right, well…" He shoved one of his hands in his pocket while the other clutched a brown paper sack. "Seeing how it's time for lunch, I figured I'd stop by to visit. I had the cook make up a couple of roast beef sandwiches this morning. Are they still your favorite?"

"Ah… yes." At least she thought they were. It wasn't as though her family ever had enough money for roast beef, and it had been a long time since those summer days when she'd badgered Jake into giving her half his sandwich while following him and Cliff around town.

She took the sack, opened it, and let the rich aroma of the meat escape into the room.

"I figured you wouldn't be able to leave the bakery in the middle of the day, but maybe we could eat in the back?"

She wiped a strand of hair away from where it was plastered on her forehead. "I'm not sure you'd want to. This time of year, that oven turns the kitchen into a steam bath."

Jake gestured for her to precede him into the kitchen. "I can always go jump in the lake before I head back to the bank for the afternoon."

She stepped into the sweltering kitchen and fanned her face. "Oh, no you don't. It's not fair of you to tell me that when you know I'm stuck here."

Jake ran a finger beneath the collar of his shirt, beads of perspiration already forming along his hairline. "Do you take a dunk in the lake before you go home every night? I would after working in this place."

She headed toward the table near the open back window—the coolest place in the kitchen, though that wasn't saying much. "It wouldn't do me any good since I go home to stand over a vat of boiling wash water."

She plopped down on a chair and cocked her head to the side while Jake took the other chair. "Do you remember that time I pushed you into the lake? If I recall, you'd been teasing me with part of your sandwich, and I'd had enough."

"Shoving me into the lake with the sandwich in my hand only made it soggy for you." He took the sack from her and handed her a sandwich. "And it was cold. I think we'd gotten snow the day before."

"We did not." She took a bite and let the rich flavors of roast beef, cheese, and sourdough bread fill her mouth.

"Clifford dove in to rescue me, and we had all but icicles hanging off our clothes by the time we walked back to my house." He spoke around a mouthful of food, his eyes dancing at the memory.

But at the mention of her brother's name, her own food stuck in her throat. "Do you miss him? Clifford, I mean?"

"Every day." He set his sandwich down. "I just wish... well, I don't suppose there's much point in wishing for anything. It's not like I can go back in time and bring Clifford back."

She set her own sandwich down, the food suddenly not as appealing as it had been a few moments earlier. "Sometimes I think God took the wrong one of us. I'm only making half the money Clifford made sailing. And Cliff used to help Ma so much. I could almost see her shoulders perk up whenever he was around, like she knew he could handle things. I don't think she's smiled once since he died."

Jake reached for the hands she was wringing on the table and rested his large one over top of them. Warmth and comfort flowed through her, along with a sense of understanding. She might have nine siblings, but she felt so very alone most days. Yet sitting here with Jake...

The bell above the storefront door clanged, and she sighed. "I need to go out there."

But she wasn't quite ready to move. It was nice spending a few minutes with someone she'd known all her life. And while talking about Clifford wasn't one of her favorite pastimes, she felt a little better for it, as though the hole in her heart had closed just a bit.

Jake took his hand away and put what was left of his sandwich back into the paper sack. "Why don't I stop by tomorrow? I'll bring roast beef again."

She scooted off her chair. "It's sweet of you to offer, but you don't need to go through all that trouble."

"Cliff would have wanted it."

But Clifford was gone now. "I really am fine, I promise."

Jake surveyed her in that quiet way he had, his gaze a sure indication that though his mind was churning, he wasn't about to speak his thoughts. "Maybe I need to stop by, not for you, but for me. It was good talking to you, Ellie. I miss your brother an awful lot sometimes, but today... our conversation... it helped."

She swallowed and gave Jake a brief nod before glancing out the doorway into the storefront, where Mrs. Kainer waited. "I suppose I can manage eating another one of those sandwiches tomorrow."

He grinned, bold and bright, reminding her of the boy that had once taunted her with his sandwiches rather than the serious banker he was becoming. "I'll see you then."

He disappeared out the back door, and she couldn't help but smile after him.

Until her gaze landed on the letter from Texas she'd left sitting on the counter—a letter she suddenly wasn't in a rush to answer.

―.―.―.―.―

Aileen trudged up the trail, one foot in front of the other as she climbed higher up the hill. How much farther to the bluffs?

Afternoon sunlight filtered through the trees around her, dusting the leaves with a glistening gold and lighting the dirt footpath ahead. Birds chirped in the trees above and a rabbit hopped to the edge of the trail, spotted her, then scampered back into the tall grass.

The surroundings should make her smile. On any other day, they probably would. But instead of curving her lips, she reached for the canteen slung over her shoulder, took a sip of water, then continued around the bend.

The final bend, it seemed, as she suddenly found herself standing on a stretch of bald rock.

She turned to take in the view, and her breath stopped. It truly was lovely. The hill dropped away at the edge of the rocks, giving her a sweeping view of the basin where Eagle Harbor lay nestled between the thick green forest and the sandy strip of beach that lined the shore. The calm waters of the harbor shimmered beside the log and clapboard town, and Lake Superior sprawled beyond, an endless expanse of blue that glinted with orange-tinted silver beneath the sun in the west.

If only Brenna and her wee ones were here to share this with her. The familiar ache of emptiness welled inside Aileen's chest, and her hand slid to the pocket in her skirt. She pulled out the letter she'd picked up from the mercantile less than an hour ago, though letter was a rather generous term for the handful of hastily scrawled sentences.

Being evicted today and staying with the Carneys tonight. Not sure where we're headed after that. Probably to Galway for factory work. Wanted ye to know.

Galway was so big, how would she ever find Brenna there? The letters and money she and Gilbert had sent last week would likely never reach Brenna now.

Aileen folded the paper and shoved it back in her pocket. Something fluttered in her stomach. Hunger? Loneliness? She stared down at the town below, the tiny houses no bigger than the toy homes in a child's play town, and blinked back the burning sensation in her eyes. Most of the townsfolk would be having dinner about now, but better she was here and hungry than in town fending off Rebekah's questions about why she was so sad.

As though Rebekah would understand. The woman was surrounded by family and friends and probably hadn't felt lonely a single day of her life.

Aileen brushed a strand of hair off her face and let the breeze rising off the water cool her. Then she turned and surveyed the rocky outcropping on which she stood. It looked as though there was a trail off to the side of the clearing. Perhaps there were more bluffs on the other side of the trees.

She followed the little path to the west, though it was probably only a trail for deer, if the tall grass feathering her feet was any indication. Just how was she supposed to bring her family to America when she didn't know where Brenna was living? How many weeks until Brenna wrote with a new address? What if it took months before Brenna could afford postage to send another letter to Eagle Harbor?

She'd wanted Brenna here by fall, all settled into her new job at the hotel. They could go for picnics amid the changing leaves, and knit caps and scarves for the children before the snow came. They could laugh over evening dinners and dream up grand futures for the wee ones.

They could be a family.

Now, she might not find Brenna in time to arrange passage before the harbor in town closed for the winter.

The trail started down the hill, twisting and curving on the slope rather than taking her to another patch of bald rocks. She hiked along as it wound its way downward and deeper into the woods. She wasn't quite sure where she was going. To a place where all was peaceful, mayhap. To a place that felt like home. Could she find such a spot in the middle of the woods with dusk approaching?

Oh, how was it she'd lived in Eagle Harbor for nearly a year and still didn't feel as if she belonged?

A rustling sounded to her left, and she froze for an instant, then blew out a breath. Probably just an animal. She stepped around a tiny sapling, its branches stretched toward the sky.

The rustling sounded again. But no, not a rustling. More like a tromping, like footsteps coming through the woods farther west. A flash of brown moved through the trees ahead.

"State yer business." The man's voice echoed through the woods, the Irish brogue bringing an odd sense of familiarity. Could it be Morley?

Mayhap. Though it could be the town vandal or some other troublemaker.

She drew in another breath, calm and slow, then released it. It could just as easily be a trapper or a hunter or a hiker. "Why is it I have to state me business? Mayhap ye should state yers first."

"Aileen? Is that ye, lass?"

Her heart stuttered at the familiar sound of her name, at the familiar lilt in the masculine voice. Then a man stepped through the trees.

But not just any man, nay. 'Twas Conan, her very brother.

The world stilled around her, no more nattering of squirrels or chirping of birds, no more rustling of leaves in the breeze. Her heart slowed too. Though it had been pounding just seconds ago, she could scarcely feel the beat of it against her chest.

"Conan." She tried to speak the word, but her throat clogged, and his name came out as little more than a choking sound. Could it truly be him? The man standing before her had Conan's brownish-red hair just a shade darker than her own. The skin of his nose and cheeks were doused with the same familiar freckles Conan had borne since he was a wee lad. Who else could it be, but him?

She moved forward slowly, as though the illusion before her would vanish if she hastened her steps. But he stood there, as real and sturdy as the thick maple beside him, dressed in brown trousers and a stained shirt that had probably been white at one point. A rifle was slung over his shoulder, and a supply pouch lay strapped about his waist. When he opened his arms, she rushed the rest of the way, wrapping her arms around his middle while he clasped her against his chest.

"Oh, Conan," she muttered into his shirt.

"There now. Don't ye be crying after me."

His strength surrounded her, filling a part of her that had been empty since the moment she'd learned of his death. The rough fabric of his shirt rubbed against her cheek, and she drew in the scent of him, rich with sunshine and forest.

"I don't understand." She pulled back enough to see his face, though that didn't stop her voice from trembling. "Last spring on the docks… y-ye died. How can ye be here now?"

His eyes, the same green shade as her own, sought hers. "I didn't know that's what they planned to tell ye. I promise I didn't."

She shook her head, thinking back to the day she'd tried so hard to scrub from her memory. The men who'd visited her from Great Northern Shipping had told her Conan's body was so mangled she'd not want to see it, and that arrangements had already been made for a grave outside of town. Evidently deaths on the docks were common enough that the shipping company had a plan in place to take care of the bodies. The men at her door had made the offer sound so kind and generous. Great Northern Shipping would see to the burial and all expenses, and wasn't that just so nice?

"But ye knew afterwards? Knew I thought ye were dead, and ye never once told me?" She stepped back from him, and the emptiness that had vanished for the few seconds Conan had held her swept back with a flood-like force. "I've been grieving for over a year, and ye didn't once think ye should tell me ye were alive?"

"Don't go getting all riled up, lass." Conan held up his hands, as though the simple gesture would somehow make up for his deceit. "We were trying to keep things quiet."

"We?" Her hands began to tremble, and she sucked in a short, choppy breath. "Who is this *we* ye're…? Wait. 'Tis Morley, aye?"

Conan slapped a mosquito on his arm. "Aye, Morley knows the whole of it."

"I saw him just last week." She spat the last words like arrows shot from a tightly strung bow. "Exchanged letters with him all winter. He had ample opportunity to let me know ye lived, and he didn't."

Yet her arrows didn't seem to pierce Conan, for he merely shrugged. "Figured everything would be easier if ye didn't know the details, that's all."

She took a step toward him and jammed her finger into his chest. "Just what do ye think is easy about being told yer brother is dead when he's not?"

Conan flung her hand away. "'Twas never me idea to tell ye I was dead. I didn't know about it until after the deed had been done. But it seemed simpler considering yer knack for questions."

"Knack for questions?" She clenched her teeth together so hard an ache formed at the back of her jaw, then spread up to her temples. If she wasn't so happy he was alive, she'd kill him all over again. He just about deserved it. "What are ye even doing here? And with a gun, no less?"

"I've got meself a good job through the end of the summer. That's all ye need to know. But I don't want ye coming into the woods again. Go back to town and pretend ye never saw me. I'll send for ye at the end of the summer."

The end of the summer was when Morley said he'd have earned enough to bring Brenna here. "I'm not going anywhere until this mysterious job of yers gets explained."

Conan had promised when he left Ireland he wouldn't stir up any more trouble, but if he...

Wait. Conan had a gun. In the woods. Could he somehow be involved with the dead man the Spritzer boys had found?

Nay. What was she thinking? Isaac had ruled that death a suicide, so the two couldn't be connected. She'd hardly be traipsing about the woods alone if a murderer was on the loose.

Conan swatted at another mosquito, his jaw as hard as her own. "All ye need to know is the job will give us enough money to buy a farm down by Milwaukee at the end of the summer."

"'Tis not worth it. Ye might not say what ye're doing, but that tells me it's illegal. It's not worth having a farm if ye have to break laws to get it." She wrapped her arms around herself. "Come back to town with me tonight and find honest work. Get your farm that way."

"It'll be yer farm too." Conan took a step toward her, then reached out and touched the side of her arm, his eyes alive with dreams she'd thought long dead. "We'll finally have property to call our own. And I'm not talking about homesteading, where it will take ten years before we have something worthwhile. Nay, we'll buy a farm outright. One with tilled fields and a strong house and even a barn. It'll be Da's dream come true for us, right here in America. Don't ye want that?"

She could almost see it. Fields rich with dirt and green with harvest. Golden rays of sun slanting over the land and kissing everything they touched. A small cottage, weathered but sturdy, with smoke unfurling from its chimney.

Except none of it mattered seeing how Conan was being underhanded about things. "Come back to town with me."

Conan dropped his hand from her arm as though her touch burned him. "Me job isn't the kind I can just walk away from, even if I wanted to—which I don't. And Morley can't leave either, so don't ye be asking him next time ye see him."

She nearly opened her mouth to ask what the job was again, but he wasn't going to tell her. "Will I see Morley about town then? And when was the last time ye saw him? Did he tell ye about Brenna?"

"Aye, he did." Conan surveyed the trees as though he expected their cousin to emerge from behind the brush. "Said ye were fixing to get yerself in a mess in order to bring her here before summer ends."

"I don't know if she can come now." Her voice wobbled, and she slipped a hand down to finger the letter in her pocket. "I just got word that Brenna and her wee ones were evicted. Her letter says she's headed to Galway to find work, but it's dated over a month ago. I don't even know where to send money anymore. Do Morley and Brenna have relatives in Galway? Mayhap someone on their mother's side?"

Conan shrugged. "Does it matter? We can't do anything for Brenna until fall. If she hasn't written to ye by then, we'll figure something out."

She crossed her arms over her chest and raised her chin. "And I already said I don't want to…"

A rustling sounded somewhere farther up the hill, and Conan's head snapped up, his eyes instantly alert. "We've been here too long. Ye need to go, lass."

So soon? She looked back up at her brother, taking in his wide forehead, firm jaw, and bevy of freckles. She'd memorized that face as a babe and loved it just as dearly as she'd loved her Da. "When will I see ye again?"

"I'll come for ye this fall, after I've bought that farm."

Yet he'd do nothing to help her now, just as he'd done nothing to help her this past year. And what if he didn't come? What if that rifle slung over his shoulder got him into trouble? What if…?

"I want ye safe, and that means ye need to be well away from me. I only need a few more months and we'll have that land we've always wanted." Conan reached out and gripped her arms, his eyes seeking hers in the growing darkness. "And don't tell anyone in town about me. Do ye hear?"

"Ye don't want me to tell me friends ye're alive?" He asked too much of her, especially considering how much she'd missed him. She should race back to town and tell Rebekah she wasn't alone anymore.

Conan's grip on her arms turned harsh. "Do ye want me to end up dead?"

She'd rather have him not working a job where he could end up dead in the first place.

Rustling sounded again, a bit closer this time, and Conan's eyes snapped back to the woods. "Promise me, here and now." The whispered words held a threatening edge. "Not a word about me to anyone, and be quick about it."

More rustling. She swallowed and looked up the hill, though in the growing shadows, she couldn't see anyone. "Fine, I promise."

He twisted his lips and ran his gaze down her. "Hike up yer skirts and move quietly, only over trails, do ye hear? Don't step on twigs or move aside tree branches. Quick and quiet now, and I'll distract him."

Him? Her heart pounded, and blood rushed in her ears. Was it someone Conan knew? "But…"

He gave her another harsh look, then swung the rifle off his shoulder, holding it with the barrel pointed down as he started through the trees.

She spun and darted into the forest, her throat thick and moisture welling in her eyes. In all the nights she'd cried herself to sleep since Conan's "death," she'd never dreamed her brother was still alive—or that once she'd found him, he'd send her away.

Chapter Ten

Twilight's long shadows stretched across the sky as Aileen made her way down the little hill where the graveyard sat above Eagle Harbor. Peepers and crickets filled the night with their song, while the sound of waves rolling into shore rumbled in the distance. The small town, with its mixture of log and white clapboard buildings, held the warm glow of lanterns and the fading scents of dinner and wood smoke.

But with Brenna lost somewhere in Ireland and Conan bidding her goodbye so easily, Eagle Harbor held little hope for her now. Why work so hard for Gilbert if she couldn't bring Brenna here and her brother intended to whisk her away only a few months after the hotel opened?

But that supposed her brother would be around to whisk her anywhere in the first place. And did she want to live on a farm purchased with ill-gotten gain? Or to live with her brother who seemed to care so very little about her?

"Aileen!"

She jerked, her heart stuttering in her chest, her feet stilling in the tall, prickly grass. Who had called her name? Conan?

A familiar form separated itself from beside one of the shadowed houses at the edge of town and started toward her, his gait clipped and fast.

"Aileen." Isaac's voice rang out against the chorus of toads and crickets.

Her heart slowed, and she drew in a calming breath as she continued down the hill.

"Are you all right?" He reached out and settled his hands on either of her arms. Though his grip was gentle, it held a certain firmness she'd not be able to easily shake off. "Where were you? Rebekah said you had a headache and were resting, but Ellie said you never came back to the bakery, and no one could find you."

"Ye were worried?" In the dimness, she could just make out the concern filling his eyes, and she couldn't stop the bit of warmth curling through her.

Mayhap she should forget her promise to Conan and tell Isaac about her brother. But what would she say, that Conan had been tromping around the woods with a gun? People did that all the time, 'twas hardly a crime.

It wasn't a crime for a person to fake his death either. Heartless, perhaps, at least toward the people who loved him, but still not criminal. "I'm sorry I alarmed ye. I was only gone a few hours and didn't think I'd be missed."

"A few hours is plenty long. Besides, it's nearly dark. The woods are no place for you at this hour." Isaac's grip on her arms tightened. There seemed to be more to his words, something he wasn't saying.

"Ye oughtn't have worried yourself. I wasn't in any danger." Except she'd thought she was, until she'd realized 'twas Conan who chased her.

But if it had been another man?

Her heart thudded against her ribs. That was something she'd failed to ask Conan. He hadn't been the only one lurking about in the woods, and whoever the other man was, Conan hadn't been too keen on her meeting up with him.

Isaac raised his eyes to the tree line now black with the shadows of night. "Did you get lost? We searched the woods, but you weren't at the river or meadow."

"We?" A lump rose in her throat. For fourteen months Conan let her believe him dead, never once checking on her or bothering to see how she fared, never once making sure she had a safe place to be. But today she'd been gone for a matter of hours, and it sounded as though Rebekah had whipped up a regular old search party on her behalf.

"How many…?" Her voice faltered, but when she looked up and met Isaac's eyes, her tongue found the words once more. "How many of ye were looking for me?"

⸱⸱⸱⸱⸱

Isaac looked down into Aileen's face. The rising moonlight illuminated her skin beneath its pale glow. He reached out and stroked a strand of hair away from her cheek, tucking it behind her ear. Then he stilled. What was he thinking to be so forward? She, of all people, hated being touched.

But she didn't move away or even flinch, just stood there, her eyes filled with… with… not longing, no, or even tenderness. Just sorrow. So much sorrow his own heart grew heavy with it. Her eyes always had a haunted look to them, but tonight was worse. The sorrow seemed to go soul deep, and the brokenness she tried so hard to hide lay just beneath a fragile surface.

"Well, who was looking for me?" She glanced down the hill toward town. "They're not still searching, are they?"

Looking for her, right. That's what they'd been talking about—before he'd gotten lost in a pair of mournful, green eyes. "Ah, Rebekah, of course, and Gilbert. Elijah and Mac, until Mac had to go to the lighthouse."

He hadn't asked his deputies to help since there'd been no proof something was wrong with Aileen. Rebekah had told him she'd gone missing after he and Granger had returned from searching the patch of beach Elijah had sent them to. They'd found a pile of empty bullet casings and footprints near the sandy cove, but nothing to indicate who'd shot at Elijah or why.

"Are they still looking?" Aileen peered around his shoulder, surveying the town.

"No, we called off the search when darkness started to fall. I spotted you while making my rounds." Probably because he'd patrolled little else besides Center Street, hoping to find exactly what he'd seen a few minutes ago—Aileen coming home well and unharmed.

"That's too many people, too much fuss." She pulled away from him and started walking, their feet soon leaving the grass and finding the packed dirt of the street. "I was fine, I promise."

As far as he was concerned, there was no such thing as too much fuss over a person gone missing. But why had she ventured into the woods?

Or maybe the better question was, why wouldn't she? The forest surrounding the town had always been safe. Aileen probably hadn't heard about Elijah getting shot at, and a suicide that had taken place eight days earlier hardly reeked of danger.

But the hairs on the back of his neck prickled, and a chill shivered up his spine. He glanced over his shoulder at the trees. Only blackness greeted him, still and deep. "You haven't yet said why you were in the woods."

"It's… it's Brenna." She reached into her pocket and pulled out a crinkled letter. "I got this after finishing at the hotel today, and I wanted some time to meself before telling others. Brenna's been evicted and went to Galway to find work. I haven't the first notion where to start looking for her in a city such as that, and I fear she won't have the money for postage to send me a letter with her new address. Now she won't even get the money Gilbert and I sent, let alone the letter about coming here."

So that explained the sadness. He reached out, took her hand, and gave it a squeeze. He then used his grip to tug her a little closer as they rounded the side of the bakery and headed to the back kitchen entrance. "I'm sure Gilbert can help you find her, but if he's unwilling for some reason, I have money put aside from my toy-making days. Surely we can hire an investigator in Ireland to search for your cousin the same as in America."

"Ye'd do that for me?" She stopped beside the door and looked up at him, a sheen of moisture glazed her eyes.

Had he said something wrong? Why was she about to cry over his offer to help? "Of course I would. Don't you want your cousin to come here?"

"You're all too good to me. I don't deserve it." She dropped her gaze and turned away from him, shoving her key in the door and swinging it open.

He gripped her shoulder before she disappeared inside. He'd not let her shut him out again. Every time he thought he might be getting somewhere with her, she said something sharp and cryptic then ran off.

"I don't know what you mean," he spoke to her back. "We treat you the same as we would anyone else. And Aileen…" He shifted so close his trousers brushed the edge of her skirt. "You deserve to be cared about. You deserve to be…" *Loved.* But he wasn't quite ready to tell her that. "…surrounded by family and friends. Life is better when you have people to share it with."

She turned to him, but the step he'd taken toward her put their faces right next to each other. Their breaths mingled as she searched his eyes. Did she realize how deep a shade of green her own were?

Even the darkness didn't mask the wide, sad beauty emanating from those emerald depths.

"Ye ought not say such things, Isaac Cummings." Her voice was shaky when she spoke, her tender breaths puffing against his chin. "If ye knew everything about me, then ye'd understand why ye should leave me alone."

She took a step back, which put her in the doorway, then took another step deeper into the kitchen before closing the door with a thud.

The lock clicked into place a moment later, and the dim flicker of lantern light floated through the window above the sink.

And still, he stood there, staring at the fading wood of the door, not quite able to force his feet to move or his gaze to leave the spot where she'd disappeared.

If he knew everything about her? *Oh, Aileen, you're more troubled than you let on, aren't you?*

~.~.~.~.~

She felt the warmth nestled beside her, the small little bundle wriggling against her chest as they lay in bed together. Aileen leaned over and pressed her lips to the fuzzy down on the top of her child's small head. The babe squirmed a bit but didn't open her eyes.

Cara. She whispered the name she'd given the child, if only in her dreams. Then she reached out and stroked a finger over her daughter's skin, smooth and soft. The child's hair was the same shade as her own, and she reached out to lay a hand atop the fuzz. Oh my sweet Cara.

Aileen jolted awake with a start, sitting up in bed and pressing a hand to her chest. Was there someone in the alley again?

Boom! Boom!

She sank back against the wall behind her bed. Not voices from the alley, but thunder. Still, she should get up and check the alley, just to be certain no one was there again. She rose on legs still trembling from being startled out of slumber and padded across the floor on her bare feet. She peeked out the window, but all was still and peaceful, or at least all that she could see.

Dark clouds from the approaching storm covered the moonlight, casting the alley into such deep shadow that even if there were men below she might not be able to make out their forms. She watched for another minute or two before turning away from the window and heading back to her bed—her empty bed that held no husband or child.

Despite the warmth of summer, her sheets felt as cold and empty as they would on a January night.

Raising a child on her own would have come with a slew of hardships. So why, oh why, did she ache so badly for the little babe she'd never even held? Why did she close her eyes every night only to imagine Cara with her? To feel her warm skin, and hear her soft, cheerful gurgles?

Aileen drew in a shuddering breath but wouldn't let the sob burst free. She ought not focus on things she could never obtain, but on things that she had here in Eagle Harbor, on the life that was laid out in front of her.

Which was why she needed to find a way to bring Brenna and her children to America. She might not be able to give her own daughter the promise of a bright, happy tomorrow, but she could make sure Brenna and her nieces got the future she and her own lost wee one would never have.

Chapter Eleven

"You planning to go back there?" Granger poured himself a cup of coffee, then came back to Isaac's desk and straddled a chair.

"Probably." Isaac narrowed his gaze, studying the map of the coast splayed over his desk and the little inlet where Elijah had been shot at.

Dusty lamplight mixed with the dying rays of sun slanting through the window behind his desk. Outside, the chatter from passersby and the occasional clomp of horses' hooves or creak of a wagon was giving way to laughter and jeers from sailors and miners headed to either the bar or brothel for the evening.

Isaac sighed and raked a hand through his hair. "I feel like we're missing something."

"I thought you and Granger searched that stretch of beach real good." Fletcher turned from where he'd been standing at the window, looking out into the street.

"We did. But I don't like that we came up empty. We know for sure a person was there." He tapped his finger against the spot on the map, then shook his head. If only the footprints in the sand and the pile of bullet casings had led them to whoever shot at Elijah. "With that and the dead body showing up a week and a half ago, there has to be something more going on."

"I don't think so." Granger crossed his arms atop the chair's back and leaned closer to the map. "That man's death was a suicide, and I'm not just saying that because it sounds nicer than the notion of a murderer skulking around. Suicide is the best explanation for what we found. And with what happened to your brother, it's not uncommon for people to pass through. We might never know why Elijah was shot at, but it's not like we found a camp."

"At least the vandal has moved on since we don't have any more ruined wagon beds or broken windows." Fletcher turned back to the window, then took a step away from it and moved toward the door. "Someone's coming."

The door to the office opened, and a tall man who looked more like a Viking than a modern-day mariner stepped inside.

"Hello, I'm Lars Norling." The man spoke in a deep voice, then extended his hand to Fletcher for a shake. "I'm looking for Sheriff Isaac Cummings."

Isaac came around the front of the desk. "That'd be me."

"I need a word in private." With his shaggy blond hair, wide shoulders, large chest, and stern jaw, he looked about ready to don a medieval helmet, pull out a battle-ax, and raid a town.

"Granger, why don't you go check on things at the Pretty Penny? Fletcher, run down to the Rusty Wagon and make sure all is calm there, then do a round. I'll come find you when I'm done here."

"Yes, sir." Fletcher quashed his hat on his head and rushed out the door.

Granger slowly pushed himself off the chair he'd been straddling, turned it around so it faced the desk, and then followed Fletcher outside at an even pace.

Norling glanced into the open door that led to the string of empty jail cells. "It's just you here?"

"For now." He may have only met the stranger a minute ago, but the other man seemed tense. What could the Viking have to tell him that was so important? Something about the body they'd found in the woods? "Can't promise how long the jail cells will stay empty though."

The man hung his hat on one of the pegs by the door. "I'm a special agent with the U.S. Customs Service. I'd like to ask you a few questions."

"The U.S...." The words stalled in his mouth. "Why is the U.S. Customs Service sending an agent here?" Unless this was somehow related to the telegram Elijah had sent.

"We believe a smuggling ring we've been trying to shut down for four years has taken up residence here." Norling pulled out the chair Granger had vacated, then settled into it. "The telegram we received over a week ago confirmed it."

"I see." Isaac walked around his desk and sank into his own chair. At least now he had a reason to justify the extra patrols and increased hours for him and his two deputies. But had he really been right about smugglers? Had that been what Aileen saw in the alley two weeks ago?

Sure, most of the men who came through town were rough, but Eagle Harbor wasn't the kind of place that attracted groups of hardened criminals. "You say you've been tracking this smuggling ring for four years?"

The man across the desk shrugged, his big shoulders rising and falling effortlessly. "Not me personally, but the customs office has been aware of the ring's activity and has had agents assigned to the case that long. Anytime we're close to catching them, they have a habit of moving their operation. Last year there was an incident near Ashland. We found the smuggling camp and warehouse, recovered over a hundred thousand dollars' worth of silver smuggled from Canada, but lost three of our men."

Something about the way the large man said it, the way his voice went raspy, caused Isaac to pause. "Were you there?"

Norling's clear blue gaze shifted down to his feet. "I was the only customs agent to survive, but the local law was there too. They only lost one man. I'm assuming I'll be able to rely on your help to catch the smugglers?"

"I… uh…" He rubbed a hand over his face. Did he really want to commit himself and his deputies to a mission they might not survive?

Ashland might have enough lawman they could lose a deputy to a criminal gang, but what would losing one person do to a sheriff's office that only employed three men? Yet he'd been elected to keep Eagle Harbor safe, and there was nothing safe about criminals hiding in the woods near town.

Isaac cleared his throat, then forced his mouth to form the next words. "Yes, we'll help. But the law here is me and my two newly hired deputies. You won't have much more than that to work with."

"Good." Norling gave a decisive nod. "Now I'm interested in any information you can provide me about Frank Ebberhard."

Ebberhard? Isaac frowned but dug in his desk for the report he'd filed on the man's arrest. There might even be a transcript of the trial around somewhere, seeing how he'd testified in it. "Not sure what he has to do with the smugglers, but Ebberhard was convicted of arson and attempted murder charges this past winter."

"Ebberhard was in Ashland last summer—one of the few smugglers' names we knew. He disappeared afterwards, and we didn't know where he'd gone until we got news of his conviction. The court report I read from the trial said you found jewelry in the cabin where he was staying. That jewelry could have been smuggled."

"I'm afraid that was taken from a woman in town." Isaac found the arrest report and slid it across the desk to the Viking. "Both the warehouse and brothel were robbed while he was here, but Ebberhard couldn't be conclusively tied to those robberies. Things like the brass chandelier and gilt mirrors from the brothel went missing, but I couldn't figure out who would take something so big and cumbersome in the dead of winter, or how the thief or thieves could make everything seem to disappear."

Norling scanned the report, then set it back on the desk. "There will be a warehouse of sorts, somewhere well protected, somewhere in the woods but not too far from shore. It's used as an exchange point, where items from Canada are brought in and dropped off. Sometimes goods from America are even stored there and a switch is made, enabling both Canadian and American tariffs to be evaded."

"The map." Isaac jolted upright. Suddenly everything Ebberhard had done and said last winter became clear.

"What was that?"

"Ebberhard was looking for a map he claimed he'd lost when we caught him."

Norling leaned forward. "What map?"

"Don't know. Couldn't get a word out of the man though he sat in one of my cells for two weeks before trial." Isaac pointed toward the door that divided the jailhouse from the rest of his office. "But it makes sense the map led somewhere significant given how badly he wanted it back."

"Did Ebberhard have any friends? People he seemed chummy with?"

"Several."

Norling glanced at the darkening sky outside the window. "Looks like we'll be paying calls first thing tomorrow morning. But you'd better dig out one of those tin stars you keep around here and deputize me tonight."

Isaac stared at the man that still seemed more a character out of a

Nordic legend than a flesh and blood customs' agent. "Why do I need to deputize you?"

"Because if this town's as small as it seems, and I just up and start asking people about ships without reason, the smugglers are going to know I'm here by nightfall. Now if I'm a deputy investigating, say, a dockworker we think might be responsible for a burglary up in Copper Harbor, I can ask about dockworkers' access to ships. I can ask about shipping schedules. I can ask if the warehouse owner has noticed anything out of place. I can ask about any number of things that will give me the information I need without causing alarm. If anyone wonders about you hiring me, tell them I have experience as a lawman."

No one would doubt that. The man carried himself with an authority people wouldn't argue with. But Norling would never blend in for the same reason. Even if he moved to Eagle Harbor and lived here a decade, his towering height and blond hair would mark him apart from the rest of the townsfolk.

Isaac shoved the report back into his bottom desk drawer. "I'll have to inform the town council, which oversees the budget for this office. I'll let them know I'm hiring you on a volunteer basis." He'd had volunteer deputies last winter too, but since he'd hired Fletcher and Granger, he hadn't needed much extra help.

Norling leaned his palms on the desk. "Then talk to them privately. The best way to catch these criminals is to make sure no one knows I'm a customs agent. Local law taking a stroll into the woods won't cause these smugglers to up and move the way having a customs man in town will. And lest you misunderstand me, these men need to be caught, not just scared off so they can move their smuggling operation to another town. We've been chasing them around Lake Superior for too many years already. It's time to end things."

But was "ending things," as Norling put it, possible with a law force of four men? It would be easier, and more feasible, to scare the smugglers off. Seemed all he had to do was start a rumor that the Customs Service had taken an interest in Eagle Harbor.

But Norling was right, the men needed to be stopped and made to pay for their crimes, not allowed to move elsewhere.

Isaac fished a tin star out of his bottom drawer and slid it across the desk toward Norling, then stood and reached for the Bible on the shelf behind his desk.

Norling stood and laid his hand on it.

"Do you promise to seek justice and uphold the laws of Eagle Harbor as a deputy?"

"I do."

"Then as sheriff of Eagle Harbor, I hereby deputize you."

"Thank you."

Isaac returned the Bible to the shelf and sat. "A couple of boys in town found a dead body in the woods last week. Looked like a suicide, considering the man's head had been blown off and we found a pistol only a couple feet from the body. Nobody in town knows who he is though. Any chance he could be tied to this smuggling business?"

"You say this man was a stranger?" Norling leaned forward in his chair and stroked his chin.

"No one in town saw him once, not even at the mercantile or bar." Isaac shifted the papers on his desk, searching for the report he'd filled out last week. "I've got a notion the man was murdered but no way to prove it."

Norling took the report and sat back, causing his chair to creak beneath his weight. "There's a good chance he's a smuggler and that he messed up and was made to pay for his mistake. We estimate this ring is moving over a hundred thousand dollars' worth of tariff-free goods every summer. Men have been killed for much less."

A shiver stole up Isaac's back. Why had the Customs Service only sent one man here? Catching these men would be too much for four lawmen to handle. "I know you want to keep things about your arrival and the smugglers quiet, but I can't allow people to go into the woods hiking or fishing without warning them of danger."

Aileen had been hiking just yesterday, and by herself, no less. He blew out a breath and rubbed at his breastbone, which suddenly ached. What would have happened had she come upon smugglers?

And what about the Spritzer boys? They hadn't been more than a hundred yards from the murder when it happened.

And that didn't take into account all the people that went foraging for berries or hiking or hunting.

"You can't say anything to the townsfolk." Norling's jaw was as hard as the blade of the battle-ax he might carry if he truly were a Viking. "These men need to be captured."

Isaac stood, his chair legs screeching across the wood floor. He leaned over the desk and stared directly into Norling's eyes. "I'm not going to let townsfolk walk into danger blind."

Except what if he could come up with another way to keep people out of the woods? And he wouldn't even need to lie, not now that he had a better guess as to what happened to the dead man.

Though the solution would open up a whole different kind of trouble for him.

The door swung open and Fletcher stepped inside. "Everything's fine at the Wagon, and I took a stroll around town too. Didn't find anything." Fletcher glanced between him and Norling, still staring at each other. "Is everything all right here? Do you need help?"

Isaac drew in a breath. "Go back to the Wagon and tell the men there to stay out of the woods. Tell them we've learned the dead man the Spritzers found was murdered, and we've reason to think the murderer is still near Eagle Harbor."

"But…" Fletcher doffed his hat and crushed the brim in his hand. "But you said it was a suicide."

Isaac clenched his jaw. "Appears I was wrong."

Norling sat back in his chair and gave a small nod. Good, the man had better be happy.

"Mr. Ranulfson won't want to hear that." Fletcher stuck a finger into his collar and tugged. "Neither will my pa. It'll send Mrs. Ranulfson and Mrs. Kainer into a regular tizzy."

Did Fletcher think he didn't know that? He could almost hear Mrs. Ranulfson shrieking at him, and it wasn't even tomorrow yet. "Spread the news. I want it around town by morning."

Hopefully the story would give them enough time to catch the smugglers while keeping the townsfolk safe.

Chapter Twelve

Elijah was out in the storm somewhere.

Isaac paced back and forth across his apartment, tromping from the small kitchen to the desk on the opposite side of the room. *Don't look out the window. Don't look out the window. Don't look out the window.* But no matter how many times he repeated the words, he couldn't help but glance at the angry clouds outside.

Dawn should have been brightening the sky already. But instead of pink and orange hues, lightning slashed from the heavens, followed by a deep thunder that shook the very bones of the building. Isaac blew out a breath. He needed to stay calm. He needed to stay in control. And that meant not letting himself have a nervous attack.

And yet his breathing came in shorter and shorter bursts. His lungs tightened until he couldn't draw air, and his vision narrowed until it turned almost black. Even if he wouldn't have glanced out the window a half hour ago and seen the life-saving crew readying the twenty-six-foot surfboat under the violent flicker of lightning, even if he wouldn't have heard his brother shout during one of those rare moments when the thunder had gone quiet, he'd still know Elijah was on the lake, putting his life and the lives of his crew at risk to rescue others from a shipwreck.

It didn't matter that the boat Elijah took was the exact same as the surfboats used in official life-saving stations all over the country, or that Elijah and his crew practiced swimming and righting a capsized boat every weekend. Taking a crew of five out into a violent storm was still dangerous. Elijah had to know that one of these days the lake would claim him as it had their pa. No man could defy that raging, watery beast forever.

Isaac reached his desk and whirled, stomping back toward the other end of his apartment.

He couldn't argue with Elijah's reasons for going out. If he'd heard Elijah's explanation for starting his life-saving crew once, he'd heard it a hundred times.

Elijah went out so there wouldn't be another tombstone at the head of an empty grave, another body claimed by the great lake to their north. He did it so other families didn't need to live through the pain that had wreaked havoc on their own family after their father's drowning.

But Elijah didn't stop to think that he was putting his family at risk of suffering that same kind of grief twice over.

Isaac stopped beside the window, staring out at the wind-lashed harbor and the white-capped waves rolling onto the sandy beach— waves that were still empty of his brother's rescue boat.

The bell beside his window trilled. He jumped, the tinny sound jarring against the noise of the storm. He looked down to see a form huddled below, cloaked in a black oilskin. Who'd be out in weather such as this? He turned for the door and hurried down the stairs. Reaching the first floor, he headed across the office then heaved open the door.

The figure rushed inside and threw off the hood of her cloak to reveal a head of deep red hair. Aileen.

"There were shadows in the alley last night, or rather this morning. I saw them just as the storm was starting and came as soon as I felt it safe." She slid the oilskin from her shoulders and hung it on one of the pegs by the door.

"Shadows? Were men running crates again?" He'd been on patrol last night and hadn't seen a ship docked after dark. If the men Aileen had seen two weeks ago had been smugglers, it would only made sense she'd see them when a ship was in the harbor.

She shook her head. "I don't think so, but I couldn't see much save for when the lightning flashed. I would've missed it entirely, except I couldn't sleep. I don't think it was more than one or two men."

A sudden burst of lightning bolted from the sky, and thunder rattled the windows.

His chest grew tight, and only half because of the storm. Were smugglers watching the bakery? Had they honed in on Aileen for some reason? "What exactly did you see? I want to know everything."

"Two shadows moved down the alley, away from the bakery. I didn't see any crates, but ye told me to let ye know if I saw anything suspicious." She twisted her skirt in her hands. "Or did I do something wrong? Did ye want me to wait until the storm passed?"

"It's fine that you came, especially if you don't mind braving the weather." Though it was a rather fierce storm to trudge through just so she could give him a report.

Perhaps more than shadows had brought her here? She'd told him to leave her alone two nights ago when he'd found her coming in from the woods, so he hadn't sought her out yesterday. But had a part of her wanted to see him again, even if she wasn't ready to admit it? Something warm swirled in his chest and he slanted her a glance.

She stood looking at one of the pictures little Alice O'Byrne had painted for him. He'd framed it and hung it on the wall, just as he'd promised. Tendrils of hair hung in damp curls beside Aileen's cheek, which somehow made the skin of her face seem more delicate than usual. Mud splattered the tips of her boots and bottom of her dress, and yet the happy yellow pattern on the fabric made her look as bright and fresh as the field full of wildflowers Alice had painted for him.

"I'm from Ireland, remember." Aileen turned back to him, then shrugged. "It rains for half the year there. If we let a storm stop us from going outside, we'd never get anything done.

The warmth inside him disappeared like the lightning flashing in the sky, there one second and gone the next. A sense of duty had brought her to the sheriff's office, not him in particular. She'd have come if Jenkins were still sheriff.

He moved to his desk to record her report, though once again, it didn't seem as though he could prove anything illegal had transpired near the bakery.

"Are ye well?" Aileen tilted her head to the side and took a step toward him.

Thunder rattled the windows again, and another vicious slash of lightning cut through the gloom outside. He glanced out the window where rain poured in torrents from the sky. Was Elijah back from his rescue yet? *Dear God, please bring him safely home.*

Aileen took another step toward him. "Something's wrong."

He swallowed and forced his gaze back to his notepad. "I'm fine."

"Then why are ye so pale?"

"I said I'm fine." Except he was never fine during storms.

"Is Elijah out on a rescue?" Her gaze drifted to the rain-plastered window. "Is that what has ye fretting so?"

"Yes." At least that was part of it, and no one could blame him. It was completely rational to be worried about his brother taking a rowboat into a rough lake to rescue sailors.

And the other part? The part that gave him nightmares and made his heart beat double? The part that made his throat grow tight at the notion of stepping into a boat? Those reactions were very much irrational, but how did one overcome such a thing?

He raised a glass of water sitting on his desk, but his hand was shaking so badly he put the cup down before it got an inch away from the surface.

"You should get home before the storm worsens." He moved toward Aileen's oilskin cloak hanging by the door. He had to get her out of his office before she realized how badly he was trembling.

"Perhaps Elijah is back now. Can ye see his boat on the beach from here?" Rather than get her cloak, Aileen headed toward the window.

Isaac clenched his jaw. "He's not back." Somehow he didn't need to be told when his brother returned, it was simply something he knew, something he felt bone deep inside him. "But it's time for you to go."

She didn't listen, stubborn woman. Instead she pressed her face to the glass and peered out the window. A second later she turned back to him, worried lines creasing her brow. "Perhaps he brought the boat in farther down the beach."

"No!" he nearly shouted despite the dryness in his throat. "Elijah always returns the surfboat to the same spot. That's his way of letting us know he's back." Isaac grabbed her coat from the peg, then stalked toward her. "Now as I said, you need to go home."

"Fine. Fine. I'll leave ye be." She came toward him then, but something about him must have given away his true state, because rather than turn so he could drape the cloak over her and fasten it about her neck, she furrowed her brow. "You're shaking. And yer forehead is sweaty. What's going on?"

I'm about to have a fit of nerves. I'll sweat and my heart will race and sharp pains will sear my chest. Sometimes my hands and feet tingle and I feel as faint as a woman in need of smelling salts. And I always have trouble breathing, every single time. But he settled for, "Nothing."

"Don't lie to me, Isaac Cummings. Ye should be sitting. Is there something I can do? Something ye need?" She glanced around his sparse office as though the plain log walls might give her an idea. "A biscuit from upstairs, perhaps, or mayhap some tea?"

Tea, the drink they gave invalids.

"I'll be fine." And he would, once the attack passed. But how long would that take? His heart wasn't even pounding yet, and once that happened, his chest would start to hurt, followed by dizziness.

"But you…" he swallowed, "…need to go." Quickly, before she witnessed the worst of his attack.

Once again, she ignored him, tilting her head to the side and studying him rather than leaving as he'd commanded. "Do ye get this frightened every time yer brother goes out on a rescue?"

Isaac looked away. "It's not your concern."

"But Elijah goes out on them quite a bit." He could feel her gaze on him, even if he didn't meet her eyes. "Didn't yer da die in a storm?"

He squeezed his eyes shut, trying to push back the memory flickering at the edges of his mind.

He'd used to love fishing, sailing, and building boats with his father. The feel of the sun on his face, the coolness of the water on his fingertips, the breeze brushing through his hair, and the wind inflating the sails on the *North Star.*

Used to. Before.

His heart started to race, and a sharp pain pierced his chest. "You have to leave. Now." The words exploded from him, angry and forceful enough they'd scare off any woman with an ounce of sense.

Aileen offered him a sad smile. "I find counting when I breathe helps. I suck in air and force meself to hold it inside until I count to ten. Then I push it back out again and count to ten once more. Try it."

Counting? He'd long known that focusing on breathing through an attack helped, but he'd never thought to add counting to it. Could something so simple be all he needed to fend off his fits?

He forced air out of his lungs in a giant whoosh, then slowly drew in a breath as she'd commanded. Before he reached five, her hand found his clenched fist. As firm and constant as an anchor weighing down a boat, she twined her fingers with his.

He sucked in the rest of the breath, holding it until ten, then blew the air out until he reached ten once more. He repeated the action and glanced into Aileen's eyes. They were rich and green and filled not with loathing or disdain or pity, but with a warmth so thick and sweet he could almost wrap himself in it. He drew in a breath for a third time, his trembling already abating, his heart already slowing.

His lifeline, that's what she'd been just now. Not the counting, but her. Much like the sailors his brother was saving at the moment, he'd needed his own rescuer, and he'd found one in Aileen Brogan.

..*.*.*

Isaac Cummings was wriggling his way into her heart, and she didn't know how to stop him.

Aileen stepped over a puddle as she made her way down Front Street toward the doctor's office on the edge of town. The waves in the harbor were rough and choppy in the wake of the storm, and the air was heavy with the scent of the lake. But the rain had stopped and the ominous thunder and lightning had moved to the east, leaving nothing more than gray clouds behind.

It was foolish to get attached to Isaac. Ten times past foolish, if she wanted to be honest with herself. There could never be anything between them—or between her and any other man. But seeing the strong man who'd shown her nothing but kindness fighting to draw breath this morning softened something inside her, and she wasn't quite sure how to harden it again.

She stepped over another puddle and moved to the side as a group of sailors passed. The boat Elijah and his volunteer crew took out on rescues rested on the beach, terrifyingly small considering how high the waves had been an hour ago. According to Isaac, the boat was a sure sign Elijah had returned, but if the worst had happened, wouldn't the other sailors return the boat without Elijah? She needed to see him for herself, if for no other reason than she could make a short visit to the sheriff's office again and lay Isaac's fears to rest.

She drew in a breath of air cool from the storm, then climbed the handful of steps to the doctor's office, knocked twice—and opened the door to chaos. The parlor was filled with men, their bushy beards and weathered faces declaring them sailors. Lindy, the doctor's wife, stood in the middle of the parlor with a platter of cookies the men seemed anxious to devour. Lindy's bulging stomach was covered so discretely by her skirt that most of the men probably didn't realize she was with child.

"Aileen." Rebekah emerged from the large sickroom on the other side of the parlor and weaved her way around the sailors, her brow knit. "What are you doing here? Did you come to help with the sailors? I think they're all fine, though a few are still waiting to see Dr. Harrington. He's in with Elijah now. Cut his arm good on a rock during the rescue."

"Will he be all right?"

Rebekah twisted her lips together and turned to glare at the door in the middle of the parlor's back wall. "I think so, though they never let me in the room for his examination, no matter how big of a fuss I put up."

If the stubborn look on Rebekah's face was any indication, the woman had put up quite a fuss.

Mabel Cummings threaded her way through the throng of men, a basket full of soiled linens in her arms.

"Do ye come to the doctor's office after every rescue, all of ye?" Aileen gestured toward the kitchen door where Mabel disappeared.

Rebekah frowned. "Of course. Wouldn't you, if you knew your brother was out in a storm?"

"I... I don't know." She looked around the room again. She couldn't see Victoria anywhere, but knowing her, she was in one of the rooms tending the sick. "Is Isaac the only one who doesn't come?"

Rebekah sighed and leaned against the wall. "When Elijah first started his life-saving crew, none of us were too keen on the idea. But we've gotten used to it over time—everyone except Isaac, that is. You'd think Pa's death would be hardest on Ma, but Isaac just pushes things deeper, lets them fester and grow instead of dealing with them. He doesn't argue with Elijah about the rescues as much as he used to, but he still hates them."

Rebekah didn't know how Isaac suffered, did she? Did any of Isaac's family know about his nervous attacks?

Aileen glanced down at her hand, the one Isaac had gripped so hard it had turned white while he'd counted through his breathing. "Mayhap Isaac doesn't hate them so much as he fears for Elijah."

Rebekah only shook her head. "It's one and the same, at least to my way of thinking. I don't know why he doesn't seem to care about whether or not the stranded mariners live or die, but he hates Elijah's rescues something fierce."

The door to the small sickroom opened and Victoria stepped into the parlor. "Dr. Harrington says anyone who still needs to be examined can go to the large sickroom, and he'll be with you in a moment. If you've already seen him, then you're free to leave."

Given the calm expression on Victoria's face and the regal way she held herself, she wasn't upset that Elijah had gone out on a rescue, or even that he'd been injured.

The door to the kitchen swung open, and Mabel Cummings emerged carrying another platter of cookies. "Here, take a cookie or two with you before you go. We've got plenty."

Half of the men filing outside turned back to snag some cookies off the platter. Aileen shifted toward the wall, giving the sailors more room to pass, but one of them paused and glanced over at her.

"Morley?" Her gaze landed on her cousin, who had a strip of linen tied across his forehead. "What are ye doing here?"

"What do ye think? Me boat got caught in a storm, and the life-savers rescued me." He came to stand beside her, hovering near the wall while sailors brushed past.

"Ye almost died?" The last word came out as a squeak.

He rolled his eyes. "I'm fine."

"What about Co—?"

Morley grabbed hold of her sleeve and yanked her toward the door, bending his head to her ear as they moved. "Are ye trying to get us in trouble? Didn't he tell ye to keep yer mouth shut about seeing him?"

They emerged into the damp morning air, and he led her down the handful of steps, his fingers biting into her elbow.

"Why are ye dragging me around like I'm some mule?" She tried jerking her arm away from him, but he only tightened his grip.

"I'm finding a place where yer questions won't get us into trouble." He dragged her around the side of the building, in the opposite direction from where most of the sailors were headed. "Honestly, Aileen, ye should do the same with me as ye do with yer brother. Nothing good will come of reminding everyone we're kin."

Morley surveyed the street as one of the sailors trotted past.

"Why should I listen to ye?" She narrowed her eyes at him. "Ye knew Conan was alive and didn't tell me for fourteen months. We even talked about him last week, and ye still let me believe Conan was dead."

"Aye, and I'd do it again, I would. 'Tis for yer own good, lass."

She took a step closer, bringing herself nose-to-nose with her short cousin. "How is it good for me brother to fake his death and ye to lie about it?"

"Because ye'll do nothing but cause trouble now that ye know." No kindness creased the faint lines around Morley's eyes as he spoke. If anything, the creases only turned firmer, harder. "Conan told me what happened in the woods. And 'tis lucky, ye are, that yer brother happened upon ye and not someone else. I'm starting to think I was wrong for letting ye call to me that day in the street. Should have just pretended I didn't know ye and gone on me way. The more people who know of our connection, the more dangerous it is."

"The more dangerous *what* is?" Her voice cracked, and she tossed up her arms. "And if these men ye're with are so terrible, then why not leave?"

"Ah, Aileen. Ever the naïve one, ye are. 'Tis not as simple as up and leaving, not once ye've started a job such as this." A hint of regret crept into Morley's eyes, and a bit of the tautness left his shoulders. "One day I'll tell ye everything, I promise. But not now. Trust me, lass. Trust me and stop asking questions."

There was almost a pleading note to his voice, a desperate look to his eyes, like the same kind of desperation Conan had shown in the woods when they'd heard someone else approaching.

And just like with Conan, she felt words of agreement tumble from her mouth before she could stop to think about them. "I'll leave ye be then, but when this job of yers is over, ye'll tell me all there is to know."

A half smile tilted the corner of his mouth, and he reached out and chucked her under the chin, just like he had when they'd been young. "'Tis a deal, cousin dearest. And when all's well and done, we'll get Brenna here too, and we'll be one big family again on a brand-new Wisconsin farm."

A family. But would moving to her brother's farm in Wisconsin help her memories from last summer fade? Her chin quivered, and she drew in a shaky breath.

"Hey, are ye all right?" Morley put his finger back beneath her chin and prodded her head up until their eyes met.

"Fine." Or rather, as fine as she ever was these days.

"'Tis supposed to be a good thing, lass, being together in Wisconsin."

Good, aye, everything would be good in Wisconsin. And she would force herself to believe it, she would. "Did Conan tell ye of Brenna?"

She wasn't quite sure what Morley's sailing job had to do with Conan stalking the woods, but if Morley knew about her visit with Conan, they must have seen each other at some point. "That Brenna's gone to Galway? I sent her money, but she'd already left before I mailed it. Do ye have any family in Galway, someone on yer mother's side, mayhap, that Brenna would be staying with?"

Morley's brow furrowed and he frowned. "Galway, ye say? Nay, we haven't any blood kin there."

"So there's nothing I can do short of getting Gilbert to hire a private investigator to look for her, or wait around for her to write me?"

"Gilbert?" Morley's eyes turned hard, any sign of warmth or tenderness disappearing behind his sharp features. "Ye mean Gilbert Sinclair? I told ye to leave off that business with him."

She dug the heel of her boot into the wet ground beneath her and planted her hands on her hips. "And I told ye I want to bring Brenna over here now, not whenever ye and Conan get around to it."

"'Tis not whenever I can get around to it, but come fall. After the close of shipping season, I'll go to Ireland and find her meself."

"Fall's too far away. We don't know where she's living or what kind of job she's working. We don't know who's caring for the wee ones while she's at work, or anything else about her situation. I'll not leave her and me little cousins to rot in the alleys of Galway. Four months is a long time, far too long to leave a woman on her own." Four months was all the longer she'd worked for Gilbert's parents in Chicago, and those days had seemed as though they'd never end. "I don't care whose help I need or how many years of me life I spend paying someone back for the money it costs to get Brenna here. I want her safe, I want her with family, and I want it now."

"Can't always have what ye want. I'd have thought ye'd learned that, lass." His jaw hard, Morley turned and stalked away, forging out into the street a moment later, and then disappearing from view.

She stared after him while hollowness welled inside her, familiar only because it filled her every time someone from her family walked away.

And because that's all her family seemed to do anymore—walk away.

Chapter Thirteen

Thump. Thump. Thump.

"Open up, O'Byrne. I need to speak with you," Isaac called before pounding again on the door to the small cabin nestled in the woods. *Thump. Thump. Thump.*

His boot heels sank into the muddy ground, still wet from the morning's storm, and water droplets glistened from the bottom edge of O'Byrne's window. What had possessed the man to build a cabin in the middle of a mud pit?

At least blue sky was starting to peek through the clouds above.

Thump. Thump. Thump. Isaac knocked again. Where could the man be? The lack of footprints in the mud outside the door told him no one had left since the storm.

"I don't think anyone's in there." Lars Norling stepped around the side of the cabin from where he'd disappeared out back when they'd arrived. "Don't think there's been anyone living here for the better part of a month."

"What makes you say that?" Isaac moved to the cabin's single window, the mud sucking at his boots.

"Privy don't smell."

"You smelled the privy?" He wanted to have a word or two with Virgil O'Byrne, sure. But he wasn't all that eager to go nosing about in the man's outhouse.

Norling leaned against the side of the small cabin, one foot crossed over the other at the ankle. "There's new grass growing on the path to the privy too. That tells me no one's been here for a few weeks."

"Could be. His children are staying with my brother, but I don't recall anything about him leaving town." Isaac cupped his hands to the glass and peered inside. The weak light from the window gave him a little glimpse of the table and chairs beneath it, but darkness shrouded the rest of the house.

"Just what type of relationship does your brother have with this O'Byrne fellow?" Suspicion laced Norling's words. "You said last night your brother is a fisherman?"

Isaac dropped his hand and turned from the window. "A fisherman, yes, a smuggler, no. He's the one that got shot at two days ago. And he doesn't have any relationship with O'Byrne, unless you call taking in his children after they were abandoned in the woods last fall a relationship."

"O'Byrne left his children?" Norling rubbed a hand over his jaw and turned to survey the towering pine trees surrounding them.

"There was an older sister, about seventeen, in charge. But yes, he left them in a shack in the woods that wasn't even fit to keep chickens." Even now, the memory of the dark lean-to with paper-thin walls caused something in his stomach to curdle. What kind of man left his children in a hovel such as that?

Evidently one who shouldn't be trusted to care for them.

"So he was gone over the summer? During the shipping season?" Norling kept his gaze fastened on the woods, almost as though he could see through them to wherever the smugglers were hiding.

"I was more concerned about how well he cared for the children than where he'd been or why. When he built this cabin and said he had a job as a lumberjack, I didn't really have reason to keep his young'uns away from him."

Norling snorted. "Sounds like he's caring for the children by asking your brother to do it."

Isaac hooked a thumb in his belt loop "I suppose that's one way to put it."

"I say we go talk to your brother."

Isaac looked around the deserted space once more, but only the rustle of wind against the wet leaves greeted him. Talking to Elijah was as good a plan as any. Besides, it would give him an excuse to see how Elijah fared. Aileen had stopped by his office earlier, bringing him a report of Elijah's injured arm. He hadn't the heart to tell her Fletcher, who served as one of Elijah's surfmen for the rescues, had already stopped with the news—just like he always did after rescues.

"He's at the doctor's, not his house." Isaac started down the narrow path that led to town. "Got himself injured on his rescue this morning."

Norling tromped along beside him, his heavy footfalls leaving unmistakable tracks in the mud. "His rescue?"

Everyone in town knew of Elijah's work, but a newcomer like Norling wouldn't. "You ever heard of the United States Life-Saving Service?"

The Viking grunted. "I work for the U.S. Customs Office, of course I've heard of the Life-Saving Service, and the Revenue Cutter Service, and the Marine Hospital Service, and just about every other water-related government service you can imagine."

"Well, Elijah doesn't work for the U.S. Life-Saving Service exactly, but he started his own volunteer life-saving team a few years ago."

"Not a common pastime." Norling's words were soft, and the man watched him while they walked, as though he knew there was more to the story.

Perhaps that was what made the man a good customs agent.

Seemed he could tell when a person left out part of a story.

Isaac watched the path at his feet. "Our father drowned in a storm."
And I didn't try to save him. But he wasn't telling Norling about how he'd failed his pa, no matter how intent the man's gaze or heavy the silence was between them. "Elijah started the life-saving team after that."

"And there was a rescue this morning?"

"Yes." Isaac's throat was thick, but he kept the panic down, focusing on the line of buildings ahead as they approached town. "I'm told my brother cut his arm on a rock."

Silence filled their steps once more as they headed down North Street toward the harbor. Like a fly to fresh apple cider, Isaac couldn't stop his gaze from straying to the bit of water just outside the mouth of the harbor, the place where he'd last seen his father alive.

He forced his gaze away. He had to find something else to talk about or his heart would start racing and sweat would cover his chest, and he couldn't afford to look weak in front of a customs agent. "You're the sort of man that stands out in a crowd. You certain the smugglers you were chasing last summer won't recognize you? All it would take is one man to spot you."

Norling took his own gaze out to the water, the gray waves still rough and choppy in the wake of the morning's storm. "For starters, Norling isn't my real name, just the one I have for this job. So the men would need more than a name to track me."

"You made up a name like Lars Norling?" Isaac scratched behind his ear. "Everyone will remember a name such as that as surely as they'll remember the Viking of a man who bears it. You should have been Richard Jones."

"Viking, is it?" The man shrugged. "Everyone remembers me anyway. I'm unmistakably Swedish, so I figure I'm better off picking a name that goes with the rest of me. If I called myself Richard Jones, you'd squint at me and wonder who my people were, why I'm so big, and what the slight accent is you hear. Going by Norling answers all those questions."

It made sense in a strange sort of way.

"But the name is just a precaution, Sheriff." Norling slowed, his lumbering gait turning into a crawl. "If we try to capture these men and fail, then I won't be around to follow them to the next town, and you probably won't be either."

"How many men?" He looked over at Norling as they neared the doctor's office.

"Pardon?"

Isaac swallowed the lump rising in his throat. "How many men have died trying to catch this band of smugglers?"

Norling looked down. "Too many, I'm afraid."

Oh, he was a hypocrite ten times over. How many times had he railed against Elijah's life-saving missions because of what another death in the family would do to Ma? Or Rebekah? Or Victoria? Or him? And yet here he was, agreeing to track a smuggling ring that the four of them had little hope of stopping.

He'd been so concerned for his family if Elijah died, but what would happen to his family if he died? Would their grief not be as bad? Would his death not tear apart the family the way Pa's had?

Except their family wasn't really torn apart, was it? Oh, there'd been a time, right after Pa's passing, where the entire world had seemed broken. But now… now everyone had moved on with their lives, and they were all probably stronger for it.

Everyone, that was, but him.

And what of his deputies? Neither Fletcher nor Granger were married, but they still had kin. Surely their families would be devastated if the worst happened, and here he was, asking them to help with an investigation that would probably end with all four of them buried six feet under.

"You all right there, Sheriff?" Norling asked.

"Fine, just fine." Isaac wiped the sweat from his brow with a shaky hand, then climbed the steps to the doctor's office and went inside, leaving the door open for Norling.

"Is what I heard about the man you found the other week true?" Dr. Seth Harrington, who had been standing on the other side of the parlor, headed straight toward them. "You think he was murdered?"

Isaac rubbed a hand over his face. With the storm earlier, he'd forgotten about the rumor, but it looked as though the story was already doing its job. "Yes, I uncovered some new evidence last night. Please stay out of the woods until we've apprehended the killer, and tell others to stay out as well."

"Of course." Worry lines wreathed the doctor's mouth and eyes. "You're probably not here to talk about the investigation, but to see Elijah. I'm afraid he's resting."

"We need to see him anyway." Norling's words came out brisk and clipped.

Dr. Harrington narrowed his eyes, his green gaze shooting to the tin star pinned on Norling's chest. "And you are?"

Isaac stepped between them. "Dr. Harrington, this is my newest deputy, Lars Norling. Norling, meet Dr. Seth Harrington."

"Glad to see Isaac's getting more help." The doctor didn't exactly smile at Norling, he extended his hand though, which Norling took. Given the slight wince that covered the doctor's features, Norling's grip was just as strong and unyielding as the rest of him.

"You can let them in, Doc. I'm awake, and I need to talk to my brother." Elijah's voice carried through the wall that divided the sickroom from the parlor.

The fist inside Isaac's belly eased at the sound of it. It was probably foolish, even weak to feel relief at something so simple as his brother's voice, but there was a difference between being told all was well and knowing for oneself.

The doc headed to the door and opened it, preceding them both into the room. "How long do you think you've been sleeping?" Dr. Harrington took a stethoscope out and held it to Elijah's chest.

Elijah lay stretched out on the bed, his long form dwarfing the small mattress. "Twenty minutes or so."

"Yes." The doctor tucked the stethoscope back inside his pocket, his large hands brisk and efficient. "Twenty minutes, plus three hours."

Elijah shot up in the bed and swung his legs around to the side, then glared at the doctor. "What'd you let me sleep that long for?"

"I told you this morning. If a man loses as much blood as you did with that gash, he needs rest." Dr. Harrington held a hand to Elijah's forehead. "No fever, and it looks like your color's coming back."

Isaac took a step closer to his brother, whose skin was almost as white as the sheets on the bed. If this was Elijah with color, how pale had he been that morning?

And just how much blood had he lost with that gash to his arm?

"I'll make you a deal." The doctor removed his hand from Elijah's forehead and studied him. "If you can walk home without fainting, you can leave with Isaac. But if you don't have the strength to make it home, you're staying put."

"I can walk home," Elijah muttered.

"I want to see it, not just hear you say it. Now I think your brother has some questions for you." And with that the doctor turned and started toward the door.

"My clothes, Doc. Where are my clothes?"

Dr. Harrington paused. "Hanging. Dry by now, I assume. But if you're asking about the necklace that was in your pocket, Victoria found it, and I sent it home with her."

"Victoria?" Elijah pressed his eyes shut for a moment. "All right. Thanks."

"Not a problem." The doctor pulled the door shut.

Elijah blew out a breath, then turned to face the room, his body tense and jaw set, as though waiting for an argument.

And why wouldn't he wait for such a thing? Isaac had spent three and a half of the past four years arguing with his brother every time he went out on a rescue. But now that his own job was about to put him in just as much danger as Elijah's life-saving, he didn't have room to rail against his brother.

Isaac grabbed the wooden chair against the wall and dragged it closer to the bed before sitting. "The fishing business must be looking up if you're buying fancy baubles for Victoria."

"It's not my necklace." Elijah drew in a breath, his chest working a little harder than it should be considering he'd not moved from his bed. "It belonged to one of the men I rescued this morning. Though I'm not sure *belonged* is the right word. I think it was stolen."

"What makes you think that?" Norling stepped closer.

Elijah's gaze fell to the star on Norling's chest. "You hire a stranger while I was on my rescue this morning?"

"Norling, this is my brother, Elijah Cummings." Isaac gestured between the two men. "Elijah, this is Lars Norling. He's from the U.S. Customs Office."

"We agreed that we were going to keep my true position secret from everyone but the other deputies." Norling's strong voice cut through the room, and his icy blue eyes held a glare.

"Elijah'd figure it out sooner or later. Besides, he's deputized." Isaac leaned forward, propping his elbows on his knees.

"No one else can know." Norling gripped the bedpost with his large, bear-like hands. "Now tell me about this stolen necklace. Any chance it was smuggled?"

Elijah raised his eyebrows. "Is that why there's a customs man in Eagle Harbor? He's looking for smugglers?"

Isaac didn't answer, and neither did Norling.

Elijah let out a low whistle. "There must have been something to that telegram I sent a couple weeks back then."

"The necklace." Norling half growled his words. "Tell me about the necklace."

"There's a ruby the size of my thumb in it, and I'm pretty sure it's real. Found it in the bottom of my boat after the men went ashore. I'm not sure which sailor had it, but I would have brought it to you earlier, had the doc not been so stubborn about me sleeping first." Elijah sucked in another breath through lungs that labored too hard, then swung his legs back onto the bed and propped himself against the headboard.

Isaac moved to shift the pillows behind his brother. "Sure you're feeling all right?"

Elijah glared at him. "I'm not a milksop."

"Right, sorry." Isaac cleared some of the tightness from his throat. "Where was the wreck?"

"That's the other part that doesn't sit right." Elijah sank deeper into the pillows behind him. "The men were in two dinghies, and they wrecked on the rocks near that patch of beach where I got shot at the other day. There was a ship out in the open water too. A big one. I could just make out its shadows. All I could think was that the men in the dinghies were taking cargo out to that ship when the storm came up. But who runs cargo from the middle of the woods to a ship in open water?"

"Smugglers." Norling's voice was as hard as the rocks that had wrecked the small vessels that morning.

Elijah yawned, then put a hand over his mouth a few seconds too late to cover it. "The men said the storm blew one of the boats off course, but another one went to rescue the first, only to end up with both boats dashed to pieces."

Isaac glanced away. He wouldn't think about how far that meant his brother's crew had to row to get to the stranded sailors, or about precisely who his brother had rescued. Elijah's missions were dangerous enough, he didn't need to be rescuing men that might well kill him if he or his crew saw something they shouldn't. "If the wreck was that far away, how did you know of it?"

"Some sailors came to my house and woke me up just as the storm started pounding."

Norling tapped his fingers against the wooden log at the top of the bed's footer. "I bet there are trails running from that beach farther back into the woods."

Isaac shook his head. "Granger and I were there earlier this week and didn't find anything."

Norling's fingers continued their tapping. "It wouldn't be uncommon for men such as these to hide their tracks well."

"Elijah, remember the map Ebberhard was searching for last winter? We think it was to a smuggling camp." Isaac leaned forward in his chair and rested his arms on his legs. "I can fill you in on more of the details later, but Norling here says the smugglers will have some type of warehouse where they're storing goods brought over from Canada."

"That so?" Now that Elijah was lying down, a bit of color crept back into his cheeks. "You need any help, let me know."

"You can start by telling us when you last saw Virgil O'Byrne." Norling came around the side of the bed and sat his large form on the edge of Elijah's mattress.

Elijah gave Norling a slow blink. For all his ruckus about being able to walk home, he looked about ready to fall asleep in the middle of their conversation. "He stopped by the house to see the young'uns last week. Asked if we could keep them awhile longer, and as you can guess, that wasn't a problem for Victoria."

"You saw him a week ago?" Norling's voice darkened.

"Why?" Elijah's word turned into a yawn. "That a problem?"

"O'Byrne hasn't been living at his cabin for a month or better, and you know he was chummy with Ebberhard." Isaac stood and moved to the window that faced the yard. "My theory is he left right after he asked you to take Alice and Toby this summer."

"A month?" Elijah shook his head. "That doesn't sound right. He's been by the cabin several times."

"So that tells us he's in the area, at least for short periods of time, but he's not living at home." Norling stood and paced beside the bed, head bent in concentration.

"He could be living somewhere in the woods," Isaac muttered the words half to himself. "Could be guarding a warehouse full of smuggled goods."

Elijah gave a shake of his head, then pressed his palm to his temple as though it pained him. "But what about Jack? Where's he in all of this?"

Isaac sighed. He'd not even thought about Jack. "Didn't you see him when you saw O'Byrne? He's not old enough to be smuggling with his pa."

"If a man thinks he can use his son to help advance his smuggling, he will." Norling stopped pacing and looked up. "Men like this aren't too picky about who they put in danger, as long as they toe the line."

When was the last time he'd seen Jack? Six weeks ago, maybe. The boy had been headed down North Street, his shaggy hair hanging over his eyes, his trousers about an inch too short for him, and his face in need of a good scrubbing. He'd waved and said hi, then asked if Isaac knew where Leroy and Martin Spritzer were.

Isaac's hands clenched into fists. Perhaps he shouldn't have let O'Byrne take his children back so easily last winter. *Dear God, please let Jack O'Byrne be well and safe.*

Elijah shoved his covers away and moved his feet to the edge of the bed. "We need to find Jack."

"No, you need to rest." Isaac jutted his chin at the bandage covering Elijah's arm from wrist to elbow. "How long until that heals?"

"It won't stop me from fishing in the morning," Elijah growled. "If that's what you're asking."

It wasn't, but he should have expected as much. His brother wasn't the type of man to let injuries slow him down. "I just want you to be well. That's all."

"Where's the sheriff?" A familiar masculine voice shouted from the other side of the wall. "Trudy Kainer said she saw him come in here, and I need to talk to him. I heard someone saying he thought the suicide wasn't a suicide anymore."

Isaac pressed his eyes shut. He should have realized Mr. Ranulfson would track him down rather than wait for him back at the office. He stood and headed toward the door, then pulled it open and forced on a smile for the town council president. "Good afternoon, Mr. Ranulfson."

Ranulfson turned to look at him, a tuft of hair sticking up at the back of his head, his neckcloth slightly askew. "Tell me I heard incorrectly. You declared that death a suicide."

"Looks like I was wrong. The death was, in all likelihood, a murder."

The man stilled, his face blanching white while he opened and closed his mouth twice before speaking. "What... do you mean *murder*? Do you... do you think this murderer is still out there? Still in the woods near Eagle Harbor?"

Isaac drew in a breath. "I do."

Ranulfson blinked, as though not quite sure what to do with that information. "Then... then you find him, Sheriff. Bring him in. That's what we pay you for, after all."

Well, at least the man wasn't threatening to take his job—not yet anyway. "I plan to, sir."

Now if only he could ensure no lives were lost in the process.

Chapter Fourteen

Aileen gripped the brush's handle and scrubbed the bristles harder against the floor. If only she could scrub away the thoughts swirling through her head as easily as she could the dirt.

Why was Morley so insistent she wait for autumn to help Brenna? He had no reason to bear a grudge against Gilbert Sinclair. If anyone had cause to resent the Sinclair name, 'twas her.

And yet she couldn't force herself to feel ill toward Gilbert. He'd only been trying to help last year, first by finding her a position in his parents' home after Conan "died," and then by bringing her to Eagle Harbor when things in Chicago turned sour.

However, none of that told her what Morley had against Gilbert. And she—

"You're supposed to scrub away the dirt. Not rub a hole in the floor."

Aileen looked over her shoulder to find Rebekah standing in the doorway, dressed in a drab blue skirt and white shirt, with a pail, brush, and rag in her hand.

"Sorry." Aileen leaned back on her knees, dunked her brush into the soapy water, and started on a new spot.

Rebekah headed across the floor, setting her pail down a few feet away.

"Ye ought not be scrubbing a floor." Aileen shifted to reach a particularly dusty stretch of baseboard. "Not a lady such as yerself."

Rebekah dipped her brush in sudsy water. "Gives me something to do since Elijah isn't fishing today and I'm not needed at the doctor's anymore. Besides, I'll only be in Eagle Harbor until fall. Maybe I want to spend as much time as I can with my friends, even if it means I have to scrub floors alongside them."

Aileen's fingers tensed around her brush. "Ye're too good to me, Rebekah. The whole lot of ye are."

Rebekah looked down, where she seemed to be rubbing her own hole in the floor. "I don't know about being too good, but I am concerned. Where did you go two days ago when you said you weren't feeling well?"

Something inside her chest pinched, and a vision of Conan filled her mind, but she'd promised not to tell anyone about him—even Rebekah. "Into the woods. I just needed some quiet, some time to be alone and think. Did Gilbert tell ye Brenna moved to Galway without leaving an address?"

"He did, and I'm sorry. I was hoping Brenna would be here in a few more weeks."

Aileen sighed and went back to scrubbing. Mayhap she shouldn't bother fighting with Morley and Conan over when Brenna came to America. At this rate, it would take until fall to find her cousin anyway.

"What did Isaac have to say about Brenna when you told him?" Rebekah rinsed her brush, then scrubbed a new section of the floor.

"Only that he'd pay for an investigator in Ireland if Gilbert didn't."

Rebekah's brush clattered to the floor. "Isaac said that?"

Aileen's cheeks heated. "He was just being kind, is all. He probably knew Gilbert would pay for everything and was only trying to calm me."

Rebekah tilted her head to the side, scrub brush and soapy pail forgotten. "You were upset when you told him?"

Upset, aye. That was one way to put it. She could still see the look on his face as she'd told him about Brenna two nights ago, the concern radiating from his gaze. Could still feel the way he placed a hand on her shoulder to keep her from fleeing, his grip just firm enough to tell her he cared about what troubled her. He cared far more than either her cousin or her not-dead brother apparently did, but that wasn't saying much.

Rebekah blew a strand of wayward hair out of her eyes. "Isaac's got a sweet spot for you. You know that, don't you?"

She'd have to be blind and deaf not to know. All those soft looks and tender smiles. All those quiet questions whispered on the street or in the mercantile, asking how she fared.

Would his kisses be as gentle as his touches? She reached a hand up and pressed it against the place on her shoulder where Isaac had settled his palm last time they'd spoken. She'd been tempted to kiss him then, just push herself up to her tiptoes, lean forward a mite, and—

"Now you've got a dreamy look on your face. I knew he should court you." Rebekah crossed her arms and gave a decisive nod, as though the action somehow confirmed she and Isaac were destined to spend a long, happy future together.

"Don't be getting no fool notions in yer head, Rebekah Sinclair." Aileen plunged her brush into the sudsy water. "I already told yer brother I wasn't worth wooing, let alone marrying."

Rebekah leaned a hand on the wet wood she'd just washed, her gaze narrowed. "Not worth wooing? You mean he's shown interest in courting you?"

Aileen set her brush on the floor and scrubbed, the bristles digging into the wood hard enough they just might leave scratches. "That wasn't me point, and ye know it."

Rebekah settled a hand over hers atop the brush, stilling her movements. "My brother hasn't been the same since Pa died. You didn't know him before Pa passed, so you can't tell the difference, but for him to care about courting a woman…" Rebekah pressed her lips together, then drew in a breath. "It's a good thing, I promise. And I can't help thinking it'd be a good thing for you to get to know him a little better. It's not as though going on a picnic or two will hurt anything."

Aileen jerked her hand away from Rebekah. "How can ye say that? Of course it will hurt things. I'm not the marrying kind, and ye know it."

Rebekah's shoulders slumped, and concern pooled in her eyes. "You ought not say such a thing. I think you'd make a wonderful wife."

"Aye, sure. Right up until I tell me husband about last summer." Aileen turned her back to Rebekah and started on a new section of floor.

"I don't suppose you've changed your mind about that either?" Rebekah's voice was soft and hesitant, a rarity for the bold woman that had somehow become her friend.

"I don't know what ye're after."

"Going to Chicago to testify."

A chill swept through her, and her fingers stiffened around the handle of the brush. "I'd get laughed out of the courtroom."

Rustling sounded behind her, then the splash of a brush being dunked into water. "Do you ever think about pressing charges of your own?"

Had she? Mayhap, in the same dreamy place where she imagined cradling little Cara in her arms. But then she'd awaken and realize the futility of bringing someone so rich and powerful to justice.

"Nay." The sharp word fell from her tongue and echoed around the room with the force of an ax striking a sapling's limb.

"I'd hoped coming to Eagle Harbor would help you get better, but last summer still troubles you."

"'Tis right kind of ye to be so concerned, it is." Aileen turned toward her friend. "But some things a woman doesn't get better from."

Rebekah hung her head, her fingers fiddling with a stray thread on her skirt. "Is there anything I can do?"

Aileen's eyes turned suddenly moist, though she'd shed enough tears over last summer there shouldn't be any left to cry. "It's not like ye can go back and keep it from happening."

"No, but…"

"Just leave it in the past, where it belongs." Aileen shoved a falling tress of hair away from her shoulder. "And no more talk of me and yer brother either."

Rebekah picked up her brush, but didn't start scrubbing. "If it's affecting your life today, then it's not truly in the past."

Aileen looked down at her hands, wet and dirty as they held the brush. "It is. Just like me mam's and da's deaths are. They're all in the past, but there's not a day they don't affect me."

Rebekah's heavy sigh filled the room. "You're not as well as you claim. And I think you're making a mistake by closing off your heart to my brother."

A mistake. Could Rebekah be right? Mayhap she should consider a future with the man who worried when she disappeared for a few hours. Who searched her apartment when she felt unsafe and walked her home without complaint. Mayhap she should consider a future with a man who loved his family so much he got physically ill when they were in danger.

But how could there be a future without first telling him of her past? And as soon as he knew that, he'd want naught to do with her.

Just like she wanted naught to do with herself.

~.~.~.~.~

The chorus of crickets and frogs mixed with the gentle lap of water against sand. Isaac stood on the beach in the gathering darkness. Above, the sky was a canvas of gray and indigo and purple. Below, the water reflected a deeper, inkier shade of the sky.

He blew out a breath and ran his hand over the hull of the *North Star* where it rested on the sand beside him, ready to be taken out at dawn tomorrow.

I can do this.

He'd not touched the boat once since his father died, yet the wood still felt familiar beneath his palm. The smoothness of the grain spoke of a vessel that had seen nearly two decades of sun and wind and waves.

His hands had helped form the hull and raise the masts. Then he'd sat down with pencil and paper to figure out the size of the sails with his pa. Starting at the age of six, he'd gone out fishing every day he wasn't in school.

Then Pa died, and everything changed. He looked out over the harbor, the water growing blacker by the second. A night was coming when he'd have to be in either this boat or another attempting to catch smugglers, which meant he didn't have time to waste.

He drew in a breath, scented with the familiar freshness that he could only describe as Lake Superior. Not everyone who stepped foot in a boat drowned. So why didn't knowing that help slow his thudding heart and rushed breaths?

Maybe once he was aboard, he'd be calmer. He'd not go far, just a few feet out from the shore, keeping the boat shallow enough he could jump out and drag it back in at any moment.

He placed his hands against the bow and dug his feet into the sand, giving it the same shove that he'd given it since he was a boy.

It slid from the beach into the water as though it were on wheels. He followed the boat a few steps into the lapping shallows, then launched himself over the side of the gunwale, landing with boots planted firmly near the mast in the center.

There, he was in a boat, in the water, and no lightning had slashed from the sky or quaking had rattled the earth. Nor was he about to drown in the two-foot depths.

So now what should he do? Sit on the bench and see if his heart slowed, if the blood stopped rushing in his ears? The panic was creeping in, climbing up his chest and into his lungs and heart, slicking his palms and forehead with sweat. But he'd not let it consume him. After all, that was the point of this exercise, to control the panic instead of letting it control him.

If he could fight through his fit of nerves with Aileen, then he should be able to do so now. He sucked a breath into a chest laboring far more vigorously than it should, counted to ten, and then headed to the bench at the stern.

The little mackinaw fishing boat rocked with his movements, and his heart upped its rhythm. Never mind that the swaying was normal. Never mind that the boat wasn't about to capsize. Now if only he could get his heart to believe it.

"Isaac Cummings, are ye in that boat?"

He turned at the sound of the female voice with the familiar accent, causing the boat to sway again, and his breath to hitch. *Rocking is normal. Nothing will happen.*

"Isaac?"

He cleared the dryness from his throat. "It's me, yes."

Aileen stood on the deserted beach, her red hair a flame against the darkening night. "I saw the boat in the water and thought it was drifting untended, so I came down to drag it ashore."

He moved to the bow, ignoring the rocking a little more this time, and leaned over the gunwale. "What are you doing out at this time of night?"

She glanced toward the lighthouse with its lantern casting a straight yellow beam into the open water beyond the harbor. "I had to visit Mac and Tressa about me rent. I'm still letting the room above the bakery even though I'm no longer working there. Then they invited me for dinner. I stayed longer than I should have, 'tis true. But Mac had the light to tend, so he couldn't walk me home."

"Wait there and let me get this to shore." He grabbed one of the paddles, still stowed beneath the back bench where they'd been kept when Pa was alive. He didn't row so much as dig it into the sand. One heave, and the boat glided back onto the beach.

Before he could stow the paddle and hop out, Aileen lifted her skirts and sloshed into the shallow water. She planted her hands on the gunwale and heaved herself inside in a move she could have only learned from Rebekah.

Her gaze skimmed over the boat before it landed on him. "I didn't think ye liked boats and water."

"That's why I'm out here. Trying to make myself…" *Like* was too strong a word to use. "Tolerate it a little better. I need to for work."

"Being the sheriff involves riding in boats?"

"Sometimes." With smugglers afoot, it would.

Her eyes searched his in the growing moonlight, and he could almost see her thinking back to his attack that morning. He'd leaned against the wall, fighting against the fear that threatened to consume him. Sweat had drenched his brow and hands, his breathing so labored he could barely draw breath.

And then she'd taken his hand in hers, gently instructing him to count to ten before dragging in another breath. He did the same thing now, pulling in a long breath and counting to ten, then letting it out and counting once more.

"I'm sorry about earlier today," his voice came out raspy and dry when he finally spoke. "I usually control myself better than that, and I don't want you to think that I... that..."

What? That he was weak? That he couldn't handle being sheriff because he was afraid of water?

"I think it must be hard to know that yer brother goes out into the very types of storms that killed yer da, even if he is doing good." Much like earlier that morning, her hand slipped into his, and she gave it a gentle squeeze. The movement also brought her nearer, close enough that when he looked down into her eyes, her breath puffed warm against his cheek, and the smell of her lemon soap twined around him. "And I think ye're brave too. Ye have to be if ye're a sheriff."

"A brave man doesn't watch his father die without trying to save him." He didn't know why he spoke the words. He'd not uttered them once since his father's death. And yet he'd carried them with him every moment of every day, a constant weight about his shoulders.

"Surely 'tis not as bad as that."

"My father was a great man. The kind of man that everybody loved. He was always going out of his way to help people. Ever since I was a little boy I have memories of people coming to our door late at night or early in the morning asking for help, wanting him to step in and solve problems. He loved us children too, almost as much as he was determined to teach us about God. We memorized Bible verses at the dinner table every night, and he included us in just about everything. I was six the winter we built this boat, barely big enough to hold a hammer, but that didn't stop him from letting me help."

With their hands still twined together, he led her to the bench at the stern, where they could sit. And this time when the boat swayed with their steps, his chest didn't tighten with panic. "I grew up on

155

this lake, spent more time on the water in the summers than I did on dry ground, and I loved it. I fished every day with my pa, but one morning, a little over four years ago, I had a headache."

He shook his head. "That's not quite true. I had a headache, yes, but I was tired more than anything. I'd stayed up late the night before, studying one of Pa's lawbooks. It was old and some of the laws and statutes had certainly changed over time, but I had plans to go to law school as soon as Elijah returned to Eagle Harbor. So when Pa roused me that morning to head out to the boat, I told him I didn't feel well.

"It was the truth, but only because I'd been foolish the night before. By lunch I was feeling better and went into town to visit Mac at the lighthouse. Rebekah came with me, saying she wanted to stop by the mercantile. She didn't go fishing as much in those days. Oh, she knew what to do on a fishing boat, but she didn't start fishing every day until after Pa died, until I stopped going out." Isaac pressed his eyes shut, but that didn't stop the vision from rising in his mind. The brutal waves and driving wind and the little boat tossed to and fro as it tried to make harbor.

"A storm blew up, quick and fierce, but I wasn't all that worried about Pa. He knew the lake like the back of his hand. Surely he'd seen the storm in the distance and was already in the harbor hauling the day's catch out of the boat. But we went up to the lighthouse tower to check anyway, Mac and Rebekah and me." The faint breeze that toyed with the ends of his hair now was so very different from the wind that had torn over the water on that fateful spring day.

"Rebekah was convinced Pa wouldn't make it. She wanted to take the Foleys' dinghy lying on the beach and try to rescue him. I told her it was foolish, that Pa could get the *North Star* into the harbor just fine, and that she'd end up killing herself if she went out." He worked his jaw back and forth, the words that had tumbled from his mouth so freely just seconds ago now deserting him.

"But yer da didn't make it back." Aileen's gentle voice echoed across the inky blackness of the water.

"No." His throat was dry, his voice rough and scratchy. "I should've listened to Rebekah. I should've gone out to save him, or better yet, I shouldn't have been studying law the night before. I should have been responsible, dependable. I should have gone out with him that morning regardless of my headache. If there'd been two of us in that boat—"

"If there'd been two of ye on that boat, ye might both be dead." Aileen reached over and rested her hand on his forearm. "Ye don't know otherwise. Ye can't."

He looked down at her hand, slender and long, even if she worked too hard for her skin to be very soft. "Maybe. But when Elijah got news of Pa's death and returned from sailing the Atlantic, he proved that a man could take a dinghy out into a storm and rescue others." Isaac glanced up at the lighthouse, then followed the beam of light that shot over the dark water to the north. "Yet when my pa needed me most, I failed him. And as if that wasn't enough, I stopped my sister from helping as well."

"Ye oughtn't blame yerself." Aileen squeezed his forearm. "Mayhap ye could have gone to bed earlier the night before, aye, but ye still don't know what would have happened had ye gone out. Could be that the lot of ye would have died, and only yer ma and Elijah would be left today."

"You didn't hear what I said, did you?" Isaac gripped the side of the gunwale with his free hand, his nails digging into the weathered wood of the boat. "It's not just that Pa died, it's that I failed him. I couldn't have prevented the storm, but I'll never forgive myself for the way I froze, my feet rooted to that platform as I stared out the lighthouse window and watched the boat capsize."

He blew out a breath, long and loud. If only he could force the memories out as easily as he could the air in his lungs. "But I'm making up for it now that I'm sheriff. I've got another chance to prove myself, and I refuse to let myself fail again. Which is why I'm sitting here in this boat, making myself face the water. Next time I'll be prepared. Next time I won't fail."

Aileen stared out over the water, black except where a beam of moonlight glistened its reflection across the center of the harbor. "Ye make a good sheriff, Isaac. There's not a person in this town who could say ye're failing at yer job."

They might if he and Norling didn't catch the smugglers, but he wasn't going to sit here and focus on all the things that could go wrong, or he'd be too forlorn to get himself out of bed tomorrow morning.

"All right, you heard my story. Now it's time for yours. What puts all that sorrow in your eyes?" If only he knew how to wipe away the sadness and put a smile there instead.

She looked down for a moment, her lips pressed into a tight line before bringing her gaze up to his. "There was… In Chicago, I…" Her throat worked up and down. "I can't."

She stood abruptly. "I know ye just shared yer story, but I simply can't tell ye mine, except to say that I'm not as good as ye think. The way ye look at me, the worry when I left town the other night, I don't deserve any of it." She twisted her hands in her skirt, a habit that was becoming all too familiar. "Ye're a good man, Isaac Cummings. Ye might not be too fond of water, but ye're still a good man. But me? I'm already lost."

He rose to his feet, his muscles stiff. Where did she come up with this tomfoolery? She'd said it two nights ago as well, right before she closed the door on him. "I might not know everything about you, but it seems Rebekah knows a whole lot, and she still cares."

Rather than answer, Aileen looked down, causing the beam of moonlight that had illuminated her face to slant palely over her hair.

He nearly reached up to finger a silver-red strand. "I'm willing to admit that my sister is far from perfect. I'm sure she'll fail you at some point, if she hasn't already. But God, Aileen, will never fail you. He loves you and He cares about you."

"Ye're wrong." Her voice emerged quiet yet hard against the still night. "God doesn't care about me. I've done too much to ever earn His care or ever be deserving of His love."

He reached out and settled a hand on her shoulder. Except his hand ended up as much on her neck as her shoulder, and the warm creamy skin above her collar pulsed against his hand.

Her gaze flew up to his, and she sucked in a breath that made her chest swell until it nearly touched his own. Yet she didn't try to twist away from him. She stayed, her face mere inches from his own, and her eyes riveted to his.

An ache built in his chest. She was listening now, waiting to soak in his next words. Somehow, if he'd done nothing else worthwhile tonight, he'd gotten her to truly listen to him. Which meant he needed to make what he said count—so he used God's words rather than his own.

"'The mercy of the Lord is from everlasting to everlasting upon them that fear him.'" The beginning of Psalm 103:17 rolled off his tongue, part of a passage that his father had made them memorize around the dinner table when he'd been about Toby O'Byrne's size.

He cleared his throat. "The truth is, none of us are deserving of God's mercy. I'm surely not." And he wasn't, not considering how he let his father die four years ago. "But God's mercy for us goes from everlasting to everlasting anyway. And you can have it just as much as anyone else."

She stood still for a moment, so still he'd almost believe she'd turned into stone if not for the warmness of her skin beneath his hand and the gentle puff of her breath against his chin. Would she take his words to heart? Forsake the heaviness that had plagued her ever since she'd arrived in town?

But then her jaw stiffened. She blinked, replacing the sincerity in her eyes with a cold resoluteness. She didn't need to step away for him to feel the distance swell up between them. "Ye said only the people who fear God get that mercy. But that's the trouble. I fear God enough to know He shouldn't waste a drop of His mercy on me. Whatever mercy ye think I can have, I'm a year too late for it. Now I'd be obliged if ye'd walk me home, thank ye."

He dropped his hand from her neck and took a step back. Take her home was exactly what he'd do, because the longer he stood with her beneath the moonlight, the more he wanted to clear the sorrow from her eyes. But with a heart as hurting as hers, he was only setting himself up to fail. And he'd already failed enough to last ten lifetimes.

Chapter Fifteen

Ellie released the giant paddle and leaned it against the side of the boiling vat, then wiped her sticky brow with her hand. Steam boiled up from the basin of wash, turning the warm air into a burning, humid mist. She should probably stir the clothes more, but her back ached, her shoulders were stiff, and her feet throbbed from spending almost twelve straight hours standing.

She moved away from the wash and leaned back against a towering pine, letting her hands rest from almost two hours of stirring different batches of laundry. She glanced at the small cabin a few yards away. The squat little pine building with cracks in the walls was the only home she'd ever known. Maybe part of her should feel guilty for seeking out the mail-order bride company and writing Sam Owens. Maybe part of her should feel guilty about corresponding with him for four months and keeping it from her family.

But she couldn't keep up with the demands of the family plus work at the bakery anymore. Everything was falling behind.

But if Sam asked her to marry him, would she really be able to leave?

Of course she could, because Ma wouldn't stay sick forever. Besides, Ma had to expect her to marry eventually. She was almost twenty.

"Ellie?"

She jolted at the sound of her name, then looked around, surveying the woods through the steam wafting from the washbasin.

"Ellie, there you are." A twig cracked and Jake Ranulfson stepped around the side of the cabin and came toward her. "I should have known I'd find you working. That's all you ever do."

She pushed off the tree, her feet suddenly not as sore as they'd been ten seconds ago. "What are you doing here?" She glanced over her shoulder at the clothes hanging on the line behind her.

He tilted his head to the side and grinned at her. "Whisking you away for the evening. Did you forget tonight is Tressa Oakton's birthday party? The entire town is already on the beach dancing and eating."

"I didn't forget. My brothers and sisters are there, all but little Lynnette." Not needing to worry about an evening meal for everyone was a blessing, and so were the few hours of quiet she was using to catch up on the wash Ma took in for pay. But she hadn't counted on her back aching quite so much, or her eyelids trying to drift closed between batches.

"You weren't planning to come?" He stepped forward and covered her hand with his wide, strong palm.

Warm tingles shot up her arm and spread to her chest.

"Come on. I want to dance with you."

"You want to...?"

"Don't look so surprised. Everyone needs a break now and then, even you." He took a step closer and stroked a bit of hair away from her face, his fingers lingering on the tender spot behind her ear.

Sam's letter in her pocket began to burn, as did the spot behind her ear where Jake's fingers rested.

"Though it looks like maybe I should do this wash for you so you can go inside and sleep." Jake slid his hand away from her ear and down her arm before clasping her other hand in his. "How much rest did you get last night?"

She looked away. Her brothers had returned late once again and been hungry for dinner. And it seemed as though Ma had agreed to take in even more laundry. Ma had tried to do some of it today, but she hadn't gotten very far. "I'm fine, but I really don't have time to dance."

"Yes, you do." He used his hold on her hands to tug her away from the wash. "You're always working, and the few times we've eaten lunch together this week isn't enough of a rest."

But she still had more wash to do, and before she could leave, she at least needed to finish the batch of clothes she'd started.

"Ellie." Ma's frail voice drifted through the cabin window. "Ellie, come take Lynnette."

Ellie pressed her eyes shut. Not again. It was impossible to hold a babe in one arm and stir the wash with the other. The steam was too hot for the infant.

"We'll bring her along to the party." Jake ducked his head until his eyes were mere inches from hers. "There's never a shortage of people willing to hold a baby."

"Ellie," Ma called again.

Ellie sighed. Jake was right. The Oaktons' party would make for a fun evening. Besides, how long had it been since she'd danced? How long since she'd done something to distract her from the constant work that piled up around her? The wash could wait for a few hours, and Leroy and Martin could help her hang it after they got back. "Let me get Lynnette and freshen up a bit. I'll be out in a few minutes."

Jake released her hands but sent her a wink. "I'll be waiting."

~.~.~.~.~

163

Aileen stood at the edge of the crowd while people milled between the food by the cookfire and the dancing on a section of packed sand. It was a beautiful evening for a party, with white fluffy clouds drifting against a blue sky turning orange with the first inkling of twilight. The bright music of the three men with fiddles tucked to their chests floated down the beach and over the water. It seemed the entire town had turned out for Tressa Oakton's birthday party, and every last person wore a smile.

The townsfolk made being happy seem so very easy, so why couldn't she find a smile to put on her own face?

Aileen turned away and surveyed the harbor, where an eagle swooped down to the water, only to emerge shortly with a writhing, silvery fish in its talons.

The mercy of the Lord is from everlasting to everlasting. Was the verse true? It seemed wrong somehow. Like there should be a point at which God would withhold his mercy. Her hand slid to her stomach. She certainly didn't deserve mercy after what she'd done.

But she'd looked up the verse last night after Isaac had walked her home. Psalm 103 didn't just talk about God's mercy, it also said He removed sin as far as the east was from the west.

Aileen kicked at a rock, but it rolled only a foot or two before settling into a new bed in the soft sand. Could God take her sin that far from her? Could God look at her and see Aileen Brogan, a simple woman searching for a place to call home, and not Aileen Brogan, terrible sinner unworthy of a husband, children, or the very home she desired?

"You're supposed to be smiling, not frowning." Mac trudged up the beach, carrying his shoes in his hand as he headed toward the lighthouse. "What's wrong? Is the fish not to your liking?"

"Nay, the fish was… um…" She couldn't claim it was delicious since she'd yet to taste it. "Well, I've yet to eat, truth be told."

"Let's get you some." Mac settled a hand on her shoulder and turned her to face the party, then guided her back toward the crowd. "I don't know how much longer they'll keep cooking."

She dug her heels into the sand. "I'm not all that hungry." In truth, it didn't seem like she was ever hungry these days. "But it smells delicious, and this was a lovely party. I'm sure Tressa appreciates it."

"She's not one to like attention, so this is the first time I've thrown her a birthday party. But she was so sick when she was pregnant last year, there were times I wondered..." His voice grew deep and his eyes took on a distant sheen. "...wondered if she'd be here to see this birthday. But here she is, dancing with Elijah." He pointed to where the pair danced. "And I have another beautiful daughter to squeeze and tickle and kiss. It warms a man's heart, I tell you. So I gave Tressa a party, because sometimes a person just needs to celebrate life."

Celebrate life. When was the last time she'd felt like celebrating anything? She cleared her throat. "Ye have a lovely family, ye do."

A grin spread across Mac's face. "I'm a blessed man, aren't I? Say, next week is the anniversary of when I proposed to Tressa. I still haven't decided what to do for it. Tressa tells me this party tonight is enough, but I think another surprise might be in order. Don't suppose you'd want to watch the young'uns on Thursday? Maybe Tressa and I could go on a picnic."

"Ye celebrate the anniversary of when ye proposed?" She'd not heard of that before.

Mac patted her shoulder, then settled his hand atop it, as though afraid she'd bolt if he didn't keep her in place. "When a woman tells you no four times before she finally agrees to marry you, you celebrate the day she said yes."

"Four times?" The couple always seemed so happy, she'd just assumed...

What? That things had always been perfect for the Oaktons?

Mayhap she'd not thought that, but she'd still not have guessed the fiery little bakery owner had turned her husband's marriage offer down four times.

"Have a heart, Aileen." Mac squeezed her shoulder again. "When a man asks you to marry him one day, take pity on the poor soul and tell him yes the first time."

She needn't worry about that. As soon as she shared her past with a man, he'd run the other direction—not that she planned to ever tell a man in the first place. Even Mac, for all his smiles and teasing ways, would probably want naught to do with her if he knew.

"Mac Oakton, are you running away from your wife's party?" Isaac trudged up the beach toward them, a small bundle of white cloth cradled in his arms.

"Forgot her present up at the lighthouse." Mac's arm finally left her shoulder, and he scratched behind his ear. "How does a man remember to plan a town-wide shindig but forget his wife's present?"

Mac waited until Isaac reached them before reaching out and gently squeezing a swaddled foot. "Is this the new Spritzer baby?"

Aileen glanced over at the babe, then blew out a breath and looked away. Sweet, mayhap, but also tiny. She couldn't be more than a handful of weeks old.

"It is. Rebekah was supposed to be watching her so Ellie could dance with Jake Ranulfson, but then the fiddlers played a song she requested, and guess who got stuck with the baby." Except Isaac didn't look all that annoyed to be holding the wee one. His lips had curled into a small smile, and his eyes had that same tender look he used with her when she was frightened or upset.

"She's a sweet one, though not quite as precious as my little Sarah." Mac dropped his hand from the babe's foot. "I've got to hurry and get back. Promised my wife another dance or ten."

He turned and left, trekking across the sand toward the lighthouse.

Aileen watched Mac over her shoulder for a moment, then glanced at Isaac, only to find him already watching her with that familiar, concerned look radiating from his hazel eyes.

"Are you unwell tonight? You were only at the party for a few minutes."

He'd been paying that much attention to her? "Nay, I'm fine." At least as fine as she ever was. "I just…" She glanced back at the revelry, where Gilbert and Rebekah danced, along with Ellie Spritzer and Jake Ranulfson, Elijah and Tressa, and a host of others. "There are a lot of people, 'tis all."

"So you're not trying to avoid me because of our conversation last night?"

Lack of conversation was a better description, considering how she'd left before sharing what had happened last summer. "I just wanted a bit of peace."

Though avoiding him wasn't exactly a poor idea.

The bundle in Isaac's arms moved, letting out a frail cry.

Isaac frowned, then looked back at the dancing. "She's supposed to stay asleep."

Aileen chanced another look at the babe. The child was so very tiny, and the shade of the downy hair on the babe's head was so very similar to her own red hue. So very similar to the shade she saw in her dreams when she ran her hand over little Cara's head.

She tore her gaze away, but staring out at the water didn't stop the pain blooming in her chest. Like a pebble striking a pond, the ripples spiraled outward, more and more of them until her entire body ached.

The babe let out another wail.

"Hold her for a minute." Isaac extended the child toward her. "Maybe she needs a woman's touch."

"Nay," she whispered, then took a step away, her arms clamped tightly around her middle lest Isaac try to hand her the babe again. She couldn't force her tongue to work, or her lungs to breathe, or her heart to start beating again. She'd seen babies since last summer, Mac and Tressa's youngest being one of them, but none that looked so similar to the infant that haunted her dreams.

"Excuse me, but I need to go." She turned and fled, walking as swiftly as she could across the warm sand that swallowed her toes with each step. She didn't care where she went, exactly, just as long as it was somewhere away from happy music and smiling faces and wee babes.

⌐.⌐.⌐.⌐.⌐

Isaac stood on the beach, as still as the stone boulders Aileen hastened toward. What had he done now? Had it been something he said? Lynnette arched her back, her tiny mouth twisting in displeasure before she let out a cry and brought her legs up to her chest.

He'd better go find Rebekah and hand off the baby before going after Aileen—not that she'd be any more willing to talk to him tonight than she'd been yesterday. He turned and headed back toward the party.

But Rebekah had already stopped dancing and was moving toward him, her gaze shifting from him to Aileen nearing the lighthouse. "What did you do?"

Isaac jostled the babe, getting her to quiet a bit. "Nothing. She just started fussing, even though you said she'd stay sleeping."

"Not to the baby, you dolt." Rebekah scowled at him but reached for Lynnette, who calmed the second she was snuggled against Rebekah's chest. "What did you do to Aileen?"

"I didn't do anything. She saw the baby and she just... panicked."

Gilbert came up behind his wife. "You'd better have a good reason for interrupting our dance, Cummings."

"I hadn't thought about a baby bothering her." Rebekah's voice grew soft. "I better go after her."

Isaac looked over his shoulder. Aileen had reached the first of the rocks that separated the sandy harbor from Lake Superior's open coast and was scrambling atop it. "Good luck."

Aileen didn't seem nearly so determined to shut Rebekah out.

"No, let Isaac go." Gilbert laid a hand on Rebekah's shoulder.

Isaac snorted. "She doesn't want to talk to me." And maybe he should be done trying to coax her into it. All she ever did was run from him.

"How can he help when he doesn't know what happened?" Rebekah shifted Lynnette higher against her chest.

Gilbert kept his hand on Rebekah's shoulder, as though afraid she'd dart off down the beach if he didn't hold her in place. "Maybe it's time Aileen tells him."

"But what if she doesn't want to?" Rebekah looked past him toward Aileen now climbing rocks.

"Look at him, darling." Gilbert jutted his chin. "He's moonstruck over the woman. He needs to know."

"What do I need to know?" Isaac hooked a thumb into his waistband. "And would you stop talking about me as though I'm not here?"

"Go find your woman." Gilbert jerked his head in the direction Aileen had gone. "And if she still won't tell you what happened last summer, then I'll give you the story when you come back."

Rebekah's eyes shot daggers at her husband. "That's not right. It's not your story to tell."

"No, but at this point, I'd say it's Isaac's story as much as Aileen's. Go on." Gilbert looked back at him, his gaze an ocean of calm. "And know that I'm praying for you."

"Right," Isaac muttered. Not that he minded the prayers, but was whatever happened to Aileen so big he needed to be covered by prayer to hear it told?

He trudged up the beach and climbed the boulders lining the shore. Gulls cried out above him, flying and dipping over the harbor, and the sun slanted its rays atop the rippling water, causing the tips of the tiny waves to glow orange.

Aileen sat alone on a long, flat rock that offered views of both the open lake and the harbor, a single person amidst an endless backdrop of rich blue.

How was it a woman could look so forlorn, so utterly heartbroken, just by sitting on a rock?

"Leave me alone." She glanced up at him, then moved her gaze out to the sea.

"Gilbert says there's a story from last summer I need to hear." He sat on the rock beside her, letting his legs drop to the boulder below.

"Gilbert wants me to tell ye, does he?" Her eyes held a mixture of rage and heartbreak, and she kicked at a pebble, sending it clattering over two more boulders before it dropped into the lake below. "Well, mayhap I should. This is getting too much, what's between us. Last winter I told ye to leave me alone, told ye I didn't want courted."

Isaac's throat turned suddenly tight, and his voice emerged raspy. "The thing of it is, I find myself falling for you anyway."

"Ye wouldn't think so fondly of me if ye knew everything."

"You keep saying that, but then refuse to tell me about it. If you're as bad as you claim, then don't I deserve the chance to decide for myself what happens next? Tell me, and if you're right and I don't want anything to do with you, I'll leave you be." But he couldn't imagine that. Whatever had happened, whatever she had or hadn't done, she'd spent the past year punishing herself for it. He'd not punish her as well.

She drew in a breath, then looked at him, her gaze flat and empty.

"I'm a ruined woman." Her voice was even and measured as she spoke, without even the barest hint of emotion. "I don't have me virtue anymore."

The words should've given him pause, should've caused his breath to still and his heart to thud, yet her confession wasn't anything he hadn't guessed. Her fear of men, her hatred of being touched in the commonest of ways, her unwillingness to be alone with him for more than a moment, they'd all told him the truth long before now. "Was it your choice? Or was the choice taken from you?"

She lurched back, though he wasn't sitting close enough to touch her in the first place. "What does it matter? It's not as though I can get me virtue back."

"It matters." To him. To God. To anyone with a good head on his shoulders.

"Why? Would ye care for me less if I made the choice? If I'd given meself to a man?"

"Probably not, but that's not the problem we're dealing with, is it?"

She looked down then, wrapping her arms around her bent knees that were tucked against her chest. "I was forced."

A burning sensation stole through him. Again, her words were nothing he'd not already guessed, but there was a difference between wondering and knowing for certain. Rage and grief and pain all mingled until the force of it was so great heat scalded the backs of his eyes. He sat there a moment, his jaw working back and forth.

Aileen had buried her head in her knees, her shoulders shaking with silent sobs.

He swung his legs onto the rock where he sat and shifted closer.

"Hey." He reached out and brushed his knuckles down the side of her cheek. "Don't cry. This changes nothing between us. I still want to court you, to know you more, to…" *Fall in love with you.*

Because he was already halfway to loving her, maybe even all the way there, if only she'd let him.

She jerked her head up, her eyes filled with sudden fury as she pushed to her feet. "Don't say that. Ye deserve someone better. Someone pure, someone who's right on the inside, because I'm far from normal in me heart."

"And you think I'm normal on the inside? You saw my attack of nerves yesterday morning, sat in the *North Star* last night and listened to my role in Pa's death." If one of them was unworthy of a relationship, then he deserved to wear that badge, not her. And yet he found himself standing to face her and reaching for her hand. "I don't care about your past, Aileen. You're the one that I want. You and no one else."

She shook her head, her eyes weighted with a sadness that seemed to grow heavier the longer they spoke. "Only because ye don't know the whole of it. There was a babe."

The air left his lungs in a giant whoosh. Somehow, in all his ponderings of what had hurt her, he'd never once thought about a babe being part of it.

She tugged her hand back from his and looked down, settling both her hands over her flat stomach. "Or rather, there should have been a babe, but I had nowhere to go, and Conan was gone. Gilbert's mother would have fired me if she found out I was pregnant. Plus I had no way to care for a child. And so I... I... I visited a brothel on my day off. A woman there claimed to have a draught that would rid me of an unwanted child."

His heart pounded. He'd heard a story once of a local woman going to Calumet to buy a potion that would cause her child to come early. "It seems dangerous to take such a thing."

"I only tried a little. The woman said it contained pennyroyal and belladonna and—"

"Pennyroyal?" He gripped her shoulders. "I've heard Dr. Harrington say it's more poison than medicine."

She angled her chin up to meet his, her eyes defiant. "It wasn't as though I had the money to traipse to a doctor and ask him what he thought about the potion."

"But you survived taking it." He loosened his hold. Perhaps pennyroyal wasn't as dangerous as Dr. Harrington claimed—or perhaps he had God to thank for keeping her alive when she should have died.

"I retched after trying only a wee bit, and so I didn't take more, but I still lost me babe a few days later. I don't know if I lost the babe natural-like or because of the potion."

"Aileen…" But his words died. For what was there to say?

"I wish I never would have tried the potion. I never even felt me child move inside me. And I miss that babe as though I'd borne it. In the dead of night sometimes, I lay there in me bed and I ache for me child. No one ever told me I would miss it so."

She looked up at him through eyes glazed with tears. "I didn't know about Eagle Harbor then. I didn't know there were places like this, where I could come and start a new life with me child. I might have lost me job in Chicago, Tressa would have still given me a job at the bakery here, illegitimate child or no. Except I didn't know. Rebekah and I weren't really friends then either. She didn't even know I was with child until after."

"Come here." He opened his arms and would have pulled her close, but she stepped away.

"Nay, I don't want tender words and strong arms and gentle hugs. I don't want yer comfort or to hear ye say everything will be all right. Because it won't." She blinked furiously, though a stray tear crested and streaked her face. "Haven't ye been listening? Ye deserve better than me. I'm ruined and broken inside."

She stood so near, and yet so very far. He could reach out and touch her, but would that drive her farther away from him? "Do you remember the verse I quoted last night? The one about God's mercy being from everlasting to everlasting?"

She looked away.

"God still loves you, Aileen, no matter what happened with your child, no matter how you were hurt in Chicago. This sadness that you carry inside you, this grief, it's not God's will for you to live this way. He has better things in store for you. Because if past sins mean people never deserve a happy future, I don't qualify either."

She sighed, invisible weights pulling down her shoulders until they hung in an unnatural slump. "It's not the same. Now please, just leave me be."

But hadn't they agreed earlier that if he could bring himself to understand what she'd done, she'd no longer run from him? And he did understand, or at least well enough that it wouldn't stop him from wanting to court her.

"Why are you...?" *So eager to refuse me yet again?*

But she'd already turned and was crossing the rock on which they stood, her feet padding quietly against the surface. Then she stepped down onto the next rock, and the one after that and after that, until her feet reached sand and the sound of the waves replaced the sound of her steps.

And he let her go. Because what was the point in asking her to stay when she didn't want to?

What was the point in telling her God would forgive her if she wouldn't listen?

What was the point in wanting to take the sorrow from her eyes and the heaviness from her shoulders, when she was so very determined to cling to them?

Chapter Sixteen

Aileen twisted in the tangled sheets, her eyes fluttering open for a second, only for her to shut them again. But 'twould do no good. The dream had been wrenching tonight, and she'd not be able to go to sleep again, no matter how long she lay in bed.

She yawned and pushed herself up, her gaze flying to the window. Had more men in the alley awoken her? Nay, she hadn't heard a thing; 'twas the dream that had done it. But not her usual dream. Cara had been older, a little girl who toddled around the house, giggling and smiling and playing with a rag doll. But there had been more babes, twins. Each with red hair like Cara's—like Lynnette's. And Isaac was there. And her. All together, a happy family with three children.

A foolish dream if ever there was one, and yet her heart ached with the happiness of it. A strange thing, that. How could a heart ache with happiness? A heart aching with sorrow or pain made sense, but not happiness. She swung her legs around the bed and padded to the window on bare feet. All was quiet tonight. Not even a glimpse of a strange shadow peeked out from behind a building.

Aye, 'twas as she thought. The dream had woken her and naught else, and she had no one to blame but Isaac Cummings.

She need only close her eyes, and she could still see him standing on the rock beside the water, his eyes earnest and voice entreating. *This sadness that you carry inside you, this grief, it's not God's will for you to live this way. He has better things in store for you.*

How easy Isaac made things seem, and not just accepting God's love, but having a home, a family, a place she belonged.

But what if, after Brenna finally arrived, she still didn't belong? What if she told her cousin what happened last summer, and Brenna wanted naught to do with her? And the same with Conan and Morley? If the lot of them ever made it to that farm in Wisconsin and they learned her secrets, would they shun her?

She shook her head. Such dark, hopeless thoughts. There had to be hope somewhere… like with Isaac Cummings. She'd told him her secret, and he hadn't turned his back on her. So what was she supposed to do now? Tell him she couldn't accept his suit because she couldn't forgive herself?

She yawned into her hand. Perhaps a glass of milk would settle her so she could sleep again. She grabbed her robe from the peg by the door and headed into the hall and down the stairs before lighting the lamp hanging at the bottom of the stairs.

Crash!

Thud!

"Ouch!"

Aileen froze, her heart pounding against her chest, and peered through the thin lamp beam into the back corner of the kitchen.

"W-who's there?"

"I'm sorry, Miss Aileen." A familiar boy's voice echoed through the kitchen. "I got here late. I promise I would've knocked had I thought you were still up."

Scraping sounded, and she stepped farther into the kitchen, where she found Jack O'Byrne righting a stool that had fallen to the floor.

"What are ye doing here?"

Two splotches of red appeared high on Jack's cheeks. "I was hungry, is all. Didn't get much to eat today. I came by earlier, just after dark, but either you went to bed really early or you were out late."

Heat rushed to her own cheeks then. She'd come home and gone straight to bed, though she'd probably been crying rather than sleeping when Jack stopped by.

"Ye're just now getting food?" She ran her eyes over the boy, but if the half-eaten loaf of bread behind him was any indication, he was telling the truth. His clothes were just as ragged as they'd been when he'd stopped by two weeks ago, and given the stains and dirt clinging to them, it didn't seem as though he'd gotten himself a bath during those two weeks either. Was it possible for a boy to look thinner in so short a time? Because she could swear Jack had lost five pounds or so.

"I missed dinner tonight," Jack shrugged and looked down. "And Pa don't feel too charitable about saving my food when I'm late."

She didn't imagine a man like Virgil O'Byrne felt charitable about much of anything, ever.

"Next time ye need inside after I've locked up, throw a pebble at me window. I'd rather ye wake me instead of making me think ye're some intruder." She pressed a hand to her heart. "Scared the life half out of me, ye did."

"I'm sorry, Miss Aileen, I promise. Do you want me to leave you money for the food? I got some." He dug around in his pockets and pulled out a handful of coins.

"Go on and take the food. I don't need yer money." Technically, the food wasn't hers to give, but she couldn't imagine Tressa taking her to task for feeding Jack. Still, she would mention to Tressa what she'd given the boy, and if the Oaktons had a problem with Jack having a loaf or two of bread, she'd pay for it.

She glanced behind him to the bread on the counter. "Do ye need more? I think there might be some leftover muffins in the storefront."

Jack laid a hand over his belly. "I had enough for now, Miss Aileen. And I'm sorry I scared you. Next time I'll throw a pebble at the window."

"Ye should leave yer da and go stay with Elijah and Victoria with yer brother and sister." She didn't like the look of Jack. True, he wasn't the only boy running around town with raggedy clothes and dirt-stained hands, but there was something else wrong, something she couldn't quite name.

"Aw, Miss Aileen. I told you already. Alice and Toby aren't old enough to earn their keep, but Pa says I've gotta. Says if I'm good for the rest of the week, I can go visit Alice and Toby though, so that's something." A bright smile filled his face.

She couldn't quite manage to smile in return. He was far too excited over something as simple as seeing his siblings. But she couldn't do much to help beyond talk to Isaac about how Mr. O'Byrne was treating Jack.

"I best be going now, but thank you, Miss Aileen." The boy pulled his cap onto his head, then turned and disappeared out the kitchen door and into the darkness.

Thank you? All she'd done was not take him to task for helping himself to some bread, when the boy clearly needed more than one meal.

⌐.⌐.⌐.⌐.⌐

"Hey, you awake up there? I'm hungry!"

Isaac blinked his eyes open only to find himself staring at the pine plank wall beside his bed.

"What time is breakfast around here?"

Isaac winced. They might have only thrown two men into jail for fighting at the bar last night, but evidently these two made more noise than a dozen of his calmer jailbirds.

"Hello? Sheriff? Can you hear me?"

He squeezed his eyes shut. The whole town could likely hear the man. And wouldn't it be just like Betty Ranulfson or Trudy Kainer to be walking by, hear the ruckus, and complain to the town council at the next meeting?

He stifled a yawn, then sat up and reached for his shirt, sitting up to button it as quickly as his sluggish fingers would allow. What time was it anyway? He snagged his pocket watch off the bedside table and glanced at it. Nine-thirty in the morning.

All right, so maybe the men downstairs had a reason to be yelling for breakfast. What had possessed him to sleep so long?

Probably something to do with staying up late to break up the fight down at the Pretty Penny, and something more to do with spending most of his time in bed thinking of Aileen rather than sleeping.

"Sheriff!" The shout was even louder this time.

He pulled on his trousers and shoved his feet into his boots before tromping down the stairs.

"I'm going to complain about being mistreated if you keep me in here any longer!"

"Me too! Since when are sheriffs allowed to starve the people they put in their cells?"

Isaac headed for the door that separated his office from the jail cells, the door he'd foolishly left open, allowing the sound to carry up to his apartment. But something on the floor caught his eye.

He paused and turned toward the folded piece of paper that had been slid beneath the door leading to the street. As he walked to retrieve it, the men in their cells loosed a litany of curses.

Picking up the paper, he unfolded it to find five words scrawled sloppily inside.

Smuggler shipment at dock tonight.

His hands shook as he stared at the words. Who had slipped this beneath the door? Why? When? It must have been some time after three in the morning when he'd gone to bed.

Could he trust it? Or had the smugglers learned that Norling was here and decided to lay a trap?

The men shouted even louder as he stood there. Perhaps the note was a trap, or perhaps it was just the thing he needed to catch the smugglers red-handed. There was only one way to find out.

Chapter Seventeen

Isaac crouched behind the rock, his deputies behind him, keeping his gaze pinned to the beach shrouded in inky blackness—blackness that would give way to dawn in an hour or so. The wind was still tonight, the water barely making noise as it lapped against the sand.

"What happens if the smugglers don't show up?" Granger asked from where he huddled behind a rock on the other side of Norling.

"We assume someone sent us here while there was activity going on elsewhere, like that inlet where the sheriff's brother was shot at." Norling kept his face directed toward the water as he spoke.

Fletcher shifted against the rock to Isaac's right. "If something was going to happen, it would've happened by now."

"Or maybe the smugglers are waiting to be sure everyone has gone home after the bars closed." It was just a guess, but if he was going to smuggle something through the middle of a town, he'd do it when no one else had cause to be outside, in the wee hours between bar closings and those getting up to work at dawn. Still, that didn't explain why the team of customs agents Norling had supposedly sent for that morning had yet to arrive.

"Either way, we stay until dawn." Norling's voice brooked no argument.

"And if the smugglers come, but not your help?" Isaac looked over at Norling. As soon as he'd shown Norling the message that had been slipped under the door, the man had headed up to Copper Harbor, where he'd sent word to Marquette.

"I sent the telegram before noon." A hint of concern threaded through Norling's voice. "If a ship enters the harbor, the Revenue Cutter Service should be right behind it."

Fletcher yawned loud enough to be heard up at the lighthouse. "How about we all go home to bed and get an hour or so of sleep before dawn?"

"No, we've got something." Isaac narrowed his eyes. At the mouth of the harbor, a shadow glided against the sliver of moon in the sky. Nearly silent, a three-masted schooner entered the harbor and slid straight for the dock before the darkness obscured it. Had he not been watching for it, he'd never have known the ship was there.

"Are its sails black?" His words were no more than a whisper.

"It's not uncommon with smuggling ships." Norling shifted beside him, his hand resting on the butt of his pistol. "They'll change the sails to white before dawn."

Which explained how the ships could come and go without Mac spotting them from the lighthouse.

"All right," Granger drawled. "We got our ship, but let's say she has a normal size crew of about a dozen. And let's pretend there aren't even smugglers from the woods coming to get what's inside."

Norling snorted. "That's unlikely."

"Maybe, but even if there are no men coming from land, that means we're four men against twelve." Unfortunately, Granger's ciphering came up about the same as Isaac's own.

"Your help had better show," he whispered to the Viking beside him.

Norling pointed to the entrance of the harbor. "Can you see it?"

Another boat with sails as black as the first glided silently between the rocks before disappearing into the shadowed darkness of the harbor.

"Except they're still on the water." Fletcher pointed at more shadows, these ones on land and taking the form of men as they moved down Front Street toward the dock. "And we'll have company on the beach in about a minute."

"Don't move," Isaac whispered, his gaze focused on the dozen or so men heading toward them. "Wait until they're on the dock and we can flank them." Though he didn't have a clue how four of them could effectively flank a dozen men.

"What if they hop on the boat and sail off?" Fletcher asked.

"What if they see the cutter and run back to where they came from before ever stepping foot on the dock?" Granger countered.

"No, the sheriff's right." Even though he whispered, Norling's voice had a firm edge. "We wait. Not only will we be able to flank the smugglers on the dock, but the cutter will probably send a crew of men to the beach in a dinghy."

"Probably?" Isaac slanted Norling a sideways glance.

The man shrugged. "The Customs Service likes to get a team of men in place before any smuggling activity, but that's not always possible if the men have to travel a distance. If nothing else, there should be men to help on the revenue cutter. They're probably climbing into dinghies and rowing toward shore as we speak."

"How many men?" Fletcher squeaked.

"Enough," Norling quipped.

Isaac shifted beside the rock. It would have to be enough. Because while the idea of four men capturing a dozen smugglers plus a ship's crew was ridiculous, it was equally ridiculous to stand by while criminals got away with thousands of dollars' worth of smuggled goods.

In the harbor, the smuggler's schooner slid into another patch of moonlight and moored itself against the dock. He had to strain his eyes before seeing that the first of its black sails was already being pulled down.

The group of smugglers on Front Street turned onto the hard path of packed dirt and rock that led to the dock, some of them rolling handcarts. Isaac looked back to the dark water. No dinghies full of men reflected in the moonlight, nor did the faint sound of oars dipping into water carry across the harbor. Was there truly a crew from the cutter coming to help?

"But I don't want to go," a familiar voice echoed through the night.

Isaac stilled, surveying the smugglers until his gaze found a short, slender form. Or rather, two short, slender forms, both of which hung back from the rest of the group, along with a large, squat man sporting a beard.

No. Not them.

Isaac's heart kicked against his chest, and sweat dampened his palms as he stared at the unmistakable forms of Leroy and Martin Spritzer.

The first group of smugglers plodded past the rocks where they hid, so determined to get to the ship that they didn't glance at the boulders by the dock. The men obscured the Spritzer boys and the smuggler from view for only a few seconds, but when they passed, Leroy was trying to jerk away from the large man, who was now dragging him toward the dock.

"You think you're big enough to fight me?" The man chuckled, then gave Leroy's arm a cruel yank. "Get on the ship. You're needed in Canada."

"You never said we'd have to go to Canada." Martin trailed behind the man dragging Leroy, evidently willing to follow his brother wherever he went.

"You wanted work, didn't you?" The man thrust Leroy forward, letting go of the boy but also propelling him closer to the dock. "Why does it matter where the work is?"

Work. Isaac swallowed. Was this the job Suzanna and Christopher had mentioned their brothers having? Why hadn't he questioned them more?

"Can't we just break another window or something?" Martin's words caused the smuggler to stop and face him. "Maybe at the bank this time? You should have heard what Mrs. Ranulfson said about Ellie after the party yesterday. She deserves a broken window or two."

"I think you've just found your vandals," Norling breathed beside him.

More smugglers passed the rocks, blocking the Spritzers from view once again, but not the smuggler's words. "The time for distractions is over. You need to go."

The last of the smugglers tromped by, revealing a defiant Leroy with arms crossed and jaw raised. "I'm not leaving my family."

"You think you have a choice?" The man reached to his belt, and a moment later the tip of a knife glinted in the small patch of moonlight. "You're going."

Run! Isaac's mind screamed the word. In the split second it took for the man to grab his knife, the boys could have run.

But they stayed where they were, Martin looking between his brother and the bearded man. "Why? W-w-what are we supposed to do in Canada?"

"You'll find out soon enough." The man jabbed the knife in the direction of the schooner. "Now get to the ship, or you'll end up like Simon."

Leroy took a step back from the smuggler. "Simon? You mean the man from the woods?"

The smuggler lunged toward Leroy, grabbing him by the arm and spinning him around so the blade pressed against the young man's throat.

"Drop the knife." Isaac stood, revealing himself behind the rock that stood chest-high, and pointed his pistol at the smuggler.

"Sheriff Cummings!" Martin raced toward him.

But the boy's shout had been too loud. Isaac didn't need to turn his head to know movement ceased on the dock, everyone suddenly still. But what was he supposed to do, hide while Leroy Spritzer got his throat slit?

"Let the boy go." Isaac stepped out from behind the rock, his heart pounding against his ribs as he cocked his pistol.

"How about you let your gun go instead, Sheriff?" The unmistakable click of another pistol being cocked echoed through the night, followed by the muted sound of footsteps in the sand. "Just bend down there and set it in the sand, nice and slow."

"Or you could do the same with yours." Norling stood now, his pistol cocked and aimed at the second man holding the gun.

The bearded man kept his knife against Leroy's throat. "Just how many men do you have behind them rocks, Sheriff?"

"Enough to see justice done." Or so he hoped.

"Freeze, and put your hands in the air." A shout sounded from the sand near where the boulders started. "This is the U.S. Customs Service! You're all under arrest."

Movement flooded the beach, but Isaac didn't turn to look, just kept his gun leveled at the man holding the knife. "Drop it, and I won't shoot."

The man muttered something, then let the silver blade fall to the sand.

The tightness left Isaac's shoulders, and his grip on the gun relaxed, though he still kept the barrel pointed toward the smuggler. *Thank you, Father.* If the Customs Service had been another two minutes, they might have all ended up dead.

"I'm so sorry, Sheriff." Leroy raced toward him. A second later, Leroy's stringy arms wrapped around his waist in a tight hug. "I was just trying to earn money for Ma, but I didn't know—"

"Sheriff, where's the jail?" A short, thin man approached him.

Only then did Isaac turn and look at the beach and dock. Men swarmed around three black rowboats, barely visible in the darkness, and more men had closed in around the smugglers trapped on the dock. Isaac drew in a shaky breath as a couple of shadowed forms jumped into the water. Shots rang into the night, followed by more splashing. It looked like the Customs Service wasn't about to let a single smuggler escape by water.

"Sheriff? I asked where the jail was." The thin man stopped in front of him and extended his hand for a shake. "The name's Linus Tate. I'm the U.S. Customs Agent in charge of tonight's operation."

~.~.~.~.~

"How could you?" Ellie rubbed the grit from her eyes as she stared across the table at her two brothers, Leroy and Martin. A dim lantern flickered on the table between them, while outside, darkness pressed against the windows of Sheriff Cummings's apartment.

Noise from downstairs rose through the floor, a commotion that didn't show any signs of dying down. Deputy Fletcher had woken her a quarter hour ago and told her she needed to come to town because her brothers were in trouble. But before they'd reached the building, she'd realized her brothers weren't the only ones who'd gotten caught. She'd never seen the sheriff's office so full before. Deputy Fletcher had taken her elbow and guided her through the throng of men downstairs, but not without one or two of them making a crude comment.

She shuddered. At least the sheriff had brought her brothers upstairs, where there was a bit of quiet, even if the dull roar of voices below still carried up the stairs.

"Go on, explain it." Sheriff Cummings leaned against the wall, his gaze burning more fiercely than the small lantern.

Martin sighed. "It was a job. We didn't ask particulars, just knew the work paid good."

"With Ma sick, we need money." Leroy spread his hands open on the table and shrugged. "You can't argue that we brought back a decent amount this summer."

"By breaking windows and taking axes to wagon beds?" The sheriff's voice cut through the room. "You both know better."

Martin looked down at the table, but Leroy kept his hands where they were, open as though his actions could somehow be excused by a simple gesture. "If you need money bad enough, you can't be too particular about what you're doing."

Tears filled Ellie's eyes. She worked for hours upon hours each day to provide for her brothers and sisters, and here these two ran off and vandalized the town because someone paid them? "Ma will be heartbroken when she finds out."

"Aw, Ellie, Ma's too sick to know what's going on," Leroy's voice held a slight tremble. "She ain't getting no better, and the doc's medicine doesn't help neither."

"As I understand it, the broken windows, the ink on Betty Ranulfson's skirts, the ruined wagon bed, and any other such incidents were cover for the smugglers downstairs." Sheriff Cummings moved to the table and leaned closer to Leroy and Martin. "You were paid to create a ruckus while the smugglers made cargo runs. Is that right?"

"I promise we didn't know what they were up to." Martin's voice cracked. "They just paid us to break windows and not get caught."

"Do you realize what would've happened had I not been there tonight? You would be on your way to Canada right now." The sheriff brought his fist down on the table with a muted thud. "These men are dangerous. If someone ever tries to pay you for doing something illegal again, you run. I don't care how much money they're offering."

"I thought they were really going to take us, Sheriff Cummings." Martin sniffled and swiped at his cheek. "Thank you for stopping them."

The muscle at the side of the sheriff's jaw worked. "I understand you boys don't have the best situation at home with your ma ill and your pa gone, but you listen here and you listen now—there are men who will take advantage of you because of it. It doesn't matter whether you're in Eagle Harbor or Chicago or San Francisco, there are always evil men who will want to use you. It's your job not to let them. I can't always protect you. It was of the Lord's doing that I was even there tonight."

"Ma and Ellie would be worried sick if we up and disappeared for months." Martin traced his finger over a scar in the table.

"We still didn't mean no harm by it." Leroy plopped his hands onto his lap and scowled.

"How could you not mean harm?" Ellie's words rang through the apartment, echoing off the stove and through the corners. "You *intentionally* broke windows. You *intentionally* destroyed a wagon bed."

Both of her brothers looked down, refusing to meet her eyes.

"What's going to happen now?" She swallowed and looked at the sheriff. "Will my brothers go to jail?"

Sheriff Cummings drew in a breath. "As far as I can tell, they didn't have a direct hand in the smuggling. From what I saw tonight, it looks like we'll be bringing one of the men up on attempted kidnapping charges along with the smuggling charges. And one is being charged with murder—a murder your brothers reported to me as soon as they learned of it." The lawman looked between Leroy and Martin. "I'm assuming those bruises I saw on your faces last week weren't from getting into a fight with each other?"

"No, sir." Martin shook his head.

"We got in trouble for telling you about the body." Leroy's mumbled words were barely discernible above the rumble of voices from downstairs. "And Harvey told us if we said anything else to you, we'd end up like Simon."

Sheriff Cummings dipped his head in a curt nod. "So you're cleared of the smuggling charges, but we still have the vandalism to deal with."

"I told you that was just a job we were being paid for!" Leroy scooted his chair back from the table, his arms crossed defiantly over his chest.

"And having to answer for it will help you remember not to break the law next time." The sheriff kept his voice even, his gaze steady as he answered Leroy, then he turned and looked at her. "They need to go before a judge and stand trial. I suspect the judge will order them to spend a certain number of hours working around town rather than serve jail time. But I'm afraid until the hearing, they'll need to stay in a cell."

"I won't do it again," Martin cried. "I promise."

Leroy dropped his arms from across his chest, his shoulders drooping. "Don't lock my brother up. He doesn't deserve it. I'm the one who found the job. He didn't want to go along, but the money was so good I talked him into it."

"I don't have much leeway on this. You'll need to stay in jail until you stand trial or post bail, and bail isn't cheap. We'll see if we can get a trial set up for the end of the week."

Leroy scowled, though his shoulders stayed slumped. Martin just kept his head bent.

"Come on, let's get you downstairs." The sheriff stepped away from the wall and pulled on the back of Martin's chair, helping to scoot him away from the table. "I'll put you two in a cell by yourselves so you don't need to worry about any of the smugglers causing you trouble."

Ellie sniffled. She should probably thank the sheriff for that small bit of kindness, but she couldn't quite force her tongue to work as Leroy and Martin rose and plodded toward the door. It clicked shut behind them a moment later.

First her older brother died, and now her two younger brothers were in trouble with the law. What was becoming of her family? What more could she do to hold things together? She laid her head on the table and pressed her eyes shut against the hot tears brimming.

She wasn't sure how long she sat there, her head cradled in her arms as silent sobs shook her shoulders, but only when the door opened again did she stem the tears and raise her head.

The sheriff crossed the room to her. "I'm sorry to have dragged you here in the middle of the night, but I really felt as though you should know now rather than in the morning when the rest of the town finds out."

She drew a handkerchief from her pocket. "Part of me wants to ask if it's really necessary they be locked up…" Rather than use the handkerchief on her face, she twisted it in her hands. "But if they'll learn this way, then it's for the best."

Or at the very least she'd tell herself that. It was easier to stomach the thought of them being in jail for a few days than thinking about her brothers in a cell later in life.

Sheriff Cummings settled into the chair across the table. "Truth is, I could probably let them go tonight if they promised to show up for court in a few days' time, especially with how full the jail is. But like you, I don't want them to do anything along these lines again.

So my thought is, treat them harsh, and they just might be scared enough to straighten out."

"What if they don't?" The words almost burned, as though saying them aloud might make them more likely to come true.

"You can't stop your brothers from making their own choices." The sheriff's jaw softened and his gaze turned gentle. "And Ellie, their choices aren't your fault."

But it felt like they were. Maybe if she wasn't so busy, she would have realized their new job was no good. Maybe if she wasn't so tired, she'd have thought to ask better questions of them.

Sheriff Cummings scooted his chair back and walked around the table, where he extended his arm. "Come on, I'll send Fletcher to walk you home. And I'm serious when I mean you shouldn't berate yourself over this. None of it was your doing."

She blinked back the tears scalding her eyes and gave her head a slight shake. If the sheriff's words were true, then why did she have this sinking feeling that she could have somehow stopped her brothers, but hadn't?

Chapter Eighteen

Elijah's footsteps thudded on the soft earthen trail as he moved through the shadowed woods back toward home. Normally he'd be out on the lake already, but he didn't have the heart to take the *North Star* out today. He rounded the final bend in the drive, then paused. Dawn lit up the sky over the lake with streaks of pink and orange and yellow that could rival the palette of any highfalutin' painter. Of course, most days he was out on the lake by the time dawn hit in full, allowing him to view a colorful sunrise over an endless expanse of sky and water.

Then again, most days the sheriff's office was dark when he passed by on his way to the *North Star,* rather than containing a commotion big enough to wake the town.

Dim lantern light filtered through the kitchen window, telling him that Victoria hadn't gone back to bed after rising to fix him breakfast that morn. He clomped up the porch steps, then went through the entryway lined with boots and winter coats before finally entering the kitchen.

"Elijah." Victoria looked up from where she sat at the kitchen table, the family Bible spread open to a passage in John. She set down her teacup and stood, coming around the table to him. "Did you come back because of me? I told you I'm fine. It's another month is all. No need to miss a day of fishing. Besides, you think I'd be getting used to it by now."

She wrapped her arms around him before he had a chance to set his lunch pail at his feet or doff his wide-brimmed hat. He slid the pail to the ground beside him, then settled his hands around her waist and drew her close. The sweet scent of her lavender water filled his senses.

"Not you, sweetling." Though the start of her monthly flow yesterday evening hadn't hurt his decision to return. Over the year they'd been married, Victoria spent at least one day a month stemming tears when they learned four more weeks had passed without a child flourishing in her womb. She'd gotten better with time though, her tears drying quicker and with less fanfare. And having the O'Byrne children around helped calm Victoria's heart better than anything he could say or do.

"Is it Jack?" Victoria rested her hands on his shoulders and pulled away from his chest just far enough to peer into his eyes. "I was just sitting here praying for him. I'm so worried. Tell me Isaac found him."

"No, no news about Jack."

Her face fell. "Oh, I was hoping."

"So was I. We need to pray harder on that end." He swallowed the lump that had worked its way back into his throat. "I came back because... Isaac almost got himself killed last night."

"He what?" Victoria's hands fisted in the fabric of his shirt. "How? What happened?"

"Smugglers."

"Smugglers?"

He winced at the high pitch of her voice. At this rate, she'd wake Ma and the children before he could tell the whole story. Then again, she wouldn't be the only one with rounded eyes and a shocked expression this morn. He and Mac knew Isaac had suspected smuggling activity near Eagle Harbor, but the news would come as a shock to the rest of the townsfolk.

"Isaac's been trying to find smugglers for almost a week now." He led Victoria to the table and sat beside her, telling her how Isaac had wondered from the beginning if the men Aileen had seen in the alley were smuggling goods, how he'd sent a telegram from Houghton to the Customs Service, and how Lars Norling had shown up a week later.

Then he got to a few hours ago. Or at least, what Deputy Fletcher had told him had happened a few hours earlier. He'd not had a chance to talk to Isaac since he was busy with the men locked up in his jail.

"When Isaac thought the Spritzer boys would end up on the ship, he pulled out his pistol and stepped out of hiding to save them." Elijah's shoulders slumped and he bent his head. "The Customs Service showed up a second later, but if they'd taken another minute or two, Isaac could have been killed."

"But he wasn't." Victoria rested a hand on his arm. "God protected him."

He shook his head, which he still kept bowed over the table. "Why did I suggest he run for sheriff? Stupidest idea ever."

Victoria's slender hand left his arm to settle on his back, where she stroked along the top of his shoulders. "Because you care about this town and the people in it, which means you want them to have a good lawman. Because you care about your brother, and you knew God had a bigger plan for him than hiding in the workshop making toys."

"Confound it. Why do you have to be so smart?"

She pressed a puckered kiss to his cheek. "To make up for how thick-headed you are?"

195

He slanted her a glance, only to see her batting her eyelashes at him. "Isaac's still in danger though. I can't help but feel like some of that is my fault. If something happens to him…"

He opened his hands, then clenched them into fists. He hated feeling so helpless. How could he stand by and let his brother work a job that put him in danger on such a regular basis? It was one thing to recommend Isaac be sheriff when there was nothing but drunken brawls and disorderly conduct to take care of. But murders and smuggling rings?

"Elijah, dearest." Victoria's sweet voice was barely more than a whisper in the quiet house. "Have you considered that Isaac's situation isn't much different than you going out on rescues?"

He pursed his lips together. "Of course it's different. I don't have a choice. If I don't go out, people will die."

"And if Isaac didn't leave where he was hiding to protect Leroy and Martin Spritzer?"

Elijah forced a breath from his lungs and stared down at the familiar, scarred table. "Maybe I never realized how hard a thing I asked of you and Ma, Rebekah and Isaac."

"It is hard knowing you're going out into such danger, but we don't stop you because God gave you an ability to help others, and wasting that would be wrong. So we cover you in prayer while you're out, and we smother you with hugs when you return." She reached over and laced her fingers through his on the table. "Ultimately, when Isaac's doing his job as sheriff, his life is in God's hands just the way yours is on a rescue."

"I'm being unfair, aren't I?"

She squeezed his fingers, then leaned over and rested her head on his shoulder, sending another whiff of lavender water wafting around him. "Horribly, but ye're also being a concerned brother, and there's nothing wrong with that."

He wrapped an arm around her shoulder and pulled her close. "I guess I need to be a little kinder to Isaac the next time he starts muttering about one of my rescues."

"That would probably be best."

He leaned down and pressed his lips to the top of her head, then closed his eyes. Life was so very fragile, and the truth was, he couldn't promise that he would survive his next rescue or that Isaac would survive another day of being a lawman. But he could savor this moment right now, holding his wife close and thanking God for the blessings He'd bestowed...

Because he didn't know how much longer he'd have them.

~.~.~.~.~

"Is it true? Are there really smugglers inside?" Mrs. Ranulfson attempted to peer over Isaac's shoulder from where she stood on the porch just outside his office. "I've never seen a real-life smuggler before."

Isaac clenched his jaw. If he'd had one person stop by today, he'd had a hundred. He didn't know quite how word had gotten out about who had been captured last night, but at this point, the entire town seemed to know. Indeed, the only thing that should surprise him was that it had taken Mrs. Ranulfson until midmorning to come snooping. And if the group of people clustered across the street was any indication, others would come snooping just as soon as Mrs. Ranulfson realized she wasn't going to get past him.

Which was why he was stationed on the porch and not inside with Norling, Captain Tate, and the captain of the cutter that had captured the smuggling vessel.

"What kind of things were they smuggling? And why were they smuggling them into Eagle Harbor?" Mrs. Ranulfson's ostrich feathers swayed on her hat as she attempted to look over his shoulder once more.

"The investigation is just getting underway. I'm afraid I don't have answers for you."

"But…" The woman licked her lips, a fascinated gleam in her eyes. "But surely you have some guess. And how did you catch them? Was it part of your normal patrol?"

"I'm not at liberty to comment." Isaac moved his gaze from the middle-aged woman to the street. Maybe if he didn't look at her, she'd give up her quest for information quicker.

Except no sooner had he looked away than his gaze landed on a familiar figure rounding the corner from Front Street onto North, the sun glinting off her deep red hair.

Aileen paused when she reached the crowd of people across the street, her brow furrowing for a moment as her head turned his direction. He'd been so busy preparing to catch the smugglers yesterday, he'd not seen her since she'd told him what had happened in Chicago last summer.

He could still see her standing on the rock, her arms wrapped about herself in a lonely hug while sorrow filled her eyes. *I'm ruined, and I'm broken inside, and I'm just plain not worthy of you. Or any man, for that matter.*

Yet now she made her way slowly toward the porch, edging around several people standing in the road. Did that mean she'd changed her mind about staying away from him? Would she consider his suit now?

"Well?" Mrs. Ranulfson stomped her foot on the floorboards. "Are you going to answer me? I asked how you caught the smugglers."

Smugglers. Right. He had a jail full of smugglers, and that's what he needed to be thinking about. Not a fiery-headed woman with cream-colored skin and haunted eyes. "I already said I can't give you details. Isn't it enough we caught them?"

Aileen's shoes sounded on the porch steps, and Mrs. Ranulfson turned. "Are you here to ask about the smugglers?" Mrs. Ranulfson pulled a fan from her handbag and began waving it rather vigorously. "If so, it's no use, he's not telling anyone a thing."

"Smugglers?" Aileen's gaze flew to his. "Is that why there are so many people about? Ye have smugglers in there?" Like Mrs. Ranulfson, she tried to peer over his shoulder and into the office.

And like he'd done with Mrs. Ranulfson, he blocked Aileen's view. Except he actually needed to have a conversation with Aileen about the smugglers. Her cousin, Morley Brogan, hadn't been caught last night, but two of the smugglers inside had mentioned him.

Had she spoken with Morley since that day on the street two weeks ago? He scowled at Mrs. Ranulfson. If only they had a bit of privacy, he could ask.

Before or after he asked if she'd changed her mind about courting? Isaac rubbed his jaw. That conversation was sure to go well. *I think your cousin is a smuggler. Has he said anything about the woods? About possibly staying out there? Oh, and by the way, do you want to go on a picnic after I track down your only family in America and hand him over to the Customs Service to be prosecuted?*

"I've need to speak to ye, Sheriff." Aileen's soft voice drew his gaze back to her. "But if this is a poor time, I can wait."

Did that mean she'd come to talk to him about their conversation on the rocks? Sweat beaded on the back of his neck, and his palms itched.

"I can make time." Because even if she hadn't come to discuss the possibility of a future together, he still needed to ask her about Morley.

Mrs. Ranulfson edged nearer to Aileen, a curious glint in her eyes. "If you didn't come to ask about the smugglers, then what did you come for? Did someone break into the bakery again?"

"I... um..." Aileen shifted closer to him. "It's not really something to be discussed openly."

Mrs. Ranulfson quirked an eyebrow, then slid her gaze between the two of them. "Is that so?"

Isaac's shoulder muscles tightened. "Granger," he called behind him. "Come watch the door for a minute."

Granger's footsteps sounded behind him. "Sure thing, Sheriff."

"Thank you." Isaac extended his arm to Aileen. "I know a place we can talk."

"All right." Aileen rested her hand on his arm.

But Mrs. Ranulfson still stood between them and the steps. He offered her a tight smile. "Didn't you say you were on your way to the mercantile?"

A slight frown creased the older woman's brow, and she looked down the street toward the shop. "Well, yes, I suppose I did."

"Have a good day then."

Mrs. Ranulfson gave a final glance at Aileen's hand resting on his arm, then huffed and trudged down the steps.

Aileen pressed a hand to her mouth and let out a small giggle.

A giggle. He'd not thought the woman had it in her.

"I'm sorry. Ye have a building full of smugglers, and here I am laughing." Her eyes smiled up at him.

"Don't apologize." If ever a woman needed more laughter in her life, it was Aileen.

He led her down the steps, then pulled her around the side of the building. They were still visible from the street, but the spot would also give them a chance to talk without being overheard. "Is everything all right?"

"I don't know." The happiness left her eyes, and she twisted her hands in her skirt. "Were ye in danger? When ye caught the smugglers, that is?"

It was a simple question, one that half the townsfolk would probably ask, yet something warm unfurled inside him at her words.

"I might not know much about smugglers in America, but the ones in Ireland who run boats to avoid tariffs, they're a fierce lot." Worry filled her green eyes—worry over *him*.

Had they been out of sight of the street, he'd reach out to touch her cheek, or perhaps lean his forehead against hers before whispering he was fine. Instead he patted her hand where it still rested on his arm. "We had help."

"I see that." She looked past him toward the sleek revenue cutter in the harbor, its sails changed to white. Even now, the schooner, still hoisting all but one of its black sails, was overrun with customs workers taking inventory of the smuggled goods. "I'll be quick then. 'Tis worried, I am, about Jack O'Byrne."

His hands tightened over hers on his arm. "You've seen Jack?"

"Aye, twice now, but this last time was two nights ago. I stopped by yesterday to tell ye, but ye were gone."

He gave a slight dip of his head. Yes, he'd been getting ready for the smugglers and had closed the office so he could track down his deputies and make plans.

"Both times Jack's come to the bakery after dark, looking for food and acting as though he hasn't eaten for days. He said he'd missed dinner with his da, but I don't quite believe him."

Isaac's muscles tensed beneath Aileen's hand. "Next time Jack visits you, I want you to keep him there, or come get me. Do something. He shouldn't be with his father, not considering what Virgil O'Byrne is involved in."

"What's Virgil O'Byrne involved in?" Aileen wrinkled her forehead. "I don't understand."

Isaac swallowed. "We believe Virgil O'Byrne is a smuggler."

"A smuggler?" She looked at the jailhouse wall behind him, her eyes wide. "Did ye arrest him last night? Where is Jack?"

"No, I didn't arrest him, and I can't find either him or Jack. They're not living at their cabin, and this is the first time I've heard of Jack being in town. No one has seen him since school got out and his pa took Alice and Toby to Elijah's."

Aileen wrapped her arms around herself and looked worriedly around the street. "I didn't know, or I would have kept Jack with me. But he's always in such a hurry to leave, so nervous, like he thinks he'll get in trouble for taking a loaf of bread or two."

"Has Jack said anything about his father, or where he's staying?" Perhaps the boy had left a clue without Aileen realizing it. "Anything about work that he needs to do in town? Anything that might hint at where the smugglers are camped?"

Aileen shook her head. "He only tells me he's hungry and that his da says he has to work to earn his keep."

Isaac raked a hand through his hair. The boy was evidently being smart about how much information he gave Aileen. "What about your cousin?"

Her gaze snapped up to his, and she stilled. "What about him?"

"Has he ever mentioned anything about Virgil or Jack O'Byrne? Anything about staying in the woods when he comes to Eagle Harbor?"

"Why? Do you think he...?" Her words trailed off, and she glanced down the road toward the harbor. "Nay."

"He was seen with a group of known smugglers earlier this week." By Elijah, who'd rescued him near the inlet.

Aileen's face grew pale, causing her freckles to stand out like burning orange coals against her skin. "He was?"

"Has your cousin said anything to you about why he's been in Eagle Harbor so much this summer? Are you sure he hasn't mentioned a place in the woods where he sometimes stays?"

"Ye really believe Morley's a smuggler?" she whispered up at him. He pressed his lips into a firm line.

She sank back against the building. "It makes too much sense, doesn't it? The way he keeps leaving and then coming back. The way he says he'll have money to get Brenna from Ireland by fall."

"Probably when the shipping season is over."

"How could he?" She bit the side of her lip, her gaze dropping to her feet. "He has to know better, and he promised…"

Isaac leaned closer. "What did he promise?"

She glanced up for the briefest of instants, tears glinting in her eyes before she hung her head once more. "That he wouldn't do anything illegal again."

Again. The word clanged through his head like the fog bell ringing by the lighthouse on a misty morning.

"And not just Morley, but Conan too."

Her brother? He'd died last spring before Aileen had moved to Eagle Harbor, but she'd said barely a word about him. "What illegal things did they do?"

"Conan kept getting into trouble with the law in Glengad. Little things, mainly fights or stealing a few pennies' worth of goods. But when Da got sick and we couldn't pay the rent, we asked for mercy from the land agent. The land agent gave us some, I suppose. He didn't evict us until after Da died—on the day we buried him."

Leaden weights formed in Isaac's stomach, and a lump climbed in his throat. Losing his pa had been hard, but he couldn't imagine losing his home on the same day he buried his father. He blinked away the burning sensation pricking his eyes and reached for Aileen's hand. She'd faced more hardships in the past two years than most people did in an entire lifetime.

"That night Conan stole money from the land agent, enough for us to buy passage here." Her voice wobbled. "I know it was wrong, but it seemed like there was no other choice. Still, I made him promise to change, to not do anything illegal once we got to America, but..."

"But now your brother's dead and your cousin is walking in his steps," he finished for her. He wasn't quite sure how they'd started talking about her brother rather than Morley. Having information about the illegal things Morley had done would be more helpful than knowing of Conan's misdeeds.

But he wouldn't ask her more now, not when the story so obviously caused her pain. Perhaps in another day or two, if they still hadn't caught the smugglers. "Is that what has you worried, that your cousin will end up in trouble like your brother?"

She blinked once, then a second time before swallowing hard. "Aye... that's what I meant. Morley is following in Conan's ways, even though he promised not to."

He sighed. He couldn't ignore that both Jack and Morley had connections to her. But in a town the size of Eagle Harbor, everyone had connections to everyone else. Still, could the smugglers somehow be using her for information and she didn't realize it? "Is there anything more you can think of?" He tried once more. "A simple piece of information might be all we need to track down the rest of the smugglers."

She looked down, her teeth biting into her bottom lip hard enough it would probably be swollen before she left. "If I knew where they were hiding, I'd tell ye."

"Even if it meant your cousin would go to prison?" He pushed himself off the wall and met her gaze.

"Aye," she whispered. "It's not me fault he started with this whole smuggling business. So I can't rightly be blaming meself if he gets locked up."

But that would mean her only relative in all of America would be behind bars, which couldn't be an easy thing for her to bear, especially not after losing her brother.

"Aileen..." He reached out a hand to touch her cheek, never mind the passersby that might see.

"Sheriff?" Norling appeared between the buildings.

Isaac dropped his hand at the same moment Aileen took a step back from him.

"There you are. Granger said..." Norling paused, his eyes narrowed as he looked between them.

"If ye gentlemen will excuse me, I best be on me way." Head down, Aileen rushed past Norling before escaping onto the street.

Norling's gaze followed Aileen as she left, then he let out a low whistle. "I see why you called Granger to the door. I'd take a break too if it meant I could talk to a woman who looked like her."

Isaac's shoulders tensed, though there was nothing inappropriate in what Norling said. The truth was, Aileen caught the eye of many a man she passed, but considering how she avoided looking at men and shrank into herself whenever one approached, most men never said more than a word or two to her.

"Who is she?" Norling closed the distance between them. "Did she have information about the smugglers?"

"The boy who went missing with his pa this summer? Jack O'Byrne? She's seen him twice. Both times he's stopped by the bakery for food after dark."

Norling rubbed a hand over his jaw. "Looks like we need to keep a closer eye on the bakery then. Maybe we can nab the boy there, then he can lead us to his pa."

"My thoughts exactly."

"There's something more," he muttered. "Something you're not telling me."

Isaac pressed his eyes shut, but no good would come of hiding the truth from Norling. "Her cousin's one of the smugglers."

Norling scowled and looked at the jail wall as though he could see through to the cells inside. "Which one? Did she want to talk to him? Is that why she stopped by?"

"We haven't caught him yet. In fact, she just learned the truth about him now."

"You sure about that?" Norling took a step back from him, suspicion lacing his words. "Could be she's in cahoots with—"

"She was the one who saw the smuggling activity in the alley and reported it. If not for her, I never would have sent the Customs Service that telegram." He blew out a breath and raked a hand through his hair, staring after the spot where Aileen had disappeared onto the road. "Besides, if you'd seen the look in her eyes when she realized what her cousin was up to, you wouldn't doubt me—or her."

"Be careful, Sheriff. Many a man has fallen for a pretty face, only to end up on the wrong end of a smoking gun."

He opened his mouth to tell Norling he was wrong, but the Viking's words held enough truth Isaac couldn't quite deny them.

Chapter Nineteen

She needed to tell Isaac the truth—even the part about Conan.

Aileen kicked at a rock in the road as she approached the bakery. The orange light from the western sun glinted off the white clapboard siding, lengthening the shadows and transforming the color of the walls into an eerie shade.

It had been two days since Isaac told her about Morley being a smuggler. Two long, sleepless days. She probably should have gone to Isaac already and confessed her brother was alive, and that if Morley was smuggling, Conan must be as well. But that meant speaking the words aloud, and she couldn't quite bring herself to do so. It also meant seeing the concern that would fill Isaac's eyes. Or would it be condemnation that she hadn't told him sooner? Then she'd have to answer the questions that were sure to follow.

But not telling Isaac meant she was hiding her brother from the law. And didn't keeping quiet make her just as bad as him?

But could she really watch her brother be locked in a cell, then sent away to face trial in some federal courtroom miles away from Eagle Harbor?

And if Conan was convicted…

Oh, she couldn't live with playing a role in his imprisonment. He might not ever forgive her. Not that she'd be able to see him to know one way or another.

Mayhap this was why Conan had let her think him dead. He must have known that if she found out what he was doing, she'd have to turn him in.

It was decided then. She'd knock on Isaac's door first thing tomorrow and tell him of Conan.

And betray her family.

She sniffled. Hopefully Isaac would understand she'd needed a couple days to think things over before coming to him. A couple of days to get used to the idea that her brother might spend twenty years in prison because of her.

She hung her head and forced her feet to move forward along the side of the bakery. Of all the illegal things to get involved with. Why had Morley and Conan chosen a crime that would get them put behind bars for half their lives?

And why did she have to know about it?

"They're scoundrels, they are," she muttered as she rounded the corner of the bakery and stepped into the alley.

"Who's a scoundrel?"

She slammed to a halt at the sight of the towering blond man standing by her door. "What are ye doing here?"

Deputy Norling's clear blue eyes were cold enough to turn the harbor to ice despite the summer weather. "I think you know."

"I don't." But she hardly wanted to talk to a lawman at the moment. Well, at least a lawman who wasn't Isaac.

"I'm here to ask some questions."

"Why?" She took a subtle step back from him. "The sheriff already asked me questions."

"And now I'd like to ask some more," he answered evenly.

She glanced around the alley, with its long shadows and eerie orange light. "Did Isaac send ye?"

The man didn't respond, just looked at her with his cold eyes.

She took another step back. He might be a deputy, aye. But he was also larger than she, larger than just about any man in town besides Mac Oakton. He could overpower her in a second. "I'd prefer to talk to Isaac, thank ye."

The man straightened, which only made him appear bigger. "And I'd prefer to ask you questions without him present."

The breath whooshed from her. Did he somehow know about Conan? "Why?"

"You know why."

"Would ye stop telling me that?" She dug the heel of her shoe into the dirt beneath her feet. "If I knew why ye were skulking about outside me door, I wouldn't waste me breath asking."

"Your cousin, Morley Brogan, is one of the smugglers."

She jolted, his words causing a fleeting stab of pain in her chest. Isaac hadn't sounded quite so accusing when he'd let her know what her cousin was up to. But she'd better get used to that pain in her heart, because the entire town would know of Morley and Conan's actions soon enough.

"I already told Isaac I don't know where Morley is." That was the truth, because Morley could be in Canada at the moment or out on Lake Superior. Just because she'd found Conan near Eagle Harbor didn't mean Morley was with him right now.

Her stomach churned. And here she was coming up with excuses for her wayward family.

"You still might have some useful information." Deputy Norling gestured for her to unlock the back door. "Now let's go inside where we can talk."

It was a simple suggestion, something any lawman would expect of someone he wanted to question. And yet her throat closed, and her feet rooted themselves to the packed dirt of the alley. She couldn't go alone with him into the bakery, but this deputy would hardly understand that.

"I... I'm not working with Morley," she stammered. And she wasn't, but oh how the words burned coming out of her. Not quite a lie, but certainly not the whole truth.

The man still didn't look any closer to leaving. Nay, he stayed planted by the door, in the same spot he'd been since she'd first spotted him, except now his lips twisted into a scowl. "Then why are you stalling?"

Why, indeed?

She drew in a breath. Mayhap it was time she told the truth, every last bit of it. If she told Deputy Norling, then she'd not have to see the look on Isaac's face when he realized just how deeply her family was involved with the smugglers. Nor would she have to answer questions about whether she was all right.

Because she wasn't. How could she be?

But Deputy Norling was all business, from his hard jaw to his cool eyes to the taut set of his shoulders. And somehow that made the task before her easier.

"The door, Miss Brogan?" Deputy Norling jutted his chin toward the locked handle.

She sucked in another breath, long and slow. It would be the first time she was alone with a man other than Isaac. But she'd left Chicago almost a year ago, and she'd not been mistreated once in Eagle Harbor. At some point, she had to stop acting as though every man she met wanted to hurt her. Let alone this deputy, who was only doing his job.

Besides, once she started talking about Conan, she probably wouldn't care who was or wasn't in the room with her.

～.～.～.～.～

Isaac rolled his aching shoulders as he plodded along the side of the bakery. He should probably be home getting a couple hours of sleep before starting patrols. Two straight days of searching the woods for the smugglers' hideout and they still didn't have a notion of where the criminals were camped. Even Norling, with all his experience, hadn't proven much help in the woods.

But it had also been two days since he'd last seen Aileen, and the look in her eyes when she'd realized Morley was involved in illegal activity still haunted his thoughts.

Isaac smothered a yawn as he rounded the corner of the bakery. Hopefully a couple of Aileen's cookies would give him the energy he needed to patrol the town tonight, though he wasn't sure how much longer he and his deputies could keep working so many hours. They searched for smugglers during the day, only to have a small break for dinner before making rounds until the wee hours of the morning.

Isaac headed toward the bakery's kitchen door. Movement flashed inside the window that stood over the sink. Probably just Aileen having an evening cup of tea. He neared the door, only to stop at the sound of voices floating through it, one feminine and one masculine. He placed Aileen's voice instantly, but it took a few more words before he recognized the male one.

What was Norling doing here? The harsh sound of Norling's voice told him this wasn't a pleasant type of call. He knocked once, then thrust the door open. "What's going on?"

Aileen sat at the table, her head hung and shoulders slumped. She looked up at him for a moment, her eyes moist with tears, before she bowed her head again.

"Sheriff." Norling stood with his arms crossed over his chest and a firm set to his jaw. "I'm questioning Miss Brogan about her involvement with the smugglers."

"I told you she has nothing to do with it." Isaac stalked toward Norling.

Norling snorted. "She might not be a smuggler, but she's more tangled in this than you want to admit."

"Surely you don't plan to accuse her of smuggling simply because her cousin is involved." Isaac crossed his arms over his chest to match Norling's.

"It's more than just her cousin." Norling shifted his gaze to Aileen, accusation dripping from his words. "But she probably hasn't told you that part, has she?"

No, he refused to believe it. Yet his throat felt dry and scratchy as he turned to look at her. "Aileen? What's he talking about?"

"I should have told ye sooner, but…" She ducked her head and traced a pattern on the wooden table.

He moved toward her, his footsteps sounding overly loud in the otherwise silent kitchen. "Is it Jack? Do you know something more about him? I told you to get me if he—"

"'Tis me brother." The words shot out of her mouth in a rush. "Conan. He's… he's… alive. In the woods."

Isaac took a step backward, as though a barrel full of copper had just rolled into his chest. The force of the invisible blow caused the bakery kitchen to tilt a moment before righting itself again. "Your brother is alive?"

Why hadn't she said anything to him?

"I told you I needed to question her." Norling's words were quiet, but they held a determined edge. "Ask where she found him. We've been searching the wrong part of the woods for the smugglers."

"Found him?" He swallowed again, his mind scrambling to keep up with the information.

Aileen kept her head down, her rich, fiery hair making a curtain between her and him. "I thought he was dead. I was told he died in Chicago before I started working for Gilbert. Before I came here."

"How long have you known he's alive?" he rasped. Maybe she'd just found out yesterday, or even a few hours ago, and hadn't had a chance to tell him yet.

"The night I disappeared and Rebekah had ye search for me. Before Mr. Norling arrived in town." She wrung her hands together atop the table so fiercely she might well break one of her fingers. "I was hiking up to the bluffs and got distracted on the way back, taking a different path than normal. I came upon a man in the woods. At first I thought he meant me harm, but there was something familiar about him."

"And you didn't tell me." The words wrenched from him, anger and pain and disappointment all wrapped together. She'd known about her brother for two weeks.

"He told me not to." She sniffled and looked up, her eyes rimmed with red and cheeks streaked with tears. "Told me what he was doing was dangerous, but that he'd be done in the fall."

"Let me guess, when shipping season ended." His words sounded as though they'd been grated against crushed mine rock.

"I didn't know what he was about. I didn't know there were smugglers or that ye were looking for them, or I might have put things together."

"Put things together? I asked you if Jack or Morley had said anything at all that might hint as to where the hideout was, and you said you didn't know anything."

"Nay, I said I didn't know where they were hiding, and I don't. I only know where I found Conan in the woods, and there wasn't a hideout nearby."

"But you didn't volunteer that information." He saw it now, how she justified the deception in her mind. He'd asked if there was any other clue he was missing, and she'd distracted him by answering a different question entirely. *If I knew where they were hiding, I'd tell you.* But that's not what he'd wanted to know. And she'd certainly had a clue she could have given him—had she wished to.

Isaac clenched his jaw and blinked away the burning behind his eyes. How much else had she kept from him? Was she withholding more information even now? Did she know where the smugglers were but didn't want to say?

Here he'd been entertaining notions of a future with her, a woman who couldn't bother to be honest with him.

"I have work I need to do. Tell everything you know to Norling." He didn't have the stomach to sit and hear more. Besides, he clearly wasn't the best person to get information from her. Norling could update him later, in that detached, monotonous tone he used when giving facts and information.

Because that was what he needed things boiled down to if he was going to catch the smugglers: facts and information, not his traitorous feelings.

"Isaac, wait." Aileen hurried from her chair. "I'm telling the truth."

"Sure you are." He stalked toward the door.

"Don't ye believe me?" She trailed after him.

He paused, hand on the doorknob, and turned to face her. "I don't know anymore, but I promise you this. If you do know more about the smugglers, and you don't tell Norling, I've got a cell with your name on it down at the jail. Hiding criminal activity is just as illegal as participating in it yourself."

He should have looked away sooner. Or maybe he should have opened the door and walked through it without stopping to hear what she had to say. Because ignoring her would be better than looking into moss green eyes that were filled with hurt. Hurt *he'd* put there.

But then, he reckoned his gaze was as hurt as hers, maybe even more so.

He forced himself through the door and shut it with a click. Norling's voice started on more questions a moment later, but Isaac simply stood there, shoulders slumped and head down as the orange hues of sunset spread across the sky and the peepers and crickets started their evening song. He'd been warned not to get involved with Aileen Brogan from the beginning. But now...

Oh dear God, please protect this town. Please give me wisdom. The last thing he needed was to fail in his role as sheriff because he'd been distracted by a beautiful woman.

And if that beautiful woman had a sincere voice and honest eyes? If she truly was sorry she hadn't told him about her brother, and if she didn't have any more information about the smugglers?

No, none of it mattered. What mattered was that she'd not been honest with him... yet somehow he'd been fool enough to give her his heart anyway.

Chapter Twenty

Ellie yawned and blinked her tired eyes as she pulled a strawberry pie from the oven and set it on the kitchen counter beside the tray of muffins. A thin trickle of fresh air wafted through the window, but the heat from the blazing oven beat it back. She used the hem of her apron to wipe her brow, then took a fork and prodded the first muffin from the tray.

The bell above the storefront door jangled, and she stilled. Could it be Jake? It was just the right time for him to stop by with a pair of roast beef sandwiches.

Except he hadn't stopped by for an entire week, not since the night Leroy and Martin had gotten caught with the smugglers.

He'd stolen her away from her vat of boiling wash only the night before to attend Tressa Oakton's birthday party. It had taken him less than a minute to convince Rebekah Sinclair to hold Lynnette, and then Jake had whisked her onto the packed sand and danced with her for four straight songs. Four wonderful songs. Had she imagined the look in his eye when he bent close and whispered that the sunset was the same color as her hair? Or when he stroked a strand of that same hair behind her ear and told her she was a good dancer?

"Hello? Ellie? Are you in there?"

Ellie straightened at the sound of the feminine voice, a sure sign

Jake wasn't the one waiting for her. She wiped her hands on her apron and headed through the swinging doors into the storefront.

Rebekah Sinclair looked up from where she stood studying the baked goods, the expensive fabric of her fitted dress contrasting with the plain wooden shelves and whitewashed walls of the storefront. "I was hoping you had a strawberry pie, but I don't see any."

"I just pulled one out of the oven."

Rebekah sent her a smile so bright Ellie almost found herself smiling back—almost. "Great! I'm hoping there'll be something to celebrate in about an hour, and Gilbert loves your pies." She glanced around the empty shop, then gave her another of those bright smiles. "You should close up and come down to the beach for a half hour or so. Gilbert is going to test one of his inventions. It'll be fun to watch."

"I need to stay and work."

Rebekah blinked. "But everyone will be down at the beach. You won't get any business."

Maybe so, but she'd still lose a half hour of work. "Maybe next time." She ducked back into the kitchen and returned with the pie.

"Have you seen how Mr. Foley's new wagon is coming?" Rebekah dug into her reticule and pulled out a bill. "I was just at the mercantile, and your brothers are doing a great job with it."

She shook her head. She hadn't even broached the subject with her brothers since their court date three days ago. The judge had ordered them to serve four months of labor, one month for each person whose property they'd damaged, plus a month for the sheriff. They'd started working for the Foleys' yesterday.

"See you later." Rebekah handed her a five-dollar bill. Taking the pie in both hands, she dashed toward the door at a pace that clashed with her expensive-looking dress.

"Don't you want your change?" Ellie called.

"Keep it. I've got to go before I miss something." And with that

Rebekah was gone, the door slamming shut behind her.

"Have fun," she muttered, then turned back to the empty bakery just as her stomach growled... for a roast beef sandwich.

Which was ridiculous, because she hadn't eaten one of Jake's uppity sandwiches for a week. There was no reason to mope because Jake wasn't here. His parents would never approve of them courting anyway.

Still, would it be too much of a bother for him to stop by and see how she was doing after the ordeal with her brothers? He'd shown her such kindness last week when he'd arrived with lunch, taken her away from the laundry, smiled and laughed and danced with her. Was there anything wrong with wanting some of that same kindness now?

Oh, she should have known not to let her imagination go free concerning Jake. She wasn't Rebekah Sinclair. She didn't have the kind of life where handsome, rich men swept in, fell in love, and solved all her problems.

No, she had the kind of life where mothers got sick, fathers disappeared, and brothers died and got tangled up with criminals.

~.~.~.~.~

Boom. Boom. Boom. Isaac lowered his pistol and squinted at the metal target swinging with the impact of his shots. Even from where he stood ten yards back, he could make out the perfect grouping of three in the center of the paper he'd tacked to the target. He should have no trouble taking down an assailant at close range. In fact, his aim with a pistol was deadly enough to defend himself even at a bit of a distance.

He holstered his gun and rolled his shoulders, tight from nearly an hour of shooting, but sore shoulders were well worth knowing he could defend himself—and others. He turned and grabbed his rifle he'd practiced with earlier, not that he really expected to be carrying it the next time he confronted the smugglers. But being a good shot never hurt anyone, especially a sheriff.

Above, the bright blue of the sky peeked through the deep green leaves shading the yard. Past Elijah's house, the calm waters of Lake Superior stretched endlessly, a deeper blue than the sky. If only the waves weren't so deceptively deadly.

But lately, the water didn't seem nearly as menacing as the danger that the smugglers posed. It had been a week since they'd captured the men on the beach, yet despite days and days of searching, they hadn't found a single clue that would lead them to the rest of the criminals. From hearing the smugglers in the jail talk, there were maybe half a dozen men left in Eagle Harbor, and another half dozen or so that moved between Eagle Harbor and Canada. If he and his deputies could catch the ones that remained here, would that put a big enough dent in the group to stop the smuggling for good?

If only he could find a way to catch all the men together at once. But at the moment, he and his men couldn't seem to find much of anything. Elijah hadn't seen anything suspicious out fishing, the nightly patrols had yielded nothing more than an occasional bar fight, and daily searches through the woods had only exhausted him and his deputies.

The men from the Customs Service had stayed in town for two days, helping search the woods. But when they hadn't found the smugglers right away, they'd transported the prisoners to southern Michigan, where those men would await trial in a federal court.

Had the uncaught smugglers moved on as well? Packed up the goods they were storing near town and set up somewhere else on the coast of Lake Superior?

Hopefully not. Norling had stayed in Eagle Harbor, though his cover as a deputy was gone, hoping to catch the remaining smugglers before they fled. But how to find them? Even the hill leading to the bluffs where Aileen had seen her brother had yielded nothing, and they'd scoured the area twice.

According to Norling, Aileen hadn't seen her cousin or her brother once in the past five days. And he'd little choice but to go by what Norling said, seeing how he hadn't seen Aileen since that evening in the bakery.

Not that he wanted to see her. What was the point? He swallowed the thickness that rose in his throat whenever Aileen Brogan came to mind. She'd been clear from the beginning that she wasn't interested in any type of romantic relationship.

And he'd been the fool who hadn't listened.

His gaze drifted to the rambling log house where he'd grown up. Was it so much to want what his parents once had? So much to want a wife to share coffee with in the morning, dinner in the evening, and a bed at night? So much to want children's laughter and shrieks echoing through his home?

Evidently so, if he expected to share it with Aileen.

He headed across the patchy grass toward the winding drive, then followed the dusty path that slithered through the woods before turning onto North Street. The Pretty Penny bar and brothel sat just on the outskirts of Eagle Harbor. Then there was the livery, the Rusty Wagon, the empty lot where the seamstress shop had once sat, the telegraph office, and the mercantile.

He slowed as he reached his office, then narrowed his eyes. There was a commotion of some sort on the beach where a crowd had gathered. Was that Norling standing there, and Rebekah beside him?

He stowed his rifle in his apartment, then tromped down to the beach. He shouldered past several onlookers before coming to a stop between Victoria and Rebekah at the edge of the water. "What's going on?"

His sister-in-law kept her eyes riveted on the harbor. "I c-can't believe it's actually working."

"I was hoping it would. Gilbert seemed rather confident about it," Rebekah muttered on his other side.

"The man's already built a crane to use on the docks down in Chicago." Lindy Harrington rested a hand on her protruding stomach. "I wouldn't underestimate any of his ideas."

Isaac squinted at the water, where a dinghy glided over the waves, fast and smooth. But that wasn't how a dinghy usually moved, even with experienced rowers. "Gilbert's out there testing some new idea?"

His stomach dipped. *Dear God, please let it be a safe idea.* The familiar wide-brimmed hats of the other two people aboard told him Mac and Elijah were with him.

"Not just a new idea." Rebekah gripped his wrist and looked at him, her eyes shining. "Gilbert found a way to put an engine on the back of the boat!"

He frowned. "You mean like a steamer engine, but on a dinghy?" Was such a thing possible? And given that ships had been using steam engines for a while, maybe the idea wasn't all that dangerous.

Rebekah shook her head, wisps of auburn hair the same color as his twisting in the breeze. "No, not like a steamer. It uses fuel oil to make energy. Gilbert calls it an internal combustion engine. Listen. Can't you hear the hum over the water?"

He tried to close out the chatter of the townsfolk while opening his ears to the water. A constant low buzzing sound greeted him. He blinked at the boat again. Could the engine go faster than a boat at full sail? If so, then trips to towns like Houghton and Ontonagon would be both quicker and simpler.

Except suddenly, the humming over the water wasn't constant. The buzz died for a minute, then started again, then died a second time. And was the boat sitting lower in the water?

221

Elijah's, Mac's, and Gilbert's frantic movements aboard the dinghy only confirmed what his heart already knew. The boat was going under.

His skin turned clammy and an iron band clamped around his chest, yet he found his feet racing toward the *North Star* sitting on the beach, his shoes pounding against the soft sand despite the fear bursting in his belly.

"I'm coming too." Rebekah's voice sounded from behind him, followed by the hurried thumping of her footsteps.

Fletcher was already at the *North Star* shoving the sailboat into the water. Waves lapped at Isaac's trousers as he jumped aboard, followed by Rebekah, who somehow managed to land on the deck just as easily as he had despite the long skirt of her fancy dress. Fletcher hopped aboard next, and Norling barreled toward them, splashing into the water and hauling himself onto the boat just as the sand slipped away beneath them.

With his gaze riveted to the swimmers making their way to shore, Isaac strode to the mast and took hold of the mainsail's rigging. The sails filled with wind and the bow turned toward the center of the harbor. Everything came back to him so easily, the feel of the rigging in his hand, the sunlight slanting onto the deck, the burst of wind that propelled the boat forward. It was almost as though the years slipped away to a time when sailing had been fun and carefree.

Almost, but the rapid thumping of his heart was new, as was the sweat slicking his hands and brow. His brothers and Gilbert made swimming to shore look effortless, moving through the water so nimbly they might all be half fish. But Pa's death proved a person could drown at any time, no matter how strong a swimmer.

Rebekah appeared beside him, an impatient look on her face. "Give this to me, or we'll miss them by a mile." She snatched the rigging from him. "I can tell you haven't sailed for years."

She called to Fletcher at the foresail before cutting the mackinaw closer to their brothers and Gilbert. The little boat the swimmers had been riding in was completely submerged. Not even an odd ripple marred the surface of the harbor over where the dinghy had disappeared. But each swell of the water over the swimmers took him back to the day the waves had washed over Pa. Four waves, that's how many times Pa had come back up before the fifth had taken him under.

It probably took minutes, but it felt like hours before Rebekah and Fletcher tightened the sails, slowing the boat.

Norling threw the anchor into the water, and Isaac rushed to the side of the boat, a rope in his hand. But Mac had already gripped the side and was pulling himself up.

"Thanks." Mac tumbled over the gunwale and landed in a sopping heap on the deck. "Would have been a long swim back to shore."

Isaac extended a hand and pulled his adopted brother up.

Mac looked around the boat and smiled.

Smiled. As though his life hadn't just been in danger.

Elijah was next, climbing into the boat on his own while refusing help from Norling. He shook the water from his hair and showed off a grin even wider than Mac's.

What was wrong with them? Weren't they the least bit concerned about drowning? Isaac threw a rope to Gilbert and hauled him over the side. But Rebekah, Norling, and Fletcher didn't seem overly concerned about the swimmers' safety either. In fact, the whole lot of them were grinning.

"You're a genius." Norling slapped Gilbert on the back. "You put an engine on a dinghy. Who would have thought?"

"It was too heavy." Gilbert looked back to the patch of water where the boat had gone down. "I thought if we could achieve greater speed with the motor, the weight of the engine wouldn't be of much concern. But having all the weight concentrated in the stern still posed a problem."

"Sounds about right." Mac held his hand above his eyes to shield the sun, then surveyed the empty harbor.

"Next time we'll leave Mac ashore and then the boat won't go under." Elijah thumped Mac on the shoulder.

Next time? Isaac clenched his jaw. Had the cold water caused Elijah to go daft? There wasn't going to be a next time. There should have never been a first time.

Gilbert rubbed his temple. "We'll get a six-horsepower engine and try—"

"How could you? All of you?" The words bubbled from his throat, dark and angry. He whirled to face Gilbert. "Are you trying to get everyone killed?"

Before Gilbert could answer, Isaac balled his hand and let it fly toward his brother-in-law's temple. His fist connected with a sickening thunk. Gilbert flew back into Mac, his eyes shut and body slumped. He would have slid to the bottom of the boat next, but Mac grabbed him and held him upright.

"Isaac!" Rebekah rushed to her husband, but sent a fiery glare over her shoulder.

"What are you doing?" Elijah's terse words rang out over the boat.

Isaac turned to face his brother, his fists still clenched. "And you helped him. Went along with Gilbert's crazy idea without any care that it might kill you."

He let his fist fly toward his brother's face, but Elijah was ready, blocking the punch with his arm. Scrambling sounded behind him, and before he could loose another punch, someone gripped his arms, pinning them from behind and yanking him away from Elijah.

"You planning to get yourself locked up in the one of those cells you're in charge of?" Fletcher's voice echoed in his ear.

"No, I'm planning to lock them up for being stupid." Isaac jutted his chin toward Elijah, Mac, and Gilbert.

"I'm a good swimmer." Elijah shook out the arm he'd just used to block the punch. "We all are. Nothing would have happened, even if we ended up swimming the whole way to shore."

"You think Pa thought something was going to happen the last time he took this boat out?" Isaac shouted the words, echoing over the water to where everyone on the beach could probably hear them. But he didn't care. How could he when Elijah was so very cavalier about losing his life? "Pa was probably just like you that day, thinking he could swim to shore if something went wrong. I bet he saw the storm in the distance and had plenty of time to get back to harbor, but he wanted to get one last net. So he stayed out longer than he should have, probably saying the same thing as you, 'I can swim to shore if something happens.'"

"It was four years ago." Rebekah rose from Gilbert's side, a measured calmness coating her words. "Whatever happened that day, we can't go back and change it. The details don't matter."

"They do when it's my fault he died." The words rasped from his mouth. His father's death was his fault, and he couldn't go back and change it, no matter how much he wanted to.

─.─.─.─.─

Thunk. Thunk. Thunk.

Isaac looked up from where he sat at his desk in his office, pouring over maps of the coast. Not that spending the past hour hunched in the same position had done any good. Smugglers could only run cargo one place along the coast between Eagle Harbor and Eagle River, and they were already watching it.

Thunk. Thunk.

"Come in," Isaac called as he rubbed at the inner corners of his eyebrows, where his muscles were tightening into a headache.

Elijah stood in the doorway, his body blocking the afternoon sun.

Of course it would be Elijah. His older brother wasn't the type to ignore an outburst like the one on the boat earlier. Isaac shifted in his chair. Maybe he should have found somewhere else to study the maps—like a cave in the forest. "I take it the doc said you could go home."

Elijah shrugged. "It was a swim, that's all. I only went to the doc's to keep Victoria happy."

But it wasn't just a swim. Isaac pressed his lips together. Why did his brother have so much trouble admitting the danger he'd been in? "And Mac's just as fine as you?"

At least the men had sense enough to see the doctor afterward, even if they all grumbled about it.

"Right as rain." Elijah leaned against the doorway, his movement sending a shaft of sun across the floor of the office.

And Gilbert? Isaac looked down. Maybe he shouldn't have punched Gilbert quite so hard—though the man had certainly deserved a good fist to his skull. "How's Gilbert's head?"

Elijah winced. "Nothing that won't heal. Pretty sure Rebekah intends to give you bruises bigger than Gilbert's the next time she sees you though." Elijah pushed off the doorframe and stepped fully inside, then closed the door behind him. "Have a few minutes?"

Isaac blew out a breath. He could say no, but what was the point? After everything he'd blurted on the boat, Elijah would just track him down tomorrow. "Have a seat."

"Wondered if I'd ever see you on a boat again." Elijah settled into the chair across from his desk. "It was good of you to sail on our behalf, though you looked a bit sick before you hauled off and punched Gilbert."

"Only over the thought that you or Mac or Gilbert would drown." Isaac clenched his jaw, causing his words to come out hard and terse. "I suppose that was stronger than the rest of it."

"The rest of what?" Elijah's words were gentle, but his eyes had that probing quality to them, the one that said he could read nearly every thought in his brother's head. "Are you that fearful you'll drown if you stick a toe in the water?"

If only his trouble was as simple as deciding he wasn't going to be afraid anymore. "Water and storms give me nervous fits."

Elijah grew quiet, thoughts churning behind his somber gray eyes. "Like... like a woman who needs smelling salts and a fainting couch?"

Isaac clenched his hands into fists under his desk. "Yes. No. I don't know, because I don't know what those women feel like when they faint." Though surely his situation was different. Surely not every woman who fainted had once seen her father drown. "My heart, it races so hard you'd think I had run ten miles without stopping. And sweat soaks my hands and forehead and chest every time. I can't stop the memories of Pa and the storm either. Can't stop myself from feeling the horror all over again.

"Or rather, I'm trying to stop it." Isaac swallowed the thickness in his throat. "I've been working on controlling the attacks. But for the longest time, the thought of being on a boat or you going out during a storm, brought them on."

"They come with every single storm?" Elijah leaned back in his chair. Was his brother thinking back to the number of storms they'd had over the past four years? The number of nervous fits that would mean?

"At first they came more often than that. With just a glimpse of the water, my chest would be drenched with sweat. But they're waning now, at least most of them. They still come whenever you're on a rescue, and I don't know that I'll ever be able to change that. But the other parts of it, the storms without rescues, or me going on a boat... well..." Isaac rubbed the back of his neck. "I've been going out in the *North Star* a bit at night, getting myself used to the feel of being on the water again."

Elijah slapped a hand on the arm of his chair. "So you're the one who's been in the boat. Here I thought Rebekah was going on midnight sails with Gilbert."

Isaac grimaced. "Should've realized you'd know someone was in your boat."

"I've known all along you didn't like the rescues. Why didn't you tell me the rest of it?"

Isaac shrugged. Why indeed? "The fits aren't exactly something I'm proud of."

"Mayhap not, but they might not be all that unusual. I worry about you too. The night after you caught the smugglers, after Fletcher told me how you nearly got yourself killed rescuing the Spritzer boys..." Elijah stuck a finger in his collar and tugged. "I know your life is ultimately in God's hands, but I was the one who suggested you run for sheriff, thinking you'd do nothing more than patrol the bars and jail an occasional thief. But now that you're tracking down smugglers..." Elijah's throat worked. "It's hard knowing I can't do much to protect you. And I realize it's unfair of me to say that considering I've spent four years telling you not to worry about my rescues."

With a lump rising in his throat, Isaac sat back and surveyed Elijah. Was this his brother's way of apologizing for all the arguments they'd gotten into? All the times Elijah had been unreasonable when he'd pointed out the obvious dangers of leading a life-saving team? If not, at least Elijah seemed willing to forge a truce. "I... thank you. I didn't expect you to understand, but knowing that you do—helps... somewhat."

"I should have thought about things from your side a little more." Elijah's voice was soft. "But while we're being honest, there's another thing I should tell you. I've never believed you were at fault for Pa's death. And I mean that."

Isaac pressed his eyes shut and sighed. Of all the things, why did Elijah have to bring this up when they were so close to reaching an understanding? "I should have been on the lake with him that day, and I wasn't."

The words poured from him then, the whole story of the day Pa died with nothing held back. Elijah didn't know how he'd stayed up late studying for law school the night before, then begged off heading to the boat in the morning. Elijah didn't even know he'd wanted to go to law school.

"And so I told Rebekah not to get the dinghy. I held her there, in the lighthouse tower, with Mac taking her other arm, and refused to even try to save Pa." Isaac stared down at his hands clenched into fists atop his desk and gritted his teeth. Elijah would never understand the frustrating feeling of standing by and watching someone he loved die. Would never understand the helplessness that had burrowed into his soul and carved out a hollow chamber.

Because had Elijah been in Eagle Harbor, he would have tried to save Pa.

Isaac brought his gaze up to meet his brother's for the briefest of instants before looking away. But an instant was all it took for the haunted, somber look in Elijah's eyes to climb inside his brain and lodge itself next to the memory of waves crashing over Pa.

"I'll tell you the same thing I told Mac when I returned home, the same thing I wrestled with those first two months." Elijah blew out a breath hard enough to rival the wind gusting over Lake Superior during a storm. "Pa's death was God's plan. I don't understand it, and if it were up to me, I'd choose to still have Pa with us. But the truth is, if there's anyone to blame for what happened that day, it's not yourself, but God, because God could have saved Pa, and He didn't."

Isaac sat back and blinked. Of all the thoughts that had run through his head regarding Pa's death, blaming God had never been one of them.

But he didn't have nearly so much trouble blaming himself. "It was like salt in a wound, you coming home and starting that rescue team. It flung all my failures back in my face. Why did you ever leave? If you'd stayed, maybe Pa would have... Maybe we'd have worked together that day, and Pa would still..."

"I thought about that for a while too, but if I'd stayed, I'd have never seen the U.S. Life-Saving Service stations on the Atlantic. I wouldn't have had the first clue how to rescue Pa. And if Pa wouldn't have died, I might not have come back to Eagle Harbor. Then I wouldn't have Victoria in my life, or the O'Byrne children. I never would've started the life-saving team, and all fifty-one of the lives I've saved since then would have been lost."

Fifty-one? A knot climbed into Isaac's throat. Was the number really so high? He'd never claim to understand all of how God worked, and he missed his pa something fierce. But what if his brother was right? What if Pa needed to die so others could live? What if there'd been a purpose in Pa's death far bigger than he'd understood? Far bigger than he'd wanted to understand until now?

Footsteps sounded on the porch outside, the clomping filling the otherwise silent office. He turned toward the door just as Rebekah burst inside.

Isaac held up his hands. "I'm sorry about punching—"

"Where's Aileen?" Rebekah's gaze skittered frantically around the office, her chest heaving. "Tell me she's here with you."

Isaac stood, the legs of his chair scraping against the floor. "No. I haven't seen her since…" *Since five nights ago, when I learned she'd been hiding her brother's whereabouts from me.* "I don't know where she is."

Rebekah's face drained of color. "Do you have a guess? Any idea where she might be?"

"Maybe the woods." *Visiting her brother.* Aileen had said she wouldn't do that, but he had no way of knowing for sure.

Rebekah whirled on her heel and strode back toward the door. "Warren just came in on one of his ships, and I have to warn her."

"Warren Sinclair? Gilbert's brother?" Elijah pushed himself to stand.

"What does he have to do with Aileen?" Isaac frowned.

Rebekah paused in the doorway and turned back, her eyes narrowed at him. "I thought Aileen told you what happened in Chicago."

"She did, but—"

"But if you need to ask about Warren, then she obviously didn't tell you the whole of it." The words flew like darts from Rebekah's mouth. She stood staring at him for a moment, her eyes fierce, as though expecting him to somehow know what she was…

Wait. Aileen may have told him what happened in Chicago, but she'd never said who'd forced her. He stumbled around the side of his desk. "Is Warren the one?"

The tears that blurred his sister's eyes gave him all the answer he needed.

"I really thought you knew," her voice trembled.

"She didn't tell me who hurt her, only that someone had." Rage swirled through him as an image of Gilbert's cold and calculating older brother filled his mind. Angelically blond hair, blue eyes colder than the harbor ice in January, and a cruel smile on his thin lips. "What do you mean Warren's here? Isn't he locked up in prison for the rest of his life for what he did?"

"She wouldn't go to the police to report what happened, and I can't blame her. It would have been her word against Warren's. The police never would have believed her."

Isaac clenched his jaw together until his teeth ached. The vile man who'd mistreated Aileen was supposed to be locked behind bars for good, never to see the light of day again. "So she didn't see justice done."

"It's more complicated than that." Rebekah raised her chin. "If Aileen had gone to the police, can you imagine the trial? What woman wants to sit before a judge and publicly declare herself ruined? She'd have lost her job, and any hope of employment, and the jury probably would've found Warren innocent because people like the Sinclairs don't get put in prison like everybody else. You should know this. You watched them get a free pass for things in Eagle Harbor all your life. Chicago isn't any different. Warren just got acquitted on a rape charge down there last week."

Isaac blinked away the burning behind his own eyes, though whether it was from rage or sorrow, he couldn't say—and he didn't have time to figure it out. "And now Warren is in town?"

"That's why I came here asking if you knew where she was." Rebekah looked over her shoulder at the street outside. "She's not at the hotel or bakery."

Isaac's heart thudded against his chest. "Then we need to find her... before Warren does."

Dear God, please help us find her. His heart might be aching over her deception, but as sheriff, he wasn't going to let any woman in this town get hurt if he could help it.

And as a man nearly in love, he'd lay down his life before he'd let the woman he cared for suffer violence again.

Chapter Twenty-One

Aileen wiped the dust rag over the top of the wrought iron bed frame. Light filtered in from the windows at the two ends of the attic, causing the cloud of dust to glimmer in the low evening sunlight.

She tucked her nose against her shoulder in an effort to stave off a sneeze. With the hotel cleaned and most of the furniture replaced, it would be ready to open in a few weeks. But this was the first time she'd come up to the attic to look at where she'd be staying—hopefully with Brenna and her wee ones.

If only she could close her eyes, wish them here, and then open her eyes to find them standing before her.

Her shoulders slumped as she looked around the long, narrow room that would easily fit Brenna's brood. She could almost see the children tucked into beds, almost hear their giggles and sniffles and excited shouts. But there'd been no word of them from Ireland.

She sniffled—from the dust, of course—and turned back to the bed. If she worked quickly enough, she might be able to finish the attic tonight. Because cleaning late was certainly better than returning to the bakery, where her thoughts were sure to wander back to a certain sheriff with unruly auburn hair, a lopsided smile, and concerned eyes.

A sheriff who hadn't looked at her once while she'd been on the beach today. Never mind that he'd only been standing two people away while they watched Elijah, Mac, and Gilbert in the dinghy. Never mind that she'd remained on shore waiting for the North Star to return while most of the townsfolk disbanded after seeing the swimmers pulled into the boat.

He'd glanced her direction once, then deliberately turned away from her.

And she was a fool for being bothered by it, because as she'd told him all along, he was better off without her. She took the rag and attacked the dust collected on the bottom rung of the bed frame. She'd meant what she'd told him the evening of Tressa's party. She wasn't worthy of him, and there were better women to pursue.

So why did his ignoring her hurt so much?

When he learned about Conan, he'd said she deceived him, but she'd never intended that. The day Isaac told her that Morley was involved in smuggling, she'd hardly been in a mood to mention her brother.

She sniffled again. Confound it all, work was supposed to have distracted her enough to keep her tears at bay.

"Well, well, if it isn't Aileen Brogan, the bonny lass from Ireland."

Aileen froze at the sound of the silky, masculine voice. Nay, it couldn't be…

Footsteps echoed behind her, the crisp, sharp sound of expensive shoes. A cold dread rose in her chest. Then the steps stopped, and the scent of familiar, overpriced cologne filled the air around her.

Her stomach churned, and a bubble of nausea swelled into her throat.

Warren Sinclair had come to Eagle Harbor.

"I've missed you." Warren's hot breath puffed against the side of her neck.

She swallowed the nausea and turned, placing a hand to her neck, where her skin burned as though he'd struck her rather than breathed on her.

She'd forgotten how handsome he was, with his light blond hair perfectly combed, his high cheekbones and strong jaw, his eyes the color of a clear summer sky.

Eyes that had haunted her nightmares for the past year.

Eyes that now looked at her as though she were a piece of meat to be devoured.

She raised her chin and forced a strength to her voice that belied the trembling in her hands. "I don't know why ye're here, but ye need to leave."

Warren chuckled, the sound quiet but mocking. "I came to visit my brother, of course. But there's nothing wrong with a man seeking pleasure while visiting family, is there?"

"Pleasure?" She spat the word and took a step back from him. "There's nothing pleasurable about ye. Now I said leave."

"I will… eventually." He took a step forward.

She took another step back, causing the back of her skirt to brush against the dusty bed.

Warren's gaze roved slowly down her, then back up again, before a grin spread across his face. "Get on the bed."

Blood roared in her ears and her heart hammered against her chest. How many times had she heard those words last year? How many times had she complied simply because doing so was easier than fighting? How many times had she refused to fight because she'd had no hope of winning?

But she wasn't alone and helpless anymore. "If ye force me, I'll report ye to the law." The words tumbled out, as hot and jagged as lightning slashing from the sky.

Warren only leaned close and laughed, his breath warming her cheeks. "It'll be your word against mine. You think the law will believe you?"

She glared into Warren's deceptively handsome face. "Aye." Because the law in Eagle Harbor was Isaac Cummings, and though he might not think too highly of her at the moment, he'd still do right by her. "Ye're not in Chicago. Ye'll be put on trial here and locked away for a long time, ye will."

A muscle clenched and unclenched at the side of his jaw. "If you report me to the sheriff, that means the entire town will find out what kind of woman you are. And you can't have that, can you?"

She gathered the spittle in her mouth and let it fly at his face.

Hardness flashed in his eyes, and he wiped the spit off his cheek with a harsh flick. Then he raised his hand and let it fly toward her.

The sound of skin meeting skin echoed through the narrow room, and pain sliced through her face. She tried to stifle her sob, but a cry escaped.

"Take a step away from Miss Brogan," a strong voice resonated through the attic.

Warren turned, shifting enough that she could glimpse the door. Isaac stood there, his pistol trained on Warren, while Rebekah, Gilbert, and Elijah crowded the top of the stairwell behind him.

She pressed a hand to her cheek and took a step away from Warren, then Rebekah jostled her way past Isaac and barreled toward her.

"Are you all right?" Rebekah's lean arms wound around her.

"Aye." Or she would be once her nerves settled.

Elijah and Gilbert came up and took Warren by the arms.

"You can't arrest me for talking to a woman!" Warren tried to yank himself free.

Isaac holstered his gun and pulled handcuffs from his belt. "I'm arresting you for assaulting a woman, which you did when you slapped Miss Brogan." His jaw was firm, his voice deep and grim, and his forehead furrowed into angry lines. She'd never seen him look so foreboding before, not even when he'd threatened to put her in jail if she hid information about Conan.

He looked at her for a moment, and the hardness left his eyes, replaced with the familiar look of concern she'd come to know so well. He shifted his attention back to Warren then, but warmth spiraled through her, and gratefulness, and contentment, and a jumble of other emotions she didn't quite understand.

But one thing she understood perfectly: she was safe tonight— and Isaac Cummings was the reason.

~.~.~.~.~

Isaac took the key Gilbert had given him and unlocked the hotel door before slipping inside and relocking the door behind him. The place was dark, but the lamplight shining through the attic windows outside had told him Aileen and Rebekah were still upstairs.

How dare Warren Sinclair come to this town and try to take advantage of a woman? Of Aileen? And the man had sought her out just minutes after he got off his boat.

Isaac dashed up the stairs, his feet pumping as hard as his blood, while rage pulsed through him. Warren had protested being thrown into jail, of course, but if the man had free rein of the town, he'd cause trouble. Slapping Aileen provided him just enough reason to keep Warren locked up.

First thing tomorrow, he'd escort Warren to his ship, which was leaving at dawn. He'd agreed to drop the assault charges in exchange for Warren leaving. As much as he might itch to see the man stand before a judge, the penalty for assault paled in comparison to having Warren paying his bail and staying in town until his court date. Hopefully Aileen would understand.

He took the stairs to the attic two at a time. "Hello, Aileen, Rebekah? Are you up there?"

"I'm still cleaning." Aileen's voice filtered over to him as he reached the top of the steps.

At the sight of her sweeping the far side of the attic, something hard fisted in his chest.

What if he'd been fifteen minutes later the last time he'd climbed these stairs?

What if he'd failed Aileen tonight the way he'd failed his father?

He squeezed his eyes shut and drew in a long, calming breath. The truth was, he'd stopped a tragedy from happening, and he was doing all he could to make sure Aileen would stay safe for as long as she was in Eagle Harbor.

But would it be enough?

"Where's Rebekah?" His voice held a raspy edge as he spoke, and he looked around the room.

Aileen attacked one of the corners with her broom, her movements so tense she might as well be using the broom to fend off a pack of hungry wolves. "I sent her home."

She'd done what? He came farther into the room. "You shouldn't be alone right now. Rebekah's probably still awake." It would be impossible for any of them to sleep tonight. "You should stay with her and Gilbert. It won't take long for one of their servants to make up a room for you."

Aileen paused her sweeping and ducked her head, never mind that she already faced away from him. "I know Warren is locked up, but... he knows that house too well. Could find wherever I'm sleeping without any hassle. I just can't..."

She was right, but staying out of the Sinclair mansion wasn't going to keep her any safer. Warren would be able to find Aileen anywhere in Eagle Harbor. The living quarters above the bakery were small enough it would take less than a minute for Warren to find where she slept. And with the lamplight shining through the attic windows, Aileen may as well climb onto the rooftop and announce her whereabouts to the entire town.

Isaac rubbed a hand over his eyes, which suddenly felt gritty. If only he could have prevented Aileen from seeing Warren at all.

She stayed in the far corner, still attacking the attic with her broom.

"I thought you'd be more distraught by what happened tonight." More distraught, and less angry. He'd expected to find her sobbing and huddled on the bed with Rebekah comforting her, to find both women's eyes red and puffy from an hour spent crying. Isaac dipped his hand into his shirt pocket and brushed his fingers over the handkerchief he'd been prepared to offer Aileen.

"If I think about it, I'll cry. But tears won't do me any good. Heaven knows, I shed enough of them last year." She gave the corner a fierce jab that probably scattered any of the dust she'd swept up.

"I had no idea he was the one who'd hurt you." Isaac sank onto an old, rectangular trunk. "If I had, I would have…"

What? Prevented Warren from coming to Eagle Harbor?

"Yer sister thinks I should press charges down in Chicago." Though Aileen's body was still turned away from him, she wasn't jabbing her broom into the corner as viciously as before.

"I know." He'd learned that when they'd been looking for Aileen earlier.

"It won't work."

"I know."

"Someone else tried it earlier this summer, and it was in all the papers. Warren was acquitted, and now her reputation is in shambles, it is."

If only Aileen's testimony—or the testimony of a similar woman—held the answer to stopping Warren. In a fair, just world, either woman's testimony would be enough to see a criminal locked away for years. But in a world where a person's wealth could make crimes disappear? In a world where a man's word was almost always believed before a woman's?

"I know," he whispered into the charged silence.

He had to find a way to make Warren pay for his crimes so Aileen had no need to fear him again.

Sure, he'd strong-armed Warren into leaving tomorrow, but justice hadn't been done. Warren would still walk free when he deserved to spend years—if not the rest of his life—in prison.

Aileen turned to him, broom clutched to her chest, and eyes haunted with shadows that went deep into her soul.

His throat grew thick. Here she'd almost been harmed, and all he'd been able to think about for the past five days was how he was mad at her.

Why had he allowed his feelings to block out her need for safety? He couldn't be a bigger fool. Maybe if he would have looked past his own anger, would have tried forgiving her, he'd have known who her attacker was and that Warren had never spent a day in prison for his horrendous crimes.

"How do ye know…" Aileen wrung her hands around the broom handle. "About the trial, that is, and the rest of it?"

"Gilbert told me."

Her throat worked. "I told meself I'd never have to see him again. There's nothing to bring him to Eagle Harbor, not with his parents selling their mansion to Gilbert. Rebekah says she and Gilbert don't even speak to Warren in Chicago."

"He'll be gone first thing in the morning. I'll escort him to the ship myself." Though it seemed like such a small promise.

And one that might not last more than a few days.

"Thank ye for earlier. For coming." Aileen brought her gaze up to meet his. "I know ye're upset with me, and I know I don't deserve any extra kindness, but I'm glad ye decided to check on me anyway."

He was off the top of the trunk and striding across the floor before she could continue with such nonsense. "I'll still protect you, Aileen, just like I'd protect anyone else in this town."

Her knuckles tightened around the broom handle. "Even if yere mad at me?"

"I'm not mad at you, I'm... hurt." And he was also being dishonest with himself, because she wasn't just another townsperson, even if his heart still ached over how she'd kept her brother a secret.

"I never meant to trick ye or mislead ye about me brother." She peered into his face, her moss green eyes searching his. "It's just..." She swallowed. "Ye might not believe me, but 'tis true, I didn't know about the smuggling."

"I believe you." He uttered the words like a caress against her skin, yet one question still burned inside him. "But when I told you what Morley was up to, why didn't you tell me about Conan?"

"Because I was shocked and still processing the notion that Conan was probably involved too. And it was all so much. For over a year, I thought him dead." Her eyes filled with tears. "I told ye before that Conan promised me he'd not do anything illegal anymore. And I was thinking about saying something to ye about Conan, but he'd made me promise to keep quiet about him being alive, and then Deputy Norling interrupted, and..."

Norling. Yes, the man had interrupted. How had he forgotten that? A growl resonated through his chest. He'd known Aileen had more to say, but with a jail full of smugglers and the Customs and Revenue Cutter Service men swarming the town, there hadn't been time to prod the rest from her.

"I'm sorry," he croaked.

She sniffled and shook her head, a long strand of hair catching on her shoulder. "For what? Yer brother's not the smuggler."

He tucked the strand of hair behind her ear. "For not giving you a chance to explain. For not listening when you said you were sorry." Because she had said she was sorry. More than once, even. He'd just been too stubborn to listen.

Too obsessed with his quest for justice to see that she'd accidentally stumbled into justice's path, not intentionally obstructed it.

Perhaps she could have told him about Conan when she'd first learned her brother was alive. But it wasn't as though he and Aileen had been close at the time. And it wasn't as though she'd known he was a smuggler. She may have suspected he was up to no good, but that was different than having evidence of illegal activity and then hiding it from the law. So could he really blame her for keeping quiet when her brother made her promise not to say anything?

"Ye believe me?" Aileen stared at him for a moment, her eyes wide and honest, and then her arms came around him—broom included—and she pressed her face to his chest.

Something thick rose in his throat, and he looked down, her hair a mass of tangled fire that was slipping from its pins. He reached behind him to wriggle the broom from her hand. Then he leaned it against the wall before bringing his own arms up to wrap tightly about her.

A woman had never felt so right in his arms. Not that he'd held that many women before, but still, he couldn't imagine anything more perfect than Aileen's rounded form against him and her head tucked beneath his chin.

"Thank ye," she whispered into his chest.

"Don't thank me." He tightened his grip around her. "I was rude and demanding and unwilling to listen to you."

"But ye believe me now."

He rested his cheek atop her head, her lemon-and-sunshine-scented hair brushing his face. "I do."

She pulled her head back and looked into his eyes. "I haven't seen either Morley or Conan since ye caught those smugglers last week. Or I would have come straight to ye."

"I believe that too." He smoothed the hair off her brow, then bent and placed a kiss on her forehead.

She froze for a moment, her breath puffing warm against his face. Then her gaze dipped to his lips, and he almost bent farther and placed his lips on hers, almost tasted the sweetness that was sure to linger in her mouth.

But her eyes still carried haunted shadows, and the corners of her mouth held a certain kind of sadness. So he settled for placing another kiss on her forehead. "I'm sorry for what happened to you tonight. I'm sorry you had to see Warren Sinclair at all, let alone face him by yourself. I'm sorry he's not permanently locked behind bars where he belongs. But you're a brave woman for refusing him."

And that made him want to kiss her all over again.

"I don't feel so brave at the moment." She looked down. "But mayhap... Mayhap we could go on that picnic ye keep talking about?"

And that was another kind of bravery right there. Hope filled his chest, like a big, puffy cloud floating across the sky on a pristine summer day. In fact, he might have just swallowed a hundred clouds for how light he suddenly felt. "Do you have any plans for dinner tomorrow?"

A shy smile crept onto her lips, and she tilted her head to the side. "I do now."

Chapter Twenty-Two

Late. Isaac glanced at the clock hanging on the wall of his office as he raced inside. He was almost an hour late to meet Aileen for their picnic. Teach him to lose track of time following a faint trail through the woods.

There'd been four sets of footprints. No backwoodsman or trapper moved with that many men. The evidence they'd found today meant smugglers were likely still in the area.

But the trail had disappeared, which meant he was no closer to finding their hiding place than when Aileen had first spotted them in the alley a month ago.

Isaac tipped open the lid to the picnic basket he'd borrowed from Victoria, just to make sure the chicken, biscuits, and pie Victoria had packed for him while he'd been gone were all in place. Not that he expected the food to crawl out of the basket, but…

Breathe, Isaac, breathe. He sucked in a long breath, then blew it out again. It wouldn't do to meet Aileen in a panic. He'd simply tell her work had taken longer than expected and offer to share their meal in the bakery instead of going on a picnic. Surely she'd understand.

Except he should probably take a bath before seeing her, sweaty and caked with mud as he was. But then they'd have even less time together, and she was probably wondering why he hadn't sent word yet. He'd spotted her farther down the beach watching Warren's ship depart bright and early this morning, but with the search in the woods scheduled with his deputies, he'd not had time to talk to her.

Had she slept at all last night? Was she calmer now? Happier with Warren gone?

Or was she frantically cleaning another room of the hotel, all the while wondering how long until that snake returned?

Because if the anger in Warren's eyes that morning was any indication, he'd not stay away long.

Shoulders tight, Isaac grabbed the handle of the picnic basket. Warren Sinclair likely considered himself above the law in all areas, not just in how he treated women. Larceny, tax evasion, fraud. He'd not put Warren past any of it. If he could prove Warren was breaking some law, then he could keep the wretch away from Aileen… and any other woman who might fall victim to Warren's evil devices.

But he hardly had time to dig into Warren's business affairs with smugglers harassing the town. Still, he could ask Gilbert if he possessed any of Warren's shipping records so a thorough search could be done once the smugglers were caught. It was a long shot, but if he could find any hint of wrongdoing, he should be able to get a search warrant for the rest of Warren's records. If the man had any documentation of illegal activities, then Warren would finally have to face justice.

Picnic basket in hand, Isaac headed for the door, but footsteps sounded on the wooden porch outside. Dear God, please don't let it be Mrs. Ranulfson come to complain about the children yelling too loudly when they play in the street.

He plunked the basket down and waited for the person to enter. What were the chances he could have them on their way in half a minute?

But instead of the knob turning, a paper slid beneath the door, folded in half just like the one that had warned him of the smuggling ship two weeks ago. Isaac rushed forward and flung the door open. But the porch was deserted, and the handful of people on the street strolled slowly by.

How could the informant have disappeared so quickly?

He strode to the far side of the porch, but the gap between his building and the next was deserted as well. He returned to his office and picked up the note, his gaze zeroing in on the same stilted handwriting he'd seen on the last missive.

Midnight at the inlet.

The inlet, as in the little beach five miles west?

He needed to get Norling and the others. Would there be enough time to bring a revenue cutter ship in? And if not, how could he and three deputies stop whatever the smugglers had planned?

He glanced to where the picnic basket sat. And how would Aileen feel about him canceling the picnic that had taken her ten months to agree to?

⌐.⌐.⌐.⌐.⌐

Where was Isaac? Aileen swiped a strand of hair from her forehead and scanned the too-tidy kitchen. Should she sweep the floor for the third time? Or mayhap wipe down the counters again? Scrub the sink once more? Oh, if Isaac didn't get here soon, she just might take a rag to the walls. Wouldn't Ellie be surprised at how clean this kitchen could be?

She headed over to the floor beneath the wooden counter that attached to the wall. She'd only swept beneath it once. If she crouched down with the broom, she could get the hard-to-reach spots a second time.

Or mayhap she should just go to the sheriff's office and…

What? See if Isaac had forgotten about their picnic dinner plans?

She hunkered down and stretched the broom out until it met the wall. It wasn't like Isaac to forget. Something must have come up.

Something with Warren?

Her breath stilled in her chest. Nay, she was being foolish to worry. Warren had left Eagle Harbor at first light that morn.

A brisk knock sounded on the kitchen door, then it swung open. Isaac stood in the doorway, his cheeks ruddy and hair a bit more unruly than usual. Mud stained the bottom of his trousers as well as his knees, and a twig clung to the sleeve of his shirt.

"What's wrong?" She straightened from her crouching position, bumping her hip on the counter.

He set a picnic basket down on the table, then came toward her. "I'm sorry, but searching the woods took longer than I expected, and now I need to go again."

The smugglers. She should have guessed he'd be busy with them, not Warren. "Have ye captured them?"

He paused for a moment and glanced around the kitchen, then shook his head. "We found a trail, but it disappeared without leading us anywhere. But just as I was coming here, I got a tip. I'm sorry I can't have dinner with you, but I wanted to stop and let you know." He gestured toward the basket on the table. "There's the food I packed, so at least it won't go to waste."

She reached out and touched the hem of his sleeve. "Don't say ye're going to go after them now?" Darkness was fast falling outside. "What if ye get hurt?"

He rested his hand atop hers, his palm warm and gentle. "If all goes as planned, they won't know we're coming. But I really must go. Elijah is readying the boat as we speak."

So he didn't plan to capture more smugglers on the beach like last time? It seemed not, if he was taking a boat. Her mouth felt suddenly dry, and something tightened around her chest. "What if the smugglers figure out ye're there? What if they shoot?"

Hardness glinted in his eyes. "Then we shoot back."

"But what if...?" She dared not voice the words. She could imagine the scene well enough, the smugglers firing from shore while Isaac and his team tried to land their boat amid a haze of flying bullets. Would her brother be out there with his rifle, shooting at the lawmen?

She stepped against Isaac's chest and wrapped her arms around his middle. Isaac couldn't die out there tonight. She'd already lost her parents, and though Morley and Conan were still alive, she'd lost them in another kind of way. She didn't know where Brenna was or how she fared, which meant she'd lost her cousin too, at least for a time.

Aileen pressed her eyes shut and burrowed her face into the solid masculine chest in front of her. She couldn't lose Isaac as well.

"Hey." He wrapped one arm around her, enfolding her in his steady warmth. Using his other hand, he prodded her chin up until their gazes met. "Don't cry, beautiful. Somebody has to protect the town or more people will end up dead."

But that was exactly what she feared. More people dead. Tonight. A tear escaped and trickled down her cheek, and she shut her eyes lest she not be able to stop another from falling.

Isaac brushed the wetness away with his thumb. "Aileen..." Her name was barely a whisper in the quiet of the kitchen, and then his lips were on hers, soft and gentle. She stilled for a moment, her muscles tensing and painful memories creeping along the edges of her mind.

But Isaac's kiss was nothing like Warren's forced and brutal kisses from last summer. Nay, Isaac's lips were tender and warm, cautious but caring.

And so she stepped closer and sank into his arms, into the kiss, into her dreams. What if she had this every day, the love of someone like Isaac Cummings? The kisses and touches of a man who cared for her? The hope of a brilliant, happy future? The promises of a thousand bright tomorrows?

Isaac's lips moved against hers, patient and tender, while his arms bound her securely to him. She curled her hands in the fabric of his shirt and breathed in the scent of earth and sun and man.

And then it was over. Isaac pulled away from her, moving his arms from her back and placing his hands on her shoulders. His eyes searched hers for a moment, two endless hazel pools of emotions so rich she could barely hold his gaze. "I need to go, but we'll talk tomorrow."

Except tomorrow seemed so very far away. She pressed the back of her hand to her mouth, half to savor the memory of his lips on hers, and half to hold onto the fresh hope springing up inside her. "The Cutter Service will help you like last time?"

His Adam's apple bobbed. "If they get here. We barely had time to send them word. Pray they come."

She swallowed the lump lodged in her own throat, though it climbed right back into her airway again. "Stay safe."

"I will." He gave her shoulders a final squeeze, then turned and strode for the door, his jaw set and back straight.

She stared at the door as it closed behind him, his words twining with hers in her mind.

Stay safe.

I will.

If only he could guarantee his safety, but he couldn't know how the night would end. Yet God knew. Dear Father, please keep him safe. Please protect him and guide him and give him wisdom.

She'd pray all night long if that's what was needed to keep Isaac alive through the night. And then, she'd head to his office first thing in the morning and see for herself that he was safe.

And if he was injured—or worse?

Her chest tightened all over again. She was falling in love with him. It wasn't supposed to happen. Not when she had so very many faults. Not when she had a past filled with shame. But it was happening anyway, despite her warning him away from her. Despite her telling herself she didn't deserve a man like him.

But the mercy of the Lord is from everlasting to everlasting upon them that fear him.

Perhaps God truly was merciful, because it looked as though He was about to give her a future she hadn't dared to dream of.

Aileen moved to the basket of food Isaac had left her.

"What do you mean you didn't get him?"

She stilled at the sound of the rough whisper coming through the open window.

"How hard can it be to hit a man over the head when he comes around the corner?" Not so much a whisper this time, but an exasperated grumble.

Fear, hot and bright, ignited in her belly. Who else but Isaac would they expect to turn a corner near her building?

"Aye, except he didn't come around the corner, he didn't." Irish laced the second speaker's muted voice. "Must have cut through the alley."

"We best find him before he reaches the others."

Her breath hitched and she clenched her hands into fists at her side—helpless fists that could do little to protect Isaac.

"Aye, and if we're too late, what then?" the Irish voice asked.

"We'll have another kind of surprise waiting for him at the inlet."

Hurried footsteps sounded on the packed earth outside, but they quickly grew faint.

Was Isaac headed to the inlet on Elijah's boat? If the smugglers had overheard her conversation with Isaac earlier, then he and whoever else was standing on the *North Star* as it shoved off would make unmissable targets.

The fear in her stomach turned to nausea, but she forced her trembling legs away from the wall, then pushed through the swinging doors that led into the storefront. Racing across the shop, she reached for the doorknob…

But stilled.

What if the men were lying in wait for her as well? She was safe inside with the door locked. What would these men do to her if they caught her trying to warn Isaac?

No worse than they'd do to Isaac if they caught him. And Isaac had already risked his life once to catch smugglers, then faced Warren last night in order to protect her. The least she could do was warn him of danger.

She slowly unlocked the door and poked her head outside. The street in front was empty, but it was busier a block down, near the intersection with Front Street. Hopefully if she hurried, she could catch Isaac before the boat left harbor. She darted through the door, her legs pumping as fast as they could onto the street. Only a few blocks and—

Thump!

Someone grabbed her from behind and pulled her backward into a soft chest and protruding stomach. She opened her mouth to scream, but a hand clamped around her lips, silencing any sound she'd hoped to make.

"And just where do you think you're going in such a hurry?" The man pulled her along the side of the building toward the alley.

There was something familiar about the voice, about the man, but she couldn't quite grasp what as she clawed and scratched at him. Despite her fighting, his grip seemed made of iron as he steadily inched her around the back of the bakery and into an alley that was far too empty.

If someone had seen her being pulled from the street or walked by and glanced into the shadows as she was being dragged along the side of the bakery, they might go to Isaac, but she couldn't hope for that.

She raised her foot and slammed her heel down into the man's shoe. He muttered a curse, his grip growing tighter as he dragged her toward the bakery door. Of a sudden, he wrenched her hair back, tipping her head up and pressing his hand more firmly over her mouth while he opened the door to the bakery's kitchen. Yanking her inside, he slammed the door behind him.

"So the shrew has claws, does she?" The man chuckled as he dragged her to the big cast iron oven that sat against the wall.

His grip around her middle loosened, and she tried to twist free, but a rope cinched around her middle so tightly the air was forced from her lungs.

The man pulled her to the floor, and then his hand left her mouth as he yanked her wrists together behind her back.

She sucked in a breath of air and loosed a curdling scream.

A slap landed on her cheek, the force of the blow knocking her head back against the stove and causing her to cry out.

"You want to be hit again?" the dark voice drawled.

Despite the pain exploding on both her jaw and the back of her scalp, she managed to shake her head, all while getting her first good look at her captor.

The balding brown hair, the squat build. 'Twas Virgil O'Byrne, Jack's father. She should have known it when she felt the large girth of his stomach pressing into her back.

"Then keep your mouth shut." The man lowered his half-bald head and looked behind her at where he wrapped the rope around the stove leg, fastening her wrists there.

He made quick work of tying her hands and middle to the stove's leg, the bindings so tight on her wrists that pinpricks tingled up and down her fingers. Then he pushed to his feet with a heavy grunt, knees popping as he stood. He ran his eyes over her and grinned. "Now see if you can get out of that."

Her head still pounded from his hand to her face, but she twisted her hands against the bindings anyway, then winced as the small movements caused the abrasive rope to grind against her skin.

O'Byrne waddled toward the door, his paunchy belly preventing him from moving anywhere too quickly. He opened it and poked his head out, and she nearly screamed. But even if someone heard her cry, they'd not be able to help before O'Byrne clobbered her again.

Rather than close the door, O'Byrne took a step back from it, and a large man with muscled forearms stepped inside. His face was creased with weathered lines that held no kindness. He took one glimpse at her, and his eyes filled with a lewdness she was all too familiar with.

Another man followed the first inside, and her blood turned to ice.

Morley.

Nay, it couldn't be.

But it was. As sure as her hands were bound behind her back, her cousin stood in front of her, his unruly auburn hair curling out from beneath his hat.

She should have known when she'd heard the Irish voice outside.

Morley's eyes widened and his throat worked, but only for an instant, then his gaze turned a hard, emerald green and he clenched his jaw.

"Where were you headed just now?" O'Byrne tromped back to her, but all she could do was stare at her cousin.

Could Morley read the pleading in her eyes?

"I asked you a question, wench." O'Byrne dug the toe of his shoe into her side, causing her to suck in a breath. "Where were you going just now?"

She glanced back at Morley, but his eyes were still hard and cold. "I had a meeting."

"You're lying." The toe of O'Byrne's shoe gouged harder into her flesh. "You want me to kick you next?"

She gasped and shook her head.

"Then tell the truth." O'Byrne kept his shoe pressed painfully against her soft midsection.

She glanced between Morley and the large man whose dark eyes and scowl told her he'd be no kinder if he were interrogating her. "I heard talking."

O'Byrne's lips thinned, but the pressure on her side lessened a bit. "Talking that made you run from the building?"

Despite the ache in her midsection, she dropped her gaze to the floor.

"To warn your lover about us?"

"He's not me lover!"

O'Byrne dropped his foot from her side and turned to the large man beside Morley. "Find something to gag her with. She comes with us."

She sucked in a breath, though it did little good since her lungs felt suddenly aflame. Come with them where? To the smugglers' camp? She tugged against her bindings, ignoring the scrape of pain along her skin as she twisted her wrists.

O'Byrne glanced back at her for a second, his bald head glistening in the light from the window. An evil smile crossed his pudgy lips before he turned back to Morley. "Go find a wheelbarrow and some burlap, and be quick about it."

But rather than head for the door, Morley held his spot. "We should leave the lass tied here for the night. It'll be a hassle taking her into the woods."

"She knows too much." O'Byrne's voice was firm and unyielding, but then he took a step nearer her, and his eyes filled with lewdness. "Besides, it's been a while since we had the company of a woman at camp."

A new kind of fear filled her, and her heart pounded against her ribs. Surely Morley and Conan wouldn't let anyone force her. She sent a panicked looked to Morley, hoping to see reassurance in his gaze, but his eyes only offered a warning, followed by a slight shake of his head.

What was he telling her no about? Resisting? She had to fight. She couldn't allow herself to be violated again.

She sucked a breath into lungs that were laboring for air, keeping her eyes pinned on her cousin, though his expression didn't change a whit. But wait, these men might not know of her relationship with Morley. After all, he'd told her to act as if she didn't know him. Perhaps Morley had been plotting ways to help her escape all this time and was only playing along with the other men. Aye, that was it. And it was why he wanted her left here. He probably planned to sneak back and untie her later.

"I said go get a wheelbarrow!" O'Byrne's shout filled the room.

Morley turned and lumbered through the door. Did that mean he was coming up with another plan? Mayhap it would be easier to escape in the woods. Darkness was falling, and the smugglers couldn't watch her every second. If Morley pretended to guard her when she relieved herself, then she'd be able to get free.

Aye, that would work. And before she escaped, she'd try to slow their progress. Mayhap she could dawdle long enough that the men couldn't return to their camp in time to warn the others that Isaac was coming.

And if she failed? Sweat beaded on her forehead and slickened her hands. Nay, she'd not think on that. Instead she'd sit here and pray—

like she'd not prayed since those endless days in Ireland when she'd begged God to spare her da's life.

Because it was going to take an act of God if she, Isaac, and the people they cared about survived the night.

Chapter Twenty-Three

Water lapped at the boat, the waves calm amid the windless night. From his spot at the stern, Elijah raised his oar and searched the shoreline, but the shadows of rocks and trees prevented him from seeing if anyone lurked inside the forest. Beside him, Deputy Fletcher helped row the small dinghy, while Norling and Deputy Granger sat one row up, surveying the shore and lake for any sign of activity. Isaac stood at the bow, as still as a statue.

Elijah dipped his oar into the water slowly so it didn't splash, a far cry from the strong rowing he and his men were used to doing when they took this boat into storms.

"I feel like we've got signs on our chests asking for someone to shoot us," he whispered to the others. He'd decided to take the surfboat instead of the North Star since its bright sails would announce their whereabouts to anyone watching from shore. But moving slowly through the open water beneath a full moon made them ripe pickings anyway.

"We probably are." That from Fletcher, whose wide eyes scanned the open water as they rowed.

"The smugglers need the full moon. They don't want to be carrying lanterns through the woods if they can avoid it." Norling pointed toward the shore. "Take the boat in. I want us to split up."

"I thought we were waiting for the Cutter Service," Isaac responded.

"If I saw their ship, we'd row toward it. But the next best plan is to split our forces. You and Granger can come in from the east and stay by the coast." Norling shoved a hand toward Fletcher. "The rest of us will row to the west, then beach the boat and try flanking the smugglers."

Split the group? Elijah's hands tightened around the oar. What if the smugglers spotted one group before the other? Five men fighting together made a stronger show than two.

"All right, we should split then. Two men on the east, and three on the west." Isaac gave a firm nod. "If the Revenue Cutter comes, we'll join their crew once they land. But if the smugglers try disappearing back to their hideout, we can follow."

Elijah's teeth clenched. "I think we should stay together." This was a dangerous mission, and the team was stronger together than apart. After all, he never split his life-saving crew…

Well, except for when he tied a rope to his waist and swam out to rescue a stranded sailor. But that was different. There weren't men waiting to kill him if he separated from the group.

But were his water rescues truly that different from what they were doing tonight? He regularly told Isaac to ignore the danger and focus on how the recues helped others. Isaac and Norling and the others were only doing the same tonight.

Fletcher dipped his oar into the water once, twice, then turned to him. "Aren't you going to turn the boat? Those rocks look like a good spot to drop them off. Can't imagine we want to take them right to the inlet before they go ashore."

Elijah spotted the large boulder that jutted up from the shallow water, creating a rocky bridge to the shore. "Right. We'll head to the rock."

"Hopefully the Cutter Service will arrive right about the time we have the smugglers surrounded." Norling kept his face turned toward the open water, probably looking for a smuggling vessel or the Cutter Service or both.

"My thoughts exactly." Isaac peered over the edge of the surfboat and into the water as though he'd never spent a day of his life terrified of the lake—let alone four years.

Hopefully the plan worked, but Elijah's heartbeat thudded against his chest as they approached the ominous rock.

Water lapped quietly against the hull of the surfboat as Isaac scrambled up, followed by Granger. His brother offered a half smile and a dip of his head, then disappeared down the other side of the boulder.

Norling and Fletcher raised their hands in farewell, but Elijah couldn't quite force his hand to release its tight grip on the oar.

Looked like he needed to do the very things he told Isaac to do whenever he went out on a rescue—pray, and trust God to protect his brother's life.

But he hadn't quite realized how difficult it was to place a brother into God's hands and trust God alone for his safety.

..*.*.*

There had to be someone nearby. Isaac peered through the dark shadows toward where a twig had just snapped. At least he thought that was the sound he'd heard a few seconds ago. The hair on the back of his neck prickled, and his blood thrummed. From his position in the brush on the east side of the inlet, he could only make out shadows of trees and bushes. The little rise where he crouched afforded him a perfect view of both the cove and the water, yet he saw no movement.

Granger squatted beside him, his eyes riveted to the open lake and his breath coming just as hard as Isaac's own. Like him, the other man must sense something was about to happen.

That they were about to catch some smugglers.

Or the smugglers were about catch them. A chill traveled up his spine, and he glanced over his shoulder, then placed his hand on the butt of his holstered pistol.

"There." Granger patted his shoulder and pointed out toward the water, his voice barely audible in the heavy silence of the night.

Isaac surveyed the lake again. And there it was, a ship with black sails, looking just like the schooner that the cutter service had taken two weeks ago. It glided closer, and he waited, the breath stilling in his chest.

Would the Cutter Service follow the smugglers in? He stared out at the dark expanse of water. No sign of another ship floating on the waves. What if the cutter men hadn't been able to ready the ship in time to set sail tonight? Were Elijah, Norling, and Fletcher all in position? Had they been able to flank the inlet?

Except there weren't any smugglers at the inlet. Isaac swallowed. Something about the situation didn't seem right. Could they be walking into a trap?

The smuggling vessel glided a little closer, then seemed to stop. Had they anchored? A vessel that large could get closer to the inlet, yes, but it wouldn't be able to pull into the shore. Isaac swept his gaze slowly over the water near the shore for signs of dinghies waiting to take cargo to the larger ship, but again, he saw nothing.

Something flickered on the other side of the cove, then went dark. Again, another flicker, then dark. Isaac tapped Granger's shoulder and pointed across the small patch of water and sand to the rocky outcropping. A small light shone, about the size of a large lantern. The light went dark for a moment, then bright again. Dark again, then bright.

"They must be sending a signal of some kind," Granger whispered.

Yes, but what did the signal say? Norling would know. But if he, Elijah, and Fletcher were in the woods, then the customs man wouldn't see it.

"I still don't see any sign of the cutter ship." Granger's voice was so low Isaac could barely discern the words.

He surveyed the water again as a sinking sensation filled his chest. He didn't see a revenue cutter either. If the customs men and Cutter Service were coming, they should have already been here.

"The ship is moving again."

Isaac swiveled his head in the direction of the black-sailed schooner. Sure enough, it was inching its way back to the open lake. A quick glance at the other side of the inlet told him that the lantern had been snuffed.

Had the smugglers on shore told the ship to leave? Did that mean he'd been spotted? Or Norling and Elijah? Or worse, were the others captured? Whatever had happened, it didn't look as though they'd be catching any smugglers tonight.

But maybe he and Granger could follow the man with the lantern back to the hideout.

"Come on." He motioned to Granger.

He moved quickly around trees and over brambles, trying to be silent while gaining ground. Darting inland, he headed to one of the spots in the cove that had trampled foliage from the last time they'd searched the area.

Isaac paused for a moment, holding his hand up so Granger stopped behind him. Eyes wide, he scanned the trees for the slightest movement—whether it be from the other team of men or the smugglers.

There, not a movement, but a rustling from behind them near the water, and a little to their west. Hopefully it was the smuggler and not Norling's group.

Isaac crept toward his right as the rustling grew louder. A faint shadow moved through the trees, but heading farther right than where he was. He snaked his way through the woods, as quietly as possible, following the faint sounds.

The rustling turned into the steady thudding of running footsteps and crunching of trampled brush. So much for trying to follow without being spotted.

Isaac dashed toward the movement, his feet pounding the ground. The man's shadow was now visible, the only moving thing between the still tree trunks.

The shadow paused for a moment. Chest heaving, Isaac propelled himself forward. A few more feet and he just might be able to take the man down if he lunged hard enough.

But the shadow darted into a thick patch of woods. Isaac followed, nothing but the trickle of moonlight through the trees illuminating his path as he struggled to keep his eyes pinned on the shadowed form.

The smuggler stumbled, possibly over a root or fallen tree.

Isaac took one step, then another, and lunged, wrapping his arms around the other man's legs.

They crashed to the ground, Isaac landing atop the shorter, bulkier form.

"Get off!" A feral growl tore through the night.

Before the man could try to roll or buck him, Isaac grabbed his wrists and yanked them behind the man's back, then fumbled for the handcuffs at his belt.

"I didn't do nothing." The man's chest heaved with his words. "Just fishin' after dark, is all."

"Here." Handcuffs appeared in front of Isaac's face, and he looked up to find Norling looming over them. "A few more feet, and he would have been mine."

"Thanks." Isaac shackled the man's hands while Granger slid to a stop beside them. "Come on, buddy, I've got a cell with your name on it and a boat waiting to take you there."

Chapter Twenty-Four

Isaac rubbed the grit out of his eyes and stared across his office at the closed door leading to the jail cells.

How long would it take for Norling to get information out of the man they'd captured?

Plenty long, if the man's behavior on the trip back was any indication. He'd tried interrogating the smuggler on the boat and got nothing but a story about how the man had been out fishing in the dead of night. The lantern hadn't been sending signals to a ship out on the water, either. He'd just been using the light to bait his hook.

"Bait, my foot," Isaac muttered through a yawn.

He supposed if Norling could get any information at all from the man, then it was worth staying up until dawn to learn of it. But considering how gray shadows stretched outside the window rather than inky blackness, dawn had almost arrived.

How much longer could the questioning take?

He glanced at the ceiling toward his apartment above. The others were all home abed. Maybe he should sleep too. If the man said anything significant, Norling could wake him.

But how exactly was he supposed to sleep? Something had gone terribly wrong tonight, and if the smuggler with Norling could provide any answers, then he would stay up to hear them. Besides, if he waited another half hour, he'd be able to visit Aileen. Let her know he was safe. She'd been so concerned for him last night. And if they happened to pick up where they'd left off, with another kiss or two…

Well, he could hardly complain about such things.

The door leading to the jail cells swung open, and Norling stepped out.

"Well?" Isaac straightened in his chair, a surge of energy rushing through his veins. "Do we know where they're hiding?"

"No." Norling's voice sounded thick and gravelly as he pulled the door shut behind him. "I couldn't get him to say much, but he did slip up once and tell me the smugglers knew we were coming."

Isaac slumped back in his chair and crossed his booted foot over his knee. "How did they know? Was the note a trap? Or did they catch the person who gave us the message?"

Norling's jaw tightened, but when he met Isaac's gaze, shadows darkened his eyes. "She. He said she when he was talking. He didn't realize his mistake, so I tried to pull more information from him before he clammed up. But the person who warned them… was a woman."

A woman? Hardly anyone knew he and his men were headed to the inlet. He'd not even stopped to tell Rebekah. Elijah would have told Victoria, of course. And he'd told…

"No," he rasped.

But the tightness in Norling's shoulders told him otherwise. "It has to be Miss Brogan. She's the only woman in town with a connection to the smugglers."

"The only woman that we know of. And she's not aided them before." But he couldn't stop the tightening sensation in his chest. What were the chances another woman had warned the smugglers when circumstances so readily pointed to Aileen?

"She wouldn't have betrayed me," he gritted through a clenched jaw.

But he was already up, pushing his chair back from his desk and striding toward the door. The dim light of predawn greeted him as he clambered down the porch steps and across North Street.

What if you get hurt? Her words from last night echoed in his mind as he raced down Third Street. Words that had led to their kiss. Her voice had been rich with concern, her eyes filled with worry. And then she'd reached out and clung to him, and he'd not been able to let her go. Even after he'd finally raised his lips from hers and stepped away, concern had rolled from her like waves off a stormy Lake Superior.

She couldn't have told the smugglers of his plans.

He reached the bakery only to find the back door unlocked and the kitchen dark and empty.

"Aileen!" His frantic shout echoed around the room as he rushed toward the stairs. Dear God, please let me find her sleeping.

He headed straight for her room, the last one on the right, and flung open the door. It held a nightgown and a familiar dress on pegs, as well as a small trunk at the foot of the bed. But the bed was made up as though it had never been slept in.

"No," he rasped through a tight throat. Had she truly gone to tell—

A hand rested on his shoulder.

Isaac swung around, his palm landing on his pistol.

It was only Norling. "She might still be in town. I'll go check the hotel, then Mr. and Mrs. Sinclair's. But if she isn't in Eagle Harbor… well, I don't think she went with the smugglers willingly."

"What's that supposed to mean?"

His mouth was grim, the hard set to his jaw visible even in the dark shadows of the hallway. "It means that a kitchen with two toppled chairs and a crooked table looks suspicious to me."

Had chairs been toppled downstairs? He'd been so intent on

finding Aileen, he'd not stopped to light a lamp or notice any details. But wait—the door had been unlocked. And Aileen was always so careful to lock it.

A cold terror trickled through him. If she was with the smugglers unwillingly, how much danger was she in?

He pushed past Norling and raced back down the stairs.

His feet landed on the floor, and he took in the state of the kitchen beneath the light of the lantern Norling must have lit. Two toppled chairs, a table that sat at a skewed angle from its usual place beside the window, and an unlocked door.

"I'll go see if she stayed with Mrs. Sinclair last night." Norling brushed past him and headed out the door.

But Aileen wasn't staying with Rebekah or cleaning the hotel or doing something else in town. He knew it as surely as he knew the sun would appear over the eastern trees in a quarter hour.

He took the lantern off its hook and surveyed the room for anything that seemed out of place, any clue that might help him learn where she'd been taken.

There, by the leg of the stove was a scrap of white fabric—like from the white shirtwaist she'd been wearing yesterday night. He walked closer, his footsteps echoing in the empty room, then bent to pick up the bit of cloth—and the clump of short, grayish-brown hair beside it.

He swallowed. There was no reason for a man with graying hair to be in the kitchen. Had Aileen yanked it off the head of whoever had abducted her? And if so, what had her captor done in response?

Dear God, how could this have happened? He hung his head and dropped to his knees. How could he have failed someone he loved so fully? And when he'd been away trying to capture the very criminals that now meant her harm?

He might as well still be standing on the lighthouse platform watching his father's boat capsize. He'd been as useless to Aileen last night as he had been to his father.

His hand tightened around the scrap of fabric from her shirt. No, he wasn't the same man he'd been four years ago. Perhaps he'd frozen on the day his father had died, but he didn't need to freeze now.

He'd told Aileen that God's mercy was from everlasting to everlasting so many times he'd lost count. Maybe it was time he claimed that same mercy for himself rather than clinging to his own guilt over his past failures.

He dropped his head between his shoulders and stared blindly at the fading wood planks of the floor. *Dear God, forgive me. I'm not sure if I should have done anything differently the day Pa died, but for four years, I've walked around feeling like a failure. Forgive me for being so focused on my own feelings that I failed to claim your mercy, your forgiveness. Extend your mercy to me now. Please. And help me find Aileen.*

The ice freezing him to the floor receded from his veins, and he stood on shaky legs. *Therefore if any man be in Christ, he is a new creature: old things are passed away; behold, all things are become new.* The verse rose up in his mind, and he almost felt the change wash over him. True, he'd belonged to Christ since he was in short pants, yet he'd willingly clung to the things of the past for too long.

But not anymore.

Now to find Aileen. There had to be more clues, something that could tell him where she'd been taken. He headed to the back door and swung it open. The first pink hints of dawn streaked across the sky, and birdsong filled the air.

He held the lamp close to the dirt outside the door, studying the mess of tracks leading to and from the bakery. There were his and Norling's footprints, Ellie's and Aileen's too, and a slew of others. Perhaps some of Ellie's siblings had visited her, or Rebekah and

Gilbert had come around the back. He'd never be able to tell who had taken her from the shoe prints.

But there was a wheel track, just one, from a single, narrow wheel. He turned and held the lantern closer to the ground. There, just beside the door, the track deepened as though the wheel had paused there, and a few feet away, two parallel marks scored the dirt—marks that could only belong to a wheelbarrow. The smugglers that had taken Aileen must have put her in a wheelbarrow to get her out of town, which meant he only needed to follow the tracks to find her.

But would the tracks be as easy to follow in the woods as they were in the alley, or would they disappear, just like all the other smuggler tracks they'd followed?

―.―.―.―.―

Pounding. She couldn't stop the pounding. Like hammers ricocheting through her skull, the beating pain was relentless. And cold. She was far colder than she should be for a summer night. And was that a rock lodged beneath her hip? Another against her shoulder?

Aileen forced her eyelids open, only to drop them tight and moan at the dim light.

"I told you she'd wake eventually. I didn't hit her that hard."

O'Byrne.

She didn't need to open her eyes to place the voice—or to recall the way he'd forced her to drink a bitter concoction he'd intended for Isaac. That had been right before he'd untied her from the bakery's stove. She'd fought him as soon as she was free, but then... then...

What had happened next?

Images flashed. O'Byrne pulling a pistol from the holster at his waist. The butt of the gun slamming into her temple. Her world going dark.

"Yes, it appears you were correct, though the effects from your blow seem to have outlasted the drugs."

The calm, calculating voice sent a chill through her despite the pain in her head. She knew that voice too. But nay, it couldn't be.

"What do you want me to do with her?" O'Byrne again.

"Leave her there."

"But…"

"I said leave her there! And get back to work. We haven't any time to waste."

The sharp bite to the words had her opening her eyes again, and keeping them open long enough to focus first on the uneven floor of rock, and then on the familiar form seated at the desk in the middle of the stone room.

She jolted upright, her heart pounding against her ribs.

As surely as she had Irish blood coursing through her veins, Warren Sinclair sat in the chair before her, his head bent over the desk as he scrawled something across a paper.

She tried to scramble away, only to find her wrists still bound together at her back. The gag that had been tied around her before leaving the bakery had been removed. But now her ankles were tied, turning her movements into a slow writhing that did nothing to move her farther from Warren. A bit of cold rock bit into her side, and she winced.

A wheezing chuckle sounded from the other side of the desk. She moved her gaze to where Virgil O'Byrne approached in the dim light, his footsteps echoing on the dank stone floor.

"How ya feeling, sweetheart? That head of yours hurting?"

She pressed her lips together, gathered the moisture in her mouth, and spit at his shoe.

Mistake! The alarm flashed through her mind only a second before his fist connected with her head.

Pain splintered through her once more, shattering into a hundred jagged pieces that ripped through her head.

She groaned as she lay back on the cold floor and turned her head into her shoulder to protect herself from another blow.

"I said get back to work." Warren's voice echoed through the dank room. "She's not worth your time. Besides, there are better places than a face to leave bruises."

Bile churned in her stomach. Oh yes, Warren knew all the worst places to leave bruises—places that would hurt for days and that no one else ever saw.

O'Byrne left, his footsteps receding on the damp stone floor until the desk blocked him from view.

She's not worth your time. Though her eyes barely opened, she glared at Warren. He still sat at the desk, writing. The room's lone lamp shone from the corner of the desk, illuminating her captor while leaving the rest of the place in dark shadows. She swallowed and clenched her teeth together. The man had ruined so much of her life, and now he claimed she wasn't worth anyone's time? If there was a reason she wasn't, then he was the cause.

"I hate ye, Warren Sinclair." She didn't speak the words loudly. Oh no, they were soft and deadly quiet. And yet they resonated through the space with such force that Warren turned her direction.

He tilted his head to the side, studying her in that calculating way he had, his eyes as cold and hard as the floor on which she lay. "Yes, I'm sure you do, Miss Brogan. But I've other matters to attend at the moment. We can deal with your hatred of me once we're on the ship."

"The ship? What are ye talking about?" She'd fling herself over the gunwale and take her chances with the sea before she spent a minute on a ship with him.

"Yes, the ship. The lawmen have done quite a good job of

thwarting my operations of late, so I'm afraid we need to move locations. Again."

"What operation? What do ye mean?" Despite the pain screaming through her head, her mind scrambled to make sense of it all. Where was she? And why was Warren here when she'd seen him leave town yesterday morn? She was missing something, something that should be fairly obvious. Oh, if only her brain would work. She didn't know whether she suffered effects from O'Byrne's cruelty or from the bitter draught he'd had her drink before leaving the bakery, but either way her mind was sluggish and hazy.

Warren pushed back from the desk, the shrieking of the chair against the floor drawing attention to the cold, odd stone that seemed more like the floor of an ancient castle than a smuggler's warehouse. "You still don't know, do you, kitten?"

Kitten. Nausea churned in her stomach, and she just might not be able to hold it in this time. "Don't call me that."

He laughed, the sound cold and dark. "And here I took you for halfway smart. Maybe none of you are as smart as I assumed or your lover would have caught me by now."

"Isaac's not—"

"Didn't you ever wonder how I made so much more money than Gilbert?" He spoke over her, as though her protest was as worthless as the dust on his shoes. "My genius brother who invents something new every few months?"

She shook her head, then winced at the jolt of pain that spiraled through her at the movement. Why would she care which brother made more money? Both Gilbert and Warren occupied a world she'd never given any attention.

Footsteps approached, and without Warren seated, she could see beyond the desk to… a curtain?

Where was she? The wall behind her was cold and damp. She

wasn't in a warehouse, but she couldn't be in a castle either. No such thing existed in Eagle Harbor.

But what about a cave? Or an abandoned mine tunnel? She glanced up at the ceiling, but it was shrouded in shadows, much like the rest of the room. But if she were in a cave or mine, it suddenly explained why Isaac had never been able to find the smuggler's warehouse, because the hideout hadn't been a building made with wood and nails, but an opening in the earth.

The curtain moved aside and Conan stepped in, a cup in one hand and a blanket wadded under his arm.

"Do you have what I asked for?" Warren snapped.

Conan glanced her direction for a moment, then looked back at Warren. "Of course."

"Good. Make sure she drinks everything. I don't want her waking again until it's time to leave." Warren's expensive shoes clacked against the rock floor as he strode from the room and disappeared behind the curtain.

Conan came closer, his eyes filled with worry. "Are ye well?"

"Aye, if ye call me head feeling as though someone split it with an ax *well*." But she could be worse, so very worse.

He squatted down beside her, setting the cup on the floor next to him. "Here, I brought you a blanket."

He smoothed the musty fabric over the cruel, uneven rocks beside her, then moved her onto the blanket and helped her to a sitting position. The feat would have taken her a quarter hour or better to manage on her own given how she was bound, yet she could hardly form words of thanks. "Ye have to help me get away from here."

He sighed, his shoulders sagging. "'Tis not so simple, it isn't. I can't just waltz out of this cave with ye in tow, at least not without getting us both shot."

"But ye're planning to help me escape?" It shouldn't be a question, shouldn't be something a woman taken captive ever had to ask of her brother. And yet here she was voicing it, a half desperate note to her voice.

"I told ye to pretend as though ye didn't know me, remember? Though I reckon the Shark would know of our relation seeing how ye worked for his family in Chicago." Conan shook his head. "Still, ye were never supposed to get caught up in this. It wasn't part of the plan."

"Plan? Have ye gone daft? If you want me safe, try working for someone honorable. Someone who doesn't kidnap people who get in his way." But her safety had never been one of her brother's concerns, or he wouldn't have left her alone in Chicago, knowing she thought him dead.

"Arguing won't do you any good." Conan set his jaw, something hard flashing in his eyes—hard, and not all that different from the cold look Warren's eyes carried. He picked the cup up from the floor and held it to her lips. "Here, drink this."

She swallowed against her dry throat as Conan held the cup to her lips. She gulped the liquid down only to spit the next mouthful out. "What swill is that? The same that they gave me last night?"

"Swill the Shark wants ye to drink, so ye best stop asking questions and finish it."

"Stop asking questions? My problem is that I didn't ask enough questions. Do ye know what kind of person Warren Sinclair is?" Do you know what he did to me? But nay, she couldn't ask that, at least not right now. "So I'll not be drinking more of the swill ye brought unless ye bother to answer me questions first."

"'Tis something to make ye sleep, is all. And I don't have much choice about giving it to ye, nor about ye drinking it. Try defying the Shark and see what happens."

"Who is this shark ye speak of? Warren Sinclair? He's the leader of this smuggling ring, is he?" He had to be, considering how he gave orders to the other men.

"Aye, he's the Shark, 'tis true." Conan raked a hand through his already mussed hair. "If ye just would have listened. If ye just would've left me alone, then—"

"I did leave ye alone," she hissed through clenched teeth. "It's not as though I went back into the woods searching for ye. Yer friends were the ones hiding beside me apartment lying in wait for the sheriff."

"But he's more than just the sheriff to ye, isn't he?"

An image of Isaac rose up in her head, his hazel eyes worried and concerned, and that troublesome thatch of auburn hair falling over his brow. "Is he safe?" She rasped the words, barely recognizing her own voice as she asked. "I know he went out hoping to catch smugglers last night. Is he...?"

"Aye, your beau clobbered one of our men, not the other way around."

She tilted her head back against the wall of rock and drew in a breath of dank, musty air. Thank you, God. At least some good had come of her defiance last night, even if her head still throbbed from meeting the butt end of a pistol.

"Now drink what's in the cup." Conan held it to her lips once more. "I mixed it meself, so I know there's not enough to do ye harm. Ye won't sleep so long with this batch either."

She pressed her lips together and stared at him over the rim of the cup. He thought telling her Isaac was safe meant she'd let him drug her? No good could possibly come of losing her senses at a time like this, but her eyelids already felt heavy, and the room had started to turn slowly around her. Had the mouthful she'd already swallowed been enough to put her to sleep?

"Don't look at me that way. 'Tis for the best, it is. I don't plan to let the Shark have ye, but we've got to wait for the right time." Conan moved the cup away from her mouth but kept it cradled in his own hands rather than setting it back on the floor. "Morley and I have already talked about it. We need to wait until we're on the ship. Then Morley will help me take one of the lifeboats, and I'll get ye somewhere safe."

"Ye're coming with me?" Hope unfurled inside her while the fog thickened in her mind. Was she being a fool to put hope in her brother? She yawned and blinked. If only her brain would focus long enough to give her an answer.

"I shouldn't go with ye, nay. There's a heap of money due me in October, and if I leave now, I won't get paid." He swallowed and ran his gaze over her, then reached out and picked a leaf from her hair. "But I can't rightly let me only sister be dragged in with a crew like ours. Before I can help though, ye need to drink this draught and go to sleep. We'll wait until the Shark doesn't suspect anything before we move."

"But what if ye can't get to me? On the ship?" Her words were sluggish now, her tongue thick and lumbering in her mouth. "What if I'm too... well guarded?"

Conan swished his hand as though her question was about as important as a buzzing fly. "He'll put ye in the hold with the cargo. There's a spot there for... ah..."

"For what? Other women?" She jerked her head up at that and forced her heavy eyelids to open. "I'm hardly the first, am I?"

"Aye, ye're the first woman. 'Tis usually men held there." Conan's eyes found hers in the dim lantern light. "But don't ye fret. We'll have ye out of the hold and gone hours before the Shark realizes it. When he does find out, he won't know where to go ashore to look—not that he'd want to go after ye anyway. He'll want to see that the cargo is hidden before he worries about anything else."

She leaned her head back against the uneven rock and closed her eyes before slurring, "I still don't like it."

"It'll work, lass. I wouldn't try it otherwise. Morley is cutting through part of the ropes for one of the lifeboats even now. We'll have ye off the ship without anyone knowing. We don't have a choice. I've got a bad feeling in me gut concerning what the Shark has planned for ye."

Aye, so did she, but she couldn't quite force her thick tongue to form the words.

"Here, let me help ye lie down."

Familiar hands touched her shoulders and slid her down onto the blanket, but before Conan released her, he cradled her against his chest and held the cup to her lips. She swallowed once, then twice, but the bitter liquid did little to quench her dry throat before the darkness claimed her.

Chapter Twenty-Five

She dreamed of nothing and everything, waking to the wetness of tears on her face, only to close her eyes and find darkness in the draught Conan had made her drink. Sometimes men's voices filled the room around her, and other times it was silent. She dreamed of her father, with his chin whiskers and his booming laugh and hearty voice. She dreamed of Conan and Morley as boys, young and happy and free to roam the fields surrounding their home. And she dreamed of Isaac, and the life she might one day have, if only…

Something shook her shoulder. "Miss Aileen."

She blinked her eyes open, only to have blackness surround her. Had night fallen already? But nay, she was in a cave or mine tunnel, where all sense of day and night was lost.

"Miss Aileen?" The shaking on her shoulder once more. "Are you awake?"

She looked to her left where a small shadow hunched beside her.

"Jack?" Her tongue felt slow and thick as she spoke his name, her brain barely managing to concentrate on the boy beside her. Still, she should have realized he'd be here somewhere. "Jack O'Byrne?"

She tried to wriggle up against the wall, but with her hands and feet still bound, she only raised herself a couple inches.

"I'm sorry they got you, Miss Aileen. But I can't get you out." He sniffled, then lowered his voice so quiet that the sound of her breath nearly blocked it out. "Maybe another day, if the Shark isn't here. But there's men everywhere, and the Shark man says you've got to be kept here with him."

You've got to be kept here with him. She pressed her eyes shut. The boy thought nothing of those words, but they caused her stomach to twist sickeningly.

Conan's plan to free her had better work. Either that, or she'd pray Isaac would find the path she took through the woods last night—not that she remembered taking it considering how she'd been knocked out.

"Everything's almost gone though, and we'll be heading out soon. Maybe…" Jack's voice grew high and pinched. "Maybe I can try to break you free on the way to the ship."

"Mayhap." Unless Warren ordered her drugged again. What if she couldn't escape after the ship departed either? What if Warren…?

Her chest tightened and the breath in her throat clogged.

"The sheriff only got one man last night, even though I left a note for him." Jack rambled on, his words coming so fast her sluggish brain could hardly keep up with them. "I was hoping he'd get more. Maybe everyone."

She shook her head, which was still aching, though not as badly as before. Now if only her lazy, drugged mind could make sense of the jumble of words. "What about the sheriff? Is he going to be here soon? Did ye tell him where we are?"

The tightness around her chest loosened, and her breaths came easier. Mayhap her situation wasn't so dire. Mayhap God would use Isaac to deliver her from Warren's clutches before she ever stepped foot on his horrid ship.

"That's the problem, don't you see? The sheriff only has himself two deputies plus the customs man. That was four men against Pa's twenty before. And even now with some of them captured, Pa's still got more than the sheriff. That's why I've been leaving notes, hoping the sheriff can pick off Pa's crew a few at a time. But I only had a chance to leave two, and now the Shark says we gotta move so we don't get caught. And Pa says I gotta go with him, but that means leaving Alice and Toby. And now you're here, and it's all just such a mess." The lad's voice went tight, and he sniffled again.

"Don't blame yourself." Aileen yanked at the bindings around her wrists, but they barely moved. "Ye said ye were slipping Isaac notes?"

Isaac had told her he'd gotten a tip about where the smugglers would be. Evidently she had Jack to thank for that, as well as for the tip that had allowed him and the Customs Service to catch the smugglers last week.

She yawned, her eyelids drifting closed for a moment before she forced them open again. But the draught was intent on pulling her back into blackness, intent on muddling her mind until her brain moved so sluggishly it couldn't function.

"Ye might not be able to get me out of here. But will anyone notice if ye leave? Can ye make it to the sheriff and tell him Warren Sinclair is in charge of the smugglers, and that he's leaving today?"

"Maybe." Jack's shadow straightened beside her. "There's still a few loads of cargo to be taken down to the beach. I can go for the sheriff, and Pa will think I'm running cargo. Aw, shucks, Miss Aileen, I should've done that hours ago. Here I was worried about you being here, trying to figure out how to get you somewhere safe, when I should have just left you be and gone to the sheriff."

Once again she pulled at the ropes binding her hands. If only she could reach out and squeeze his hand, pat his head, even give him a hug. Instead she winced at the pain that bit into her flesh. "Don't spend time apologizing. Just go. As fast as you can."

She closed her eyes to the sound of quick footsteps echoing on the cave floor.

～.～.～.～.～

Isaac curled his hands into fists as he stared at the stream. Oh, he could follow the wheelbarrow tracks all right, right up until they disappeared into the water flowing down the hillside.

"I've been up and down the bank for half a mile, and I don't see any tracks," Elijah called from where he, Mac, and Gilbert stood on the opposite bank.

Sunlight slanted through the trees above them, filtering down through lush, thick leaves to land in patches and angles along the sandy ground and stream. Birdsong surrounded them too, a happy chorus of chirping that only made the fear in his gut grow heavier.

Isaac pressed his lips together and surveyed the ground on the opposite bank for some sign that he and the others might have missed. But the only tracks he found were the ones made by his search party.

He had to find Aileen before she was harmed, but each moment they lingered put her in more danger. *Dear God, please keep her safe.*

Was it too much to hope that her cousin and brother would protect her? They'd certainly given little thought for her safety up to now.

"I don't understand." Granger sloshed through the shallow waters of the stream with Norling at his side. "The tracks just disappear."

Isaac shook his head and stepped into the water, where he could get a clear view downstream without bushes obscuring the shoreline. The coolness made his toes turn numb while the warm air caused sweat to trickle down his neck. "They had to get out of the stream at some point."

But where? Which direction? He made his way south along the stream, leading farther inland.

"Do you think they followed the stream all the way down to the lake and then took a boat?" Elijah rolled his neck, then leaned back against a large maple tree.

A sinking sensation started in Isaac's chest and dropped into his stomach, then clear through to his knees. *Please, God, no. Not the lake.*

But considering how the tracks disappeared, it seemed the likeliest answer.

"We need to split up." Norling's command filled the forest. "Elijah, Gilbert, and Fletcher, you're with me. Since you know the coast well, we'll head down to the shore and see if we can find a place the smugglers might have beached a rowboat."

Sweat coated Isaac's forehead and trickled between his shoulder blades. If the smugglers had forced Aileen onto a boat and taken her into the wide, open lake, they'd never find her.

Elijah pushed himself off the tree. "If that's the case, then we need to find where they brought the boat ashore again."

They were more likely to catch a unicorn in one of Pa's old bear traps. But still, they had to try looking. They couldn't just abandon the search because the odds seemed impossible.

God, are You up there? Are You listening? I'm here, trying to do right by Aileen, trying to find her. I didn't give up like I did the day Pa drowned. But You have to help us. We can't do it without You.

Norling shifted in the icy stream, his eyes following the winding path down the hill toward the open water. "If it looks like there was a boat at the mouth of the stream last night, we'll go back to town and get the *North Star*, then search for Miss Brogan from the water."

"And you want me, Granger, and Mac to follow the stream inland?" Isaac looked upstream to where the water disappeared around a bend of thick pines. "Look for tracks there?"

Norling gave a curt nod. "Search carefully anywhere tracks would be easily concealed, like brambles or a thicket."

"Brambles and thickets. Right. If we leave the riverbed for any reason, we'll mark the path so you know where to follow." Though something told him he'd end up back with the others soon enough, spending days searching the coast for any sign of smugglers taking Aileen ashore.

"Sounds good." Norling sloshed out of the river and climbed onto the bank beside Elijah and Gilbert. "If we go into town for the *North Star*, we'll leave word with Mr. Foley at the mercantile."

"It's a plan." Isaac gave a curt nod, then turned back to the stream and started inland, Mac and Granger with him.

They walked for an hour or better, searching every thicket they came across, only to find no tracks on the other side. The sun beat down upon their backs and glinted off the water with a nearly blinding brightness. Squirrels nattered above them and scampered through tree branches, while birds chirped merrily as they passed.

Isaac scowled at a sparrow perched on a sapling limb. Did the entire forest have to seem so wretchedly happy?

"Time for lunch." Granger sloshed out of the water, hoisted himself atop a rock, and pulled a sandwich out of the pack he'd been carrying on his back. "I'm hungry."

"Finally." Mac tromped over to Granger and dug another sandwich out of the pack. "I was starting to think Isaac wanted to starve us."

Isaac wiped the sweat from his brow with the back of his hand. How could the others eat knowing that Aileen had been captured? Weren't they worried about her? But even if he couldn't stand the thought of filling his belly, he could use a rest and a gulp or two of water.

He sat down on a large boulder beside the rock where Granger had sprawled, and that was when he saw it. A large shoeprint in a small patch of earth between two of the rocks. He stood, his gaze running up the sloping bank that was almost entirely rock, then scrambled over to the next boulder, and the one after that and after that until he reached the top.

"Here," he panted as he focused on the mess of footprints in the dirt. "They did leave a trail, and they went this way."

There wasn't a wheelbarrow anymore. They must have ditched it somewhere in the woods, likely near where they'd gotten into the river. But there was a distinctive set of the same three footprints they'd been following before. But there was no set of feminine footprints. Was Aileen no longer with the men? Had they dumped her somewhere? A chill rushed through him. There was only one reason for dumping a person in the woods.

But maybe they hadn't dumped her. Maybe they'd carried her. Still, there could be no good explanation for Aileen not walking on her own.

Granger and Mac hurried up the bank behind him, then both men crouched to study the prints.

"Well, I'll be," Mac muttered. "Sneaky louts."

"Professional louts." Granger shoved the last of his sandwich in his mouth and choked it down. "I'd given up hope."

Leaves rustled and footsteps pounded farther up the path. Isaac reached for his gun as Mac and Granger pushed to their feet. But the gait of the person rushing toward them was too light and quick to belong to a man their size.

"Aileen?" Isaac called.

A short, thin form burst through the trees instead.

"Sheriff Cummings! Sheriff Cummings!" Jack O'Byrne slid to a halt in front of him, then doubled over to catch his breath, his narrow chest heaving. "You gotta come quick. They've got Miss Aileen!"

Chapter Twenty-Six

Aileen swallowed against the gag biting into her mouth and surveyed the trees. Where was Jack? Had he been able to find Isaac? If not Isaac, someone else?

"Move faster." Behind her, Virgil O'Byrne planted his large hands on her shoulders and gave her a shove.

She winced, her wrists twisting painfully against the rope binding them behind her back, and stumbled forward over the rock-strewn path. Her head still pounded from the effects of the draught.

She cast another glance at the forest surrounding her, but no shadowed forms of men with guns drawn and tin stars on their chests rushed toward them. And no shouts to halt echoed through the woods.

Dear God, please let them find me.

"I said, faster. We don't got all day." O'Byrne grabbed her by the elbow and dragged her down the slope toward the blue water sparkling between the trees. A handful of men traipsed in front of them, all carrying cargo of some sort. O'Byrne had roused her from slumber a half hour ago, cut the bindings around her feet, and gagged her before telling her it was time to leave. She'd only gotten a few glances at the old mine tunnel where the smuggled goods had been stored, but those glances had been enough to see the big, cavernous room of rock was empty of everything but the curtain and desk Warren had used as a makeshift office.

Which meant once she reached the water, the ship was likely to depart.

O'Byrne dragged her another few steps, and the panic in her chest climbed into her throat. Mayhap God had forsaken her. Mayhap Jack and Isaac and Conan and Morley would all fail and she'd meet her end at Warren's merciless hand. Mayhap she'd been right all those times she told Isaac she was past God's mercy…

Or mayhap she'd waited too long to claim it.

Oh, how different things would have been if she'd accepted Isaac's suit last winter. They might even have been married by now, and then she never would have been kidnapped. She would have told Isaac about Conan as soon as she'd realized he was alive, and the entire smuggling ring might have been caught weeks ago.

She could see it so clearly in her mind—one different choice six months ago, and her life might now be on a different path. One that would have brought happiness and fulfillment rather than loneliness and heartache.

God, I want another chance. I know I don't deserve one, 'tis true. I know I've done nothing but waste the chances You've given me. But if You wouldn't mind giving me some mercy, letting me have one last chance, I promise to take it and be grateful. And if that chance just so happens to include Isaac Cummings, then that would make me the most blessed person alive.

It came back to her then, a verse she'd heard not from Isaac, but as a wee lass sitting on a parish bench beside her father. *Though your sins be as scarlet, they shall be as white as snow.*

God could do that, even with the mistakes she'd made since coming to Eagle Harbor. *Take my sins and make them white as snow, please. I want to be whole and clean and… forgiven.*

She drew in a breath of summer air fresh off the lake, and a sense of peace flooded her.

But it lasted only until O'Byrne jerked her ropes again and sent her stumbling toward the beach.

⌐.⌐.⌐.⌐.⌐

"This is more dangerous than any rescue I've ever gone out on with Elijah." Mac whispered the words from his hunched position shrouded in the bushes.

"I know." Isaac surveyed the flurry of activity in the inlet below the rocky outcropping where he, Granger, and Mac all huddled. Crates and crates and more crates filled the sandy beach, each being loaded into dinghies and rowed to the three-masted schooner anchored in the mouth of the inlet, only fifty yards or so from shore.

"There're too many to take by ourselves," Granger whispered from beside him. "We have to wait for help."

"We are." Though it galled. Isaac fingered the butt of his pistol. He'd be able to pick off half a dozen men before being discovered. But what would happen then? Plus the smugglers had Aileen—at least according to Jack. He'd not gotten a glimpse of her himself. Was she already on the ship? Or had she yet to board?

Jack had made it sound like the smugglers planned to bring Aileen to the ship right away, which was why he and Granger and Mac had come to the inlet rather than look for the abandoned mine tunnel Jack had given them directions to.

He'd then sent Jack to find Norling, Elijah, Gilbert, and Fletcher and tell them to take the *North Star* to the inlet. But he'd been crouched here with Mac and Granger for almost a half hour without any sign of help coming. Had Jack not been able to find them?

A deep, familiar shade of red flashed through the trees near the beach, and his throat caught. Men loaded the last of the crates into one of two remaining dinghies and pushed off the beach, but Isaac kept his gaze riveted on the forest where something had just moved.

There, another flash of red and a bit of white. And then Aileen was standing on the beach, her hair disheveled and falling in tangled strands down her shoulders and back, her white shirtwaist untucked from her skirt.

Isaac started to stand, but Mac grabbed his arm and tugged him back down. "No you don't."

"But they have her."

"Giving us away won't do her any good."

A large, burly man—Virgil O'Byrne?—dragged her forward toward the single boat remaining on the sand, and she was soon flanked by two other men.

She was barely on the beach for half a minute before she was in a boat rowing out to the big schooner. Isaac clenched his teeth. Even if he'd been lying in wait right next to the water, it would have been impossible to charge the men before they'd whisked her off.

But he wouldn't let himself fail her. "Let's go."

"Where?" Granger's brow furrowed. "You can't mean to board the ship."

"I sure don't mean to let her sail away on it."

Mac shook his head. "The time to stow away on a ship is before people get there, not two minutes before it's ready to set sail."

Isaac looked at the ship, its sails already unfurled, getting ready to depart with the next burst of wind. "I have to try."

He pointed to a rope ladder hanging down the side of the ship. The ladder passed near two different portholes before disappearing over the top of the gunwale. They could sneak into either of the portholes and wait for the perfect time to free Aileen. "Either of you two up for a swim?"

He glanced down at the blue water shimmering below them,

water that was plenty deep below the small bluffs. Then he stood and dove into the depths before Granger or Mac could stop him.

~.~.~.~.~

Something was wrong. From where she stood atop the poop deck, Aileen swept her gaze over the main deck of the schooner, where men were busy taking crates down into the cargo hold. She was supposed to be down there too, wasn't she? Hadn't Conan said she'd be held with the cargo?

That's where he and Morley were supposed to find her when they helped her escape.

But instead of being taken below deck and into the hold, O'Byrne had dragged her up to the top deck, then handed her off to Skees, the brute that had helped capture her last night.

Her hands were finally free—O'Byrne had untied her when she'd needed to climb the ladder into the ship—but having the bindings gone did her little good if Skees refused to take his eyes off her.

"Stop fidgeting." The man tightened his grip on her upper arm. "I'll tie you up again if I need to."

"Or ye could let go of me." Aileen tried to wriggle away from him. "It's not as though there's somewhere I can run."

And there wasn't. Even if she tried jumping overboard, her skirt and petticoat meant she had little hope of out-swimming the sailors who would jump in after her. And that was if she could make it to the gunwale without Skees or someone else catching her.

Conan had been right about the best time for escape. It would be once they were at sea, when no one was paying her any mind and she was forgotten in the bowels of the ship.

Provided she made it into the bowels of the ship.

Skees sneaked an arm around her waist, then pulled her back against him. Rancid breath wheezed into her ear. "Now why would

I let go of you? Looks to me like you want to be held closer, sweetheart."

She elbowed him in the gut, but all he did was grunt, then squeeze her harder against him. She would have tried wrenching away, but the sound of a door closing resonated from the cabin below, and bootsteps sounded on the stairs. O'Byrne emerged onto the poop deck, followed by an immaculate looking Warren, sporting a three-piece suit that didn't seem to have a speck of grime from the mine.

The familiar sound of expensive shoes clacked against the deck as he neared, and he trailed his gaze quickly down her. His face remained expressionless, but something told her he saw everything—her fear of what would happen next, her revulsion as she arched her body away from Skees, her determination to escape before Warren could hurt her again.

"Put her in my quarters." Warren muttered the words as though they were a mere afterthought. As though she were as insignificant as one of the crates being ordered about. Then he turned and moved to the top of the narrow stairs leading down to the main deck, talking to O'Byrne beside him.

Her heart hammered against her chest and blood roared in her ears. She wasn't going into his quarters. Not today. Not tomorrow. Not ever again.

Skees loosened his hold on her waist and shoved her forward. "Ya heard the man. Into the cabin, wench."

No! She rushed toward Warren instead and shoved him as hard as she could. "I'm not going to be yer wench."

He fell forward and his hand shot out to reach for the railing at the top of the deck, but missed.

She teetered at the top of the steps and almost missed catching the rail herself.

His body hit the stairs with a crack, his neck bending at a harsh angle, and a ghastly shriek filled the air. He rolled twice more before landing on the deck below with a sickening thud.

Then he was still. Too still.

She gripped the railing tighter, her nails digging into the weathered wood. Had she killed him? She leaned over to get a better look. But nay, his eyes were open, looking straight at her.

The men hauling cargo rushed forward, everyone surrounding him until they blocked him from view.

"What have you done?" O'Byrne yanked her off the railing and grabbed her wrist, twisting it around behind her back until she yelped with pain. His breath puffed hot on her face, then he leaned over the rail and called to his men. "Is he dead?"

"No," the man standing nearest Warren's head called up to him. "But he says he can't feel nothin'. Says he can't move neither."

She blinked again, her throat thick. Had she paralyzed him? She stood as still as though she'd been paralyzed herself. She shouldn't wish ill on another person. Shouldn't wish another person dead, or hurt so badly they would never recover.

But if Warren truly was paralyzed, then he couldn't take her into his quarters and hurt her. And not only her, but he'd never be able to hurt another woman again. And mayhap he couldn't lead a smuggling ring either. If he was paralyzed, he'd have to lie in bed all day and rely on others to tend him.

A shadow moved over her, dark and large enough it covered all of the men hovering below. She looked up to find another ship blocking off the entrance to the rocky inlet, coming so close it looked as though they might crash.

"This is the *USRC Rush*." A masculine voice projected from the other vessel. "Surrender your weapons."

The sleek bow and low hull told her the boat was built for speed. Had Isaac directed the Revenue Cutter Service to the inlet? Her heartbeat slowed, the rushing sound in her ears quieting.

"Do we fight?" One of the men below reached for his pistol.

O'Byrne glanced at the ship, then down at Warren. "No. Not unless you want to end up dead or like the Shark."

A half dozen men wearing blue uniforms and white tricorn hats swung over on ropes from the *USRC Rush*. The cutter men still onboard slid planks over the side of the cutter to connect the two ships, and a torrent of sailors rushed across.

Tears sprang to her eyes. She was safe. Truly safe. She'd been so certain, when climbing the ladder to the ship, that any chance she had with Isaac was over, that her very life might be over. Mayhap she'd protected herself from Warren's advances by shoving him down the stairs, for a while at least, but the other smugglers would likely have hurt her. Yet each man in a blue uniform who crossed onto the ship further strengthened the hope that had sprung up in her heart the instant the voice from the revenue cutter had filled the harbor.

A few of the smugglers grabbed their pistols, but the number of cutter service and customs men made any hope of fighting futile.

O'Byrne released his cruel grip on her arm, and she sank against the railing. Quick and heavy footsteps sounded behind her, and she turned to see O'Byrne and Skees both running toward the side of the ship.

"Up here!" Anger filled her voice as she waved at the customs men. Did Skees and O'Byrne think she'd let them escape after how they'd treated her? "They're trying to jump overboard."

A trio of men charged up the stairs and burst onto the poop deck, then raced for where O'Byrne was moving his large girth toward the other side of the gunwale.

"Miss Brogan!"

She turned and surveyed the main deck, her gaze landing on the only man from the cutter not wearing a blue uniform.

Deputy Norling dashed up the stairs. "Where's the sheriff?"

"Ye mean Isaac?" She glanced around the ship again, her chest tightening. "He's not here. Is he... is he supposed to be?"

"Jack said he would be."

"Ye saw Jack?"

"Yes, we were headed back to town when he found us. Said he'd already seen the sheriff and that he was going to rescue you. Elijah, Gilbert, Fletcher and I were to take the *North Star* and meet him here, but we got back to town just as the revenue cutter was pulling into harbor."

"I... Oh." Her mind raced to follow all the details. Jack had certainly succeeded in getting help, but where was Isaac?

"Are you all right?" Norling rested a hand on her shoulder, turning her just enough so their eyes met. "Did the men hurt you?"

She touched the rope burns on her wrist with a hand, then reached up to the spot beside her temple where O'Byrne had hit her with the butt of his gun. "The men were too busy moving cargo to bother with me at first. But once we got to the ship..."

Her throat turned tight, refusing to let a single sound slip through her mouth. She looked down, to where Warren now lay abandoned by the other smugglers. His skin held a grayish tint and his eyes were closed, but even from the deck above, she could see he struggled to draw breath.

"I... he... that is..." She gulped in a lungful of air. "I shoved him, and I don't think he can move. But he meant me harm, and I was so angry." She pressed a hand over her mouth and squeezed her eyes shut, but she could still see the image of Warren in her mind, lying on the deck below, gasping for air. "I never intended..."

"That man needs attention," Norling called over the deck. He waved at some men below then pointed to where Warren lay.

Norling turned back to her, a firm, but worried expression on his

293

face. "Aileen, if he's truly the man in charge of this smuggling ring, he's looking at death by hanging in a few months anyway."

"But he has to go to court for that, and here I just…" She sniffled. "Do ye think he'll be able to move again? Mayhap he's just hurt, mayhap if Doc Harrington treats him…" But if Warren recovered and wriggled out of yet another criminal charge, where could she possibly go that he'd not track her down and make her pay for what she'd done?

Norling dug around in his pocket and pulled out a handkerchief, then tucked it into her hand. "Here, dry your eyes, and don't worry about him. He's our concern now. Let's get you to the cutter, make you some tea. Don't suppose these criminals bothered to feed you, did they?" He settled his big hands on her shoulders and turned her toward the stairs.

Yet the view of the deck swarming with cutter service men only caused her to still again. "But where's Isaac? Do ye think the smugglers caught him?"

A new worry flamed in her chest, worry that was almost worse than the fear that had consumed her when she'd been bound on the floor of the cave. Was Isaac lying somewhere in the woods, broken and bloody? Or worse, with a bullet hole in his chest? He must need help, or he would have already been here.

Norling patted her shoulder. "We'll find him. Maybe we just beat him to the inlet."

She drew in a shaky breath. "I can't go anywhere until I know he's safe."

"Don't be foolish. You need food and drink." Norling shifted so that he stood in front of her, then bent his head and looked into her eyes, but not in a compassionate kind of way. He might well have been Dr. Harrington inspecting a bruise given his official, detached assessment of her. "Did the smugglers make you drink something? There's something off about your eyes."

She stomped her foot on the deck. "I'm not the one who's missing. I'm not the one ye need to worry ab—"

"Aileen!"

At the sound of the familiar voice, her heart stopped. She turned and peered over the railing in the direction of the shout. It took only a moment to spot Isaac, though he'd yet to find her. He stood beside the door in the deck floor that led to the cargo hold. Wet hair was plastered to his head, and his clothes were sodden too, his shirt half-sticking to his chest.

She raced down the stairs as Mac and Granger shoved through the door, both just as wet as Isaac.

Isaac had spotted her and barreled through the cutter service men toward her. Then he was wrapping his arms around her and pulling her into a hug. The water soaking his shirt was cool, and yet his embrace couldn't be warmer, his arms couldn't be steadier, his grip couldn't feel more perfect.

"Ye're here," she whispered against him. Her legs turned suddenly weak, her body as limp as his sodden clothes.

"Of course, I'm here. Did you doubt I would come for you?"

She buried her head in his chest, shaking it slightly. "Nay, but I worried what might have happened while ye were trying, I did."

He leaned down and kissed the crown of her head, then stroked a tangled strand of hair behind her ear. "Nothing happened except me saying a few hundred prayers God would keep you safe."

She closed her eyes, sinking deeper into the warmth still emanating from his body despite his damp clothing.

A muted voice—Norling's—sounded somewhere above her head, then she felt the rumble of Isaac's voice in his chest as he answered, but she couldn't make sense of the words floating around her. Indeed, they didn't matter. There was only one thing that mattered—God had given her the second chance she'd prayed for.

And she didn't intend to waste it.

Chapter Twenty-Seven

He'd thought there could be nothing worse than knowing the woman he loved was kidnapped. But he'd been wrong. The worst part was listening to her recount all the things that had happened to her—or nearly happened—while he'd been unable to find her.

Isaac squirmed in his seat next to the bed as he listened to Aileen explain to the customs agent what had happened in detail. Seeing her slumped on one of Dr. Harrington's sickroom mattresses, her vibrant hair fallen around her in a tangled mess and the purple bruise marring the skin beside her left eye, had made his jaw clench and his hands ball into fists. But the stories she was telling made it hard to remain seated and not head out and see justice done immediately—his own form of justice.

What kind of brother drugged his sister? Maybe Conan really did have some cockeyed plan to save her after drugging her, but that didn't make up for what he'd done.

Isaac reached over and gripped Aileen's hand, but that only caused him to notice the rope burns around her wrist again. He drew in a breath. How hard she must have struggled to rub her skin raw.

"And then I pushed him, I did. He tumbled down the stairs and landed on the deck below." Aileen worried her free hand in the folds of her skirt, her shoulders slumping. "Mayhap I should be sorry I did it, but part of me—"

"You shouldn't be sorry in the least. There's nothing wrong with defending yourself." Isaac tightened his grip on her hand, giving it a firm squeeze. If only he had arrived on the deck sooner, then he could have dealt with Warren himself. "There's nothing wrong with trying to stop a monster from hurting you."

She glanced over at him, the skin beneath her eyes smudged with shadows. "I'm not sure what I expected to happen when I shoved him, but I just couldn't contain meself after he ordered me to his room."

Isaac glanced over at the customs officer perched rigidly in the wooden chair beside him, notepad in hand, dutifully recording every last word Aileen spoke. What were the chances the man would mind if he reached over and pulled Aileen into his lap while she finished her story?

But the officer looked up before Isaac could do more than rub his thumb over the back of her hand.

"About your brother and cousin, Miss Brogan." The man pressed his spectacles higher on his nose. "Do you have any idea where they might be?"

"Are they still unaccounted for?" Worried lines furrowed Aileen's brow.

"Afraid so." The customs man positioned his pencil over the notepad.

Isaac stifled a yawn and rubbed his bleary eyes. No wonder the Customs Service had brought so many men. There were too many angles of this investigation for one person alone to keep up with—especially when that person hadn't gotten any sleep the night before. Last he'd known, Morley and Conan had been seen in the cargo hold of the schooner, stacking crates before the revenue cutter arrived. But the customs men hadn't found them aboard ship.

Aileen slipped her hand from his, then pushed herself off the bed and went to the room's single window. "Conan said something about cutting the ropes to one of the lifeboats so we could escape, but that's all we had time to talk about."

"The Customs Service doesn't have any idea where they might be?" Isaac covered another yawn with his hand, then stood. Maybe he wouldn't feel quite so tired if he moved.

"Sure we do. Somewhere with the missing lifeboat Miss Brogan just spoke of." The officer scrawled something more on his paper. "The Brogans were probably below deck when we captured the ship, and after hearing the commotion above, sneaked out one of the portholes to the lifeboat."

Aileen turned from the window, her arms wrapped around herself. "I'm not covering for them, if that's what ye're thinking. I didn't even see them on the ship. I assumed they were below deck, which is where Conan said I'd be taken. But Warren..." She swallowed, her face losing the bit of color that had seeped into it on the trip back to Eagle Harbor.

"It's all right, love." Isaac went to wrap his arms around her, then brought her against his chest, customs agent and propriety be hanged. He reached up and gently traced the bruise on her face with his thumb. "No one thinks you helped them escape."

Isaac looked over her head and glared at the officer. "Do we?"

The man rolled his eyes, then flipped back through his notepad and studied it for a moment. "All evidence seems to indicate the two escaped on their own."

"And your notes clearly state Aileen was held against her will, correct?" The last thing he needed was for the Customs Service to think she had taken part in the smuggling efforts.

The man sighed and scratched the side of his head. "They do. I'm just trying to make sure I have all the needed information, Sheriff. It's not my job to incriminate. We have lawyers for that."

"What happens if ye don't find me brother and cousin?" Aileen pulled back to look at the customs man.

"We'll find them." The man didn't even glance up as he answered, just studied his notes. "Where were they living before they came to Eagle Harbor?"

"Conan was pretending to be dead for the past year, so I don't know where he stayed. I can give you Morley's address in Chicago though."

"If you could write it down for me please." The agent tore a piece of paper from his notepad and handed it to Aileen. She headed to the bedside table, her footsteps slow and sluggish, then yawned before scrawling the address on the paper.

She returned the paper, and the customs agent folded the single sheet before sticking it into his breast pocket. "Can you think of anywhere else your cousin or brother might go?"

Aileen's shoulders rose and fell in a small shrug. "Conan wanted to buy a farm in Wisconsin, but I don't think he had a specific place in mind. When he talked about escaping from Warren, he said the three of us would go west."

"West?" The man blinked through his spectacles. "Did he say anything more specific than west?"

Aileen stifled a second yawn and slowly shook her head.

"You've asked enough questions for now." Isaac sent another glare toward the customs agent, then rested a hand at the small of Aileen's back and guided her toward the bed. "You should rest, love."

"Actually, she needs to be examined," Dr. Harrington spoke from where he stood in the open door. "Which means both of you should leave."

The customs man closed his notepad and stood. "I'm done, but be advised the captain might have more questions for you later, Miss Brogan."

"Thank ye." She sat on the bed and gave the agent a slight nod before he left the room.

Dr. Harrington took a stethoscope out of his medical bag, then raised his eyebrows. "Sheriff Cummings, you'll need to leave as well."

"Right." He'd probably tarried too long here as it was. There were smugglers locked in his jailhouse, customs and revenue cutter men swarming his office, and a ship filled with illegal goods to be guarded.

But then he glanced back at Aileen, sitting on the bed with her shoulders caved inward, and couldn't quite make himself take a step toward the door.

Stethoscope still in hand, Dr. Harrington moved to the edge of the bed, but looked at him rather than his patient. "I only let married couples and family stay while someone is being examined."

"I plan to marry her." The words fell from his mouth before he thought to rein them in.

Aileen drew in a sharp breath, and he slanted another glance at her. She looked back at him with her mouth slightly open, but some of the sadness had left her gaze.

He scowled. She deserved an official proposal, not something that had accidently slipped out. But that didn't change the fact he wanted to be involved in every part of her life—and that he didn't want to leave her now.

"You aren't her husband at the moment." Dr. Harrington hardened his jaw and jabbed a finger toward the door. "Out."

"Isaac, I'll be fine, I will." Aileen moved her legs onto the bed and curled them against the mattress, shifting herself so she faced him straight on. "I've told ye, naught happened to me."

"Are you sure?" he whispered, his throat suddenly thick. She wasn't hiding something because she was afraid of what he might think, was she?

"I'm fine, I am."

"Given that bruise next to her eye, I wouldn't say nothing happened." The doctor placed a firm hand on Isaac's shoulder and shoved him toward the door. "But I can't tell you if that's the worst of it unless you let me examine her."

"All right, all right. I'm going." But he stopped in the doorway and turned back to the doctor. "Her wrists. She has rope burns there. Do you have some kind of salve for that?"

Dr. Harrington crossed his arms over his chest. "What do you take me for? A quack?"

"No, not a quack. I just…" His gaze fell to Aileen again. She had hung her head and was sitting on the bed with her knees pulled up, arms wrapped around herself. Confound it. He should be the one hugging her so she didn't have to hug herself. "Are you sure I can't—?"

"Yes." The doc's jaw clenched. "Don't you have a jail full of men to attend?"

And a head customs agent to talk to. He should probably have a conversation with the captain of the revenue cutter as well. How long did the Customs Service plan to hold the smugglers in Eagle Harbor? He'd need to arrange for meals the entire time the prisoners were here. Did he need to arrange food for the customs and revenue men too?

Isaac pressed his lips together into a hard line. Once he left, he'd be busy for hours when all he wanted was to be with Aileen. But then, the sooner he left, the sooner he could return.

He took a final glance at the woman he loved then stepped backward through the door. It shut immediately and a lock clicked into place.

"I want to see her as soon as you're done," he called. "And I expect a full report."

No answer.

He yawned, scrubbing a hand over his face. Now to face the chaos at his office—if only he could convince his aching feet to move. Maybe the doc's wife had some coffee brewing. He'd need about ten cups if he planned to stay awake long enough to deal with the mess awaiting him. He headed toward the kitchen and cracked open one of the swinging doors. "Hello?"

"Come in." Lindy Harrington stood kneading bread dough at the table. Little wisps of golden hair framed her face, and a band of sweat streaked across her brow.

"Sheriff." She straightened and wiped her hands on her apron. "Are you looking for Warren Sinclair?"

"Warren." His blood rushed hot enough he suddenly didn't need coffee to stay awake. "I hadn't really planned to talk to him."

But maybe he should. After all, he'd known Warren Sinclair longer than any of the customs men. Perhaps he could get more information out of him than someone else. "Where is he?"

"Sometimes Seth puts the gravely ill patients in our room." She nodded toward the door on the far side of the kitchen. "Your Deputy Norling just left a few minutes ago. Word's been sent to Gilbert, but he's not here yet."

"The doctor doesn't expect Warren to live?" Not that he was surprised. Warren's skin had held the gray pallor of death on the ride back to Eagle Harbor, his breaths had been shallow and raspy, and he still hadn't been able to move his arms or legs.

Lindy settled her hands atop her protruding stomach, her eyes misting. "Seth said if a person's spine is injured somewhere high on their back, it can affect their breathing. Something about the lung muscles not working as they should, along with the arm and leg muscles. After a day or so of the lung muscles not working properly…"

"I see." It made sense in a sickening sort of way. Isaac moved toward the door that led to Warren's room. "I'll peek in, just for a minute."

To say goodbye in peace? To chew him out in anger? He wasn't quite sure what he'd do, but something felt unfinished between them, and this might well be the last chance he had to see the other man.

The room was eerily quiet, and the sour stench of death clung to the air. Sunlight shafted through two windows, painting the bed in light, yet nothing about the bed seemed cheery.

Warren lay there, his eyes shut and hands resting over his chest. It was an odd position for a man to hold while sleeping, but then, if Warren couldn't move his arms, he probably had little choice about where they rested.

Isaac stepped closer, the tightness in his jaw and shoulders slowly loosening as he ran his eyes down the strong, lithe body that would soon be buried beneath six feet of dirt.

He couldn't quite make himself feel happy about Warren's condition. But he couldn't quite feel sad either, considering how Warren had hurt Aileen. Knowing he'd never be able to hurt another woman again. Warren might not stand in a court of law to answer for his crimes, but God had seen to it that Warren answered for them in another way. Isaac swallowed. Perhaps relief was the emotion swirling through him, quiet and subtle, assuring him he'd have no reason to either fear or fight this man in the future.

Warren's eyes opened into two thin slits. "You," he rasped. "Where is she?" He cast his eyes about the room.

Isaac took a step back from the bed and plunged his hands into his pockets, where his fingers balled into fists. "If you mean Aileen, she's none of your concern."

"The strumpet should be… be… taken out back and… shot." Despite Warren's obvious struggle to both talk and breathe, no pain creased his face, only anger. "She did this to me."

"And what would you have done to her if she hadn't pushed you down the stairs first?" The words slashed from his mouth like an ax at full swing.

Warren's lips twisted together, but rather than answer, his eyes shifted to the door. "You…"

Gilbert stepped into the room.

"This is…" Warren tried to cough, but couldn't quite get his lungs to expel whatever was trapped inside them, and a wretched gurgling cut off his words for a few seconds. "…all your fault."

"Funny." Gilbert's voice cracked, and his throat worked as he surveyed his brother. "I could have sworn you were the one in charge of the smuggling ring, not me."

"Because of you." Warren spat the words with a sudden burst of force. "Always coming up with an invention. Always coming up with a better way to make money."

"I don't see what my inventions have to do with anything." Gilbert approached the bed. His jaw was hard, but it clenched and unclenched as though he fought to control the emotions that had to be swirling inside him.

"I had to make more money than you… or Father… Father would have given you…" Warren closed his eyes, his lungs laboring, but again, no discomfort crossed his face, just anger and loathing.

Isaac glanced at the door. Should he get the doctor? Perhaps if Warren were sitting up, he could expel some of the fluid that seemed trapped inside his chest.

"Are you talking about which one of us Father gave his shipping company to last year?" Gilbert's brow furrowed.

Isaac looked down at Warren's form, which still seemed too strong and hearty for him to be dying. Rebekah had said something last summer about Warren and Gilbert being in a competition for who would run their father's shipping empire, but he hadn't paid all that much attention. He only knew that Gilbert didn't work for his father now. He was a partner with two other men in some kind of invention company, where they developed things like cranes and pulleys and boats with motors on the back of them.

Gilbert sucked in a long, slow breath through his nose, his jaw still set. "Tell me you didn't start smuggling so you could show a bigger profit margin with the ships Father gave us."

Warren's hard eyes gave all the answer Gilbert needed.

"I never wanted a part in Great Northern Shipping. I couldn't have stood to work that closely with Father." Gilbert lifted a shoulder in a careless shrug, as though one of the largest shipping companies on the Great Lakes didn't matter a whit to him. Then again, for someone as whip smart as Gilbert, maybe it didn't.

"I'm much happier now, doing what I love, and having Rebekah in my life." Gilbert looked down and blinked, the muscle at the side of his jaw pulsing again. He wasn't exactly sobbing over his brother's deathbed, but considering how controlled Gilbert usually was, he might as well be. "They tell me..." Gilbert cleared the raspiness from his voice. "They tell me your lungs have been damaged."

"I'll recover." Warren's neck muscles strained, and the veins at the sides of his brow bulged as he struggled to raise his head a few inches off the pillow. "I'll call for the best doctors in Chicago. And once I'm out of bed, you'd better hide. Because I'll come..." A half cough, half choking sound cut off his words, and his head dropped back to the pillow. But the movement did little to stop the coughing, which didn't subside as it had last time.

Gilbert turned to him, an aching softness in the blue eyes that usually appeared so bored and cool. "Fetch the doctor."

"Already on it." Isaac strode for the door, but opened it only to find Dr. Harrington striding through the kitchen, medical bag in hand.

"Lindy says Mr. Sinclair's coughing is growing worse."

"It is." Isaac stepped to the side so the doctor could enter.

Warren's terrible, gurgling hacking filled the room.

"Gilbert, do you want to stay? I'm afraid this might not be pleasant." Dr. Harrington spoke over the coughing sounds as he strode to the bed and set his medical bag on the little table against the wall.

Gilbert turned away from his brother, a sheen of moisture glazing his eyes. "No, I think I'll go. Will you send word when... if...?"

"You'll be the first to know." Doc Harrington patted Gilbert on the shoulder, then stepped right up beside Warren and positioned his stethoscope over the man's lungs.

Isaac held the bedroom door open for Gilbert, and the other man strode past him. But even when he closed the door, the sounds of Warren's gasping and coughing still emanated into the kitchen.

Lindy stood near the table, the bread dough forgotten, and a look of sympathy on her face. "I'm sorry, Gilbert. I know those words don't sound like much, but I truly am sorry."

"Thank you." Gilbert squared his shoulders started for the door that led to the parlor.

"Sheriff?"

Isaac moved to follow Gilbert, but turned back to Lindy.

"I just checked, and Aileen is sleeping. Perhaps you can give her time to rest before visiting again?" Lindy smiled at him so sweetly he found himself agreeing.

"Will you send word to my office once she wakes?"

Lindy gave him another soft smile. "Of course. I'm sure she'll be asking for you anyway."

"Thank you, now if you'll excuse me." He darted through the kitchen doors and caught the door leading outside just before Gilbert pulled it closed.

"Wait." He caught his brother-in-law by the arm before Gilbert bounded down the porch steps. But when Gilbert swung around, his eyes red with unshed tears, Isaac suddenly had no words. What did a person say in a situation like this, and to the man who had married his twin sister, no less? Lindy was right. *I'm sorry* seemed so very trite. "I… uh…"

Gilbert gave a small shake of his head. "You don't need to say anything. Truly. There's no part of this situation that words can fix."

Isaac dug his hands into his pockets. "I was hoping Warren would regret things, maybe show a bit of remorse." Maybe that's what had propelled him to Warren's bedside earlier, the hope that even someone as cruel as Warren would change for the better at the end. The hope that someone like Warren would claim God's mercy for himself.

"Me too." Gilbert looked off into the distance, his gaze roving the harbor. "But you heard him. He spent his last words blaming me for the smuggling ring he's run for four years. I think he regrets getting caught and getting injured, not the smuggling." Gilbert's Adam's apple bobbed, and his voice grew soft. "And not what he did to Aileen and others like her."

Something hard fisted in Isaac's chest, and he suddenly found it impossible to swallow. "I don't understand how a man can be so evil."

Gilbert heaved in a breath. "There was a part of me that thought—that hoped—things would be different when I walked into that room. But my brother isn't going to change, and I can't make choices for other people, only for myself. So I'm choosing to go home and spend the evening with my wife who loves me. I'm going to hold her extra tight and kiss her extra long and send a slew of prayers to God thanking Him for giving me a woman who's better than I deserve. And you should do the same." Gilbert clapped a hand on his back. "Worry about what you can change. Not about what you can't."

Isaac could only nod. When had Gilbert become so wise?

"Head back to your office and deal with whatever mess is waiting for you. And when Aileen wakes up, go see your woman. I'm off to see mine." Gilbert turned and jogged down the steps without waiting for a response, his gait a little too fast for a dignified businessman.

But the perfect pace for a man who was in love with his wife.

Isaac trudged down the steps and turned the opposite direction toward his office. But something told him that when he returned later, his steps would be just as quick as Gilbert's, if not a little quicker.

Chapter Twenty-Eight

Elijah yawned and blinked the sleep from his eyes as he headed up the winding trail to his house. His shoulders ached, his feet screamed, and his head pounded as though he'd been up for the past forty hours—which he mostly had. The sooner he climbed into his bed, the better.

Yet he really couldn't force himself to move much faster on account of Jack, who stumbled along the packed-dirt trail beside him as though he'd not gotten any sleep for three days, instead of two. "You sure you're all right?"

"Just tired," the boy answered on a half yawn. "And hungry."

And in need of a bath, a new pair of clothes, and a haircut. The boy had never looked so unkempt, not even when Lindy Harrington had first found him and his siblings living in a hovel in the woods.

And yet, Elijah had never been prouder to say he knew the lad either. "You did well today. Real well. If not for you, we might never have caught the smugglers." His throat grew tight at the thought. He might not love Aileen Brogan the way Isaac did, but that didn't mean she deserved to be abducted by the likes of Warren Sinclair.

"How are Alice and Toby?" Jack looked up at him, concern written across his weary eyes.

"They've been worried about you, but besides that, they're fine.

Might be napping, though I don't see any harm in waking them this once if you'd like to check on them."

Jack nodded and trudged over the sparse lawn toward the cabin. "That'd be nice, if you don't mind."

Mind letting an older brother be reunited with his siblings? "Not at all," he croaked as they climbed the porch steps and stomped through the entryway.

Victoria stood in the kitchen, her back to them while setting the kettle to boil. At the sound of the kitchen door closing, she turned, a smile on her face, though her eyes held worry and questions. "Did you find…?"

She pressed a hand to her mouth and gasped. "J-Jack?"

Jack was reaching the age where boys liked to be taken hunting and fishing, liked to start trailing after their pas rather than clinging to their mas' skirts. But he didn't have any trouble racing to Victoria and wrapping his arms around her in a hug.

"Are you all r-right? Where have you been? I was so w-w-worried." She brushed a hand over his hair, then stroked his arms and back, as though seeing Jack alive and whole wasn't quite enough for her.

"I was with my pa, but Deputy Norling says I don't have to live with him no more." Jack had pulled away long enough to answer her question, but then buried his face in her side again.

"You don't need to live with your pa?" Victoria's eyes met his above Jack's head, a fragile hope kindling in them. "Does that mean…?"

Elijah cleared the grit from his throat. "Looks like Virgil O'Byrne will be locked up for a good long time. Once he's convicted at trial, we'll be able to file for adoption, make everything official." He blinked against the moisture that suddenly welled in his eyes. "Jack did right well today, Vic. He's the reason we caught the smugglers.

Him alone. When he realized they had Aileen, he ran away and found Isaac, then found us."

Victoria opened her mouth, but before she could ask more, Alice's voice drifted from down the hall. "Mr. Elijah's back!"

Two running sets of little feet pattered toward him, and Alice and Toby both launched themselves at his legs. He bent to sweep them into his arms.

"We prayed for you." Alice placed a kiss on his cheek. "That God would keep you—"

"Jack!" Toby cried, his little legs scrambling to get down.

Alice turned her head, spotted her brother, and started wiggling too. "Let me go."

He set them both back on the ground, and they raced to their brother, who'd finally released Victoria, but only so he could hug his siblings.

Elijah's eyes met Victoria's, and he blinked away the infernal moisture that kept making his gaze grow fuzzy. "They're going to be ours."

She pressed a hand to her mouth and gave him a slight nod as tears tracked down her face.

He stepped around the huddled young'uns and settled his arms around her. "Don't cry, sweetling. This is a happy day."

"I know, it's just…" She plucked the handkerchief from his shirt pocket and used it to dab her eyes. "For so long I wanted a babe of my own, but seeing the children here, like this…" Her throat worked, and she blinked furiously as more tears slipped down her cheeks.

"God had it planned better than we realized." He stroked an errant wisp of hair away from her brow.

"He did. I never should have doubted Him."

"Nor should've I." He gathered her closer and cradled her head against his chest. "I'd forgotten how good God's blessings are."

But standing in the kitchen of the home where he'd grown up, holding his wife while looking at the children that would soon be his... he'd never felt so blessed.

~.~.~.~.~

He'd asked it.

Ellie stared down at the letter quivering right along with her shaking hands. But she didn't need the bold, strong letters to be still in order to read them. *Will you marry me?*

"Excuse me, miss."

She jolted and looked up to find two sailors staring at her expectantly.

Because she was blocking the doorway of the mercantile. Heat exploded onto her cheeks. Teach her to open a letter and start reading while she walked. But she'd been in a hurry to get home after working at the bakery—at least until she'd gotten Sam's letter.

"Sorry," she mumbled, then stumbled through the door and to the far corner of the porch, where she sank back against the outside wall of the mercantile. She sucked in a breath through lungs that seemed suddenly starved for air, then forced her trembling hands to still and her gaze to focus on the remainder of Sam's letter.

Maybe I didn't make my intentions clear enough last time, which is why I've yet to get a response from you. But now that I've got ranchland, I'm going to need a wife. After I finish this next drive to El Paso as a cattle hand, I plan to put up a house. It'll be a nice one, I promise, with a room just for the two of us. I've already got the spot picked out on a little rise overlooking my land—our land. Because after writing you for these past months, I'd love nothing more than to share my home and my land and my life with you, Ellie Spritzer.

Ellie gulped. *Nothing more than to share my life with you.* How did a woman refuse words as sweet as those?

"Ellie?"

She stiffened, her hand curling against the crisp paper, and looked up into the familiar brown gaze she'd not seen for a week and a half.

Not since the night her brothers were caught with the smugglers.

"Are you...? That is, what I meant to say was..." Jake sighed and doffed his hat, crushing the brim in his hands much the same way she'd crushed the letter. "I'm sorry I haven't been by to see you in a few weeks, but..."

"But what, Jake?" She narrowed her eyes at him.

"But my parents saw us dancing the night of Mrs. Oakton's party, and... um, they think I'm not focusing on the right things." His voice turned tight and raspy, and he stuck a finger into his collar and tugged. "They think I might be getting a little distracted and... ah... I'm going back to Chicago early. Pa has a friend with a bank there who needs help before school starts, and I ..." His words died again, and he offered a small shrug, as if his rambling somehow made everything better.

She shook her head. Sure, there'd been a part of her that had dreamed something more than friendship might bud between them. A small part. A part she'd known not to pay any mind. His smiles had been nice, as had his roast beef sandwiches, and the time they spent sharing memories of Clifford. But people like Jake Ranulfson, who wore tailored suits and spent more money on food for one meal than her family did for an entire week, didn't plan futures with the likes of her. Maybe Elijah Cummings had married Victoria, and Rebekah had married Gilbert Sinclair. But they were the exceptions.

Still, he could have at least stopped by to tell her why he hadn't visited for lunch rather than leave her wondering for a week.

Jake opened his mouth as though to say something more, but closed it and slid his hat back on his head, a hat that probably cost more than every last stitch of the clothing she owned. "It won't always be like this, Ellie. I need to obey my parents now, but I'll be done with school in another year, and maybe then—"

"I won't be here in a year." She looked down at the letter in her hand. "Thank you for the sandwiches, and sharing your memories of my brother, but the truth is, I've been exchanging letters with a cattle hand in Texas for some time now. A cattle hand who will soon have his own ranch and needs a wife, and well…" She swallowed and looked up at him, meeting his soft brown gaze for what would probably be the last time. "Sam just asked me to marry him, so it looks as though I'm off to Texas."

"Texas?" Jake whipped his hat back off his head and took a step closer to her. "That's clear on the other side of the country. You can't go traipsing off there by yourself. Besides, how much do you know about this… this… this stranger?"

She raised her chin. "I know he's honest and kind and a hard worker, God-fearing too." What more could a woman like her ask for in a man?

Jake hooked a thumb through one of his belt loops and scowled. "I don't like it. How do you know he's not trying to take advantage of you?"

She huffed out a breath and scowled. "Jake Ranulfson, is it really that hard to believe someone kind and honest would be interested in me?"

He shook his head, his eyes getting all soft and concerned again. "No. Ellie, it's just… I'll worry."

"No, you won't." She pressed her eyes shut, trying to forget the smile on his face when he'd danced with her at Tressa's party, the tenderness in his eyes when he'd reached out and fingered a strand of her hair the morning she'd greeted him with half her hair down. She raised her eyelids and met Jake's gaze squarely. "You'll go to Chicago and forget all about me."

314

His eyes swept down her in a familiar sort of way that told her he remembered the lunches and dancing just as fondly as she did. "I could never forget you, Ellie."

"Then how come I haven't seen hide nor hair of you for the past week?" The words hurt as they fell from her lips, but Jake could be nothing more than a friend. He might think about her fondly on occasion when he was lonely in Chicago, might even whisper pretty things to her when he came back to Eagle Harbor during school breaks, but when the time came to pick a wife, he wouldn't be desperate enough to tie himself to her.

Oh, why had she let Jake get so close?

"I was wrong not to come by." He took another step toward her, bringing them near enough they'd cause a wave of town gossip within the hour. "I should have come to see you anyway, never mind my parents."

"No, you're right for minding them. Heaven knows your parents have likely been biting their fingernails watching you spend so much time with me."

"This isn't about my parents."

"No, it's about me, and you. And what's best for both of us. Which means I'm going to Texas, and you're going to Chicago." It was the way things had to be. She couldn't ask Jake to thwart his parents over her.

She peered up into his eyes one final time, etching the soft brown of them into her memory, then raised onto her tiptoes and placed a kiss on his cheek. "Good-bye, Jake."

She ducked her head and stepped around him, descending the porch steps with nary a glance over her shoulder.

Chapter Twenty-Nine

Isaac sat on the rocks near the lighthouse, the wind off the lake toying with his hair while the waves lapped at the boulders below. To his left, a trio of gnarled pine trees fought over which one would twist itself the most out over the waves to get the sunshine it needed. Beyond, the water stretched in a vast expanse that seemed to never end.

His gaze landed on the familiar spot where the *North Star* had capsized, dumping his father into the angry waves. But his breathing didn't shallow, his heart didn't race, and sweat didn't slick his skin.

No, it didn't hurt to look at the spot anymore, or even to remember.

His father had led a rich life and had left a legacy that lived on in him and Elijah and Rebekah and Mac. Perhaps Pa's time had ended too soon, but there was hope beyond Pa's death. Days turned into months, and months into years, and years into decades. And he wasn't going to let that one day of his life control him anymore. Wasn't going to let what he'd chosen to do—or not do—define him.

"Goodbye, Pa," he whispered into the breeze.

A rustling sounded behind him, and he looked over his shoulder, half expecting Mac or Elijah to have spotted him from the lighthouse and come to keep him company. But Aileen was there instead, her hair a fiery orange glow beneath the setting sun. She sat beside him on the sun-warmed rock.

"The doctor finally let you go?" He'd gone back to visit her yesterday evening, after he'd sweet talked Mrs. Kainer into fixing an extra batch of food for all the men and gotten a report on everything the customs and revenue cutter men had pieced together. But Dr. Harrington had been insistent she stay longer for observation. The good doc had been just as insistent when he'd stopped by after breakfast that morning, and she'd been sleeping heavily when he stopped in at lunch.

"I finally convinced him that naught happened to me, at least naught beyond being frightened and deprived of sleep." She slipped her hand into his and looked toward the setting sun. "It's so peaceful here. I know the sun sets every day, but I doubt I'll ever tire of watching it."

His hand tightened around hers. "Come back and watch it with me tomorrow?"

She looked up at him with eyes as green as the water was blue. "There was a time when I didn't want to think about tomorrow, so stuck on the past, I was."

He stroked his thumb over the back of her hand. "I wasn't so different myself, if you recall."

"But tomorrow comes anyway, doesn't it? Ye keep quoting that verse about the Lord's mercy being from everlasting to everlasting, but there's another Bible verse, one about the Lord's mercies never failing, about them being new every morn."

"'It is of the Lord's mercies that we are not consumed, because his compassions fail not. They are new every morning: great is thy faithfulness.'" He shrugged, a bit of heat creeping up the back of his neck. "It was another one Pa had us memorize."

She rolled her eyes. "Aye, is there any verse in the Bible ye don't know?"

A pair of eagles cawed, then took flight from the top of the gnarled pine tree beside them and swooped over the water.

Isaac smiled, his heart light enough to soar through the sky beside the regal bird. "Probably. Might take a while to find one though."

"Stop teasing." Her elbow nudged him in the ribs. "I'm trying to tell you something important. That I don't dread tomorrow anymore. I look at it, and it's full of hope, and new things, and… ye." Her last word was barely more than a whisper, but she scooted around on the rock so she faced him fully. "At least I want it to be full of ye. I know I'm not perfect. I've made my share of mistakes but—"

"As have I." He laid a finger over her lips, soft and delicate beneath his skin. "You saw one of my attacks. I was weaker than a nervous woman in need of a fainting couch and smelling salts."

She tilted her head to the side, a tender smile whispering across her lips as she must have remembered what he'd looked like that morning Elijah went out on a rescue. "Ye were never that weak."

But he was, or at least he had been. "When I realized the smugglers had taken you, my first reaction was to give up. I felt like I'd already failed you, just like I had with my pa." He looked back out to the mouth of the harbor, to the patch of water that had haunted so many of his dreams. "All I could see in my mind was my father's boat capsizing, over and over again. And it felt like I'd made the same mistake with you, like I had no choice but to stand by while you perished."

She swiped a wayward lock of hair off his forehead. "This from the man who dove into the water from a bluff and sneaked aboard a ship to rescue me."

"And I would have, if the Cutter Service had taken fifteen minutes longer to get there," he muttered.

"Aye, ye would have, 'tis true." She cupped his cheek with her palm. "But let's not talk about that anymore. I'm still trying to tell ye something, I am. Now if ye would just stop interrupting."

"Go on then." Though she'd better hurry, because with her face so near his own, he was about two seconds away from sweeping her onto his lap and finishing the kiss they'd started two nights ago—the one he'd cut short so he could catch smugglers.

She swallowed, then dropped her hand from his face and glanced to the side, as though she was suddenly unsure what to say.

The trouble was, drawing back from him wasn't going to get them kissing any faster. What were the chances she could tell him while snuggled on his lap?

But then she sucked in a breath and spoke. "The answer's yes."

"Yes?" And now she was talking in riddles.

"About marrying. In the doctor's office yesterday, ye said ye planned to marry me, and I just want ye to know I'll say aye." Two splotches of red climbed onto her cheeks, and she squirmed on the rock beside him. "When ye get around to asking, that is. Not that ye have to ask now, but… well… what I mean is… if ye've still a mind to marry me despite me turning down yer suit so many times, then I've a mind to let ye."

He planted his hands on either side of her lap and leaned forward, caging her in. "I planned to ask you all fancy. Maybe buy you a bauble or have Rebekah's cook make up a special meal."

She stared up into his face, their lips so close the slightest movement from either of them would have them kissing. But instead of leaning forward, she reached up and stroked that obstinate patch of hair away from his brow again. "Yesterday, when I was in the cave, when the smugglers were taking me to the ship and I didn't know where ye were, I realized I should never have said nay to ye courting me, not even last winter."

His chest tightened until he could barely breathe—and it wasn't the same kind of tightening that accompanied one of his attacks. "I was so worried when I couldn't find you. But I intend to keep you safe by my side from now on."

To prove it, he gathered her into his arms and shifted her onto his lap, then pressed his lips to hers. She tasted of sweetness and light and good. Of hopes and dreams. Of everything he'd ever wanted for his future. She reached up and wrapped her arms around his neck, her fingers toying with the ends of his hair, then sighed contentedly.

He didn't know how long he held her there, his lips probing hers, their breaths intertwined. It felt only like seconds, but if the heaving of his chest was any indication, he'd kissed her far longer than was proper. And yet he couldn't quite make himself pull back. He'd meant every word of what he'd said. He didn't plan to let her go ever again—which meant he felt no need to unwind his arms from her at the moment.

But she eventually pulled away and rested her head on his shoulder. Her shoulders rose and fell with another peaceful sigh, and she stared out over the water. The sun was sinking into the horizon, painting the rocks and water with its fiery brush, and bidding farewell to another day. But it would rise again in the morning, just like God's mercies.

"Marry me, Aileen Brogan." He ducked his head so his mouth was beside her ear, his voice little more than a whisper. "Spend the rest of your life with me."

She raised her head from his shoulder and met his eyes. "I can't promise to make a perfect wife. There are memories from my time in Chicago that I can't erase no matter how hard I try to put them behind me."

He stroked a wisp of hair away from her face. "I don't expect you to be perfect, love. Just mine."

After all, maybe that was the most beautiful part of God's mercy.

Not that it made people perfect, but that it could take broken people, make them whole again, and give them a happy, bright tomorrow.

A smile spread across Aileen's face, as vibrant and beautiful as the setting sun. "Aye, Isaac Cummings. 'Tis yers I am."

He leaned down and rested his forehead against hers, then smiled. Because with Aileen by his side, he had a whole host of bright tomorrows ahead of him.

Epilogue

Six Weeks Later

Thwack. Aileen sliced through the cabbage with bold strokes of her knife. *Thwack. Thwack. Thwack.*

The tangy aroma of cabbage juice filled the air of the small apartment above the sheriff's office, and her stomach growled at the familiar scent of the food she'd eaten nearly every day in Ireland—a food she hadn't consumed enough of since she'd moved to America.

Beside her, the pot of water she'd set to boil was beginning to hiss and bubble. A cabbage, a rutabaga, some potatoes, and a handful of carrots, plus the beef round she'd spent the past three days corning. She and Isaac would have a feast for kings, they would. Her mouth started to water, which was a bit of a shame considering the food needed to boil for two hours or better before it would be ready to eat.

Footsteps sounded on the stairs, then the apartment door opened behind her.

She turned as Isaac stepped inside, and her stomach fluttered. Mayhap her stomach would stop getting antsy eventually, but ever since their wedding three weeks ago, she hadn't been able to look at her husband without odd sensations consuming her belly, and her heart growing so full it just might burst from her chest and run straight to him.

"I thought I heard you up here. Did you sneak in while I was talking to Mrs. Ranulfson?" He started toward her, that familiar thatch of auburn hair falling over his brow.

"I wanted an early start on dinner. 'Twill take a good bit to cook." She turned back to the cutting board, but before she could pick up her knife, Isaac came up behind her and wrapped his arms around her middle.

"Cabbage... again?" he choked.

She could hear the wince in his voice. She shoved her elbow back and jabbed him in the stomach. "Stop. I've barely eaten any since coming here. Just wait until I boil it with the beef I've been corning. Ye've never tasted anything so good."

"You're forgetting I grew up on Ma's fish dinners, love. Meat boiled with cabbage can't compare, no matter what you do to it."

"Oh, and have ye ever had corned beef before?"

He stroked a strand of hair behind her ear. "Ah... does it have fish in it?"

She scowled and reached for the uncut half of the cabbage.

"Come on." He dropped his arms from around her waist, but gripped one of her hands in his. "I have something to show you."

"I should get this started so it can simmer first."

He reached for the damper on the stove and turned the handle down. "No, I need to show you now."

She furrowed her brow. "Ye do realize I'm in the middle of cutting a cabbage?"

He didn't even try to hide his grimace. "The cabbage can wait, I assure you. But this apron needs to go." He stepped behind her, his fingers fumbling with the tie at her waist. Then he leaned his head down, and his lips grazed the tender place where her shoulder met her neck.

A shiver travelled through her, followed by a rush of warmth. "Isaac…"

She glanced at the bed wedged into the corner of the small apartment. Was that what he intended to show her, more about the joy of intimacy when willingly explored in a marriage? He could do so all day long and she'd not utter a word of complaint.

But instead of kissing her neck again, he pulled away, lifted the apron strap over her head, and tugged her toward the door. "Let's go."

She sighed, her gaze still latched on the bed. "Aye, but later can we…?"

"Are you asking me to bed you, wife?" He stopped in the doorway, a slow smile spreading across his face.

"I… um…" Heat flamed onto her cheeks, and she glanced over her shoulder at the bed once more.

He chuckled, the sound happy and deep. "And this from the woman who wouldn't even rest her hand on my arm six months ago."

She squirmed. "I just…"

But he cut off her words with a kiss so tender it stole the breath from her lungs and thoughts from her head. She stepped in closer, reaching up to twine her arms around his neck while his scent surrounded her.

He pulled away before she could link her arms, a small growl sounding from his lips. "Come, before I forget what I'm about."

He grabbed her hand and led her down the stairs and through the sheriff's office below. Afternoon sunshine greeted them as they stepped onto the busy street. He wove around a wagon and a group of schoolboys headed to the beach before turning down Fourth Street. "I got a telegram from the Customs Service this morning. The pair of men in Duluth they thought might be Conan and Morley? Turns out they were another pair of Irish immigrants."

She slanted a glance up at Isaac. "So they're still free?" She couldn't help but be a little happy. Her brother and cousin needed to pay for their crimes, 'twas true, but she wasn't exactly eager to see them locked up for a decade or better.

Isaac's jaw was grim, his eyes focused on the road ahead. They passed Center Street and the bakery without him slowing, though he kept his hand wrapped around hers, their fingers laced together. "Not sure you can say a man is free if he's running from the law, but they haven't been caught yet."

"Do ye think they made it out West?" Was it wrong to hope they stayed free and reformed their ways? Was it wrong to hope they would both find women who made them as happy as Isaac made her?

"Could be, lots of places for a man to disappear out there, but the Customs Service hasn't stopped looking for them yet." Isaac slowed as they approached a small two-story house on the far corner of Fourth and Cedar.

Rather than the white clapboard or rough logs that made up most of the buildings in town, this house was painted a soft yellow. Flowers had been planted in the beds on either side of the front door and in flower boxes hanging off the two front windows, giving the house an extra burst of color. Thick woods started just past the small yard, providing a rich backdrop of green to the already charming home.

Isaac started up the path to the door, which had been painted to match the summer grass.

"Are we making a call?" She slowed her steps, but he plowed right up the walk until they stood on the small porch.

"You could say that." He took a key from his pocket and inserted it in the door, then held the door open for her. "Ladies first."

She stepped inside only to find the front parlor completely empty. No coat tree or sofa or hutch. Nothing except bare walls painted a rich cream color. She turned back to Isaac, still standing in the doorway with the key in his hand. "I don't understand… is this… for us? Have ye bought it?"

"I know it's not a farm in Wisconsin, and it's certainly not a farm in Ireland, but well…" His throat worked, and he held open his hands to encompass the room. "I want you to have a house, and this one seems like a good fit."

Her throat grew thick, and the breath stopped in her lungs. "Nay, it's too much. There's room aplenty for us in the apartment above yer office. And if we can't live there for some reason, there are servants' quarters in the hotel."

But she couldn't help looking around the empty room. She could already see a sofa against the far wall and a coat tree beside the door. Perhaps an arm chair in the corner, and if there wasn't room for a hutch in the kitchen, one could be placed against the third wall between the two windows.

"But we don't own the apartment above my office or the servants' quarters of the hotel. I know there isn't much land, only five acres of woods behind the house, but anything with more land was too far outside of town considering my job." His voice was low and gruff as he spoke. Then he closed the door behind him and came toward her. "This is your dream, isn't it? To have a home that belongs to you and no one else?"

"Aye." She forced her voice to work past the tightness in her throat. "'Tis as ye say."

"If you like it, we can buy it. All I need to do is go to the bank and sign the papers."

"'Tis everything I've ever wanted." But that wasn't quite true, because while she may have wanted a house, she hadn't dreamed of a husband in so very long. She pushed up on her tiptoes to kiss his cheek. "Nay, 'tis more than I ever thought I would have."

He caught her before she could drop back to the ground, wrapped his arms around her, and gathered her close. The kiss was hot yet soft, tender yet insistent. He tilted her head so their lips met at just the right angle. She raised her arms and linked them about his neck, then pushed higher onto her toes in an effort to get closer. A soft groan rose from his chest, but that didn't stop him from shifting her back farther in his arms, until she had no balance left but relied entirely on him to keep her from falling.

The door burst open behind them.

"Isaac!" Rebekah's voice filled the room. "Ye've gone and ruined the surprise!"

Isaac slowly took his lips from hers and straightened, setting her on her feet once more, but in no hurry to pull away completely. He glanced toward the door. "How was I supposed to know she would start dinner two hours early? I had to find a way to stop her."

"Next time take her for a walk on the beach. You've messed everything up." Rebekah's lips pressed together in a flat line.

"What are ye talking about?" Aileen moved her gaze between her husband and Rebekah, who stood with a crate filled with foodstuffs in her arms. "Are we eating dinner here?"

Isaac stroked a hand up her arm, then down again, keeping her pinned against him. "Yes, and we're having fish. Not cabbage."

She rolled her eyes. "Cabbage is healthy for ye. Keeps a man hale and hearty, it does."

"Rebekah. Where do you want...?" Gilbert stepped into the doorway carrying another crate, but when his gaze landed on her, he paused. "Oh, I suppose that answers everything."

Answered what? Why was everyone upset she was standing in the house Isaac wanted to buy for her?

A glimpse of reddish blonde hair and pale skin flashed just beyond Gilbert's shoulder, and her breath caught in her chest. "Brenna?"

It couldn't be, yet she knew that shade of strawberry-blonde hair as well as she knew her own deep red tresses. She wriggled out of Isaac's hold and rushed toward the door, barely giving Gilbert a chance to step aside before she barreled into the sunshine.

"Brenna!" She threw herself into her cousin's arms. "Ye're here. But how…? When…?" Her throat closed, cutting off her words.

Brenna chuckled, wrapping her in arms that had grown thinner in the two years since they'd last seen each other. She still smelled of Ireland, of salty seas rather than fresh ones, and bogs and peat and sunshine. "That investigator yer friend hired found us straight off, he did. We'd only been in Galway a few weeks."

"And I don't want to go back," a young voice sounded from somewhere near her waist.

Aileen pulled back from Brenna far enough to see little Nora standing beside them, her hair a flaming bright shade that met somewhere between Aileen's and Brenna's locks.

"Everything in that city stinks like coal smoke." Nora's arms were crossed tightly over her chest, and her chin was tilted upward.

"And there's nowhere to play." This from Cathal, who must have grown a foot since she'd last laid eyes on him. He approached holding a little girl's hand. "Just houses and houses and more houses."

"Don't forget about the neighbor who yelled at Mam whenever Ide would cry." Another boy skipped toward them, a colorful rock in his hand. He'd been so young when she left Ireland, she barely recognized her cousin's third child, Daithi.

"That doesn't sound like a fun place to live." She crouched down to the children's level, then looked directly at the little girl in a threadbare dress with light hair like Brenna's. "Ye must be Ide. I'm Cousin Aileen. 'Tis right lovely to meet ye, lass."

Ide tucked her chin into her shoulder and looked down at the ground.

"Ide, she's kin. Ye need to hug her." Nora threw herself into the open arms meant for Ide.

Daithi joined the hug a moment later, then Cathal.

"Oh, I missed ye all so much, I did." Aileen squeezed her cousins so tightly they squealed.

"We missed ye too, Cousin Aileen." Nora hugged her tighter.

Little Ide came up and wrapped her arms around Aileen's neck, her grip hesitant and fragile.

Tears sprang to Aileen's eyes, but with her arms still wrapped around the children, she was helpless to stop them as they crested and streaked her face. Then she looked up to see Isaac standing beside them, watching her with such tenderness that tears crested anew.

Voices sounded from behind her, and she looked over Cathal's shoulder to find Elijah and Victoria headed up the steps with the three O'Byrne children they were adopting. And Mac and Tressa were making their way down the street as well, their four children in tow. Just behind them were the Harringtons, and it looked like some of the Spritzers were coming too.

How had she ever thought of leaving Eagle Harbor? It was rich with friends she was growing to care more about every day, and it had family too, both her family from Ireland and the family Isaac brought into their marriage. She wiped a tear from her eye and glanced back up at Isaac. Her heart had never felt so full, and she had God and His mercy to thank for it. God, mercy, and the wonderful man committed to giving her a life more abundant than she'd ever dreamed possible.

Want to find out what happens to Ellie when she goes to Texas?
Don't miss the new Texas Promise Series coming in 2019.
The small-town stories start with Ellie Spritzer and Sam Owens in
Tomorrow's First Light.

Sign up for my author newsletter to be notified when
Tomorrow's First Light releases.

Thank You

Thank you for reading *Love's Bright Tomorrow*. I sincerely hope you enjoyed Isaac and Aileen's story. This novel concludes the Eagle Harbor Series—at least for now—but I hope you'll journey with Ellie Spritzer to Texas for the first novel in my new Texas Promise Series, *Tomorrow's First Light*.

Want to be notified when *Tomorrow's First Light* releases? Sign up for my author newsletter. Subscribers also get a free copy of *Love's Violet Sunrise*, a prequel novella to the Eagle Harbor Series. Sign Up Here.

Be sure to add author@naomirawlings.com to your safe email list so that the emails go through. I keep all subscriber information confidential.

Also, if you enjoyed reading *Love's Bright Tomorrow*, please take a moment to tell others about the novel. You can do this by posting an honest review on Amazon or GoodReads. Please note that to leave a review on Amazon, you need to go directly to Amazon's website. Your e-reader may ask you to rank stars at the end of this novel, but that ranking does not show up on Amazon as a review. I read every one of my reviews, and reviews help readers like yourself decide whether to purchase a novel. You might also consider mentioning *Love's Bright Tomorrow* to your friends on Facebook, Twitter, or Pinterest.

Author's Note

I hope you enjoyed the conclusion of the Eagle Harbor Series. I'll admit, writing this book was quite the undertaking. I wanted to finish the series in a way that would resonate with the readers who have come to love the rustic town of Eagle Harbor and all its inhabitants. However, when it came time to actually give Isaac and Aileen their happily ever after, things got really difficult. Both Isaac and Aileen had endured much in the novels preceding *Love's Bright Tomorrow*. I wanted them to find happiness, peace, and contentment. I knew God could give them those things if both of them would turn their hurts and burdens over to Him. But I also knew it wasn't going to be an easy journey for either character.

I trust Isaac and Aileen's story illustrates how God can give healing and strength to those who turn to Him, no matter how hurt a person might be. One thing I discovered while writing this story is that mental illness, such as depression and suicidal thoughts, are real risks for women who are raped, and they are equally serious risks for women who have abortions. If you or someone you know fits one of those conditions, it's important to get help. Suffering in silence and isolation will likely make these problems worse. There are numerous support groups available for both rape victims and post-abortive women. One of the best places to start is with the Christian organization Healing Hearts Ministries.

As Aileen discovers in this novel, God's mercy is from everlasting to everlasting. I'm aware *Love's Bright Tomorrow* is a work of fiction, but in real life, there is still no sin too great or trauma too deep for God to overcome. The path to healing and hope may not be easy to tread, but the end results will be well worth the difficult journey.

Thank you for visiting Eagle Harbor with me in this novel. I hope you've enjoyed the conclusion to the Eagle Harbor Series, and I hope you'll follow Ellie Spritzer when she heads to Texas as a mail-order bride in *Tomorrow's First Light*, releasing in the winter of 2019.

Other Novels by Naomi Rawlings

Texas Promise Series

Book 1—*Tomorrow's First Light* (Sam and Ellie)

Book 2—*Tomorrow's Shining Dream* (Daniel and Charlotte: releasing 2020)

Book 3—*Tomorrow's Constant Hope* (Daniel and Keely: releasing 2020)

Book 4—*Tomorrow's Steadfast Prayer* (Harrison and Alejandra)

Book 5—*Tomorrow's Lasting Joy* (Cain and Anna Mae)

Eagle Harbor Series

Book 1—*Love's Unfading Light* (Mac and Tressa)

Book 2—*Love's Every Whisper* (Elijah and Victoria)

Book 3—*Love's Sure Dawn* (Gilbert and Rebekah)

Book 4—*Love's Eternal Breath* (Seth and Lindy)

Book 5—*Love's Winter Hope* (Thomas and Jessalyn)

Book 6—*Love's Bright Tomorrow* (Isaac and Aileen)

Short Story—*Love's Beginning*

Prequel Novella—*Love's Violet Sunrise* (Hiram and Mabel)

Acknowledgments

Thank you first and foremost to my Lord and Savior, Jesus Christ, for giving me both the ability and opportunity to write novels for His glory.

As with any novel, the author might come up with a story idea and sit at her computer to type the initial words, but it takes an army of people to bring you the book you have today. I'd especially like to thank Melissa Jagears, my critique partner for *Love's Bright Tomorrow*. I'd also like to thank my family for working with my writing schedule and giving me a chance to do two things I love: be a mommy and a writer. Also thank you to Roseanna White, Lynnette Bonner, and Victoria Naegele for assisting with the editing and providing early feedback. And finally, a special thanks to my former agent Natasha Kern for encouraging me to keep working on the Eagle Harbor Series.

About the Author

Naomi Rawlings is the author of numerous historical Christian novels, including the Amazon bestselling Eagle Harbor Series. While she'd love to claim she spends her days huddled in front of her computer vigorously typing, in reality she spends her time cleaning, picking up, and pretending like her house isn't in a constant state of chaos. She lives with her husband and three children in Michigan's rugged Upper Peninsula, along the southern shore of Lake Superior where they get 200 inches of snow every year, and where people still grow their own vegetables and cut down their own firewood—just like in the historical novels she writes.

For more information about Naomi, please visit her at www.naomirawlings.com or find her on Facebook at www.facebook.com/author.naomirawlings. If you'd like a free Eagle Harbor novella (Mabel and Hiram's story), sign up for her author newsletter.

Made in the USA
Coppell, TX
13 April 2020

20017664R00201